The World of Evendaar

Book One

# The Child Revealed

A. R. Winterstaar

Cover Illustration by Anastasia Ward (akward13@live.com)

First Published 2014

Third Edition, May 2018

ISBN: 0991479459

ISBN-13: 978-0991479450


Evendaar Publishing

www.evendaar.com

# CONTENTS

# DEDICATION

Monica Hall

My dear friend, and a true queen if grace, humor and a great nobility
of the spirit are all the attributes required for the job.

# THE PROPHECY OF THE END OF THE WORLD

*A child born into the Golden Age shall be stolen from the Light and hidden from the eyes of the world.*

*Seek this Hidden Child when the three Signs of the End of the World appear.*

*The First Sign shall be from Hell when the Shadows will move within the deep places and seek their dominion over Men in the coming days of Darkness.*

*The Second Sign shall be of the World when a tempest shall eat the sun and the skies themselves will weep and strike at the ground with their power bringing seven Days of Night.*

*The Third Sign shall be from Heaven when the Seven Sisters will dance across the skies and uncover the One Path to the Child.*

*Only the Hidden Child shall defend the Throne from the Favored and cast the Shadows into the Light to restore the Glory of my Chosen Ones on the Throne of my Kingdom.*

*Beware and rejoice, for only in the greatest darkness does the brightest light shine.*

*Taken from "The Prophecy of the End of the World," printed by Pere Manus and dictated by the Child Prophet Celestina and voice of the Goddess Serena - 31— Year of our Goddess Serena*

# CHAPTER ONE
## "This Special Day"

Adele sat at the extraordinarily shiny table and looked down at her image, dark and distorted, in the black glass. She flinched away from the expression of bewilderment holding her face tight. Those swollen eyes and sunken cheeks belonged to another woman. A woman who had lost her life and still couldn't work out how it had been taken from her. She was ashamed for her reflection and turned away.

It was done.

The lawyers packed up their folders and shuffled their papers back into their designer briefcases, studiously avoiding eye contact with everyone else at the table.

Done. Just like that.

Adele looked across at her husband. Ex-husband. She watched Justin as he spoke quietly to his lawyer. He'd gotten a haircut. It looked good, suited him. She hated herself for wanting to touch those blond curls. The same curls that sat on the head of their youngest daughter.

She could tell the exact moment he realized her gaze was on him, even before he looked up. She saw his shoulders raise and his jaw tighten. When had he started hating her? He lifted his eyes to hers and she didn't recognize what she saw flickering in their sea-green depths.

She knew what she must look like to him as she sat there at that fancy table in her cheap, ill-fitting pantsuit. She had only bought it because her housewife-wardrobe of jeans and T-shirts wouldn't cut it on this special day. She knew her eyes were pleading with him to stop. To make this all okay.

What she wouldn't give for one of his wicked smiles and a wink.

Something. Anything.

Anything that would tell her they could go home together now and everything would go back to normal, just like every other day of their seven-year marriage.

But Justin was looking down at the table now, his hands covering the place where his own reflection would be.

"Mr. Marlock will stop by in two weeks' time to take the children for the weekend, as per the custody agreement," said Justin's lawyer, his voice too loud in the small room. He smiled broadly at Adele. She thought he looked vaguely familiar. Was he one of Justin's old school buddies? Justin leaned over to whisper something.

"Err, correction," said the lawyer. "In three weeks' time, as my client will be out of town on business. Apologies for the oversight, Justin."

Justin nodded magnanimously and smiled. Yes, they were definitely friends.

Adele looked back at her own lawyer. A stolid woman with short, graying hair and hands that rasped when she rubbed them together. All her promises of "I'll make sure you'll get what you deserve from the bastard" tidied away in a little manila folder covered with too many colored paper clips. Daria Millens wasn't Adele's friend.

Did she get what she deserved from Justin?

She got her children. Those three glorious, relentless bundles of energy that needed to be fed, clothed, comforted, and driven about in her old Volvo. She got their tiny, crumbling, old bungalow. She got to do it all on her own. Alone.

Adele almost jumped out of her skin when Daria Millens nudged her in the ribs.

"Mrs. Marlock, we can go now. We are all done here…it's finished."

*Finished.*

Her marriage to Justin Marlock was finished.

She was finished.

Adele stood unsteadily. Her wedding ring cracked on the glossy black glass as she grabbed the edge, smearing the surface with her fingerprints.

"I think…I just need…" Her voice sounded squeaky behind the sharp ringing in her ears as the world shrank down to a pinpoint.

"Sit down, Adele!" insisted Justin's disembodied voice. "She does this all the time, please don't worry about her."

"Someone to hold me," Adele whispered, before the blackness pulled her under and she hit the floor.

# CHAPTER TWO

## "The Oppressive Atmosphere of the Grey Palace"

Prince Rainere twisted and thrashed against the silk sheets of his bed. His long black hair dashed against the whiteness like a spreading stain. Sweat drenched his body and, though he slept, his limbs jumped with a palsy that knew no rest.

Grotto watched as the wizard, Ohren, set up his bottles and vials of tinctures. Their tinkling sounds and his young master's groans were the only noises to be heard over the sounds of the storm raging outside the window. Grotto moved to the bedside to hold his master's hand and tried to slow the man's trembling with the small gesture of comfort.

Ohren caught Grotto's wrist.

"Grottonski, he must have no more after this, you understand? He is not nearly so strong as his father was, and it would mean a painful death for him if you insist on it again."

"It is not me who does the insisting," snapped Grotto, wrenching his arm away and reaching for Prince Rainere's hand again. He was incensed that this St. Lucidis wizard would dare to even mention Prince Rainold in his master's presence.

But Ohren would not be so easily thwarted. He leaned over and caught Grotto's eye.

"Do not forget, I know who you are, old man. I know where you are from and I know your debt here is greater than mine."

Despite his strong words, the wizard's hand shook slightly around the vial of blue liquid as it flashed and popped with odd little explosions. He quickly poured it into the open mouth of the sleeping prince. Both men clamped their hands to the prince's arms when he convulsed frantically as the potion hit the back of his throat. A froth appeared at his lips and his eyes flew open, wide and panicked. Then, almost as suddenly, his body relaxed again, his eyes closed, and his breathing became steady.

Ohren quickly and quietly packed his paraphernalia back into his black bag. His odious work here was done. However, as he reached the door his hand hesitated on the handle. He turned to speak, but closed his mouth again when he saw that the sharp eyes of the prince's manservant were already upon him. Ohren coughed, feeling a fool in front of the older man. He frowned gruffly to hide his discomfort, but his voice held a note of pleading.

"I'm in deadly earnest when I say this to you, Grotto. Another dose of the Blue Tonic and that boy you call your master will not wake up next time. Please do not call me on such an errand again."

Ohren didn't wait for an answer before he turned and left the room. He hurried down the torch-lit corridors of the palace, his footsteps muffled by the threadbare carpet. He found his way with long-practiced ease but, as ever, he shuddered when he passed under the eyes of the ravens which lined the sunless hall. Though they were made of stone, they always made his skin crawl.

Ohren swore bitterly under his breath, cursing the Sacred Oath he had made one hundred and forty-five years ago to a man now dead and gone from this world. But it was a promise that could never be broken, so Ohren was trapped into performing this wretched task tonight. The only comfort he could take in this situation was that the prince was surely near the end of his strength, and he would not last much longer in this world. Finally, Ohren would be free.

If the Goddess Serena would just take mercy on him.

Determinedly keeping his gaze on the rough-hewn stone of the steps, Ohren slipped out the exit, into the portal, and away from the oppressive atmosphere of the Grey Palace.

# Chapter Three

## "Her Fingers Danced Well Shy of the Glimmering Lights"

Adele was floating, looking down at the golden light that shielded her little house, surrounding it in a protective barrier. She had made it so her babies could sleep safe while she left them tonight.

Looking up, Adele could see the stars, so many millions of them. Here in her Dream World, they shone and pulsed with the energy of the Universe, so much more clearly and brighter than in the real world.

Adele smiled at the joy she felt, surrounded by the energy of the stars. It was amazing. She felt so alive and strong, even though a part of her knew she still slept in her bed in the softly glowing house below her.

Adele sensed, rather than saw, the path that floated above the twilight-darkened streets of her suburb. She raised her arms up to catch the breeze that would lift and carry her away into the gloaming distance.

To her right, the ocean glimmered out past the twinkling yellow lights of the town. To her left, rolling hills lay buried in their nighttime shadows.

Adele could feel the cool breeze blowing more strongly now, yet it didn't chill her, only took her higher into the sky and made her nightdress flap against her legs. She twisted lightly in the air, weaving through the current and breathing in freedom on the vanilla-scented air.

All at once, she saw the great castle in the distance. Its black rock glowed dimly with a greenish hue. The lines of the pinnacles and turrets were as familiar to her as her own home was. She felt drawn to this place. It was where she always wanted to go in her dreams.

Adele arrived at the castle in moments, and dropped lightly down to the roof of a battlement. The stars blanketed the sky here, too, thick and heavy. She stretched her hands up to try to touch them, and chuckled when her fingers danced well shy of the glimmering lights.

To her right, the door of a turret flew open, banging back against the stone wall with a force that cracked the wood.

He was here.

The figure stood still in the doorway, cloaked in shadows. Adele's joy bubbled up inside of her. She beckoned to him, smiling.

"It's me, Adele."

The figure stepped out and advanced slowly toward her. He was always so shy at first.

But it was him. The man of her dreams, both waking and sleeping. His chest was heaving as if he had exerted himself running up the stairs. He stopped when he was just a few steps from her. Her heart thudded. He was close enough that, even in the dim twilight, she could see the sheen of sweat on his forehead. His cheeks were flushed and his eyes were intense with emotion as they bore into hers. Adelena reached to touch his cheek. He flinched but allowed her hand to come close. He closed his eyes as she felt the air where his face should be.

Disappointment bloomed inside her.

"I can't touch you tonight," she breathed sadly, her voice thin and reedy, as the wind snatched her words away.

Once, she had. Just once, she had dreamed of his arms around her and felt the heat of his chest pressed against her cheek. There had been a strong scent of rosemary in the air but also something sharper, more bitter than any herb. The moment had ended too soon and she had woken in her bed wracked by a grief she barely understood.

But this moment, here with her Dream Man, standing on the roof of his castle, trying to speak. This dream she had dreamed a thousand times. Always so close but never touching. Always speaking, but their voices soundless to the other.

She watched as he realized her hand would not touch him. His eyes darted from her floating hand back to her face. His pain was so palpable she could feel it twist in her own chest. Tonight he looked frail. Though he was well over six feet tall, his posture was stooped and he bent down as if to cradle her in his arms. The hair that flowed over his shoulders was long and unkempt. His face was thin and haggard. But his eyes, as always, kept her transfixed. Though she could only guess at their color, she could not look away from their smoky depths. Adele shivered for a reason that had nothing to do with the cold.

Her Dream Man seemed seized by a sudden desperation. He clutched at her still-raised hand and watched as again his fingers moved through it unheeded. He was talking furiously now, gesticulating wildly, eyes narrowed as the wind whipped up in response to his emotion. He looked enraged, but Adele knew that this was just another version of the same dream. She had nothing to fear from her Dream Man or his passion. Oh, but his passion was so wild and beautiful.

"I can't hear you," she murmured and made to place her hand on his lips, stepping into him, as she had done another thousand times, to quiet his rage.

She could see the fine stubble on his chin. His Adam's apple bobbed gently as he swallowed. He dropped his head down to hers. She saw herself reflected in his dark eyes. Her long hair tangled about her heart-shaped face, her hazel eyes shadowed and wide over thin cheeks. She did indeed look pale and ghostly, which was all she was on this rooftop under the stars. A ghost.

She reached up on her tiptoes and watched as his mouth formed words she hadn't heard in years. Words of love and desire. His lips were so close to hers now. So close.

Just as Adele thought she could feel his breath in her mouth, a violent wind snatched at her. Like a paper doll she was lifted up on its current and taken high up above the parapet.

Her Dream Man threw his arms up, trying hopelessly to catch her. But he never had, and he never could. She was a ghost here, after all. Adele knew the wind had come to take her back home. Her babies were waiting for her, and though she was happy to return to them, her heart ached for her Dream Man and his passion.

As she was whipped away, Adele turned back to see the desperate anguish of the figure on the castle battlements, left howling in pain and cursing the stars as he watched her recede into the distance. Arms clasped tight around himself, he walked slowly backward to the broken doorway of the staircase, his gaze never leaving the sky.

# CHAPTER FOUR

## "Three in the Morning"

Adele woke with a jolt. She sat up in bed and automatically looked at the digital clock on the bedside table. 3:01 a.m. Shit. Justin still hadn't come to bed. She strained to hear where in the house he might be. When she remembered, the knowledge hit her like a cold slap in the face.

He wasn't here, and he wasn't coming home ever again.

Despite the fact that he had spent the last year of their separation sleeping at his parents' house nearby, most nights she could pretend that he was just away on a work trip and coming home soon. Some nights he did come home, his key turning in the lock around midnight, the scent of alcohol clinging to his clothes and the tears in his eyes telling her he was so, so incredibly sorry. Their reunions were always fast and frantic, yet deeply unsatisfying in so many ways, leaving Adele feeling insulted and frustrated as Justin snored beside her. In the morning, he was always gone.

*Divorce.*

Adele still couldn't quite work out how it had happened to her. She had believed in their marriage. Sure, it might have felt like hard work at times, but wasn't that true of all young marriages? She had three small children to look after, and he'd had his burgeoning career. Wouldn't you expect the dry patches to stretch into months? The frantic sex of their trial separation was the most action she'd had since Stella, their youngest, was born.

Justin had kept repeating that what they had together just "wasn't enough for him anymore." Really? So, did that make him greedy or her pathetic for accepting less than perfect? Why was she happy to settle for him while he wanted to search for happiness without her?

Maybe he had already found his "happiness." Maybe his "happiness" wore skinny jeans and still laughed at all his jokes. Adele thought of Justin's new haircut and winced.

*But wouldn't I trade in Justin for my Dream Man?* A quiet voice inside her asked. *To be with someone who loves me with such passion would be incredible.* Her Dream Man's face floated in her mind.

"And I am free, too. Now," whispered Adele to herself as bitter tears tracked down her cheeks. "But my Dream Man is just that, a dream. So really…I have nothing."

She dropped her head back on her pillows and squeezed her eyes shut, tight against the world, in an attempt to stave off another 3:00 a.m. panic attack. They came so regularly now. Adele pulled her faded floral comforter up over her shoulders and breathed deeply. She forcefully turned her mind back to her dream.

Ever since she had started that guided meditation class six months ago, she had been having more and more lucid dreams. This one, for instance, had seemed so vivid she could almost smell the vanilla still in her hair. She had read about astral traveling, when the spirit leaves the body and travels about in different parts of the world, or even to other worlds. It was hardly an exact science, but, regardless, Adele took a sliver of hope that she might be traveling to somewhere real in her dreams.

But of course not! It was all rubbish. The truth was that she was a divorced mother of three who was very soon going to go broke if she didn't keep her head out of the stars and start thinking about getting her life back together.

Adele thought miserably about her unfinished Environmental Sciences degree and her university years as a barmaid on campus. She had gotten pregnant so young, there hadn't been time to start any sort of career even if she had known what it was she wanted to do.

Then there was the house. They had bought their little bluestone bungalow when it was the perfect size for a family with just two kids. They had both been full of enthusiasm about how simple the renovations would be. Now, one more child and three years later, the kitchen was still a 1980s monstrosity and the bathroom had that horrible pink toilet. The two eldest children were squashed up in one of the three tiny bedrooms, and the baby in the third one. Adele's eyes traveled to the four painted squares of color untidily decorating her bedroom wall. She just couldn't decide which color she wanted the most; which color that could turn her tiny, overstuffed bedroom into an elegant boudoir. But she couldn't even think about buying paint now, not with all those horrible sounds the water heater had been making. No doubt, that ancient machine was on its last legs, just like the dishwasher in the kitchen.

Adele scrunched her eyelids together and fought to breathe normally as she felt anxiety crushing the bottom of her lungs and the sharp ringing in her ears rise in pitch.

To calm herself, she conjured the image of her Dream Man's face. High cheekbones, regal nose, his chin sharp and strong, his perfect lips, always moving in the words she longed to hear. But it was his eyes, eyes that flashed with such intensity, which she clung to in her memory. It was his eyes that made him seem so real to her. Surely, she didn't have the imagination to create such incredible power and beauty. Even as a phantom, he took her breath away and made her heart pound. *If only he was here to bring some love into my life and rescue me from this terrible emptiness...*

A piercing cry broke her thoughts.

It was Stella and her night terrors again. Adele rolled out of bed and shivered at the feel of the cold floorboards underfoot. Justin must have turned the heating off the last time he was here. Adele snarled to herself. *Jerk.* She had no idea how to turn it back on.

Adele moved down the short corridor to the baby's room, her way lit by little fairy and car nightlights. She cursed softly when she stepped on one of her son's little transformable robot cars. *Damn, those things had sharp corners!*

The door to Stella's room was ajar, and Adele found her baby shaking and sobbing in the corner of her bed. She leaned over the wooden side of the crib and scooped her daughter into her arms. Stella gave another shriek of fear as she was picked up, and her eyes flew open.

"Sssh, my darling girl. Sssh, Stella Bella," Adele crooned as she stroked her baby's back. Stella buried her head in her mother's neck and her panic began to subside. Adele sat down in the old rocking chair in the corner of the room and rocked until Stella's sobs had given way to tiny snores.

It was only when Adele was sure her daughter was asleep that she let the tears prick her own eyes. Maternal guilt welled up inside of her at her own rotten disloyalty.

*I have love in my life*, she reprimanded herself silently. *I am loved unconditionally by three little people who need me to be strong for them. I can't lose my head in the clouds dreaming of dark strangers, and I can't lose myself grieving for Justin. I just have to accept that he doesn't want me anymore…*

She bit her bottom lip as it trembled and, in the dark of the night, finally admitted to herself the one thing she had been prepared to overlook for the sake of her children's happiness. The one thing she had ignored as she fought for the last year to keep her family together.

*I don't love him anymore either. And now I'm free of him…*

Adele almost gasped at the hard honesty of her admission. Relief began to trickle into her thoughts between the fear and grief. Yes, her marriage had failed, but she was still a mother and that mattered more to her than anything else in her life.

Adele thought of her children. Natalie who, at six, was as sharp and sensitive as Adele herself, and was probably much smarter. With her long dark hair and bright-green eyes, it was a wonder to Adele that someone as plain as she was could produce a child so beautiful.

Aaron, her second, had been born not even eighteen months after his sister. A winter baby, he had spent the first six months of his life in and out of hospital fighting every infection that blew in on the cold winds that shook their windows and crept in under the doors. Adele had insisted on heaters in every room of their drafty little house, but Justin had resented the expense and only acquiesced after Aaron's left lung had collapsed from pneumonia. But that didn't stop Justin from switching off the system at every opportunity, even when he didn't live here anymore. Adele winced when, as if on cue, Aaron let out a chest-wracking cough from his room across the hall. He whimpered in his sleep, and she heard his bed creak as he turned over, no doubt throwing his pillow to the floor.

Stella, the baby she held in her arms, was just two years old and the result of the one and only time Adele had stood up to Justin. Up until then she had been grateful that he stood by her, and let him run the family and her life. He was the only one working and bringing in any money, after all.

When that test had shown two little blue lines, her joy was indescribable and his despair was awful. They had stood staring at each other over the ugly pink toilet in their bathroom, a room far too small to contain all of their emotions.

"We can't…you'll have to," he'd said, staring horrified at the little white stick trembling in her hand.

"I won't," she'd answered fiercely, shocking herself as much as him. "I never will. Ever. So don't ask me to."

He'd shut down then, she remembered him sulking for months and refusing to help…even when she got so sick she couldn't get out of bed…even when she got so big and tired and cried all the time at the end. Instead he had worked later and later at the office, and started going away on weeklong trips for work. Her guilt at insisting on the third baby, and the extra financial burden, stopped her every time she wanted to ask that he do something, anything, with the children. But no. She had brought this on herself. It wasn't his fault she had wanted the baby. But it was her fault she had kept it.

Adele stroked Stella's soft, damp curls and tried to remember the Justin she had first met. He had been so wild and fun. Her quiet spirit had gravitated to his carefree nature and the wicked smile that had made her melt. Everybody who met him loved Justin, but it was only Adele who had wanted to keep him all to herself.

Justin had married her because she had asked him to. Justin had had a baby because she had wanted one, then two, then three. Now he only wanted one weekend in two to visit them. Adele suppressed a sob, and it sat like a rock in her chest. She had given him a burden too heavy to bear, and she had given her children a father who hadn't wanted them in the first place. The Justin she had seen in the lawyer's office today was the man their marriage had made him.

*I've screwed this up for everyone* she thought miserably as the cold reality of her life surrounded her in the darkness. Adele felt a deep heat suffuse her chest as her breath became ragged. She fought hard to push down on the anxiety, which tried to rip a hole in her control. She breathed deep and thought of flying…flying on a vanilla-scented breeze…until a normal rhythm returned.

Adele placed the snoring toddler back in her crib, her arms shaky from holding Stella so long. Stella was getting so big now.

Adele checked that the other two children were sleeping soundly in their little bunk beds before shuffling back to her own bed. The clock face was blurry to her exhausted eyes. It didn't matter what the time was, she was going to be tired when she woke up, anyway. She was always so tired lately. She limped to the bed and lay down. Briefly, she fantasized about ringing her mother and asking her to come over to help with the kids this weekend, as if they had a normal relationship. But it would never happen. Adele's adoptive parents were both academics with itchy feet who couldn't stay in one country for longer than a few months. They were probably still in the city right now but she couldn't be sure, as sometimes they forgot to tell her when they changed jobs or took on new research projects. They had been so disappointed when Adele had thrown away her first degree while she was still so young, to "squat and reproduce," as her mother had put it. *They had yet to meet Stella, and the baby was already two years old!*

Her life had never been what one would call stable. As an only child, Adele had found the constant moving around with her parents difficult. It had been hard to make friends, and always being "the new kid" had left her with a permanent sense of self-consciousness.

Now she was twenty-nine, and she had hardly a friend to call on or family to back her up when times were tough, and times were so tough right now.

Adele rolled onto her back and stared up at the glass chandelier as it tinkled in the breeze from the window draft.

Her attempt at making a family of her own had failed, and now she was left in the rubble of her bad choices. All she could do was hold on for dear life and hope something good happened soon.

Adele sighed deeply. Hoping that something good would happen soon was the way she had always haphazardly run her life. It was a baseless hope that she was made for better things, that something crucial was finding its way to her, if only she had the patience to wait long enough. It was this same hope that had made her decide to ask Justin to marry her, and kept her having the children one after another. It was this quiet, determined optimism that Justin had loved her for, and then eventually couldn't stand. But she couldn't leave the children's lives to an open fate, she had to make an actual plan. They needed her to be the mum and the dad now that Justin had abdicated his role by leaving them. They needed her to return the stability that had been taken out from under all their lives.

At three in the morning, this was just too much to take. The tears leaked from her eyes and made the pillow damp, but Adele snuggled down and ignored the discomfort. She squeezed her eyes shut tight and imagined the gray castle where her Dream Man lived; hopefully she could see him again tonight. *Hopefully something good would happen…*

# CHAPTER FIVE

## "Though It Was Fickle, the North Wind Could Not Lie"

Prince Rainere stared out the window of his chamber. He looked over the palace gates to the Dark Forest, and the sharp spines of the Black Mountains beyond it. The clouds hung heavy and ominous in the sky, threatening more of the flooding rain, which had plagued the countryside for days.

Rainere tapped his fingers against the windowpane in a sharp tattoo. The dream he'd had last night played over and over in his mind. Perhaps it was the rejuvenating effects of the Blue Tonic, but his dream had been so vivid. He shook his head to clear the image, but behind his closed eyes, all he could see was her face. Her face, with the wide dark eyes, happy laughing eyes. Delicate features made her look like a beautiful doll. She was so petite and came no higher than his shoulder. She always looked fragile to him, breakable. He couldn't guess her age. Perhaps she was just a girl, but her eyes held a wisdom that told him she was probably an older spirit.

He had dreamed of her hundreds of times. Sometimes the dreams were just a flicker of movement. Only flashes of her turning this way and that, as if she were caught in the surface of a bubble as it floated away from him. But now, more often, the dreams were tantalizingly clear.

He remembered the lace trim on her dress as it lay against the skin on her chest, framing the curve of her breasts beneath it. The way her long, dark hair fluttered in the breeze, blowing across her soft cheek. The hand she had reached up to touch his face with was so perfectly clear, he could have traced the delicate webbing of veins that throbbed just under her skin.

*It was intolerable!* He wanted to be distracted from these tortuous musings that plagued him.

19

Rainere slammed the window open, shaking the glass in its frame. He let the sharp air cool his flushed cheeks as he breathed in deep of the wind from the north.

The North Wind always spoke to Rainere.

He stared hard, looking beyond the invisible air about him to the whorls, gusts, and eddies whirling past. Today, the North Wind spoke of snow and the deadly cold polar winds that screamed across the tundra beyond the Black Mountains. It described the waking of the great ice bears and their hunting across the arctic snows, killing anything that moved and spraying the ice with the red, red blood. The North Wind laughed heartlessly at such sport.

Closer to home, it whistled and whispered about the ravens nesting in the palace turrets and of a strange wind that had blown in, ruffling their feathers and whipping their nests apart.

"A Spirit Wind," whispered a whorl to an eddy.

"A Spirit Wind," answered the eddy. "Not us, not I, the North Wind."

Rainere froze and concentrated on the words heaving about him on the breezes.

"A Spirit Wind brought a spirit from another world…"

"Not us, not I…"

"Chased her away we did…not our Spirit…not our world…"

"T'was a she-spirit on her Spirit Wind…we chased that she-spirit away…"

"Not us, not I…back to her world she will go."

"Who is she?" shouted Rainere as his hair blew about his face and he leaned dangerously far out of the window.

But the North Wind did not answer the questions of mortals, or even Immortals, but only spoke to those who could listen, and now it had no more to say. It blew away, shrieking in delight, as the West Wind came chasing it.

Rainere pulled the window shut, his mind reeling. This was the first proof he'd had that he wasn't entirely inventing this woman who haunted his nightly dreams and dominated his waking thoughts.

Was she this spirit the North Wind saw last night?

She had to be! The North Wind had tasted her and, though it was fickle, the North Wind could not lie. If she was real, spirit or no, she could be found, and Rainere was certain he had the means of finding her.

# CHAPTER SIX

## "The Prophecy of the End of the World"

High Wizard Ohren leaned back in his chair with a groan. He looked around his study and rubbed his eyes. The light had grown even dimmer in the room as the storm howled outside his window.

Ohren usually felt so cozy in his little attic room. Hidden away at the top of a tall tower, it was his office as much as it was a place to hide from the rest of the Golden Palace and his daily responsibilities as the High Wizard of the High Wizards Council. But today, the tiny space, with its walls of bookshelves and haphazardly squashed-in desks, felt claustrophobic.

Another clap of thunder rattled the windowpanes and set two of his weather contraptions whirring and whizzing on their brass wheels. Ohren stood up and stretched his long arms above his head. Another groan escaped him. *I'm getting old*, he thought, with not a little irritation.

He moved to pull yet another lantern from the shelf by his window. Though it was the middle of the day, the storm clouds covered the sky so darkly that it might have been late evening. He glanced out of his little window but couldn't see anything except rain, rain, and more rain. Like someone was endlessly throwing buckets of water at his window.

Ohren snorted. "The entire kingdom will wash away at this rate," he muttered.

He couldn't remember a time when it had rained so hard or for so long. How incredibly tiresome and dreary it all was.

Ohren returned to his table with the new lantern and put it with the two already there. He spread out the celestial map he was marking, but it bounced out of his hands and fell to the floor, rolling under the table.

Ohren cursed and gave up on chasing it. It was rubbish, anyway. He'd been trying to chart the celestial paths for this month, but he'd obviously made a mistake somewhere, as the map made no sense at all.

He slumped down in his chair, absently spinning a tiny sphere on the great brass contraption that sat in front of him. Taking up almost the entire length of the table, it was made up of thousands of spheres and disks of varying sizes, all revolving around one another in tidy little clusters of satellites and stars. At the center of this model of the galaxy was the largest disk, its engravings showing the large land mass and myriad island groups that made up the world of Evendaar.

Ohren stared into the three-dimensional star map, trying to divine where he had gone wrong. He carefully corrected the orbit of the sphere he had set spinning, and frowned darkly at the ancient contraption. *Maybe it was finally failing after all these years?* It had to be over a thousand years old, at least.

But it was impossible to decipher. That six stars could fall into alignment so close to Evendaar was improbable, but that a seventh would cause a lunar eclipse was unthinkable. Such a thing had never happened. Ever.

Ohren ground his teeth in frustration and swore again. Suddenly, what should have been a peaceful day's work in his study was making him furious. He resisted the urge to swat at the pesky stars again and force them out of alignment by his simple desire to make it so.

A tapping sounded at his door.

"Come in," growled Ohren, hoping it was someone he could yell at.

The door creaked open to reveal a man so old it was a surprise to many that he could still stand, let alone walk unaided.

"Good afternoon, High Wizard," rasped the elderly gentleman as he tottered into the room, his arms filled with scrolls. Without being invited to, he wandered over to a desk and heedlessly dropped the scrolls onto it. Unfortunately, the desk was already covered in piles of books, and the scrolls tipped off and all over the floor.

"I thought I'd bring you my list of those students I feel might be of use to you as apprentices, High Wizard."

Gnarled fingers dug about in his top pocket and he pulled out a piece of paper along with his glasses, which he perched on his nose. The paper shook slightly as he held it out to Ohren.

*Apprentices! Damn it all!* Ohren had forgotten about choosing his apprentices for the year. It was all a complete waste of time, of course, as no one was born with enough magic in their blood these days, let alone the aptitude and strength needed to complete the training itself.

Ohren sighed crossly and snatched at the list.

"You are welcome, High Wizard," croaked the old man civilly, giving a low bow and almost tipping over.

"What's all this mess on your floor, Ohren? A man could trip over on this lot. Look…scrolls everywhere!" He bent down very slowly to pick some of them up.

"Oh, leave them alone, Gorrik," huffed Ohren. "You'll break a bone kneeling down like that."

He perused the list of students in the Accadaemia and snorted. *Just as he had thought!* No one had shown the slightest talent for advanced magic in this year's intake. He huffed again and threw the paper on the table.

"You'd better be careful, wizard. The wind'll change and your face will be stuck like that," observed the ancient Gorrik drily as he climbed carefully to his feet with a scroll in hand. "I saw that happen to a boy once in my student days. Grant, I think his name was...could've been a Belvoir."

"Really? Did things like that happen at the Dawn of Time?" retorted Ohren.

"Oh, you have no idea," answered Gorrik with a sniff, not at all offended.

Ohren let out a guffaw and gave up teasing his old friend before he had really gotten started.

"Tea, Gorrik?" he asked, heading toward the fireplace.

"Hmmm, yes, why not," agreed Gorrik as he examined the scroll in his hands. "If you don't have anything stronger, of course?"

Ohren arranged the tea things, throwing leaves and hot water into the pot along with a glug of something golden that perfumed the air with the scent of rich spices.

"Here you are, old man." Ohren placed the spiked tea a safe distance from Gorrik's elbow. "Don't bother reading that, Gorrik, you'll just be wasting some of your last precious minutes in the world."

Ohren sat back in his chair, facing the model of the Celestial Skies, and blew on his steaming cup.

"I've obviously made a mistake," he said. "But where and how, I don't know. I've brought up the last ten years of charts for the same months, but something is definitely off this year. Maybe the model is breaking down?"

"Hmmm...it is never good to feel we are more clever than the Gods, Ohren. They don't tend to like that," sniffed Gorrik, as he turned the scroll around. "Aha, that's it!"

"What is?" asked Ohren hopefully.

"I had it upside down," said Gorrik in a tone usually reserved for children, as he glanced at Ohren over his glasses.

Ohren snorted and went back to gazing morosely at the Celestial Skies, its stars and moons orbiting one another with maddening patience. There was nothing connecting them together, no rods or pulleys. Though the knowledge was long lost, the model had reputedly been created using an Infallible Spell, a gift from the Gods to one of the Marchant ancestors. The Infallible Spell was just that, infallible. It should keep the little spheres turning about one another until the end of time.

*Perhaps the end of time has come?* He thought, and snorted again.

"Stop making that noise," croaked Gorrik. "It's disgusting."

Ohren dropped his head in his hands and glared balefully at the window.

"It's this damned weather! Six days it's been raining like this. Six! We are going to wash away at this rate," he growled.

"Six days, you say?" asked Gorrik, his expression suddenly sharp and his milky eyes alert. "Do you fancy there might be a seventh day of thunder and lightning?"

"What? I don't know, probably." Ohren's tone was doleful. His petulance made him seem like a much younger man. Younger than his long gray beard and wrinkled skin would suggest. He watched Gorrik shuffle over to the window.

"Do you think it might be accurate to describe this six-day storm as a tempest, perhaps? What with the sun being covered by darkness, the flooding rain, and the electrical storms…one might even call this the Seven Days of Night, if one were so inclined."

Ohren sat up slowly in his chair, his expression wary.

"You've finally cracked, old boy. You can't be serious?" snapped Ohren, but there was no venom in his tone as his mind worked furiously over the calculations.

Gorrik shrugged. "Perhaps. Maybe I'm just a crazy old historian with too many ghosts chasing through my head. But I'm looking at a six-day storm and a star chart telling me that the Seven Sisters are falling into alignment tomorrow at…" He checked the chart. "Just before midnight, our time."

Ohren blanched beneath his pale beard. His blue eyes stood out like sapphires in his white face.

Gorrik came back to the table and slurped his tea.

"Well, the good news is you haven't wasted a morning's work. The bad news is you've predicted the end of the world, and you've only given us thirty-six hours' notice."

He threw back the rest of his tea and smacked his lips.

"But that would mean…the Hidden Child." Ohren's voice was only a whisper. "Gorrik, we aren't ready—none of us are prepared for the start of the prophecy!"

Gorrik nodded calmly. "If a tree falls in the forest, is it silent because there is no man there to hear it?" His mouth quirked up at the side. "Can a prophecy still be fulfilled even if there is no one there to watch it unfold?"

"No," groaned Ohren. "Oh please, Gods, no! Gorrik, what do we do?"

Gorrik shrugged again and handed the star chart back to Ohren.

"The Gods won't help us now, boy. They gave us the prophecy, and the Celestial Skies, what else do you want them to do? Wipe our asses for us?" He chuckled darkly.

"But…I—I need time to prepare," stammered Ohren. He stood and sent his chair crashing to the floor. "Damn it, Gorrik, we have to do something…I must call the High Wizards Council together."

"Wonderful!" Gorrik rolled his eyes. "You can all argue with each other until the end of the world."

He patted the high wizard on the arm, but his voice was grave. "You know what needs to be done, Ohren. And only you have the power to do it."

Ohren's eyes filled with fear, and something else unrecognizable.

"But I'll need him...I'll need his help."

Gorrik cocked his head and raised an eyebrow. His look was so searching that two spots of hot pink bloomed on Ohren's pale cheeks. He dropped his eyes.

"You were a boy then, Ohren," Gorrik said softly. "You are a man now, and besides, we have no time to find him. You must try without him as best as you can. Certainly your brother can help."

Ohren closed his eyes and grimaced as if in pain, but when he opened his eyes again they were clear and focused.

"I will need your assistance in the Spell of Retrieval, Gorrik, but it will be dangerous for you, you understand?"

"More than me, you will need one of The Blood, Ohren." Gorrik frowned.

Ohren shook his head. "I will only need The Blood itself, not the body it came from, and I have that."

Gorrik opened his mouth as if to ask a question but closed it again and shrugged. As he turned to leave, he gave Ohren a wink. His good humor was at such odds with the wizard's fear.

"I'll be down in my chamber enjoying a bottle of the finest Firewhiskey I've ever had the pleasure to taste. I've been saving it for a special occasion for over two hundred years now...the end of the world seems special enough, I think." Gorrik smacked his lips as he opened the door. "Send for me when you need me."

"Gorrik," called Ohren from where he was standing frozen at the table. "What if we fail? What happens if..." His voice choked off.

Gorrik smiled and his face folded back curiously, like a concertina.

"Well, my friend, it's a big bottle of Firewhiskey, so we'll go out the way we came in, crying and laughing." He stepped out the door. "Good luck!"

# CHAPTER SEVEN

## "The Prince Was a Queer Bird"

Prince Rainere walked from his bedchamber through the dark, dusty corridors of the Grey Palace to the west wing and home of the Great Library. He was certain he could find something there on communicating with spirits or demons to help him speak to his Dream Woman, maddening though she was.

Arriving at the enormous six-paneled double doors, Rainere was irritated to notice his breathing was too rapid and he felt overly warm. The brief respite of the Blue Tonic was already waning. He gave the door an almighty shove with his shoulder but only managed to open it a crack. Another shove and there was just enough space to slip his slim frame through.

The Great Library was a huge echoing hall lined entirely with rows of bookshelves reaching up to the vast cathedral ceiling. Threadbare carpets of gray and red lined the cold flagstone floors, and moth-eaten curtains of ancient velvet hung limply against the enormous floor-to-ceiling windows. They were pulled back, though precious little light filtered in as the storm raged outside.

With a flick of his hand, Rainere lit the candelabras nearest to him, and those along a large desk close by. The flames were an odd green color but the light burned yellow and was perfectly useful.

The prince closed his eyes and stretched his arms out by his sides. He allowed his power to race free of his mind, feeling it surge up and down the aisles of bookshelves searching for the psychic trace that would signal the type of knowledge he was looking for. After what felt like a moment but could have been an hour, Rainere pulled his power back into himself and opened his eyes. He dropped his arms and groaned. Hundreds of books lay piled untidily on the long tabletop, the floor around it, and the chair beside it. He pinched the bridge of his nose and cursed softly.

Shaking off his despair, Rainere knocked a few books off the spindly chair and sat down. Grabbing the first book off a pile by his elbow, he began his search.

*      *      *

Grotto watched his master from the gap in the doorway. The doors had been made from stone and wood, and were much older than he was. Over the years they had been imbued with so many magical protections that even just standing this close to them made his skin crawl. Because Grotto wasn't of The Blood like the prince, he couldn't cross the threshold. But he didn't need to be close to his master to see the shaking hands and sudden shivers that tormented the man's body.

The back of the prince's neck was visible as his lank hair parted to show the family crest tattooed there. The dark lines flowed beneath his collar and down each side of his spine to cover his entire back. The tattoo was actually a spell, and one of the strongest of its kind: an immortality spell. Magic itself etched into flesh and one of the most powerful gifts the Gods had given the Marchant family. Yet despite this terrible magic, Grotto's master was looking decidedly fragile. That wizard, Ohren, was right: the prince couldn't take much more of the Blue Tonic. It was such a poor substitute for what the prince really needed.

Immortality was a gift and a curse from the Gods. Only a God had the strength and stamina to live an endless life. Naturally more delicate, humans struggled with maintaining their bodies to withstand the centuries of life given to them. However, a millennium ago, the Eldar Marchants had happened upon the Gift of Life, allowing them to live endlessly in perfect health. The secret of the Gift had been closely guarded by the family ever since. But this prince of the Marchant family, and last heir of The Blood was a queer bird, and refused the succor of the Gift. Instead, he preferred to suffer the side effects of his aging frame and bolster his strength with the use of the Blue Tonic. It was a terrible compromise. The Blue Tonic was a poisonous opiate that induced a great lethargy in the body and created confusion in the mind. The mental fog was accompanied by a dismal paranoia and hallucinations.

Grotto sighed. He blamed the Blue Tonic for his young master's obsession with this woman who infected all his dreams and disturbed his waking moments. It was unhealthy, is what it was. If the prince needed a woman, he should just take a woman. There were plenty of slatterns in the nearby village who would count themselves lucky to be the bedmate of a Marchant prince, even in these times.

But, no. The prince had mooned about the palace for months pining for this phantom spirit. Grotto was afraid the poor young prince's mind truly was coming apart. Despite his better judgment, Grotto had had to call the wizard last night. The prince had become insane with pain and had insisted on taking more of the Blue Tonic.

Grotto could not deny his master anything.

But that pompous wizard had looked at Prince Rainere like he was no better than a dog, while his poor master had moaned and writhed on the bed, suffering the agonies of his immortality.

Oh, but he had been such a bright young thing not too many decades ago. Proud, and so exceedingly clever. Even after the events of his childhood, Rainere had remained curious, seeking out knowledge in every corner of the Grey Palace. He was powerful, too. His magic had come in even greater and faster than his father's had, once the immortality spell had been fixed on him when he was just thirty-five years old. The prince had been strong then, despite what that wizard had said when he compared Rainere to his father, Prince Rainold.

Grotto knew better than some nasty kingdom wizard just how powerful his Prince Rainere could be. Grotto had served the royal Marchant family for three generations, coming into service when Rainere's grandfather still reigned.

Grotto ground his teeth when Rainere began muttering fiercely to himself, dashing through book after book, before throwing each one behind him. Unheeded, the books rose up and floated slowly back to their shelves. Grotto flinched when the prince let out a sharp cry of frustration. One of the lanterns nearest to Rainere exploded, and green fire flew out and over the table. Where the droplets touched paper they flowed harmlessly off, bunching together and gathering in a pool away from the books. Not so the prince, who swore at the burns on his skin and smoking patches on his shirt.

Grotto closed his eyes wearily and shook his head. If only Prince Rainere had been just a *little* like his father. Prince Rainold would never have allowed himself to degenerate into this state, and the sort of delirious lethargy that his master lived in.

Mind you, Prince Rainold would never have been able to be manipulated into going along with the Prophecy of the End of the World and the plan to save the House of Marchant that Grotto had devoted his entire being to creating. Rainold had been a far more selfish creature than his monkish son. Grotto thought about how much of Rainere's condition was his own fault but decided quickly that it didn't matter.

Come tomorrow when the Seven Sisters covered the face of his Moon Goddess, Lune, the Prophecy of the End of the World would begin when the Hidden Child was returned to Evendaar. The powerful Empress Ka-kik would make it so. Then the prince would once again sit on the throne of Unisia, and he could mumble and mutter as much as he wanted and no one could do a thing to stop him.

Grotto's shoulders straightened as he thought with dark pride of what was to come. A Marchant would once again rule the kingdom of Unisia.

Oh, that he would see such a day in his own lifetime! Nothing could stand in their way. After all, it had been foretold in the Prophecy of the End of the World. All Grotto had to do was keep Rainere alive long enough for it all to unfold as it should.

*     *     *

Back in his chamber, the prince pushed away the tray of food before him as his stomach protested the idea of eating. Rainere screwed up his eyes as he felt the familiar pounding at the back of his head, and feared the pain that was to come. He walked to the window and rested his hot forehead against the glass, letting the fierce rain beating against the glass vibrate into his mind.

This fog, this awful fog that consumed him and drove him mad. There was no escape. No relief.

Prince Rainere sensed more than saw the rising of the sun, as there was no break in the darkness of the storm. He tried to avoid the pain a little longer by focusing his thoughts on his Dream Woman.

"Who are you?" he whispered, his eyes closed. His visions of her were so vivid, so solid. She was absolutely otherworldly but not, he thought, from the Netherworld. But how? From where? And how could he find her?

"If only I wasn't so tired. My head aches and my skin burns…why couldn't I find anything useful in the library? I can't be the only Marchant in two thousand years who wants to capture a spirit from another world…why? Why? Why?" Rainere muttered uselessly.

He traced the map of scars on the back of his right hand. They shimmered silvery against the white of his skin. With a distant expression, he watched his hands tremble as they vibrated with the last of the magical traces he had encountered in the old tomes and scrolls. Some of the traces he had barely felt, while others had literally burned his fingers with their power. Most of the texts he had examined today were to do with either folklore or war weapons. Two completely disparate topics. The war-weapons books were the most aggressive about protecting their secrets, and Rainere had had to be extremely careful when examining them. His mind recoiled at the hideous nature of the weapons, both biological and mechanical. He shuddered at the spell which when cast caused unborn babes to die in their mothers' wombs, and at the weapon that could ensnare a particularly malignant demon that was small enough to fly into the ear of its victim and take control of its brain.

It was sickening to him that so many of his ancestors had put most of their considerable power and intellect into creating weapons to destroy humankind in such wicked ways.

The other subject that reoccurred just as often was folklore. More interesting, but equally useless. He pulled a tiny lavender-colored book from his pocket. It had been bound in cloth and handwritten in some kind of berry juice, if his sense of smell could still be trusted. A book of prophecy, it had been scrawled by a barely literate priest from the wailings of a young girl who'd claimed to be the human Voyce of the Goddess Serena. It was a common enough end-of-the-world prophecy, and not particularly imaginative. Certainly, there was nothing in it about how to capture a wandering spirit. Rainere threw the book onto his desk, where it knocked over a cup of water.

"Master?" Grotto interrupted his musings. "Perhaps you would like to break your fast with something hot?" Grotto set another tray of food next to the untouched one on the table.

Rainere flinched at the clatter of metal cutlery and the clinking of porcelain. Everything was suddenly so loud, but still Grotto sounded very far away when he spoke.

"Maybe just a bite, master, and then a brief rest. Master has had a long night and needs his sleep."

Grotto observed the prince out of the corner of his eye as he set the hot soup and bread out on the table. The prince was pale beyond even that determined by his lily-white ancestors. His eyes were glassy and wore dark shadows beneath them. It was clear the prince was nearing the end of his strength for the day, though dawn had just broken.

But Grotto's heart clenched painfully in fear when the prince swayed on his feet and staggered toward him. He caught the prince and held him as if in an embrace.

"May the Goddess help us all if my master doesn't live past this day," prayed Grotto aloud, as he pulled the larger man to the bed with a strength that belied his stooped frame. "And may the Goddess forgive me if I let the prince break his Sacred Oath to the empress, alive or dead."

He rested Prince Rainere's head on the pillow as gently as a mother would. There was no time to waste. He must take the prince to the empress now in case the worst should happen. But first there was much to prepare. Grotto ran from the prince's chamber and down the dusty hall, his coattails flying out behind him.

Prince Rainere lay on the bed, pale and feverish, his light breaths hitching every now and then.

Outside, the seventh day of the tempest raged and raged against the dawn.

# CHAPTER EIGHT

## "No More Time for Prayers"

"Do we have everything we need?" asked Ohren of the other two men with him in the small, dank dungeon room.

"For the last time, brother!" snapped the man who could have been Ohren's reflection. "We do not have everything we need, we don't even have half of what we need, and we should *not* be doing this!"

Ohren wiped his hand over his face and down his beard. He turned to his twin and understood that behind his anger was the fear they all shared.

"Orestes, we must do this," sighed Ohren. "The End of the World is coming tonight. You've studied the prophecy as well as I have. Our only chance of saving life as we know it is by bringing the Hidden Child back to Unisia. The Gods gave us the only knowledge we will ever get about how to save ourselves. We have to try because we are the only three people alive who know who the child is and where she was hidden all those years ago. Only we can attempt the retrieval when the Seven Sisters move into alignment in…" He checked the timepiece he'd brought. "…twenty-eight minutes."

"But that's what I'm saying, Ohren!" shouted Orestes. "You are going to attempt one of the most dangerous pieces of Dark Magic you've ever tried, and you are basing this whole endeavor on conjecture and your own overblown arrogance. Prophecies aren't like fables. They aren't meant to be taken literally!"

"This one is," muttered Ohren, adjusting the sandy edge of the Circle of Power and fanning the flames of the four little fires he had built there. Over the fires, he had placed rosemary, sage and salt crystals in three separate brass bowls. There was an empty bowl waiting for the last ingredient, which would be added before the incantations were said.

Huffing after his shouting, Orestes finally gave up trying to sway his stubborn brother. He resorted to glaring furiously at Ohren as the other wizard fiddled with the little twigs for the fires.

A soft hiccup broke the tension.

"Drink, anyone?" asked Gorrik, and belched meaningfully, as he proffered the bottle.

Gratefully, Ohren took a swig of the Firewhiskey, and after a moment took another. He gave the bottle to Orestes.

"You'll kill us all down here, Ohren, and not one damn person is going to know why we died," said Orestes quietly. "You are leaving the kingdom without its high wizard and its high magistrar..."

"And its oldest history teacher!" Interjected Gorrik, wagging his finger, the slight motion causing him to fall off his low stool.

The two brothers' eyes met across the dim firelight.

"You did the right thing sending that baby away one hundred and forty-five years ago, Ohren. Do not bring her back here now. It's over!"

Ohren shook his head. "No, Orestes, I set this prophecy in motion when I sent that child away. I changed our destiny. Don't you see? I'm responsible for all of this! I need to stop the end of the world coming, or I need to try," he faltered, his voice cracking. "And I need your help, brother, just as I did last time."

There was a long moment of silence.

Orestes shook his head and threw his hands in the air.

"Well, at least I'll go out with a bang," he said, a smirk pulling at the side of his mouth as he took a long pull on the bottle of Firewhiskey.

"Or we'll survive and the whole of Unisia will live happily ever after," replied Ohren with a relieved grin.

"Either way, I'm enjoying being flat-on-my-ass drunk," sniffed Gorrik from the floor where he now lay.

The twins took each other's hand and moved to sit around the Circle of Power, careful not to touch the flames. Gorrik shuffled over, reverentially placing the bottle of Firewhiskey before himself as he struggled to cross his legs. With a tiny golden knife, Gorrik sliced his hand open and held it over the empty bowl. Great splotches of black blood dropped into the crucible. Ohren leaned over and, while chanting a quiet incantation, emptied the last ingredient from a little glass vial into the bowl to mix with Gorrik's blood. Gorrik tied up his hand with a handkerchief and watched as Ohren took a burning twig from the fire and lit the blood mixture. The flames jumped into the air for a moment before settling back into the bowl. Twin columns of smoke, one of green, one of gray, rose up and twirled about the rim of the bowl, images appearing and fading as they moved.

"So pretty," murmured Gorrik, his glassy eyes hypnotized by the dancing smoke. He held out his hands to the two wizards. Ohren and Orestes each took a gnarled old hand, and immediately all three men sat bolt upright, their eyes raised to the ceiling.

The power flowed through Ohren like an electric current, freezing his spine and jumbling his organs. He felt his bowels contract painfully.

There was no more time for prayers.

No one could help him now that he had committed his brother and his oldest friend to the Spell of Retrieval. He focused his thoughts on the incantation, forcing the words out through his clenched teeth. The star chart he had spent the last day memorizing was etched in his mind as he worked to separate his power from his body and send it out across the sky…the heavens…the universe. He sought the psychic signature of the child he had hidden all those years ago. He found it, blinking like a star in a distant galaxy. His power headed to the source. He was close…so close…and then a force rushed up in front of him.

Back in Unisia, in the little basement room, Ohren whimpered in pain, sweat dripping down his face.

Ohren's power sought a path around the force that prevented him from moving. He didn't recognize the energy signature, but it had to have come from the same world that he did. The force moved toward him, and all of a sudden, everything went black.

Ohren's body succumbed to the strain. He slumped to the floor. Orestes and Gorrik both screamed in pain.

# CHAPTER NINE

## "The Spell of Retrieval"

"This won't hurt my master, will it?" asked Grotto anxiously as he watched the Royal Guards of the Empress Ka-kik place Prince Rainere upon the ceremonial stone table.

The table was more like a slab of rock. Its sides were rough and unshaped, but the surface was covered in intricate patterns that acted as a network of runnels to the gutter carved at the four edges. At each corner was a stone lip, under which four fires had been set in bronze crucibles.

The smell of rosemary and sage caught in Grotto's throat, making him cough and his eyes water. The salt in the crucible hissed and spat.

"Yes," replied the empress from where she sat at the head of the table.

Grotto looked up hopefully.

"This will most definitely hurt him. He will have felt no pain like it in his young life." Her voice clicked and rasped as her tongue stumbled clumsily over the words of the humans' language.

The empress looked down at the sleeping prince, her face a mask. The white-and-yellow-painted bodies of her shamans stood to attention next to her, her royal guards retreated behind them. The empress placed her front feelers against Rainere's temples. She hovered over him, breathing in his breath through the pores on her black legs.

"He is weak," she hissed in irritation. "He might not be strong enough for the journey back, Grottonski."

"His body has been sorely tried by the Blue Tonic," protested Grotto.

"He is a Marchant prince, and he promised us this thing he would do for us. It will be a very bad thing if we perish in this spell with him," hissed the empress. Her royal guards shuffled and clicked in consternation at their leader's anger with the old man.

Grotto swallowed nervously and fought the smoke in his throat for a breath. He remembered suddenly how very far down under the earth the center of the nest actually was. His Goddess Lune was covered tonight by one of the Seven Sisters...no one would see him perish if the empress decided to devour them both.

"I have brought him the Gift of Life," croaked Grotto, gesturing at the covered bundle laid out behind him.

"Ah, so it is not a tribute for me?" snapped the empress, raising herself up on four legs.

Grotto swore inwardly. He had forgotten a gift for Her Royal Highness. He cleared his throat and tried to keep his expression cold.

"The Gift of Life is for the prince after the ceremony to prevent his death. Unless, of course, his death could benefit Your Majesty?"

"Nasty Grottonski," snapped the empress again. "You know I need this Marchant prince for our destiny."

Grotto breathed out slowly. Empress Ka-kik was as nervous as he was. One of the shamans leaned forward to whisper to her. She nodded.

"It is time!" she screeched, stepping back from the table as her two shamans stepped forward. They held large golden knives and in unison sliced Prince Rainere on each side of his neck, each wrist, each hip, and each ankle. Muttering their rhythmic incantations, the shamans took sticks from the fire and blew the smoke over the prince's insensible body. The blood, which had been trickling out slowly from the cuts, now leaked out more rapidly until it gushed down to the table. Grotto watched in horror as too much blood raced down in rivulets to spill over at the corners and fall into the fires.

Grotto shivered as the empress, the shamans, and all the other spiders in the cavern started a high, eerie keening. The sound stabbed at his ears and sent his pulse racing.

Prince Rainere lay as if he were dead.

Empress Ka-kik stepped forward and, still keening, laid her face over the prince's. As she breathed in his breath, she stiffened suddenly and raised her eyes to the ceiling.

The Spell of Retrieval was cast.

Frozen with fear, Grotto could only remember the journey his life had taken to get him to this evil cavern.

He had been there the very night that Prince Rainere had been born. It had been a night much like tonight. A storm had raged outside, shaking the windows and making the servants mutter. The princess's dying screams had set Grotto's teeth on edge as they echoed through the palace. The sound of Rainere's first cry had mingled with his mother's last.

He had been such a quick little thing, his bright eyes catching Grotto's as his tiny fingers squeezed Grotto's own, holding on for dear life. At the same moment, Grotto had felt his own heart squeezed in that little viselike grip. He had spent every waking minute since then serving his young master, guiding and training him in the traditions and ways of the royal Marchants. He had worked so hard to instill in the child the values and beliefs that had been held sacred by the family for thousands of years.

And now here he lay.

*The last Marchant prince and final hope of the family, bleeding to death on a stone slab in the Spider Peoples' nest, dying for a promise the prince had made to keep himself alive one hundred and fifteen years ago.*

Grotto felt a tear run down the leather of his old cheek.

"Forgive me, my prince. I could not see you forsworn…but the prophecy will save you. It has to…"

# CHAPTER TEN

## "He Wasn't Alone"

Rainere was running. Running as fast as he could through the Black Forest. He leaped over logs and dodged around the enormous Bolar Pines in his way. Looking up he could see the stars luminous overhead. He saw the leaves of the trees move in a breeze his body couldn't feel.

*I am well again!* thought Rainere with a fierce joy, letting out a howl that didn't reach his own ears. It mattered little that he knew it was a dream and that magic held him here. He saw traces as it glittered greenly on the edges of his vision.

The forest ended and he stood at the edge of a meadow. The grass waved and rippled rhythmically in an invisible breeze. The moon sat huge and voluptuous in the sky but dark, as if veiled by a blue shade.

*The Seventh Sister covers the moon,* thought Rainere, though he didn't know where the knowledge came from. *I haven't much time, I must find her!*

A shadow in the form of a great horse appeared over the land and caught Rainere's gaze.

*It was time.*

He ran to catch the shadow as it passed over the swaying grasses.

One jump, two jumps, and Rainere leaped onto the back of the shadow creature. He sat bolt upright as his power fused with the magic in the shadow. Faster than thought, they shot up through the sky, passing through the heavens, out of their galaxy and into another. A bright light raced before them. It glowed with the heat of a sun and had a tail like a comet.

"Faster, we must go faster!" Rainere urged his mount. It was a race now, and he had to be first.

The stars flashed by him as he managed to pass the speeding comet. The shadow he rode screamed in anger and pulled up short in front of the comet, dancing and rearing.

"No!" shrieked Rainere. The comet was traveling too fast; a collision would kill them all. The shadow horse wouldn't move and fought Rainere's control. It reared and struck out with its forelegs, challenging the comet.

Rainere could feel the heat from the comet on his face; already it was singeing his skin.

He leaped from his mount, down and away into the nothingness of the Universe. He heard the shadow horse scream in rage.

Then...

He floated in crystalline silence, surrounded by the pale light of an infinite number of stars. Suddenly, he wasn't alone.

The voice that spoke was female and filled up the emptiness in his soul. "Come to me, my prince."

*It was Her voice. The woman of his dreams had come to lead him home!*

Prince Rainere felt an unimaginable joy. The voice was a rope to guide him. He clung to it and pulled himself along until he reached a glass wall in the middle of the universe.

*That was odd.*

Rainere pushed at the wall. He kicked it and shoved it with his hands. He tried to fly up and around it, or under it, but the wall had become a bubble. Inside, he could see Her. He kicked harder at the wall, howling in frustration. He had to tell her he was coming for her...she had to know he could hear her.

"My prince…come to me, my prince!" Her voice echoed more softly now. She was crying. Crying because she didn't know he was there to take her. He wanted her so badly it hurt him in a place he hadn't known existed in his soul.

The bubble of glass was shrinking beneath his hands. The comet flashed past, smashing into him, and the bubble exploded.

Rainere's scream rent the silence and sent him spinning away through the stars. He struggled to get back to the broken bubble, his arms flailing to hold on to something. As the tears coursed down his face, he saw it was too late. Fragments of glass drifted about him, floating and spinning, reflecting only the stars back at him. She was gone. The comet had destroyed Her…

And now he was destroyed with Her.

Rainere stopped fighting.

He knew that if he didn't find the shadow horse, he would float endlessly in the stars with no way to return home. Stuck in the nothingness forever.

He knew all of this, and he didn't care.

She was gone.

The voice that spoke to him next was a vibration in his mind. It wasn't Her voice and he didn't want to listen.

"Prince Rainere, the stars are no place for a Marchant prince and the royal sovereign of the Seven Kingdoms of Evendaar…Master of the Grey Palace and Leader of Those Who Remain in Darkness…Caretaker of The Blood."

Rainere didn't take even a moment to consider the voice that spoke to him as he floated in the stars. He was lost, gone, shattered like the fragments of glass that surrounded him.

"Your love has called to us, last prince of Marchant, and we have heard you. It is decided that you shall be returned. As it is foretold, so shall it be."

A surge of hope buffeted Rainere's desolation and knocked him sideways. He tried to right himself, but with no horizon, there was no right way up.

"I hear you," he struggled to say. "Please! Please give her to me! I want her...I need her." His teeth started to chatter as though with the cold.

"You are dying, last prince of Marchant. Allow the Gift of Life to save your body, and I shall return your soul."

Rainere felt himself enclosed in a soft golden glow.

"Sleep, last prince of Marchant, for when you wake you will need your strength."

Immediately, a dull lethargy weighed heavily on Rainere's limbs.

"Who are you?" he murmured. "How can I thank you for giving her to me?"

The voice laughed and the sound was like a star softly exploding.

"We are called many names, all of which we are none. You may call me by the name of your love, for as you love her so you will be loving me. But be warned, last prince of Marchant. She will not be alone, as you are not alone. Only you can fight those she cannot see to keep her safe with you."

"But who will—"

"Sssshh, last prince of Marchant, sleep."

And the darkness was the blackest Rainere had ever known.

He slept.

# CHAPTER ELEVEN

## "Come To Me, My Prince"

Adele woke in the night and immediately checked the clock. It was 3:00 a.m. She groaned and lay gently back down on her pillow, hoping the movement wouldn't disturb any of the little ones nestled around her.

Outside, the storm seemed to get wilder. A rumble of thunder rattled the windows, and Stella whimpered in her sleep. All three of the children had been odd this afternoon, whiny and needy by turns. Then when the storm broke, just after dinner, it had all gotten a bit hysterical. Hence, they were now sleeping in her bed.

Adele sighed. She had fallen asleep herself in her clothes after reading and singing lullabies until she was hoarse.

She tried to pull off her uncomfortably tight jeans, but it was just too difficult to do lying down. Besides, she decided, she couldn't be bothered getting up and changing. It was too late, anyway. She lay back down on her pillow and closed her eyes, determined not to let her anxieties wake themselves up before she could go back to sleep.

It was cozy in her bedroom as the storm raged outside. It was easy to imagine the air golden and glowing, protecting them from bad dreams and dark thoughts. Adele reached out gently and made sure she was touching each of her children. They were all that was left of her family, and they were all that mattered.

Unbidden, an image of her Dream Man came into her mind. She smiled at the idea he might be part of her family, too. She needed him…he was her escape from reality.

Adele relaxed her face, her neck, her body, her mind.

*My prince. Oh, my prince,* she thought, her mind exploring his face in her memory. *Come to me, my prince, riding on your white horse, come and rescue me.*

Lying in her bed Adele, grinned. *I'm an idiot,* she thought, stifling a tired giggle.

There would be no prince on a white horse to rescue her, or at least not in this lifetime. She was all alone with her children and there was no one to save them but her now. She would have to be her own hero.

Adele didn't even notice the tear as it dripped from her eye. She turned into her pillow and, with her body wrapped around her three babies, she drifted into sleep.

It was quiet when it happened.

The sound that the universe makes when it rips cannot be heard by human ears.

There was just the gentle music of a wind chime and the murmur of voices from a distant shore as Adele and the children were surrounded by an intense white light and sucked through to another world.

# CHAPTER TWELVE

## "Welcome To the Golden Palace"

Adele felt the room warm and dark around her. She had dreamed such vivid dreams and was too exhausted to open her eyes yet. Her limbs felt like lead, but when she reached out, she recognized that each of her three children lay sprawled about her. She let sleep take her once again.

*     *     *

A strange smell woke Adele the next time. It tickled and irritated her nose like cheap incense. She coughed and brushed at her face. She'd had the oddest dream of a dark room, fire and chanting, and glass. Lots of broken glass. She coughed again and breathed more easily. Sleep stole her once more.

*     *     *

Adele was a little alarmed when she woke the third time. Instinctively, she knew she had slept too long. Her head felt heavy and her mouth was dry and furry. She tried to open her eyes but they seemed glued together. At least her body didn't feel so lethargic now, and she reached up to rub her face with her hands.

It was only then that she felt a gentle breeze wash over her. Her heart stopped beating. There was only one window in her bedroom and it was always locked.

*Oh God, who opened it?* She sat bolt upright in bed and then froze again. It seemed to take an awfully long time for her brain to process what she saw before her.

Adele and the three children were lying on a giant four-poster bed, covered in a purple-and-gold bedspread of the kind Adele couldn't afford. In fact, it looked like one of those fancy Italian brands. She really hoped the children weren't dribbling on it, as it probably had to be dry-cleaned…

With a supreme effort, Adele forced her mind to stop gibbering and take in the rest of her surroundings.

It was an enormous room and had been decorated sumptuously in gold and rosewood furniture. It looked like they could be in a European castle or some American millionaire's home. Everything sparkled and glittered with wealth.

*What. The. Hell?*

Adele counted doors, looking for the exits.

There were two sets of double doors, one in front of the bed and one to the right of her. There was another single door to her left. But despite how many there were, they all seemed miles away from the bed.

*You could almost fit our whole house just in this bedroom,* thought Adele, gazing around dazedly.

A tinkly noise brought her attention behind her, to yet another set of double doors, this time of glass, which led out to a balcony and were open to let in the breeze.

*Oh God, where are we?* Thought Adele, only vaguely aware that she should be feeling slightly more terrified than she currently was. But knowing herself like she did, no doubt catatonic fear wasn't far off. She decided to do some exploring before it set in and rendered her useless.

Adele slowly pulled her legs out from under Natalie, who didn't stir at all. She felt a weird sense of vertigo as she dropped down off the high bed, and planted her bare feet in the plush golden carpet.

"Don't scream," she admonished herself in a whisper, as a wild feeling of hysteria quickened in her chest. "Just don't bloody scream. I need to find out where we are. Maybe I should try the balcony first?"

The direction gave Adele a sense of purpose, and she focused hard on putting one foot in front of the other until she could reach out and touch the gauzy curtain blowing in the gentle breeze. The balcony beyond the doors was more like a terrace, and despite craning her neck, she couldn't see an end to it on either side.

*Where are all the people? And why is it so quiet?*

Nothing stirred in the room itself, and there was no sound but the little crystal wind chimes tinkling. A horrible thought occurred to Adele, and she quickly checked the children and was relieved by their quiet snores.

An hysterical laugh bubbled up in her chest.

"Stop it!" she warned herself firmly. "This is just a dream…a really, really vivid dream. Maybe I can go out on the balcony and try to fly home…but what about the children? Can they fly, too?"

Adele stepped forward and out the doors onto the balcony, but having braved that much she couldn't make herself go any farther.

Despite the weirdness of her situation, she could still appreciate the beauty of the day. The sun shone out of a deep azure sky and the gentle breeze was soft and fresh on her face. She jumped when she heard a bird singing from the balustrade.

She had never dreamed of the daytime before.

Adele pulled back from the balcony doors, absentmindedly taking in the elegance of the gold door handles and the fragile texture of the pink curtains. Someone had spent a lot of money on this place. She walked back to the bed and her sleeping children, noticing now that even the bed sparkled in the sunlight. As she came closer, she realized it was made of glass, or maybe even crystal. *Impossible!* Her hand ran over the intricately carved bedpost. She closed her eyes as she swooned slightly, pressing her head against the cold surface.

*Wakeupwakeupwakeup!* she prayed.

Adele's stomach gurgled loudly. Suddenly she felt…real. She held her breath as her stomach continued to growl and her bladder began to complain. Never once had she felt hungry in a dream. Not once…not ever. Adele's head started spinning again and she willed herself to let her breath go and take in another one.

"If I'm really real and really here…then the kids are real, too?"

She reached out and touched Aaron's shoulder. She felt the warm reality of him as he twitched under her hand.

Adele felt the walls close in on her and her breath start coming in short, sharp bursts as the enormity of the situation came crashing down on her.

All four of them had been abducted and taken somewhere far away. She didn't know how she could be sure, but the breeze that blew in the window did not smell like the dust and eucalyptus of home.

Adele struggled with herself as panic threatened to release the control of her bladder.

*How the hell did they get us here? Why were we all asleep? Were we drugged? We're all still in our pajamas so when did this happen? God, I really have to pee. Maybe a drug cartel or an arms dealer or…* Adele thought, frantically trying to come up with a reason for their abduction. *But why would anyone like that want to take us? We don't have any money for ransom, nor does anyone we know. Maybe Justin sold us into slavery?*

But no, that was too ridiculous.

Adele realized she was trembling. Her heart raced and she clasped her arms around herself to keep from falling apart.

Adele heard a voice. She froze. A second voice joined the first. Adele's terrified senses picked up the sounds coming from behind the double doors to her right. She had never been so scared in all her life.

Her maternal instincts melted the icy grip of fear when she realized she was on the wrong side of the bed. She forced her legs to move so she could stand between whoever was coming through that door and her sleeping children.

She had no idea what she would do if armed men entered the room.

A new terror sliced through her as other voices joined the first two. It was too difficult to tell what language they spoke but they were getting louder. Suddenly, the voices fell silent.

Adele braced herself. A ringing started softly in her ears but she couldn't afford to faint now. She glanced back at her defenseless children, and anger started a slow burn somewhere deep inside her. Adele took strength from its heat and spread her arms, like a mother bird protecting her young.

Frantic thoughts buzzed through her head. *God, I must look stupid! What if they have weapons? Somebody help us!*

The door handle turned.

A small rotund woman in a sparkly gold dress poked her head in and opened the door wide. She stepped into the room and was followed by a much taller man. The two of them stood facing Adele at a safe distance, their expressions watchful. Waiting.

Adele remained in her defensive pose, eyes wild, with barely a breath in her lungs. Another moment passed.

The little woman stepped forward and dropped into a deep curtsy before standing up again. Her eyes were a soft lavender-blue and were scrunched at the sides in a way that suggested her face was most comfortable when smiling. Her mouth twitched at the corners now as if to prove that. Something about the woman oozed comfort and joy, from the bouncing blonde curls piled high on her head to the little hands clasped in front of her plump bosom. Adele guessed she might be in her early fifties, but with rosy cheeks and that puffy gold dress, it was hard to be sure.

Adele sniffed at the fragrance that drifted over to her. The lady smelled of peaches.

Adele fought an hysterical urge to leap into this woman's arms and sob all her fear onto that well-cushioned shoulder. She managed to restrain herself, but the effort caused her to start shaking again. Never moving her eyes from the two figures before her, Adele slowly dropped her fatigued arms to her sides. With this semblance of strength gone, Adele felt she had to react strongly in another way.

"Who are you?" She whispered, her voice was hoarse and dry.

The stranger took another step forward and curtsied deeply again. Her dress rustled prettily. But Adele's eyes didn't miss the restraining hand the tall man placed on his companion's elbow.

*Are they afraid of me?* She wondered.

"Oh, Your Grace! We are so mightily honored to have you here with us. Again, I mean. So honored," the lady gushed, her expression radiating happiness and sincerity. "We are also honored to welcome you to the Golden Palace, and your ancestral home." She blushed after her little speech and dropped into another curtsy.

The outward appearance of respect helped to dissolve some of Adele's more bizarre theories about their situation, but her brain still churned wildly, wondering what this meant for the children.

"Why are we here?" she croaked, her throat clearing slightly.

The older woman's smile froze just a little, and she threw a quick look at the man behind her.

"Your Grace has returned home," she repeated, gesturing about the room with her small hands. "It is a miracle that after all these years, we have you back again."

Her blue eyes twinkled and Adele realized she had tears in them.

"Who are you?" repeated Adele slowly.

"Oh! My apologies, Your Grace! My sincerest, deepest apologies, Your Grace. I have forgotten to introduce myself, of course." The woman blushed even more deeply, the pink flush staining her chest.

For some reason her discomfort made Adele feel slightly more at ease.

"Your Grace, my name is Dolores Ollenby of the St. Lucidis Ollenbys from the Blue Hills…down near the Belvoir Estate." She drifted off upon realizing Adele wore a nonplussed expression. With a quick "Er-herm," she squared her shoulders and continued.

"I am the Head Keeper of the royal household and Matron of the royal nursery and I am Your Grace's servant in all things," she finished in a rush of breath and dropped into another deep curtsy. She rose, waiting for a response.

Adele stared.

"I'm here to assist Your Grace and the little Majesties in any way I can now that you are all awake." Dolores Ollenby gave a little wave to someone behind Adele.

Adele spun her head to see her children all sitting up in bed, wide-eyed and staring. With one movement, they all turned to look at her. She saw her own shock and uncertainty reflected in their faces, and it nearly killed her fragile composure. She shuffled back up onto the bed and gathered them in her arms. Stella buried her face in her mother's neck while Natalie and Aaron moved in to her sides. Holding her children like this made Adele feel braver, and that helped her manage her longest question yet.

"What do you want with us?" Her voice wasn't far from normal now.

Dolores Ollenby looked slightly confused but hid it with a big smile.

"Well, Your Grace, I believe that question might be better answered by the high wizard here than by myself." Dolores Ollenby gestured to the man behind her and moved out of his way with a little bob.

The man stepped forward and commanded Adele's full attention so directly she wondered how she could have looked away from him before.

He was very tall, well over six feet. Long white hair, which hung to his shoulders, framed a narrow face, and a long gray beard fell past his chest. Despite the full beard, she could see he was smiling at her. Under bushy eyebrows vivid blue eyes sparkled, almost hypnotizing her with their intense color.

Although he was so imposing, his smile was radiant, and Adele was shocked to see Aaron respond and smile back.

"Welcome, Majesties," he began, spreading his arms and bowing low. "Welcome to your kingdom of Unisia on the world of Evendaar. I understand that you must be very confused by your sudden arrival here, but I must say, you all look to have recovered very well from your incredibly long journey."

His voice was clear and sonorous, but Adele was having a hard time concentrating on full sentences, as her mind kept shrieking at each strange word.

*Unisia? Majesties? Evendaar?*

"Allow me to introduce myself. My name is Ohren and I am the Head of the High Wizards Council of Unisia. I have many other titles but the only other one you need to know is that I am your friend. It was I and my brother wizards who brought you here to this land and your native world of Evendaar."

He paused and let this sink in. His concerned eyes found Adele's, and for a moment, she felt she might drown in the iridescent blue of them. She shook her head, blinking, and the moment passed.

"Mummy, where are we?" piped up Natalie, her voice squeaky from sleep.

Ohren smiled broadly. "It is nowhere on your Earth world, Your Grace. You have all been brought back to your ancestral home on Evendaar."

"My name isn't Grace, it's Natalie," said Natalie boldly.

Ohren bowed again. "It's an honor to meet you, Princess Natalie."

Natalie giggled and the sound seemed incongruous to Adele, who was still trapped by her disbelief.

"Of course this has all got to be overwhelming for you, Your Graces. But we would not have brought you here except in the case of our greatest time of need. The Hidden Child is returned and will sit on the throne of Unisia once again, and we welcome you back with all our hearts."

The silence that fell after his speech was total. Adele couldn't understand how he could keep speaking yet make less and less sense.

A small gurgle broke the silence. Stella raised her head from her mother's neck and looked at Aaron, who shifted uncomfortably.

"Mummy, I'm hungry, aren't I?" he whispered loudly.

Adele roused herself from her mystified reverie. She looked down at her little boy with his sleep-rumpled hair and his worried green eyes. His vulnerability strengthened her.

"Of course, darling," she soothed him, brushing his hair out of his eyes. "We'll get something for you."

"And me," murmured Natalie.

"Me," added Stella.

Adele forced her voice to sound smooth and calm. Addressing the Wizard Ohren, she felt a sickening thrill of nerves.

"The children are very hungry. Do you think it would be possible to feed them?"

The wizard raised an eyebrow.

"I should think it would be more than possible, Your Grace." He bowed slightly to the pink-cheeked woman, who was waiting with clasped hands. "Mrs. Ollenby?"

Mrs. Ollenby beamed as if all her Christmases had come at once.

"Well, of course, Your Grace! We have a small dining room for you through the doors here, and I will have luncheon set up in a moment."

"No!" said Adele much louder than she meant to. "We'll just eat in here."

She wasn't sure why she felt it safer to eat on the bed but at least here she knew. Out there, beyond the doors, could be any number of surprises.

"But of course, Your Grace," acquiesced Mrs. Ollenby immediately, smiling at the children and clapping her hands. "We shall have a meal for you in just a twinkle."

She winked at Natalie but seemed unperturbed by the lack of response.

Another man stepped into the room, eyes downcast. He was dressed all in gold and white, like he was going to a fancy party. Mrs. Ollenby didn't turn to look at him, but spoke quietly over her shoulder.

"We will bring in the luncheon things to the bedroom for their Graces' meal."

The man stepped out, but not a moment later six men dressed exactly the same way came into the room carrying silver trays.

Adele jumped at the sudden entrance of so many people and squeezed Aaron's arm, making him yelp. Ohren moved close to the bed, his arms held behind his back in an obvious effort to seem nonthreatening.

"Calm yourself, madam." His tone was gentle. "You have all been on a very long journey and have slept for over a day and a night. It is important that you should eat and regain your strength. No one seeks to cause you any harm here."

He stared intently into her eyes and Adele felt herself falling into the blue again. "You are safe now, Your Grace."

Adele felt the tension in her back loosen its hold slightly. She realized the tall stranger had a point. She would need to maintain her strength if she was to remain vigilant in this alien environment.

A small clammy hand touched the back of her neck and Aaron whispered in her ear. Adele felt extremely uncomfortable making requests of these strangers who held them captive, but the children had needs. She decided to use the same mannered attitude that had been shown to her.

"Excuse me…uh…sir," she began. "The children would like to use a bathroom before they eat."

"Of course, Your Grace, of course, most natural." The wizard beamed at the children. "And very healthy, too. It's a wonderful sign, as it means all of your organs are functioning well after the journey, just as we hoped…"

"High Wizard," interrupted Mrs. Ollenby as she bustled past him and put her arms out to Aaron to help him down off the bed. "Children do not like to wait for bathrooms, if you don't mind?"

Wizard Ohren stepped back out of the way as the family struggled off the high bed.

"Quite right," he agreed, still smiling.

Mrs. Ollenby rolled her eyes and tsk'd disrespectfully.

"Wizards!" She smiled. "They get so excited about very mundane things. Here we go, everyone!"

Mrs. Ollenby had led them through the single door, to the left of the bed, and into a cavernous bathroom. An enormous bath took up most of the floor, but a line of three vase-shaped pots was attached on one side of a wall and Adele made a beeline for them.

Adele allowed Mrs. Ollenby to help her get all the children on and off the pots and watched as the lady worked the complicated system of taps to get the water temperature just right for washing hands.

When they reentered the bedroom, she saw the bed had been transformed. A feast had been set up at the end of it with glass plates, silverware, and real crystal glasses placed on individual trays, ready for each of them. The cushions and pillows had been moved to act as seating behind the buffet of food.

"My's hungry," burst out Stella, frightening her mother but causing a ripple of merriment around the room.

"Of course you are, dearest," chortled Mrs. Ollenby. "Up you hop, everyone on the bed and eat anything you like. We have a little bit of everything here, as I didn't know what your favorites would be."

The food in front of them smelled delicious, but Adele felt it was only wise to examine everything before allowing her children to touch it. Most of it looked familiar, like the vegetables and fruit, for instance. There was a grain dish, which looked like sand but tasted nutty and was similar to rice. Adele heaped the children's plates with what she felt comfortable with but stayed away from the meat dishes. While they ate, Mrs. Ollenby kept up a chatty monologue explaining what everything was and which utensil was used for which food. She poured juice and set water for them all, and Adele eagerly slaked her thirst.

She took the time now that she felt less desperate to observe her surroundings.

*They keep calling me "Your Grace,* she thought. *And this room is certainly sumptuous enough for royalty. Everyone is being so polite and there are so many servants here. Everyone speaks English but these people could be from so many different races.*

She looked around at the different features and skin tones of the men who were waiting on her and the children, all dressed in gold and white.

*But where are we, really? Maybe this is just a big hoax and a compère is going to jump out from behind a door shrieking that this is all a joke.*

Adele looked around, searching for cameras that might be hidden in corners. Maybe someone had broken character and was wearing a digital watch?

But no. The beautiful room around her remained completely unfamiliar.

She watched as Mrs. Ollenby walked over to where the wizard was standing by the balcony doors.

*Wizard?*

She was so confused. Did *wizard* mean the same thing here as at home? Another phrase filtered through her unconscious: *greatest need.* What was all that about? Adele was sure it could only mean something dangerous. She choked on the piece of bread she was eating as her throat closed over.

*Oh dear God, someone help us, please!* She thought wildly.

"Your Grace?" The wizard spoke softly but Adele was alarmed that she hadn't heard his approach. Panic gripped her with fresh strength.

"If you'll allow an old man to sit with you, I will answer some of your no doubt more pressing questions before the coronation."

Adele shuffled back on the bed as Ohren perched himself easily next to her. She wondered at his familiarity. He was obviously the one in charge in the room, but the respectful way he spoke to her was sincere, and would have been charming if she wasn't so terrified. He certainly didn't look like he was about to attack her or the children.

"We have a legend in our land, a prophecy, if you will," began Ohren in response to Adele's silence.

"What coronation?" Adele blurted out.

"Wouldn't you prefer I started at the beginning of things, Your Grace?" the wizard asked kindly.

"How about we just skip to the part about when we can go home again, Wiz...zard." Adele stumbled over his title; this was all just too ridiculous.

"Please, Your Grace." Ohren raised his hand as she opened her mouth to speak again. "We have only a little time and much to say."

Adele nodded slightly, cowed by his aura of authority.

"As I said before, my name is Ohren and I sit at the head of the High Wizards Council, which is one-half of the governing body of Unisia. One hundred and forty-five years ago, civil war threatened the kingdom and a violent coup was launched on the leading royal family of St. Lucidis. Our queen was with child at the time the Golden Palace was stormed by the insurgents. The shock brought on an early labor and the queen birthed her daughter that very day. Terrified the insurgents would kill her baby and true heir to the throne, the queen asked the Wizards Council to hide her baby somewhere she could never be harmed. Unfortunately, the Wizards Council had been influenced by elements that supported the insurgents' coup. So, those in the inner circle made a decision that instead of simply hiding the Princess they would send her away through time and space to another world entirely. To the world of Earth, where she would be safe."

The wizard paused and gave a deep sigh, and Adele saw worry etched across his face.

"Weakened by her daughter's birth, the queen died that very night. But the king and the family of St. Lucidis fought on, defending the palace and winning the battle. They retained the palace and their seat of power, but they had lost their only heir of royal blood. Unfortunately, the king died soon after the victory. The kingdom was left to be run by the Wizards Council, and a Regent placed next to the Throne by a common vote by the heads of Evendaar's four royal families." He paused again and looked Adele clear in the eyes. She saw blue fire burning there.

"You, Adelena, are the baby who was sent away so long ago. You are the heir to the throne of St. Lucidis and the rightful Queen of Unisia by dint of the purity of your bloodline. The kingdom is facing a dark time, and we need a leader to show us the way back to the light."

Adele sat back on the enormous bed, clutching her children, completely and utterly stupefied.

*I have to say something and stop this madness*, she thought, overwhelmed by the insanity of Ohren's words.

Natalie got in first.

"So my mummy is a queen now?" she asked, gazing up at Ohren with her big green eyes.

"Yes, little one." Ohren smiled kindly. "At least, she will be as soon as we can attend her coronation."

Adele finally got her mouth to work. "What?" she spluttered.

"Your coronation, Your Grace. All is in readiness, and we are due to begin, now-ish."

"Now-ish," repeated Adele stupidly.

"Mummy, the coronation is when they put a crown on your head." Natalie's eyes lit up with excitement.

"What? Why do we need to do it now?" Adele asked.

Ohren's gaze flicked to the door more than once, giving him a slightly shifty look.

"Because the time is right and your subjects are waiting," Ohren explained, quickly getting up from the bed and checking a timepiece in his pocket. "We gain nothing from waiting, I'm afraid, Your Grace."

Very quietly, more servants filed into the room; this time all were women. They either held huge bundles of velvet and lace in their arms or carried wooden trays of beautiful shoes and jewelry. Mrs. Ollenby clapped her hands and bustled forward.

"If High Wizard Ohren will excuse us, it is time for the royal family to dress for the ceremony."

The women carrying the clothes moved to the bed.

Adele's patience snapped. "Wait just a minute!" she shouted and climbed off the bed. "You mean to tell me that you put me on Earth as a baby but now you want me back as the heir to your throne on this alien planet, Um...usia?"

"Unisia," corrected Mrs. Ollenby with a smile.

"And now I need to be the queen right here, right now?"

"Your grasp of the situation is admirable, Your Grace, given the strangeness of your circumstances." Ohren beamed at Adele.

"But how do you know you've got the right girl?" she asked, baffled into curiosity by the wizard's happiness.

Ohren smiled even wider. He moved forward and took both her hands and gave them a squeeze. His hands were warm and so big they covered hers completely.

"Why, Your Grace, the Gods showed us the way to you, and the Gods do not lie."

He squeezed her hands again.

"We also performed the Blood Ceremony, and it's indubitable: you are of the royal St. Lucidis line. You are your father's daughter."

He stepped back to allow Mrs. Ollenby to present Adele with her dress.

Adele shook her head wildly. She felt like a child but the idea of getting naked and dressed again was too much right now.

Mrs. Ollenby paused in the face of Adele's reticence.

"Just put the robes over their clothes, Mrs. Ollenby," said Ohren and walked back over to the double doors, stealing a glance into the other room beyond.

"Time is of the essence, dear lady," he called and sent the serving women and Mrs. Ollenby into a frenzy of activity.

"I'm sorry to be so rough, Your Grace," said Mrs. Ollenby with an apologetic grimace as she pulled a dress over Adele's head. The material was a heavily embroidered gold brocade, studded with glittering stones. It didn't completely cover Adele's old pink T-shirt, but a lace collar was fastened around her neck with a huge pearl chocker to add to the disguise.

Adele watched anxiously as the children were gently prodded and pulled into their own gold lace dresses and pants by the serving ladies. All three children looked very serious but didn't seem frightened any more. Adele yelped as her hair was brushed and twisted high up on her head, and fixed in place with a gold net. A large gold cape was placed on her shoulders and fastened by a linked gold chain across her front. It was a truly enormous costume, and as Adele crumpled handfuls of the purple silk lining in her hands, she felt pulled down by the sheer weight of it.

"I'm sorry, Your Grace," apologized Mrs. Ollenby when she saw Adele's discomfort. "It really is an awfully heavy cloak, but it was made for monarchs much larger than yourself, you see."

The lady moved off to finish tying on the little purple lace capes around the children, knotting big silk bows under their chins. Adele would have laughed at the sight of them all dressed up in flowing lace and bows, but the situation was just too weird for laughter.

"We weren't expecting to have to dress any little ones, but as long as they are matching for the ceremony, that's all that really matters," said Mrs. Ollenby, eyeing her handiwork critically.

"But I look like a girl, don't I, Mummy?" complained Aaron when he caught sight of himself in a mirror.

"Well, I look like a princess," said Natalie, preening in front of the same mirror. "And I *am* a princess, if Mummy is a queen."

"Hey, I guess that's right," agreed Adele, taking her cue from the children and acting along. She moved to take the lace cape from Mrs. Ollenby, who was trying to dress a squirming Stella. She tied the silk bow under Stella's chubby chin, smoothing the cloak down over her Hello Kitty pajamas and gently pulling some of the snarls out of her blonde curls.

"Now you are a princess, too, Stella Bella," Adele whispered, kissing Stella on the nose.

"Yes, but only a baby one," agreed her big sister reluctantly.

"I'm a princess, too, aren't I, Mummy?" insisted Aaron, stepping in front of Natalie at the mirror.

"No, Aaron, you are a boy, so that makes you a prince, not a princess," corrected Natalie in her bossiest voice.

"I said that!" cried Aaron, "I said, I'm a prince."

As the all-too-normal sounds of the children bickering filled the unfamiliar room, Adele counted the exits one more time.

But what could she do?

No matter how kind her captors were, they were still not going to let any of them go home. She was trapped. They were all trapped.

# CHAPTER THIRTEEN

## "My Dream…She Has Left"

Rainere slept as still and cold as the dead.

Grotto stayed in the armchair before the fire, holding his lonely vigil and watching the expressionless face of his master for any flicker of movement. Occasionally he would get up to force water between the prince's ice-cold lips, and tried to keep him comfortable with piles of heavy bed furs. A huge fire burned endlessly in the grate, and the flickering light gave the prince an artificial appearance of warmth.

When there was no other way to serve his master, Grotto sat on his knees and prayed to the Goddess Lune. If only his master could be brought back to him whole in body and mind.

It had been awful in the cavern of the Spider People.

When the empress had collapsed during the Spell of Retrieval, her shamans had rushed to her side, leaving the prince unguarded. Grotto had felt true fear as he had looked down upon his prince, so white and bloodless, on that ancient table. With shaking hands, Grotto had been able to give the prince the Gift of Life, and his old heart had almost stopped when his master had risen to take the Gift in his arms and absorb the rest himself before closing his eyes again. With the nest in an uproar over their empress and the failure of the spell, Grotto was able to hoist the prince over his shoulder and somehow stagger back up the tunnels and outside to their waiting horses.

Getting back to the Grey Palace had been a nightmare, with Grotto afraid that every bump and low-hanging tree would knock the unconscious prince from his saddle.

But even back in the safety of the Grey Palace, the battle wasn't over yet. Grotto feared his prince was too weak to return to the land of the living. The Dark Magic of the Spell of Retrieval had been too strong; too much blood had been lost from his body, already strained by the effects of the Blue Tonic.

Still, Grotto did not give up hope.

And on the second morning, his faith was rewarded when the prince awoke.

Grotto was dozing in his chair by the fire. His chin slumped to his chest, his legs sprawled and almost touching the grate. A noise roused him and instantly his head turned to the prince. Faster than thought, Grotto sprang to the side of the bed, and something akin to joy lit up his soul.

"Master?"

Rainere didn't turn his head to the sound of Grotto's voice. His dark eyes only stared sightlessly at the ceiling.

"She's gone," he said and his voice was desolate. "My Dream…she has left…gone…where can I find her? The Gods spoke to me but I can't find her."

Grotto was confused. "Master, if you speak of the Empress Ka-kik? The empress yet lives, master!"

But it was too late. Rainere had passed out again. Grotto placed his hand over the prince's mouth and felt the breath only lightly against his skin.

"Oh please, Gods, don't take him yet," begged the old man, his voice the only one in the deep silence of the room.

*    *    *

It wasn't until the next day that Rainere woke again.

The prince opened his eyes. He was back in his own chamber, in the Grey Palace. He was back with the world.

"Thank the Gods, I am returned," Rainere groaned aloud, and the words scratched at his dry throat.

The memory of the Goddess's voice reverberated around his head, and he shivered. The power in her voice had made him feel so tiny, and so insignificant. But he had been saved for a reason. He had to rescue his Dream Woman from the bright comet who had taken her.

Rainere struggled to sit up, and groaned at the stiffness in his muscles. He swung his legs over the side of the bed, and the feel of cold stone under his feet made him flinch.

The gray light at the window showed it was probably midafternoon. The patter of rain against the window beat almost in time with the ticking timepiece above the fireplace. Rainere listened to the gentle sounds as his shivering grew more and more violent. He knew unless he warmed up that the cold would soon paralyze him.

It took all his strength to rise and stagger to the fireplace. The blaze had burned down to a pile of glowing embers, and Rainere reached in to take the hot coals in his hands, blowing on them to make the sparks dance. Instead of burning his flesh, the light appeared to leach out of the coals and transfer into Rainere's long white fingers. When the first coals turned black, Rainere dropped them on the hearth and picked up another handful. The heat slowly returned to his body, and Rainere's shivering finally abated. He stood and returned to curl up on his bed before the threatening nausea overwhelmed him. Closing his eyes again, he breathed in deeply, and tapped into the power that lay at the center of his core. It leaped to his thought and made him start. Physically he felt wrecked, but this surge of magical strength could only come from one source. He opened his eyes and looked about with a new clarity. Something had changed within him, despite his failure within the spell.

Rainere considered what he knew.

It must have been the Spider Empress who had cast the Spell of Retrieval, fusing her power to his. But she hadn't been strong enough to carry him, even with his blood fueling her spell. Clearly, the spell had been poorly constructed—her horse form hadn't been nearly fast enough to ride in the stars. If only he hadn't been unconscious when she had cast the spell, maybe then he could have succeeded in getting through the glass wall and to his Dream Woman first. If only.

*"Come to me, my prince…"*

Rainere ground his teeth in frustration. She had cried out for him as he wept for her. Even the Gods had heard the two of them.

*Next time, she will be mine*, he vowed silently. I will do whatever it takes to rescue her.

The voice of the Goddess had told him he would find her, and it was doing no good to be lying in bed. He had to get started.

Rainere pulled himself up again and swallowed the bile that filled his mouth.

"Grotto!" His voice was harsh and croaky in the quiet room.

In irritation, Rainere uttered a small summoning charm and added a little tweak to let Grotto know to answer immediately. He was surprised again at how quickly his power flowed at his command. Within minutes, Grotto was at the chamber door, rubbing his head where his hair had been pulled and cursing his rotten luck that the prince had woken just when he'd had to answer a call of nature.

"Oh master, you are finally awake! I had so feared that…" Grotto trailed off as he took in Prince Rainere's expression. He dropped to his knees.

"Master, forgive me. I had to keep you to your oath to the Spider Empress. She needed you immediately to fulfill the prophecy. But you were unconscious from the poison of the Blue Tonic. They needed The Blood for their rites…I couldn't let you break your oath to aid them in their time of need."

Prince Rainere pulled himself up to stand and sneered at his old servant, but his vitriol was for himself. He had been so weak. While he'd been unconscious and helpless, they had taken his blood for one of their barbaric and primitive rituals, and like a cheap whore his spirit had turned away, and let them.

Grotto crawled on his knees to the bedside.

"Please, master, do not blame yourself…it's the Blue Tonic that brings you so low."

"But it wasn't the Blue Tonic that brought me back, was it, Grotto?" The prince's eyes were shadowed. He already knew the answer.

Grotto blanched. "I had to, master." His voice was plaintive, begging. "You needed the Gift of Life so badly…they had taken so much of The Blood from you when their empress collapsed. There was no time for you to heal naturally."

"Their rites failed, anyway?" said Rainere bleakly, sitting back down before his shaking legs betrayed him.

"I fear that the Spell of Retrieval they tried only failed because another power, which had also cast the same spell, intervened…or at least that was as much as I could gather from the shamans as they tried to resuscitate their empress."

Rainere's gaze became thoughtful.

"Who were they trying to retrieve across the universe?"

Grotto shrugged and got off his old knees now that Prince Rainere's dark humor may have passed, but he kept his face averted from the prince as he answered.

"It was said that they were looking for the Hidden Child of the Prophecy of the End of the World. As to who stopped them, it could only have been the wizards."

The prince raised an eyebrow. "I have heard of this prophecy—but the child was called the Lost Child."

"Lost or hidden, it is still the same prophecy, master," said Grotto. "Empress Ka-kik sought to bring the Hidden Child back to this world to fulfill the prophecy, which says the Child will bring the Dark Powers back to the throne of Unisia."

Rainere barked a mirthless laugh.

"That's what they wasted The Blood on!" he sneered. "Well, my Oath is fulfilled. They will have no more of it again."

He had a brief memory of a little lavender book that had contained a similar prophecy. He had put it somewhere…perhaps on his desk, or in a pocket?

Rainere got up and walked to the window. After the initial shock of waking wore off, his legs felt more solid and his heart beat strongly in his chest now. The miserable fog of the Blue Tonic had completely dissipated, and a healthy hunger burned in his belly, despite the nausea. Rainere felt strong and whole again.

The Gift. The cursed Gift had done this to him. How many times had he spurned it, preferring the chemical-induced health of the Blue Tonic to the moral complications of using such a precious resource? And now he was awash with it. He breathed deep and felt the Gift pulsing through him.

The prince looked out over the soft gray of falling twilight. His gardens were already cloaked in shadows.

"I think perhaps that my Dream Woman might be this Hidden Child the empress was searching for."

Grotto didn't like the dreamy note in the prince's tone.

"Your guess is better than mine, master, but like I said before, that phantom was just—"

"But she isn't a phantom, Grotto," corrected Rainere, speaking to his own reflection in the window glass. "She is real. The Gods told me so when I was out beyond the stars."

Something shifted in the bottom of Grotto's gut.

A secret, long buried, shivered and made him feel ill. *If the phantom which had plagued the prince's dreams was actually…? But no, it couldn't be.*

Grotto's thoughts turned wildly, and he forced his body into action to disguise his disquiet. He went to the bed and began to remove the old sheets.

"Be that as it may, master, you will need to regain your full strength before you do anything else tonight. And it might be wise to find out if the wizards at the Golden Palace were successful where the Empress Ka-kik was not, in retrieving the Child of the Prophecy. I will run your bath and have dinner served for you in the Glassroom…it will do you good to get out this chamber."

The prince nodded absently, already distracted by the conundrum in front of him.

How was he to find his precious Dream Woman now that he knew there was a very real possibility she was in Evendaar?

\*       \*       \*

The Glassroom was dimly lit by a large candelabra that sat on the dining table in the middle of the room. Three walls and the ceiling were made entirely of glass panels, and they reflected the candlelight back into the room, lending an eerie feeling of depth where there was none. Hundreds of plants lined the walls in deep trenches and in pots on pedestals, but they were withered and mostly dead. The room was once a thriving greenroom filled with elegant trees and precious flowers, but it had been left untouched since Princess Rainella, Rainere's mother, had died. It had been her favorite room, and it was now Rainere's, if for no reason other than it was one of his only tenuous connections to her.

His long hair hung, damp and shining, down his back, and he was dressed warmly in a heavy silk gown and leather slippers. Sitting at one end of the dining table, Rainere stared at a fixed point in the distance as he steadily ate the plate of meat and vegetables that had been set in front of him. Grotto stood behind his chair ready to fulfill any need he might have. At a pause in Rainere's chewing, Grotto doused the prince's meat with gravy before he continued eating. The prince didn't appear to notice.

It was only a loud knock at the door of the Glassroom that woke Rainere from his sleepless dreaming. Grotto opened the doors but stepped back in surprise when he saw a brightly-dressed messenger at the door led by a gray-faced house servant.

"'is 'ighness 'as a visitor," growled the sullen servant before turning on his heel and vanishing down the hall.

The pink-cheeked messenger and Grotto stared at each other in silence for a moment…then another…

"For Gods' sake, let the man in," said Rainere, hiding his curiosity with a bored tone.

With a start, Grotto came to his senses and stepped back smartly to allow the man to come in.

Rainere watched the messenger with cold eyes. He hadn't seen an official messenger in St. Lucidis livery in the halls of the Grey Palace in over one hundred years. The shiny gold and purple of the man's clothing was odd in the somber atmosphere of the Glassroom, with its dark windows and dead foliage.

Grotto took his place behind the prince's right shoulder and glowered at their visitor, who shuffled and ruffled himself in preparation for his speech. It appeared he had the very good sense to be extremely nervous about delivering his message.

"Er-herm…to His Royal Highness, Prince Rainere Rainov Lucien Grey Marchant, Immortal Wizard and Last Prince and Head of the Marchant family, Steward of the Grey Palace and Leader of the Star Seeker Clan…"

The prince rolled his hand in a signal for the young man to get to the point.

"Er-herm, er-herm," coughed the messenger, his pink cheeks blushing even hotter. "I, Odell Bluewin of the St. Lucidis family, have been entrusted with the duty, and pleasure, of informing His Royal Highness of the most wonderful and immediate joy bequeathed on the kingdom not three days since…er-herm…due to the bountiful goodness of our Gods and our Wizards Council." Grotto snorted quietly. "The good Princess Adelena has been returned through the wise and mysterious ways of the wizards. The princess, having passed the Ceremony of the Blood and been indisputably proven to be the daughter of the last, and late, King Octavius III, is being crowned as we speak in the presence of High Wizard Ohren and all the honorable dignitaries of the Court of the Golden Palace. You are hereby invited to the ceremony of homage to our new queen, and the subsequent ball, to celebrate the queen's coronation. Long live the Queen Adelena Olivia Serena St. Lucidis!"

The messenger finished the last bit in one breath and his face was quite purple by the end of his speech.

Whatever Rainere had been expecting to hear, it certainly hadn't been that!

He picked up his fork and absently twirled it in his hands. His mind was racing.

*A new queen has been brought to this world and crowned already by the Wizards Council?*

*The memory of a bright white comet streaking toward the glass sphere and his Dream Woman inside it.*

*"My prince…"*

"Adelena," the prince whispered, and her name, and all the pieces in his mind, clicked into place like a puzzle suddenly arranging itself.

The ghost of a smile flickered across the prince's face.

"Er-herm, er-herm, the Ceremony of Homage will take place in one week's time, and the royal interviews will be conducted on the day following the ball. I have Your Highness's official invitation and itinerary of events here...should Your Highness not wish to attend, there is a notice to be signed under the first page." The messenger sounded hopeful it would be used.

With a flick of his hand, Rainere motioned for Grotto to step forward and accept the invitation. The messenger flinched as Grotto snatched it out of his shaking hand.

"And now, Odell Bluewin of St. Lucidis, you have discharged your duty admirably." Rainere took his eyes from the messenger as Grotto handed him the parchment scroll. "I thank you for the invitation, and when you go back to the Golden Palace, you will tell the wizards that the Marchant prince will be attending this Ceremony of Homage to our new queen."

He could hardly suppress the energy surging through his body with excitement at the news, but he kept his manner controlled.

"My man, Grottonski, will take you and your entourage to the kitchens for refreshments before allowing you on your way. I will not have it said that the Marchant family does not provide hospitality to its guests, no matter how lowborn. We are not monsters, after all."

The poor messenger looked as if he would rather jump out of a window than go anywhere with the formidable Grotto, but he acquiesced with a polite bow.

"Your Highness is too kind." He followed the manservant out of the room.

Left alone, the prince pulled the ribbon from the scroll and slowly unfurled the paper. The magical seal broke at his command with a small crackle. He read the document three times before he could take in any of the information written on the golden paper. His hands shook as adrenaline suddenly spiked through his body. He leaped up, sending his chair crashing backward to the floor, and began pacing the Glassroom, cursing aloud.

"Gods, this is impossible! The wizards have taken her for their own…are they seeking to avoid the prophecy being fulfilled, or trying to fulfill it? How much do they know? Why do they have this knowledge in common with the Spider People? What am I missing here? Where did I put that little lavender book of prophecy?"

Rainere paused in his pacing as a thought struck him.

"Adelena. Her name is Adelena."

His heart ached; finally, he had her name after all this time.

"She is here in the world, my world…and so close." Rainere turned in the direction of the Golden Palace. She was only two days' hard ride from him now but three by the carriage he would need to take as required by his station. He already chafed with impatience.

"But the wizards have her, and they've crowned her queen! Why would she want to be their queen?"

There were just too many questions to satisfy his burning curiosity. But above all else, she was here in Evendaar. He just had to get to the Golden Palace to see her.

His gut churned with excitement. The anticipation until he found her was going to kill him, and Goddess help anyone who tried to stand in his way.

"Adelena," he whispered and imagined holding the real woman in his arms. "I'm coming, Adelena. I'm coming."

# CHAPTER FOURTEEN

## "Long Live the Queen!"

Adele felt trickles of sweat chase each other down her spine. Her shoulders ached under the unfamiliar weight of the enormous cape, and her new shoes pinched mercilessly.

"Mummy?" a tiny voice squeaked behind her.

Adele tried to turn around to face Natalie, but with her great long train in the way, it was a struggle. She made it far enough around to see Natalie's worried face. Stella and Aaron stood beside their sister, looking thoroughly bemused.

Adele forced herself to smile brightly.

"Isn't this fun, guys?" she lied. "What a beautiful room this is! Look at the ceiling."

Adele allowed herself a moment of honest awe as she, too, looked around the new room they had entered. It was beyond gorgeous, with stunning deep magenta rugs and couches covered in rainbow-colored silks. The ceiling was sparkling with iridescent blue and purple lights, which shone brightly, even in the late-afternoon light. Great crystal chandeliers hung low, providing even more sparkle in a room that positively glittered with beautiful furniture and gorgeous artworks.

If only the room hadn't been filled with people.

With Ohren at her side, guiding her by the elbow, Adele and the children made their way across the hushed room to the balcony through French doors. With a quick glance, Adele surmised this balcony was even grander than the one outside the bedroom. Unfortunately, it too was filled with people. As the family walked out into the sunshine, a unit of armed men stepped in neatly behind them, giving Adele another surge of terror.

"Don't worry, Your Grace," whispered Ohren, sensing her fresh panic. "They are your Queen's Guard and are only here for ornamental purposes today."

Adele cast an eye over the six tall, burly men. Their plumed helmets rustled in the breeze and their swords and metal chest-plates gleamed in the sun. They wore simple tunics of polished leather with a short fringe over dark leather pants. Even their skin was polished, and Adele watched the light glisten on their heavily muscled arms and shoulders for a moment. They looked at a point over her head and marched in an odd short step, keeping close behind the children. Adele noticed Aaron staring at the soldiers, already wearing an expression of worship.

Ohren got her attention again with a quick jab of his elbow, making Adele trip over her own shoes on the golden carpet. The people closest to her started whispering, and she was sure she heard a few giggles.

*Perfect! Thanks, Wizard*, she thought crossly, cringing with embarrassment despite her fear.

Adele stopped at the foot of a dais of three steps. At the top stood a tall figure wearing robes of gold and white, carrying what looked like a scepter in one hand and a globe in the other. Adele had to squint to look up at him, but as he had the sun behind him she couldn't really see his face.

Adele felt Ohren nudge her again, more gently this time, in the direction of the golden steps where she would have to kneel. Thankfully, four ladies rushed forward to adjust her massive skirts so she could get down. Adele checked behind again to see that the children were all right and saw Stella sitting down, her dress all puffed up around her, while Natalie and Aaron stood over her, white-faced and holding hands.

The priest, or whoever he was, raised his arms for quiet. In the silence that fell, Adele heard a low rumble below the balcony. Shouts, strains of music, and bursts of laughter floated up to her.

*It's a crowd of people down there!* She thought in shock. *It sounds like they're having a party.*

Adele closed her eyes and swallowed down her nausea. A breeze cooled her sweat-streaked brow and surrounded her with the fragrance of something delicate and floral, something familiar. Vanilla.

Her eyes snapped open as the priest began to speak.

"We have before us the heir to the throne of the kingdom of Unisia. The heir has been returned to us from across the stars and has come home to rule over the people and the four royal families of Unisia with the Constitution, the Gods, and our love to guide her."

Adele quailed beneath the volume and strength of his words.

*Oh Christ, what am I doing here?* She felt a desperate urge to get up and run away from this ceremony but had a sick feeling it was too late for running.

The priest continued, but Adele couldn't concentrate as her mind spun, reviewing everything that had just happened this morning.

*Woke up on an alien planet, had lunch, became Queen of the Aliens.* It could have been hilarious but Adele only wanted, more than anything, some privacy so that she could throw up in peace.

To keep her mind off her nausea, Adele concentrated on tensing and relaxing her knees, as it was uncomfortable to kneel like she was. She glanced out of the corner of her eye at Ohren but he remained unnaturally still, his expression solemn and his eyes trained on the priest.

Adele tried to focus on what the priest was saying, but he was now speaking in a language she didn't understand. It sounded Germanic, or maybe Latin, and he was waving his scepter around a lot. Suddenly, he turned to face Adele. With the sun behind him, all she could see of his face was his glowing blue eyes. He paused, and Adele heard the rustling and whispering of the crowd around them intensify. Her heart thumped hard in her chest. She swallowed.

"Adelena Olivia Serena St. Lucidis, daughter of King Octavius and Queen Olivia of the family St. Lucidis, and true heir to the throne of the kingdom of Unisia, do you solemnly vow to care for the people, the families, and the Kingdom of Unisia until the last breath should leave your body?"

Adele swallowed. *For the safety of my children*, she thought.

"I do," she answered squinting up at the priest. "And God help me."

The silence that followed Adele's quiet agreement lingered. She began to get nervous that she was supposed to say something else. Adele glanced over at Ohren and saw he was locked in a staring contest with the priest. She didn't have a minute to puzzle it out when the priest spun around, arms raised, and bellowed to the crowd below: "People of Unisia—I give you your queen. Long live the queen!"

The roar that rose up from the mass of unseen people below rocked Adele. Ohren took her elbow to help her to her feet and up the three steps to the top of the dais. The priest stepped aside for her. The roar became even louder when she got to the top and looked down at the people. The sound thundered through her chest and raised the hairs on the back of her neck.

"Long live the queen! Long live the queen!"

Adele's eyes filled with tears.

*These people really think I'm their queen!* She just couldn't understand it. *They've been duped as well as I have.*

She didn't even raise her hand to wave.

"I hope you know what you are doing here, young woman," said a deep voice beside her. "Or Goddess help us all when the truth gets out."

Adele turned in shock to the priest. *If he knew she wasn't a queen, then why had he just made her one?*

Ohren stepped up beside her as the priest exited the dais. He clapped his hands in glee.

"That's it! You are the queen and no one can do a thing about it. No one can take what is rightfully yours."

Adele looked at Ohren suspiciously as he helped her down off the dais, the words of the priest ringing in her ears.

The priest was waiting for them at the bottom of the steps. Adele actually stepped back, fearing he might be violent, so angry was the look he blasted them with. He grabbed Ohren's arm and pulled him aside.

"I don't like surprises, Ohren," he hissed through clenched teeth. "And I don't like you going behind my back. You promised me—"

"I promised nothing," interrupted Ohren, stepping up to the man who was his exact replica, right down to the long beard and gray brows beetling over electric-blue eyes.

"She needs to be protected, and this way I can hide her in plain sight."

"You put her on the throne!" hissed the priest. "She couldn't be in a worse place. Think of the prophecy, Ohren!"

Adele stared as the twins faced off under the hot sun. They were exactly alike except for their clothes. Adele couldn't tell any difference between them at all. They were hissing at each other so quietly now she couldn't hear a thing. She decided it was time to go.

Adele turned around to scoop up her children, but there was nowhere to go. A large crowd milled about them, casting the family sidelong looks and there was no clear path to the doors.

Adele's paranoia grew and she had a hard time ignoring the ringing in her ears as the panic started to clutch at her chest.

A figure suddenly cast the little family in shadow, blocking out the sun with his height. Adele jumped, fearing it was the angry priest again.

"May I be of some service, Your Majesty?" It was one of the Queen's Guard, his helmet's purple plume fluttering in the breeze.

"We need to be...to get back inside," stammered Adele, eyeing the sword and lethal collection of knives strapped to the man's waist by a shiny leather belt.

"It would be my honor, Your Majesty."

The big man turned and barked a command. In seconds, a path down the gold carpet was cleared for Adele and the children.

Under the gaze of the hundred or so curious aristocrats, Adele fled inside, pulling her children with her as fast as the stupidly heavy cape would allow her.

The darkness of the room after the glare of the sun outside blinded them all for a minute, but the guard showed them safely to a couch where Adele could put the children down. Mrs. Ollenby dashed over with a tray of drinks and sweets, and helped the children take off their capes and bows.

After seeing that the children were more comfortable, Adele turned back to the guard who had helped them.

"Thank you for your help just now, Mr....um..."

The guard dropped to his knee, his head bowed, and his arms held straight by his sides.

"Your Majesty, my name is Ohrig of the Family St. Lucidis, title heir to Ontessa. I am ranked Major in the Unisian Army and General in the Queen's Guard. I will be honored to lay down my life for you and your family, Queen Adelena Olivia Serena St. Lucidis." He stood and shouted, "Long live the queen!"

The shout was echoed by the other Queen's Guardsmen circulating the room, causing people to spill their drinks and titter.

"Right. Thank you. That's…um…very kind of you," stammered Adele, taken aback by the passion of General Ohrig's promise and all the shouting.

She looked up at him. He wouldn't have cleared six feet, but was built so broadly that he had the presence of a much bigger man. In the natural light of the room, she could see that he was older than her, maybe pushing fifty? His dark-brown hair was cut close and generously sprinkled with white and silver. His eyes were a blue so pale they looked as though they had been bleached by the sun. His skin was weathered and tanned a deep golden color. His chin had been freshly shaven, but he had missed a bit just under the very tip of his chin.

The detail struck Adele as endearing. Something about this man made her feel safe. Maybe it was the rippling arm muscles, or maybe it was the gentle expression he wore as he watched the children cuddle into Adele.

*He obviously likes kids, and if he is our personal guard, I had better keep him close until I work out how dangerous this place really is for us,* thought Adele. The decision helped untie some of the knots in her stomach, until she heard a shout from the entrance.

"Where is she? Where is she?"

Ohren hurried to Adele's side.

"Please ignore everything this man coming toward us now has to say," he whispered, tickling her ear with his beard. "I will explain everything later."

"Oh Christ…" muttered Adele as her nausea returned.

The crowd parted as the man stalked through, searching the room with his eyes until he found Ohren.

"You!" he spat, pointing his finger at the wizard. "What have you done?"

Adele was starting to feel like one of the children among the giants of this world. She looked up at the man shouting at Ohren. He was at least six-foot-four's worth of broad shoulders and well-muscled anger. He had tawny blond hair which hung down to his collar, and his blue eyes were blazing. He would have been gorgeous if it wasn't for the ugly sneer marring his perfect features.

"Where is she, wizard?" he snapped, glaring around at the crowd. "Where is this alien interloper you have just crowned as our queen?"

Adele got the distinct feeling he was playing up to the curious crowd, as he spread his arms and shouted theatrically.

Confused by his anger, Adele looked around the room, too, before she realized he was talking about her. She was the alien interloper!

*Oh. Crap.*

Ohren was calm and collected before the younger man's rage. Although Adele didn't know the wizard well, she could tell he was feeling smug and was hiding it badly.

"Calm yourself, my Lord," soothed Ohren. "Her Majesty is here, with us." He gestured in Adele's direction on the couch.

"What? Where?" snarled the blond, looking over Adele's head.

Adele felt even smaller than usual. God, this was humiliating! She watched the angry Adonis search the room for someone who might look the part of a queen, as she most obviously did not.

Ohren frowned and admonished his foe like a child. "Now, now, my Lord, let us not succumb to dramatics." He shook his head, trying to suppress a smile. "May I present Queen Adelena Olivia Serena St. Lucidis, our once-lost heir, now recovered and crowned this very day."

Adele couldn't take her eyes off the lord, as he finally understood that the tiny brunette in the purple cape before him was his queen.

When his fierce gaze fell on Adele, she had to fight the urge not to gasp. He reminded her intensely of a lion she had once seen at the zoo. The cold savagery in his gaze was hypnotic, though now the sneer on his face was replaced by a look of contemptuous surprise.

"Is this her?"

Ohren's frown deepened. "Your Majesty, may I present Lord Orgustus Olivier St. Lucidis, your very distant nephew, by my reckoning. I do apologize—he normally has better manners than this."

Lord Orgustus flashed his attention back to Ohren, releasing her from his gaze.

"You have gone too far this time, High Wizard. You have crowned this—this imposter—as our queen without my approval—or the approval of the High Court—without a Blood Ceremony or the Goddess's blessing. Nothing! I will see her deposed this minute—"

"Easy, my Lord," interrupted Ohren in a warning tone. "Your father, the First Regent, attended the Blood Ceremony and signed his name verifying the queen's legitimacy. All the paperwork is in order, I assure you."

"But this tiny woman doesn't even look like us! How can she be St. Lucidis? She could be Marchant for all we know. What of the Goddess's blessing?" Lord Orgustus raked his gaze up and down Adele as she suppressed a shudder.

"The Goddess spoke volumes with her silence," answered Ohren vaguely.

*What Goddess?* thought Adele, feeling thoroughly sick now. She had been put through a Blood Ceremony? *Seriously? That sounded horrible.*

"I am the Second Regent and hold the real seat of power in the court, High Wizard. I should have been told about her, and about all of this."

"I'm telling you now" Ohren shrugged.

Lord Orgustus went very red in the cheeks and a vein throbbed at his temple.

"You will answer for this, wizard," hissed the lord. "Queens can be crowned and usurpers can be deposed just as easily." He spun around, his shoulder cape whipping out behind him as he stalked off through the crowd.

"What a jerk," whispered Adele in awe.

"Quite, Your Majesty." Ohren gave her a rueful smile. "I do apologize that my first coronation gift to you should be an angry lord, but there will always be those who are disturbed by your arrival."

Mrs. Ollenby touched Adele's arm.

"Your Majesty, are you quite all right? You've gone white as a sheet," she asked with a concerned frown. "High Wizard, the queen is exhausted. I believe the court should be escorted from the royal quarters. They can all gawk at the royal family at the coming ball."

"Very well," agreed Ohren, and gestured to General Ohrig. The two men moved off to manage the crowd.

Another of the Queen's Guardsmen appeared to help Mrs. Ollenby and Adele find a path back to their bedroom next door.

Adele headed straight for the big glass bed, pausing only to pull off the horrible cape and heavy gold dress. Standing in her T-shirt and jeans, she felt the world sway around her. She had just enough energy left to climb into the big bed and pull her children in after her.

"Can I get you anything, Your Majesty?" asked Mrs. Ollenby, as she pulled the heavy curtains closed against the setting sun.

"Home," answered Adele, already close to sleep. "We just want to go home."

# CHAPTER FIFTEEN

## "She Is My Destiny"

In his study, Rainere leaned back in his armchair by the fire. He felt warm, hot even. He stared into the flames and turned the royal scroll over and over. It was his first real link to Adelena.

"Adelena," he whispered, enjoying the taste of her name on his lips. He closed his eyes and conjured her face in his mind.

Suddenly his eyes flew open. Someone was in the room with him.

"Hard day, m'liege?" a rasping voice inquired from the direction of the window. Rainere flew out of his chair and faced the intruder, attempting to hide his disquiet with anger.

"Schiss," he snarled. "What are you doing here?"

"Expecting someone higher up the chain, m'liege?" sniggered Schiss with a cocky look. "Well, I am all you'll be getting for now, m'liege, and be thankful for it. I could well have been an assassin for all the mood the Nest Council is in."

Schiss's large round eyes narrowed to slits.

"They think you have betrayed the Spider People and gave the Hidden Child over to your own people."

"My people?" Rainere asked in genuine surprise.

"Yes, m'liege, the humans are your people, aren't they?"

"The humans are not my concern, as much as they are not my people, Schiss. I'm an Immortal, not a human—the Nest Council knows that."

Schiss shrugged. "Well, yes and no, m'liege. Yes, you are immortal *now*, but you did used to be human *then*. The Council is now doubting your loyalty, because the exact human female they have been searching for—and that you helped *nearly* secure last night—has actually ended up in the glass bed of the queen of Unisia."

Schiss gave a casual sniff. "You can see their point, surely?"

Rainere pierced Schiss with a sharp look, and his mind raced ahead to the many consequences of the situation.

"Do *you* think I gave the wizards Ada—the Hidden Child, Schiss?" Rainere's voice had become dangerously soft as he rose from his chair and eyed the smaller man from his full height.

Schiss took a step backward and banged into the window frame behind him. He held up a skinny hand in a gesture of peace.

"No, of course not, m'liege," he said, suddenly aware of his precarious position, alone with a powerful immortal. "I'm simply telling you what the Nest Council told me to tell you." He hunched his spindly body in anticipation of a strike and dropped his eyes to the floor.

"They don't believe you have fulfilled your Sacred Oath," he said in a low voice.

Prince Rainere stood perfectly still. His face wore an unreadable expression. With a sharp crack, all the mirrors in the room exploded.

The prince walked calmly to his desk. Grabbing a black feather pen, he shook the glass shards off a fresh scroll of paper and wrote with preternatural speed.

Schiss waited, still and silent in his place at the window, sending a quick prayer to his Dark God that the prince wouldn't make him explode next. Why, oh why, had he been so cocky? He should have known a Marchant prince would never be cowed, no matter how much trouble he was in.

Rainere finished the letter with a flourish and sealed the scroll with black wax and a small spell. He rose from his desk and thrust the letter at Schiss.

"You will take this to the Nest Council and the empress immediately," he ordered, as he opened the window behind Schiss. "I will follow later to reassure the empress personally."

A cold wind blew in as if it had been waiting for this very opportunity. Fat drops of rain spattered on the floor and gusted about the two figures. Rainere studied the heavy cloudbank hovering over the Grey Palace. He leaned out to listen to the tales of the North Wind, but the news was garbled and confused.

The prince held out his hand to Schiss, palm up.

"Now, Schiss!" His dark eyes flashed with impatience.

"Of course, m'liege. Farewell." Schiss nodded and, with a pained expression, shifted back to his spider form with a squelchy *pop*. On Rainere's hand sat a skinny black spider with a gray stripe down its abdomen. With a few muttered words, Rainere cast the spider into the gloam of the darkening skies. He watched to make sure Schiss had disappeared into a portal before closing the window against the rain.

Pressing his back to the glass, Rainere barely took a moment before he gave vent to the rage that boiled inside him, burning in his veins. He raised his arms and screamed a long clear howl of pure frustration. The crystal chandelier in the ceiling above his bed exploded into a thousand pieces, the force bringing it down and taking a chunk of the ceiling with it.

*How can they do this to me?* He thought as he dropped to his knees in the rubble. *How long do I have to keep paying for my sins in this world?*

Rainere moaned and hugged his arms about his chest.

"And now my Dream Woman is here. I cannot let her be touched by this evil. I must keep her safe from them all."

A low gasp from the doorway distracted him.

"I'm all right, Grotto, I did this to myself," Rainere said, gesturing to the mess, but the words rang true in the shambles of his heart, too.

"Pack my bag," he commanded, pushing himself to his feet again. "And find my cloak. It's bitterly cold in the Spiders' Nest at night."

Grotto looked worriedly at his young prince.

"Are you sure that's wise, master, given the current state of politics?"

"Grotto, I know what I'm doing." The prince brushed himself off and searched for his things in the rubble. "I have a chance to right the wrongs done to me, and I intend to do everything in my power to finally free myself of the Oath to the Spider People. I cannot have it hanging over me or Adelena, any longer."

The prince sounded completely crazed to Grotto, who didn't like the wild look in his master's eyes as he moved about the room covered in gray dust like a ghost.

*He looks like his father*, thought Grotto with a shiver.

"I don't wish to speak out of place, master, but—"

"Then don't," snapped Rainere.

But Grotto hadn't gotten to where he was by being easily scared by Marchant princes. He tried again.

"But I must suggest the very real possibility that the phantom of your dream is *not* the Hidden Child now sitting on the throne in the Golden Palace. Until we get to the palace, we cannot know who the Child really is."

Rainere froze and turned to face his long-suffering manservant. It was only because concern for the prince radiated from his very being that Rainere softened toward Grotto and answered with words instead of an incantation.

"You are right, Grotto, she might not be the Hidden Child of their ridiculous prophecy, but she is my destiny…my Adelena."

He loved the sound of her name no matter how many times he said it.

"She is mine. I know it, Grotto. Now I need to convince the empress to let me have her, while also giving that Spider what she wants most: the kingdom of Unisia. If I can promise her that I will fulfill her wretched prophecy, then I will have a better chance of protecting Adelena from whatever the empress plans to do with her. The wizards no doubt want the same thing but in reverse. These politics have nothing to do with Adelena and nothing to do with me. I must save her from them all." Rainere stood in the center of the room with his fists clenched tightly by his sides. Illuminated by the fire, he seemed to glow with the intensity of his words.

Grotto bowed his head; he knew when a fight was futile with the prince and acquiesced, for now. "I will find your winter cloak, master."

"And Grotto," called Rainere as he continued to pick through chunks of broken plaster, "Find the royal tailor. As the storm may have washed the roads away, it could take three days to get to the Golden Palace by carriage, and that means we only have three days to prepare my wardrobe and luggage to be there in time for the Ceremony of Homage."

"Yes, Master." Grotto bowed and slowly took his leave, bent under the new worries he now carried on his shoulders.

"Aha!" said Rainere softly as he found what he had been looking for. He held a perfectly round crystal ball in his hands, and blew the dust off it. Inside a tiny blue flame burned, flickering and rolling, as if in a breeze. It was precious to the prince, as it had been a gift from his father so many years ago. He brushed off a place for it on the mantelpiece and watched the little flame for a moment before gently setting it down and walking away.

He had much to prepare.

# Chapter Sixteen

## "Tea and Handkerchiefs"

Adele woke with a start. The gentle gray light of a new day filtered into the room through a gap in the curtains. Automatically, she raised her head to check the bedside alarm clock and for a second forgot entirely where she was. She lay back on her pillows and waited for her brain to catch up.

It only took a moment before the stress-induced nausea cramped her stomach and she remembered what had happened the day before.

*What am I going to do?* She thought hopelessly. *This is all too weird and crazy. How the hell am I supposed to cope with all this? How am I going to get us all home again?*

For a moment, Adele thought about home: its endless routines, the dishes in the sink, and her permanently tear-stained pillow. Justin. Would he be looking for them by now? Oh, no, he had that work trip. He wouldn't even drop by for another three weeks yet. She tried to recall any friends who might miss them. Maybe some of the mums from school would notice she was gone? But Adele had lost touch with the few friends she'd had from before the kids. Nowadays, she didn't have time for Facebook or coffees or drinks out anymore. Not with raising three little ones practically solo. What would she really be going back to?

"God, what am I thinking?" she said to herself. "I can't do this queen stuff, either. I can barely keep my own bills paid and house tidy. How can I cope with a whole country?"

Adele groaned. The world did not make sense.

"Why am I thinking about this like it's all real? Odds are I'm lying in a hospital bed somewhere, having hit my head. This is all one big massive delusion. I am no one's queen!"

Stella shifted in her arms, the little girl murmuring in her sleep. The sound was so sweet and sleepy, it made Adele's heart clench and she forgot her nausea and cuddled her baby, inhaling her warm, peachy scent.

*Whatever has happened to us, it feels very real and I'm going to have to find a way to cope here. I need to find out what they want from me and how to give it to them as quickly as possible so they'll let us go home soon.*

Decision made, Adele felt strong enough to disentangle herself from the mess of warm bodies and climb off the bed.

She padded across the floor and peeked cautiously into the sitting room beyond the double doors. She stepped through, closing the door quietly behind herself so as not to wake the children.

The room seemed so big without all the people in it from the ceremony yesterday. Though the new dawn could be seen through the windows and French doors, the chandeliers remained lit and rainbows of light decorated the carpets on the floor. Adele noticed there were several doors leading out of the room in all directions, and that there was an area, like an enormous bay window, on the other side of the room. She spied a long polished table and matching chairs in the alcove. A dining area, perhaps?

Adele trailed her fingers over the wall nearest to the door through which she had just entered. The silk wallpaper and gilded wainscoting felt cold to the touch. Adele shivered. She looked around the room and felt awed by the display of wealth around her. The heavy velvet and brocade curtains at the French doors pooled on the ground in gorgeous great heaps, and Adele thought idly of how much the children would enjoy jumping in all that soft fabric. Not to mention leaping on the dozens of overstuffed armchairs and couches that were dotted about the room in conversational clumps.

At the thought of her children, Adele remembered why she had braved the trip out to this room by herself.

"Hellooo?" she called out nervously.

Four liveried servants leaped immediately to attention before her, scaring the wits out of her. They had been standing in a neighboring doorway. How had she not noticed them before?

"Oh! You frightened me!" she exclaimed, putting a hand on her pounding heart. "Please don't jump like that."

But the four men remained standing silently in a line, arms by their sides, heads bowed.

"Could someone please go and find the wizard for me?" Adele asked, not sure which gentleman to address.

"Which wizard would Your Majesty wish I seek out?" asked the man at the end of the line.

"God, you mean there's more than one?"

"Yes, Your Majesty. The High Wizard Ohren is in residence at the Golden Palace, but the other three wizards of the Council are at the Accadaemia, the University," he added.

Adele finally caught his eye.

"You can call me Adele, you know…I'm used to that more than Your Majesty." She tried to smile kindly but his reaction surprised her. The gentleman dropped to his knee and bowed deeply, his chin to his chest.

"If it please you, Your Majesty, to serve you in my fullest capacity and stand by your side is an esteemed honor. To presume any further would be an insult to you."

Adele didn't know what to say as he climbed back to his feet, eyes still averted. Why was everyone so crazy passionate here?

"Um…if you feel so strongly about it, sure…I mean, fine…thank you, I guess."

There was an awkward silence.

"Can you tell me your name, maybe?" she asked more timidly.

"Head Steward Roberts, Your Majesty, and these are Stewards Hollis, Turner, and Franks." All the men bobbed their heads without looking at her.

"Nice to meet you," offered Adele to the silence.

"Well…um…Roberts, could you get the Wizard Ohren for me now, please?"

The steward bounded to the door so quickly Adele jumped again. He placed his hand on the door handle and opened it to reveal the wizard already on the threshold about to knock.

"The High Wizard Ohren, Your Majesty," called Roberts, not missing a beat, and he stepped smartly back to allow the wizard to enter.

"That was well done," said Adele and was rewarded with a quickly stifled smile from the steward. The human gesture reassured her.

Ohren strode into the room with a bounce in his step. He was dressed more casually today, in black pants and a deep-violet robe of the kind English professors wore, over a loose white shirt. His blue eyes trapped her in their laserlike focus.

"Feeling more rested today, Your Majesty?" inquired Ohren cheerfully. "Anything we can do to make you feel more at home?"

"I'd love a cup of tea," answered Adele. "Milk and sugar?"

"Absolutely!" Ohren signaled over Hollis, or maybe Franks.

"Tea and a spot of breakfast for the queen, please."

Hollis or Franks nodded and left. The remaining three stewards quietly stepped to the other doorways, awaiting the next order, still as statues.

"Thank you, Ohren," said Adele with relief. She walked to the open French doors and looked out at the balcony where she had been crowned just yesterday evening. It was completely pristine, not even the gold carpet remained.

"Are you all right, Your Majesty?" asked Ohren kindly.

"Lost, terrified, and exhausted, actually," answered Adele more sharply than she meant to. She squinted at the rosy glow lighting the horizon. The sun looked exactly the same here as on Earth. "Tell me honestly, Ohren, are we prisoners here?"

"Prisoners, Your Majesty? No, of course not!"

"Then let us go home. I just want to take my children home now before they get any more frightened by this madness." Her voice shook with a fear she couldn't hide.

"Your Majesty Adelena," began Ohren. She felt him walk up behind her and place his warm hands on her shoulders. He turned her to face him. Adele looked up into his incredibly blue eyes and saw kindness and sympathy there.

"Child, you *are* home," he said softly. "This is your world and your birthright. We kept you hidden on that other world for too long, I know, but the portents didn't arrive until recently. We brought you back because we need you. Your people, your nation—we need you to lead us through the coming days. You will be our guiding light, Your Majesty."

Adele hiccuped a sob. "But I can't do this, don't you see? I can't even keep my own house or life together. How can I help you by being a queen?"

Ohren folded her against his chest.

"There, there," he soothed her as she tried to fight her emotions.

"This just so crazy…" Adele wiped at her eyes but more tears fell.

"Please, Your Majesty, sit down." He led her to a puffy couch covered in a bright-green paisley velvet. "Tea will be here soon, and you will feel better." He handed her a handkerchief and she had to smile.

"I'm sitting in a palace on an alien world, and you still have tea and handkerchiefs here."

Ohren smiled back. "We are not barbarians, madam."

He sat down in a pink wingback armchair opposite her and crossed his long legs out in front of him. His hands made a pyramid over his chest as he regarded her.

"Queen Adelena, let me tell you the full story of your birth."

"And how do you know my name?" she interrupted. "I know I never told you that yesterday."

Ohren smiled again, but this time his eyes wore a distant expression.

"I knew your name because I was there when your mother named you."

"Oh." Adele felt like the wind had been knocked out of her.

Ohren took a deep breath and began:

"About one hundred and fifty years ago, the last King of St. Lucidis sat on the throne. King Octavius III was a black-tempered and fickle man, more obsessed with his own appetites than running the Kingdom. The King had very base leanings, and the Court of the Three Families despaired of him ever finding a wife and providing heirs. But eventually he found a highborn lady to accept him. Lady Olivia was a widow with two grown sons of her own. The queen was a kind and gentle woman; and, though near the end of her childbearing years, she endured the attentions of the King long enough to gain and lose six pregnancies. Against my advice, she attempted a seventh time, and this time the child quickened in her womb and grew well. The queen was overjoyed with her success.

"However, the political climate in Unisia was getting more and more unstable. Certain factions in the Court were influencing the King to allow the Marchant family to participate once more in Kingdom politics. The last Marchant king, Rainov the Cruel, had been defeated only one hundred years earlier and the Marchant family was exiled from society. So the memories of their cruelty and abominations had yet to fade.

"Fearing that the King might allow a return to Marchant rule, the other three royal families, led by the queen's own sons, rose up in a violent coup to depose your father, King Octavius, and his supporters. When Olivia's sons heard that a child had been born to their mother and King Octavius, her younger son went wild with rage. An heir strengthened the King's position exponentially. I heard through the serving women that the son, Otto, was going to kill the baby.

"The queen was thoroughly weakened by the birth and couldn't defend you. She begged me, as I sat at her bedside, to hide the baby where no one could find it. Just to keep you safe until the danger had passed. I did as she asked…"

Ohren's voice had dropped to a whisper and his face was pale as if he was reliving that terrible night all over again. He blinked, revived, and cleared his throat.

"My brother and I, with the help of some others, sent you away to another world in a parallel dimension to our own. I had studied the physics and knew that time passed more slowly on that world. I had hoped to bring you back when you were still young. I never imagined I would bring you back as a fully grown woman of thirty years with three children of her own."

"Twenty-nine," corrected Adele absently. "I'll be thirty next year."

Ohren smiled. "Of course, forgive me."

"Your brother is the angry priest from yesterday, your twin?"

"He isn't a priest, but I would like to see his expression at being called such." Ohren chuckled. "No, my brother Orestes is the Magistrar of the Court of the Golden Palace. A kind of law-keeper, if you will, and a judge. But he is also a damn fine wizard when he practices."

"And Lord Orgustus?"

Ohren sighed. "Lord Orgustus is a direct descendant of Otto, Queen Olivia's son. It was Otto and his brother Orwin who placed themselves at the head of the court as regents after the King died. That branch of the St. Lucidis family has been in charge for the last one hundred and fifty years."

"Until I came along," added Adele. "No wonder he hates me."

Ohren sat forward in his chair.

"He is angry now, Your Majesty, but he doesn't have to be. It is my sincerest hope that you can win him over and have him support your position as queen of Unisia. A united kingdom is vitally important right now."

Adele frowned. "Why was your brother so angry?"

Ohren waved his hand as if it mattered little.

"He hadn't been prepared for me to crown you so early, that's all. But he recognizes you are the true queen—please be assured of this."

Adele took the cup of tea that was handed to her by a young woman in a gold dress and white apron. She nibbled on a piece of toast.

"What's with all the O names?"

Ohren smiled.

"It denotes one's position in the Family of St. Lucidis. Only those with the true royal blood of our family running through their veins can be called by a name beginning with O. Your mother actually called you Olivia Adelena Serena, after her mother before her. It's a precious family name."

"I don't think I can rename myself," frowned Adele.

Ohren smiled and this time his eyes crinkled at the edges. When he smiled like that, Adele could see that he had been a good-looking man not too many years ago.

"That won't be necessary."

Ohren watched as the young woman before him sat back, curling her legs under herself and considering everything he had just told her. He waited for the real question he was hoping she would ask, at the same time praying she wouldn't. His answer was by necessity going to have to be a string of half-truths and disseminations, just as his description of her birth had been.

When she sipped at her tea, he noticed the cup shook ever so slightly. He could tell she was overwhelmed by everything that had happened to her in the last few days. He could only hope that she would show the strength of her true heritage and cope with the new world she had been shown.

*Come on, Adelena, you can do it. Put the pieces together for me*, he thought.

Adelena looked up from the carpet and struck him with her hazel-eyed gaze. With a slim hand, she pushed her hair back behind an ear. Her little shoulders were hunched against anymore bad news.

"Why do you need me now?" she asked, her voice trembling. "What is it that you want me to do?"

Ohren poured himself more tea and tried to ignore the shiver of premonition that gripped him. Nothing he had done by putting a new queen on the throne in Unisia was right. *But*, he assured himself, *everything I have done and will do is only ever for the good of the nation and for the world of Evendaar.*

"We need you to lead this kingdom against the forces of Darkness," he answered. "The kingdom is a place steeped in power and magic. Our world is very close to the home of the Gods, and our somewhat glorified position brings those who would covet and steal our wealth. But the people of our kingdom have lived in peace for over two hundred and fifty years, despite the minor coup, and they are not prepared to defend themselves from what lurks in the darkness of our world."

"You are talking about magic forces, I guess, not invading armies from other countries?" asked Adele, cheeks pale and eyebrows raised.

"Exactly." Ohren nodded. "If you could be our beacon of goodness and light, the people would have someone to stand behind. Someone to fight for, and someone to fight for them."

Adele gave a slightly hysterical giggle.

"I can't fight magic, Ohren, I'm just an ordinary person."

"But you aren't, Your Majesty." Ohren shook his head emphatically. "You are the daughter of King Octavius and Queen Olivia, and both were extremely strong in magic. You were special even before you were born, that's why I had to hide you. To save you, so you could return and lead the kingdom when we have need of you most. The portents suggest—"

"Portents? Ohren, please, I don't understand these words." Adele raised her hand and shook her head.

Ohren took a deep breath; this next bit would be tricky.

"It is my belief, Your Majesty, as a reader of prophecy, that there are those who will seek to pull the kingdom into the Dark Days and out of the Golden Age we live in now."

He checked Adele's expression but she stayed silent.

"I, and my closest colleagues, believe that retrieving you from across the stars and crowning you queen will help to avoid the worst of what may be to come."

"So…" interrupted Adele, "most of my job is already done just by sitting on your Throne?"

Ohren smiled, relieved by her summary.

"Exactly. But you will not be alone in this task. I will stand by your side and teach you the magic that you do not yet have at your command. I will be with you every step of the way."

They sat for a moment in silence, sipping their tea and avoiding each other's eyes.

"So I'm just a figurehead?" asked Adele quietly.

"Er…" Ohren was unsure what to say. "In a way…"

"Good," sighed Adele, a shy smile lighting her features.

*Gods, she looks like her mother*, thought Ohren and winced at the twist of old guilt in his gut. Hopefully he could serve the King's daughter better than he had Queen Olivia. Ohren blinked to dispel the vision of her mother that Adelena's smile conjured up for him.

"I couldn't do anything else useful, I'm sure, so let's just keep it simple, okay?"

"By all means, Your Majesty," agreed Ohren, somewhat bemused.

Although he had promised to help her, he hadn't expected she would have no interest in the role of queen. Was she really so disassociated from her heritage? Ohren was slightly stunned. He'd never had anybody voluntarily hand him the ultimate power of the kingdom before. A warm glow of satisfaction began to burn in him. Everything was going according to plan. In fact, it couldn't be going better.

Long live the queen, indeed!

# Chapter Seventeen

## "A Dreadful Welcome"

The journey from the Grey Palace had been a long and frustrating one. The roads were badly damaged after the week of severe storms that had wracked the country, and several times Prince Rainere had to alight and help the drivers haul fallen trees and logs from the roads as they passed through the Dark Forest, which surrounded the Marchant lands.

When their small party finally reached the King's Highway, travel became much easier because crews had been working to repair the storm damage and clear the road for the hundreds of Unisians making their way to the capital city, Concordis. The busy traffic was no trouble to the prince, as the crowds all made way for his black carriage, sometimes pulling right off the road to avoid having any discussion about it. Despite the years that had passed, the Marchant black was still recognized and universally feared. Glancing out the window, Prince Rainere saw men cross themselves with the Sign of the Goddess and mothers pull their children close as he passed by. Though he sneered at their peasant ways, he was sharply reminded of why he lived a life so solitary and isolated.

He was not welcome here.

Late spring sunshine bathed the countryside, illuminating the vibrant greens and golden browns of the fields by the roadside. Though the rain had damaged the constructions of men, nature rejoiced at the abundance and dressed the land in bright flowers of every color. Flocks of birds took to the azure skies, filling the daytime hours with their songs, and the air was redolent with the herbs that grew thickly by the side of the road.

Yet despite his interest in the unfamiliar beauty of the lands surrounding him, the prince itched to speed up their pace. He forced the drivers to keep going as late as they could into the night to make it to the Golden Palace on time for the Ceremony of Homage for his Adelena. Three days of travel seemed an eternity to wait after the years he had dreamed of her, and Rainere kept his temper badly. By the morning of the third day, he was almost beside himself with nerves and anxiety. Fortunately, their haste had served them well, and they reached the palace on the morning of the ceremony itself.

As their carriage passed by the capital city and joined the line of other carriages making their slow and inexorable way to the Golden Palace, Prince Rainere fussed with his jacket and refused to acknowledge the crowds of gawking and pointing citizens that lined the road. He was a freak to these people. A walking ghost from the past, come to pose for their amusement.

Prince Rainere fought to control his anger by focusing on what he would say to Adelena when he finally saw her in flesh and blood. Anxiety ruled his thoughts.

*Would she even recognize him as he would her? Had the wizards poisoned her against him already? Would she seek to follow the prophecy as the wizards did? Would she even speak to him at all, knowing who he was in this world?*

He took a deep breath and sought to calm himself. Of course she would know him. The Gods had promised him he would have her. It was foretold.

*She was so close now.*

Rainere looked through his carriage window as the Golden Palace came into view. It seemed to glow in the morning sun as the mica crystals buried in the white stone glittered gold in the light. He had never visited the palace before and was awestruck by the sheer enormity of it.

As they filed ever closer to the great gates of the palace, Rainere counted the number of carriages in the queue before their own, and tried to recognize the family name and title of each aristocrat by the flags they displayed. It looked like every member of each Family had gathered today for this momentous occasion. All for his Queen Adelena.

A wide golden carpet had been laid down the front steps of the palace, and people were taking their time ascending them, enjoying being seen as much as taking in the scene. Heralds lined either side of the carpet playing a welcoming salute each time someone stepped out of a carriage.

Rainere's natural reticence balked at the public display and he sneered at the ostentatious pomp and ceremony of the St. Lucidis family.

"I will not be a part of their little playacting, Grotto; take us around the side to the stables."

Grotto banged on the wall of the carriage, signaling the two drivers to move on. With petty satisfaction, Rainere watched the consternation that his leaving the line caused in the forecourt. He was more than happy to avoid the scrutiny of the court of the Golden Palace for as long as he could.

Grotto sniffed, alerting the prince to his disapproval.

"Master, with so much at stake here, we gain nothing by shirking protocol."

He was rewarded with a bone-melting glare.

Grotto bowed his head, but he risked a glance up again through his eyelashes and caught the look of uncertainty that flitted across the prince's face. He breathed a silent sigh of relief. The prince had understood his warning.

Rainere hated to be scolded like a child when he already felt so unsettled by this day. He was used to his solitary existence, and as their carriage pulled into the busy stable yard, the noise and chaos heightened his nerves. But Grotto was right. Rebelling against protocol was not the way to make himself stand out. He must get close to the queen, not alienate himself from her court. There would be plenty of others lining up to smear his Family name without adding to the scandal himself.

The carriage finally drew up to the entrance at the side of the palace. The drivers jumped down and knocked on the door to give the all clear. Grotto stepped out first and lowered the steps for the prince to descend more elegantly, then fell in behind the prince's right shoulder.

"Grotto, please make sure it is only my drivers who handle the horses."

Grotto looked over at the four rearing and kicking steeds that had sent all the stable hands running for cover.

"But of course, master," he said, nodding at their drivers, who immediately brought the horses under control.

Rainere braced himself as he turned to the entrance and saw the small honor guard of St. Lucidis servants hurriedly arranging themselves about the door.

A nervous squire of no more than sixteen years stammered the official welcome, mostly looking down at his feet. One of the trumpeters gave a halfhearted salute but trailed off midway after a look from Rainere.

Rainere let Grotto accept the official offer of hospitality in typical style.

"A dreadful welcome, indeed, for His Royal Highness Prince Rainere of Marchant," Grotto snapped. "I hope the Royal Marchant Quarters have been prepared for His Highness."

The squire looked up with a stricken expression.

"I have His Highness's itinerary right here, sir." The poor boy fumbled with the unfurled scroll and almost dropped it.

"As you can see from the map, His Highness isn't—"

"I know where the Marchant quarters are, boy," Grotto growled, snatching up the scroll and imperiously directing the other stewards to help with their trunks and luggage.

Prince Rainere cast an eye over the young squire and stewards as he passed. All five of them stood gawking with their mouths open. He almost smiled. Most of them probably hadn't known until today that he actually existed, outside of dark rumors.

In his fluster, the squire had forgotten his manners as official guide and had to sprint past the royal party to stay abreast of Grotto, who was stalking down corridors and hallways as if he owned the place.

As a child, Rainere had been made to study the floor plan of the Golden Palace, as it once had been the ancestral home of the Marchant monarchs. He had seen pictures and maps but nothing had prepared him for the overwhelming opulence and grandeur of the architecture inside the palace: twelve-foot gilded ceilings, walls lined with enormous painted murals of paradisiacal scenes, and vast windows framed by heavy brocade curtains fringed with gold. Everything sparkled in the sun as it streamed in through the glass windows. Rainere felt disconcerted walking on such highly polished floors, fearing to slip, but the carpets were so deep he thought he might trip if he didn't watch his step carefully again.

Rainere watched as their little party passed by a wall of mirrors down another carpeted hallway. He couldn't help but notice how odd he looked with his pale skin, black clothing, and long, dark hair. The people bustling through the corridors about him were all brightly dressed in their best festival clothing and greeted one another with shouts and laughter. This was a shiny modern world, and Rainere felt like a walking antique.

His nerves made him impatient for the quiet of his rooms, and when he looked up and noticed that Grotto was arguing with the young squire, he approached them.

"Grotto?"

"This boy tells me we are not staying in the Marchant quarters but instead they are putting Your Highness in the east wing," Grotto spat, infuriated.

"I'm so sorry, Your Highness," stammered the boy, close to tears. "This wing has been given over to the new royal family. Only official staff may walk these corridors today, and every day of the festival. I was trying to explain to your manservant that you have very nice rooms—"

Prince Rainere held up a hand to stave off more excuses.

"The queen is just down this corridor?" he asked.

"Yes, Your Highness, fourth door along—I mean, yes…" The squire blushed furiously at giving the exact location of the new queen.

*She is so close now*, thought Rainere and his heart started thudding uncomfortably.

"I see," he replied, feigning disinterest. "Very well, lead on, boy."

Weaving past Grotto, who was still muttering about the dishonor and insults to The Blood, Rainere followed behind the squire but kept finding excuses to glance back. He didn't see her.

# CHAPTER EIGHTEEN

## "Naturally a Plain Person"

Adele sat on the couch surrounded by her overexcited children. They jumped and yelled around her, trying to push one another off her lap.

"Stop it!" shouted Adele over the din they were making. "Or I will tell Mrs. Ollenby not to give you your great surprise this morning!"

All three children sat down meekly. They had been expecting Mrs. Ollenby's "great surprise" since yesterday. Adele hated to yell at them in front of a room full of people, but they were all getting a bit mad with the excitement in the palace in preparation for the second coronation and Ceremony of Homage that was to happen today. Hundreds of guests had been invited from all over the kingdom for the weeklong festival. Most guests were staying in the palace itself, causing all sorts of chaos. The palace had been buzzing for days now, and her children with it.

Strangely, the children had accepted their arrival in Unisia with a confidence that Adele found hard to accept, even though she was completely grateful for it. The little ones had found so much to love about the palace and being treated like royalty, but Adele waited for the day when they finally asked to go home again, and for their father.

"Hello, royal family!" Mrs. Ollenby sang out from the doorway, sending the children into hysterics again.

"Our surprise! Our surprise!" They chanted, bouncing on the couch. Adele only narrowly missed an elbow to the head from her crazed son.

Mrs. Ollenby hefted an enormous basket covered by a tartan blanket.

113

"Now who's been a good little prince or princess?" she asked with mock seriousness, her cheeks pink with pleasure.

"I have, I have!" howled the children.

"Well…" Mrs. Ollenby paused dramatically, "with Her Majesty's permission, of course?"

"Go on," said Adele, smiling and enjoying every minute of her children's joy.

"Who likes puppies?" cried Mrs. Ollenby, uncovering the basket and three tiny puppies.

The children fell on the basket with shrieks and cries of "Mine, mine, mine!"

It was all too much for Stella, who promptly burst into tears.

Just as Adele reached for her baby, the new nanny, Seraphina, swooped in to pick up Stella and comfort her.

Adele was about to protest, but when she saw her normally shy baby bury her face in the pretty redhead's neck, her emotion changed to one she didn't recognize.

*Am I jealous?* wondered Adele. She felt she should be grateful for the help, but she couldn't shake the unease she felt seeing her baby in someone else's arms.

"Your Majesty?" Mrs. Ollenby interrupted Adele's uncomfortable train of thought. "The puppies were a gift from Prince Bertrand Belvoir II, of the Belvoir family, as your homage gift. These pups are quite rare, you know, and bred from the prince's own stock."

"They are gorgeous, Mrs. Ollenby. I'll have to remember to thank him when I meet him at the ceremony. The children have never had a pet before, let alone once each."

Adele smiled at the squeals of joy as the little tan-and-black puppies cavorted with her children.

"Now while the children are occupied, if I could have your undivided attention for a moment, I would like to show you the wardrobe my team and I have designed for you for all the different events to be held this week."

"Of course." Adele swallowed her nerves. She hated dressing up, and she was dreading the idea of being the center of attention for an entire week.

Over the last seven days, she and the children had managed to feel at home in the large suite of rooms and enormous balcony of the royal apartments, but Adele had been too nervous to go wandering about the whole palace, despite urging from Ohren to explore their new home.

Mrs. Ollenby had been in every day, conducting interviews and introducing her to all the members of staff Adele needed to meet. Hundreds of people passed through their rooms, and Adele had given up on asking names. One of the first items of business had been to choose a nanny for each of the children. Adele had chosen three lovely young women from the same town, Seraphina, Siobahn, and Caitlin. They were girls from "good families" who "knew children" and were "used to hard work," but Adele had chosen them for their smiles and easy way with the kids. However, leaving her children was just not an option for Adele, so mostly the nannies just stood around dying for something to do.

Ohren popped in most mornings, too. He gave Adele lessons on the history of Unisia and its four royal families: the Belvoirs, the Carparells, the reigning St. Lucidis, and the outcast Marchants. He also introduced her to Tilburn, her majordomo and now near-constant companion, who tutored her on the upcoming ceremonies and the etiquette involved in being the queen of an entire kingdom. He was a bossy little man and his lessons were as much a trial as they were interesting to Adele. But at least he gave her practical help in how to fudge her way through all this queen stuff.

"Your Majesty!" trilled Mrs. Ollenby, regaining Adele's attention as the lady ushered in at least a dozen women, all pushing mannequins ahead of themselves. They rumbled across the floor until they stood in a line in front of Adele.

Adele stared dumbfounded at the parade of glittering, gem-encrusted, rainbow-colored gowns.

"My God," she whispered in horror. "You expect me to wear these...things?"

Mrs. Ollenby surmised, incorrectly, that Adele's shock was in fact awe and smiled even more broadly, clapping her hands with delight.

"Your Majesty, your seamstresses have worked tirelessly day through night to prepare these gowns for you. Of course you can change anything you like, but I can assure you these gowns are the very height of fashion in Unisian court society, and some are even a bit ahead of their time," she said proudly.

Adele watched as the children dodged about the mannequins chasing their puppies and getting chased in turn by their nannies.

"Not on the dress!" shrieked one of the pale, tired-looking women (definitely one of the overworked seamstresses) as one of the puppies took a squat near the golden train of a gown.

"Oh dear, I really didn't think this through. Maybe the puppies should have come after the dresses," said Mrs. Ollenby, dabbing at her forehead with a lace handkerchief. But the crisis was safely averted.

The ensuing minute of drama had given Adele a moment to come up with a polite way of letting the lady down gently.

"Mrs. Ollenby, I can see how much work you have all put into these incredible gowns...and they are extraordinary...it's just that I am naturally a plain person. I think something simpler would suit me better. This one for instance." She pointed to a shimmering gold dress with a long train of layered purple feathers, gathered under a big bustle of violet silk. "It's just not *me*."

Adele needn't have been so delicate with Mrs. Ollenby's feelings, as the dear lady had no intention of being thwarted.

"Plain is for nightgowns, Your Majesty," Mrs. Ollenby scoffed. "But these gowns are fit for the queen of Unisia. Now let's see the shoes and jewelry together with some of my favorites."

Adele was bustled behind a makeshift screen, still blushing and trying to defend herself from the ten seamstresses who began to disrobe her immediately.

After what felt like an hour of strapping, tying, and poufing, Adele was allowed to step out from behind the screen and was presented with a mirror. Her jaw dropped at the image before her.

The children gathered around her.

"You don't look like you, but you look better than you normally do," said Natalie with the sledgehammer honesty of a six-year-old girl.

"You look like Rainbow Barbie!" crowed Aaron, dancing a little jig of excitement.

"Barbie," agreed Stella, still holding Seraphina's hand.

"I look like...like..." Adele was at a loss for words.

With her hair piled up and her shoulders exposed by the low neckline, Adele noticed for the first time how delicate her collarbone looked. She gazed into her own hazel eyes and almost smiled. The bright purple of the silk actually suited her pale skin, and the blush of embarrassment had given her cheeks a pretty glow. Adele was quietly pleased to see that her small bust pushed higher than usual made her waist seem tiny. She looked...

"Like a queen," answered Mrs. Ollenby gently, and adjusted the emerald necklace at Adele's throat.

Adele narrowed her eyes, and found herself again in her normal frown. "I might need a bit of lipstick, though," she said doubtfully.

"Well, of course, Your Majesty, every lady needs a bit of help. That's what your team is for."

"My team?"

"Please let me introduce you to your dressers: Piers and Julian."

Two beautiful young men stepped forward, wearing bright colors and powdered faces.

"And Katie, your perfumier and assistant dresser."

Katie was blonde and shorter even than Adele. She gave a sweet smile and dimpled adorably.

"And your ladies-in-waiting, Lady Cara and Lady Lisbeth, who you already know." Adele smiled at the dour old dames who both curtsied stiffly.

"Well, you all have your work cut out for you," said Adele, still embarrassed for herself in front of these glamorous strangers. Adele winced at the polite giggles in response to her comment. She couldn't get used to the fake laughter every time she said something only halfway funny.

She turned back to the mirror and saw a beautiful stranger stare back at her.

"I wasn't joking," she muttered.

It was going to take a lot more than a big dress and lipstick to convince Adele she was a queen.

# CHAPTER NINETEEN

## "Adele Concentrated on Breathing"

*The Throne Hall was more like a cathedral than a mere hall,* thought Adele as she surveyed the stained-glass windows above her. She tried to make out the images in the glass, but the noise of the crowd distracted her. Hundreds of aristocrats from all over Unisia were crammed into wooden pews, shuffling and chatting, waiting for the new queen and her children to come down the aisle and be crowned in front of them.

Wizard Ohren had explained that they hadn't been able to locate the crowns in time for the shotgun coronation last week, hence the need for a second coronation.

"It's a nice diplomatic touch, actually," he had said, "Then the families all feel like they have been a part of the beginning of your reign instead of excluded from it."

Adele concentrated on breathing as she stood at the grand double doors leading into the Throne Hall. The gold dress she wore was truly enormous. It hung heavily on her small frame, the bustle digging into her back uncomfortably. Adele fought the urge to throw a temper tantrum, pull the scratchy pins from her braided hair and wipe off all the greasy makeup she wore. The ringing in her ears came and went sporadically. Adele just prayed she wouldn't faint in front of the entire kingdom of Unisia.

The children fussed and fidgeted behind her and, despite her usual reticence, Adele was grateful that someone else could carry Stella for the ceremony, as an anxious queasiness threatened to overwhelm her.

"You look divine, Your Majesty," whispered Mrs. Ollenby, giving Adele's elbow a little squeeze.

"Yes, very nice," said Ohren, somewhat more casually, as he watched for Tilburn's cue. Powerful strains of music from an orchestra began, causing a hush to fall over the crowd.

"Majesty, it's time!"

With one last rustling adjustment, they were off down the aisle.

Adele was concentrating so hard on every measured step down the golden carpet that she almost didn't register her audience. But as she came into view, a loud "Ahhhh!" reverberated around the lofty hall. Adele blushed furiously beneath her makeup.

For an instant, she felt almost like a bride at an extravagant wedding. Her own marriage had been a little civil ceremony that they had shared with only Justin's parents and a couple of his close friends as witnesses. Her parents hadn't even shown up. At the time, she hadn't been able to shake the feeling that it had been more Justin's day than her own.

But today, *today*, everyone was here just for her.

The comparison made her push her shoulders back and walk a little taller in her narrow shoes. She approached the throne at the end of the aisle, climbing the steps to the top of the dais with only a little wobble. A flurry of activity ensued as four ladies-in-waiting stepped in to pull, tweak, and drape Adele's train so she could sit down on the huge golden throne. A small step had been pushed up against it, as her feet couldn't touch the ground. The children were arranged in much smaller, more comfortable chairs behind the throne and propped up with cushions and bolsters, a veritable army of nannies and ladies-in-waiting surrounding them, along with the Queen's Guard, standing to attention, on either side,

Adele could feel Ohren's eyes upon her and looked up at his bright smile.

"Your Majesty has never looked more beautiful, I'm sure," he reassured her warmly. "Just remember, you need to radiate strength now. These aristocrats are meeting you for the first time. They need to see you as a worthy queen and strong leader. Don't let them down." He gave her an encouraging pat on the arm and fell back as Tilburn stepped up to give his speech.

The little man was in his element, his cheeks pink with rouge and pride. He for one was thrilled to have a "proper" royal family on the throne in the Golden Palace Court and to be able to put his intense etiquette training to good use. Finally, he had the status he had always craved as majordomo. Tilburn shook out his ruffled sleeves, and began the speech he had rehearsed for days.

Adele couldn't focus on Tilburn's voice. Instead, she concentrated on avoiding the combined gaze of the entire crowd. She resolutely stared at the back of the room, counting the multicolored banners that hung over the great doors, representing the four royal families and all the various non-royal lines within the families. Her gaze traveled to the ceiling and she almost gasped in awe. Adele had never been to visit the Sistine Chapel, but if it was anything like the painting before her eyes, she felt she hadn't missed out on anything. The Goddess Serena, after whom she had been named, stared down at the congregation with a beatific smile, surrounded by hundreds of smiling cherubs and animals of all descriptions. Adele recognized some of the creatures from the mythical stories of home: fauns, griffins, and an enormous smiling minotaur; but others she had no idea about. In the center of the piece, cradled in the Goddess's arms, were four beautiful women, their faces frozen in expressions of rapture. It looked kind of erotic to Adele, not at all like the images of religious rapture that she was familiar with. Adele shrugged mentally and dropped her gaze back to the hall. The mass of people before her had been packed in on dark wooden pews, and colored sunbeams streamed in through the stained-glass windows to light the air above them, as if the entire crowd wore a halo of gold.

Adele was surprised from her daydreaming when Tilburn finished his speech and a huge noise erupted. It took Adele a moment to realize it was the sound of thunderous cheering and applause. She gazed down incredulously at the crowd and through blurry eyes saw a sea of smiling faces.

*They actually want me?* Was the single thought that flickered through her shell-shocked brain before she felt Ohren place the golden crown upon her head.

Now that she had twice been made queen of this alien world, Adele felt the weight of the responsibility almost pinning her to her seat. She nodded her head slightly and felt the heavy crown shift and wobble. The velvet rim under the metal band pushed her hairpins deeper into her head and Adele bit her lip to keep from groaning in discomfort. Everyone around her was smiling and clapping. Adele smiled wanly at the crowd and gave a little wave to acknowledge their cheers and started a louder swelling of noise.

This was just all too incredible to believe.

Tilburn stepped up and silenced the raucous congregation with a dramatic flourish and announced that the Ceremony of Homage would commence.

A line began to form down the middle of the aisle as the princes, dukes, lords, ladies, and other titleholders of the four families each took their place in the queue to swear fealty to their new queen. Adele let out a small gasp of dismay as she realized the people she thought were leaving were in fact joining the line as it reached outside the doors of the Throne Hall and into the enormous antechamber beyond.

"Hand, Majesty," prompted Ohren when Adele failed to notice the approach of the first supplicant. Adele was wearing a ring on her left hand, a gold band topped with a huge purple stone. The ring was far too big for her, having belonged to her father King Octavius, and was tied to her finger with a purple ribbon to keep it on. Much to Adele's mortification, every supplicant had to kiss the enormous ring.

She smiled shakily at the lord kneeling before her, but as he lifted his bowed head, she found herself trapped in the angry gaze of Lord Orgustus. His expression was fierce as he held his mouth in a hard line of tight-lipped fury.

Adele could feel herself trembling in his warm grip as he took her hand. His eyes never left hers as he raised her ring to his lips and muttered the promise of fealty. Adele remembered her line at the last minute.

"As your queen, I accept your loyal fealty," but her voice sounded quavery and weak.

Whether by accident or intent, Lord Orgustus missed the ring entirely and he kissed her hand instead. The contact made Adele shiver, a movement not lost on the lord as he straightened before her and bowed again.

"My...queen." The hesitation sounded slightly menacing, and Adele felt herself quail under his icy blue stare.

"My Lord, please!" whispered the Majordomo furiously. "Off the dais now, if you please."

Adele leaned back and tried to catch her breath with her heart sitting squarely in her throat. The ringing sounded sharply in her ears and the room began to swim before her eyes, warning her she was getting dangerously close to fainting.

"Well done," Ohren murmured, interrupting the start of her panic attack. "Just a little louder next time. Carry on, you are doing wonderfully."

Adele felt her heart rate slow a little at his praise, and she tried to refocus on the next gentleman in front of her. The first ten men were the most important in the kingdom, Tilburn had told her earlier. So she tried to make a good impression by smiling and keeping her voice steady.

*Just keep going,* she told herself. *This is just one more day, as weird as all the others in this mad world.*

The line stretched on and on, and Adele lost track of the time until she heard the children start to fuss and whine. Failing to get much of a reaction for their noise, Aaron and Natalie began pretending to fall off their chairs and giggling at the sound of the thump. Adele knew from long experience that this game would only end with someone crying.

"Ohren...Ohren," Adele whispered. The high wizard was sitting beside Adele on a much smaller version of her throne and greeting all the supplicants as they approached her. At Adele's interruption, he leaned forward and gave her a frown.

"The kids are getting bored now, do you think they could go back to our apartment before they hurt themselves?" she asked.

Ohren shot a glance behind himself and his face broke into a grin at the silly antics of her children.

"Of course, Your Majesty. Mrs. Ollenby herself will escort them back to your quarters."

Adele returned her attention to the ceremony, wincing only slightly at the ecstatic cheers of her children as they escaped their dull duties of sitting down and being quiet.

Tilburn surprised her by stepping forward to announce the next supplicant much more loudly than he had the others. This time he practically shouted: "The First Peer and the Head of the Marchant family, His Royal Highness, Prince Rainere Rainov Lucien Grey Marchant. If it would please His Highness to approach the throne..."

A rustling murmur filled the great room as many of the guests turned to watch the Marchant prince walk down the aisle. Adele looked on with interest herself. Ohren had told her that the prince was the last Marchant left alive in the whole of Unisia. After her brief history lessons, she had felt sorry for him. He was, after all, an orphan carrying the weight of his family's terrible history on his shoulders.

"He's not here...he's not here...typical Marchant arrogance," muttered Tilburn, agonized by the break in protocol, and the huge gap in the line.

Adele finally saw a figure make his way from the front of the Hall. He was dressed head to toe in black, and stood out dramatically from the gold finery and color of the room.

*Like a crow among parrots*, thought Adele idly as she watched the prince's slow approach.

His bearing was regal and his tread was steady as he walked, seemingly unaware of the stir he caused in the crowd, though the whispers and chatter grew louder as he passed by. It was only when he was halfway toward her that Adele realized that the prince wasn't wearing a hood but it was his long black hair that fell on either side of his face.

Her breath caught in her throat, and her heart started to beat a rapid tattoo again.

Adele drank in the sight of him like a dying man does water. That chin…those dark eyes…the pale, angular cheekbones…it seemed both an eternity and no time at all when he reached the dais and slowly climbed the steps.

Adele trembled as she gripped the arms of her throne, her knuckles white, to stop from leaping out of it and into his arms. In the bright light of the hall, she could see the true color of his eyes like she never had in the twilight of her dreams. They were a deep moss green, forest green, green like leaves in a shadow.

"Majesty, hand!" whispered Ohren sharply.

Adele raised her hand and flinched when the prince's larger, cool one closed over hers.

They were touching. Finally, they were touching.

When he spoke, his voice was gravelly and hoarse, and though she had never heard it before, it seemed as familiar as her own.

"I swear fealty to Queen Adelena St. Lucidis on behalf of The Blood and Marchant family. By all the Gods of this world"—he looked up at her, his lips poised above her ring—"and the next."

Adele watched as his lips close over the jewel of her ring. She felt a sudden heat sweep her body, like a fever, as sweat slipped down her back and under her bodice.

*He is here, he is really here!*

He was exactly as he had appeared to her in her dreams, but in the reality of the Throne Hall he was clean-shaven and his long hair shone under the lights. He was dressed simply in a well-cut black suit of velvet which fit his form in a way that was completely distracting. A single brooch, a silver dragon, at the clasp of his satin shoulder cape was his only decoration.

"Rainere." His name was barely a breath on her lips.

"Adelena," he whispered, and in his eyes, she could see the same recognition and fierce joy that fired her own soul.

They had found each other.

"Er-herm…" Tilburn cleared his throat. "Thank you, Your Highness." He nodded to Prince Rainere that it was time to move along.

The prince gave Adele a deep look that made her eyes fill with tears.

"Don't go," she whispered, refusing to let go of his hand. She felt him squeeze back and had to bite her lip to keep from crying out. Here was a piece of her home, a real piece of her own world, before all the craziness in Unisia began, but better because he wasn't a dream anymore. He was real, and he recognized her, too…but that didn't mean he wouldn't disappear in a puff of smoke and be gone forever.

"Tonight." He murmured, looking down. His lips barely moved but it was enough of a promise for Adele. She forced herself to release his hand. Like everyone else in the Throne Hall, she watched him walk back down the aisle, but she was probably the only one who felt a desperate need to run after him and never let go.

"My Lord!" snapped her majordomo, making Adele and the next gentleman in line both jump to attention. Tilburn had obviously been repeating himself and was now terribly annoyed.

"Are you all right Your Majesty?" asked Ohren quietly.

Adele nodded dumbly, not trusting herself to speak.

Ohren let out a dry chuckle. "Don't worry, my queen, a Marchant prince has that effect on most of us. But I promise you won't have to see much more of him."

Adele gave Ohren a wan smile. How could the wizard be so clever yet misunderstand her so often?

She tried to turn her attention to the rest of the line of waiting aristocrats, but every time someone kissed the ring it was Rainere's lips she saw. Every time someone took her hand in his or her old dry one, it was the weight of Rainere's squeeze she relived time and again.

The next hour passed so quickly that Adele didn't realize they had reached the last supplicant until she heard Ohren say, "Bertie, you old imp! I was looking out for you with the rest of the Belvoir peers. Why didn't you stand up as the head of the family?"

Prince Bertrand II of Belvoir grinned and gave a nonchalant shrug. He barely reached the high wizard's shoulder but did not seem at all in awe of Ohren, as most people were. He looked to be around the same age as the wizard, but he was clean-shaven and wore his white hair tied back in a neat braid. He was dressed brightly in the green and brown silk of the Belvoir family, in a manner that Adele had come to accept was modern fashion in the court, but his shoulder cape hung with a rakish twist and his grin was wide and infectious.

"I didn't want to take any of the glory away from the young ones. You know it's my grandson who will be taking the reins from me soon. And I had a nice little snooze at the back of the Hall while all the boring stuff was going on. I only just woke up as the stewards were cleaning up back there. Besides"—he turned his birdlike gaze on Adele—"I wanted to meet your little princess from another world. All very interesting, this business, wizard."

The little man looked Adele over with a big smile on his boyish face so she didn't take any offense. It was almost a relief to meet someone who found the idea of her being queen as preposterous as she did. Someone who wasn't Lord Orgustus, that is. She held out her hand to shake.

"Adelena Lucidis." She smiled. Adele didn't think twice about giving her maiden name. Marlock and the husband who went with it were just so far away from her now.

"Prince Bertrand II of the family Belvoir of Belvoir Estate, but please call me Bertie." He turned her hand over and kissed the back of it quickly. "It's a pleasure to meet you, Your Majesty; an enormous surprise, to be sure, but a pleasure all the same."

He tossed a look over his shoulder at Ohren and gave Adele a wink. "Last year the wizard there honored us with magical sky fire for the Solstice festival, but this year it seems we are to have a brand-new queen. Heaven knows how he will top this next year?"

"Now, now, Bertrand, no seditious prattle here," said Ohren and clapped the old man on the back, almost knocking him off his feet. "Don't make me have to imprison you for treason."

Bertie and Ohren chuckled together as if this was an old joke. In such casual company, Adele felt comfortable enough to stretch her sore back and yawn broadly. As she wriggled her numb behind, she noticed that the huge crowd had already left the hall, and Tilburn was packing up all his scrolls with the help of two young squires.

"Ohren, I'm going to go back to the rooms to see if my children are okay," Adele said as she stepped down off her enormous throne. A thought suddenly occurred to her.

"Bertie, you are the one who gave us the basket of puppies for my children this morning. I have to thank you very much for them. The children were so excited to have pets, they've never had any before."

"Yes," agreed Ohren drily. "Because we don't have enough animals running around the palace growling and trying to mark their territory."

Bertie guffawed loudly. "Yes, and how is Lord Orgustus treating you lately? Still your right-hand man?"

"It would seem I have to lead Her Majesty back to her quarters," answered Ohren loudly, clearly changing the subject though he was still smiling. "And shall we see you at the ball tonight, old man, or are you going to leave that for the youngsters, too?"

"I'd never miss a party like this one, Ohren, you know that!" Bertie grinned cheekily and gave a deep bow. "Save a dance for me, my queen?"

"Of course." Adele smiled and curtsied a little.

"You, too, High Wizard?" asked Bertie, giving Adele another wink and making her giggle.

Ohren rolled his eyes and didn't deign to answer, leaving Bertie to chuckle at his own joke as he and Adele left the dais.

As they headed out of the Hall and back down the long corridors to the royal apartments, Adele became very aware of the six men of her Queen's Guard marching in tight formation around them.

She nudged Ohren with her elbow.

"Why do we have a military escort today?" she asked quietly. "Is it not safe in the palace anymore?"

She hadn't seen much of the Guard at all after the day of her first coronation.

Ohren leaned down a long way to whisper directly into her ear.

"The Queen's Guard have been in charge of guarding empty rooms and statues for years, Your Majesty. You'll have to forgive them for being a little proud and overzealous on such a special day as your coronation."

Relieved, Adele nodded. She promised herself she would thank General Ohrig and the rest of the Guard for standing at attention all day behind her throne. That must have been incredibly dull.

As they walked, Adele looked around corners and doors for Rainere. She chewed her lip and frowned. She had only seen him for a few moments but already she was finding it hard to control the flapping of the butterflies in her stomach. He was here and he actually lived in this world, and now he had a name: Prince Rainere.

What could it all mean? How much crazier was her life going to get?

Adele sucked in her breath when she saw a tall dark figure ahead of them, but it was just a steward in the dark blue of the Carparell family. Her chest tightened painfully as disappointment crushed her.

"Tonight," he had said. Maybe at the ball they could find some time to talk? Maybe she could dance with him?

Adele frowned more deeply and tasted blood on her lip. She stopped biting it. She instantly hoped the mark wouldn't show tonight. She wanted to look her best when she saw him again. Adele grinned at her own foolishness but picked up her step to back to the apartments. She had only a few hours to get ready for the ball, and she wanted to give Julian and Piers as much time as she could to prepare her.

For the first time since she had arrived in this new world, Adele was looking forward to a royal function instead of dreading it.

# CHAPTER TWENTY

## "Between the Gods and Prophecy"

Prince Rainere managed to maintain his self-control for the entire length of the Throne Hall and the antechamber beyond it where Grotto waited for him. Desperate for privacy, he glared ferociously at the beautiful blonde woman who curtsied deeply to him as she stood next to Grotto.

"Your Highness, please forgive me for my boldness, but I would like to introduce myself—"

"The prince has no time for you, Lady, excuse yourself now," snapped Grotto. He had seen the expression on Rainere's face. The prince was in a state of high agitation, and it was up to Grotto to get him back to their rooms before he made a spectacle of himself and the name of Marchant. Grotto groaned internally at the news he knew was coming.

The two men exited the antechamber under the curious gaze of the nobles waiting there but by none more closely than the pretty blonde who had been so rudely spurned. Obviously, this Marchant had no better manners than the rest of his predecessors.

Back in their apartment, Grotto carefully closed the doors as his master began frantically pacing the rooms. His pale cheeks were flushed, and his eyes glittered with excitement.

Grotto poured the prince a glass of wine and murmured a quick prayer to the Moon Goddess Lune. He only wanted the best for his young master, and if the boy loved the Hidden Child that the Spider Empress wished him to be joined with, then so much the better. Grotto had almost cursed aloud when he had finally lay eyes on the new queen. Her face so different yet as familiar as another in his memory. Though it was not destiny, but rather the machinations of evil wizards, if Grotto could orchestrate the marriage of his master to this new queen, imposter though she was, all would be well. The prophecy stated that the Hidden Child would join with the Chosen Ones and bring the forces of Darkness back to the land. The last Marchant prince was the only Chosen One left in Unisia. Though the choice was obvious to Grotto, a marriage was going to be incredibly difficult to bring about, as his master only sat on the fringes of Unisian court society. To present him as a suitor for the queen would be a delicate process.

Unfortunately, it was Grotto's experience that Marchant princes in fits of passion were always poor decision makers, and right now their hopes all rested on the prince's ability to control the situation and not indulge himself in this fantasy which had plagued him for so long.

"It's her, Grotto. Adelena is my phantom woman. She's the one who has haunted me all these years!" Rainere's voice was low but Grotto heard the yearning in it. "She has been brought here to me…"

"By the wizards?" asked Grotto drily.

"By the wizards, yes, but only because they think she is the Hidden Child of their Prophecy," agreed Rainere, stopping briefly to gulp down the goblet of wine Grotto handed him.

"As the Spider Empress believes, also," Grotto gently reminded him.

The prince made a noise of derision and threw himself into an armchair by the fireplace, staring intently at the cold grate as if there was a fire there.

"They all think she is here for their purposes, but I know better. The Gods told me she would be put here for me. Though she wouldn't be alone…"

Rainere glared at the tidy pile of logs and dried herbs.

"Regardless of who surrounds her, she will be mine, Grotto. I am sure of it. After all, the Gods told me so."

"Do you not think that perhaps the Gods have placed this woman, the Hidden Child, before you, Master, so that you could, together, fulfill the Prophecy of the End of the World? It would make sense…"

"It makes no sense, Grotto. Don't be a fool! The prophecy is an ancient account of the babblings of an insane maiden, scrawled down by a foolish monk. Surely you cannot mean to tell me that you give this rubbish as much credence as the Spider Empress does? She is completely mad!"

Grotto hid his disappointment well. Though he had hoped that the prince would finally accept the truth of the prophecy when he met the false queen, it was of no account if he did not. Just as long as he acted as was necessary to fulfill the predictions. The Spider Empress would not allow a second failure on the part of the prince, and had demanded that he continue to keep his Oath to her. Keeping his master focused on this would be Grotto's main concern.

Grotto moved across the room to pour another cup of wine for the prince.

"Master, forgive me. I'm from an older time, when prophecy was as common as the Old Tongue. Of course, you are right to think as you do, but still, we must show caution. The Spider Empress will expect us to respect the course of the prophecy and use it to guide us in our dealings with the new queen."

Prince Rainere gave a shallow nod. Grotto was ever the voice of reason. What did it matter if the Spider Empress thought he was following her damned Prophecy of the End of the World? All that mattered was that he had finally found Adelena, and she him. The Gods had been right. She would be his.

# CHAPTER TWENTY-ONE

## "To Dance With a Dream"

Adele's stomach squirmed. Behind the great gold doors of the ballroom, she could hear the party in full swing. Her stomach writhed again. Somewhere in there, Rainere was waiting for her. The anticipation was almost painful. Adele smiled down at her shoes and resisted the urge to bite her bottom lip. She would only chew off her lipstick.

Adele had surprised Mrs. Ollenby tonight by choosing a gown of deep violet, the bodice tight against her ribs and glittering with rubies and tiny jet stones.

"But you said you wanted something more modest, Your Grace," argued Mrs. Ollenby, offering up a candy-pink gown with a high neckline and frothy lace roses decorating the shoulders. "The violet is an elegant choice but you will hardly stand out. It's so somber!"

"But that's exactly why I will stand out, don't you think?" countered Adele. "Everyone else will be dressed like peacocks, and I'll be different."

Julian and Katie had laughed and agreed with her.

"The violet is gorgeous with her hair and, besides, in such a dark color she might catch the Marchant prince's eye." Everyone had tittered at Julian's joke, but Adele's stomach had dropped to her feet.

She patted her full skirt nervously. She was always dreadful at parties, as her natural self-consciousness worked overtime and ruined all the fun. She nudged Ohren with her gloved elbow.

"Ohren, you wouldn't happen to know where I could get a drink before we go in, do you?" she asked quietly, watching her guards and ladies-in-waiting chatting noisily.

*They've been with me all week and I can't even remember their names,* she thought, feeling suddenly lonely among all the people. She hoped Rainere was close by inside.

Discreetly, Ohren proffered a small silver bottle.

"Here, Your Majesty—but just a taste. This is very strong stuff. I brew it myself." He tapped the side of his nose with a grin.

Adele took a delicate sip. The liquid filled her mouth and seemed to swirl about of its own accord before running down the back of her throat. Adele coughed automatically, but a burning warmth was already spreading throughout her limbs and rocketing down to her feet.

"Oh my God, Ohren, it tastes like it's alive!" Adele checked her feet to make sure they hadn't melted.

*Wow, pretty shoe*s, she thought happily.

Ohren chuckled and gave her a nudge.

"Majesty, you are shouting."

"Whoops, sorry," giggled Adele, and grabbed the old boy's arm, giving it a squeeze. She actually liked Ohren. Despite the fact he had pulled her out of her own life and into this insane one for his own crazy purposes because he was, well, crazy, she really, really did like him.

Tilburn poked his head through the doors. Adele giggled at his shiny red face.

"The Court is assembled, Your Majesty. We are ready for you now."

Adele heard a voice call, "Fall in!" and her six massive Queen's Guardsmen lined up, three on each side of her and Ohren.

"No fluffy helmets tonight, General Ohrig?" asked Adele conversationally when she saw the burly man to her left.

"No, not tonight, Y'Majesty," answered the general, cracking a smile which he quickly stifled again.

*Good, at least he knows how to smile,* thought Adele. *Everyone has been so damn serious all day. It's time to have some fun!*

Even though she was ready for it, Adele was still surprised when the great doors were pushed open and the huge glittering ballroom was revealed. The members of the court had arranged themselves away from the queen's entrance, but were still close enough to see everything she might do.

Adele searched her mind for her earlier nerves but found nothing except a jumpy excitement. Falling in with the footsteps of her armed escort, Adele stepped out into the ballroom to thunderous applause. She nodded and bobbed her head, smiling at all the well-dressed people before her.

A cloud of perfume assailed her senses and, because of it, Adele realized her majordomo was right next to her.

"Should I make a speech or something, Tilburn?" she asked gaily.

Tilburn couldn't hide the horror in his expression.

"No, Your Majesty. Gods, no! And please, for the love of all that's holy, stop waving."

How funny! Adele hadn't even realized she was waving. She gave the distraught gentleman a little wink, to let him know it was all right to let his tightly curled hair down a bit. But he must have missed it because he dropped his scroll and took a couple of tries to pick it up again.

Adele and her retinue made their way to the center of the room so there could be more clapping as she stood and nodded at everyone in the room smiling, smiling, and smiling. She didn't hear when the dancing was announced, but a sharp jab to the ribs alerted her to the elderly gentleman waiting patiently in front of her to take her arm.

It wasn't Rainere, and Adele bit her lip. Her tipsy joy was based on seeing Rainere as soon as possible.

It did not occur once to Adele that she actually didn't know how to dance properly on Earth, let alone at a coronation ball in the kingdom of Unisia. But she had a vague idea about letting the gentleman lead, and for most of the night it worked wonderfully. The chat between her partners was very basic and mostly involved them blessing her reign, to which she would thank them for their good wishes before it was time to change partners again.

Hours later, as a clock rang in midnight, Adele finally found herself without a partner but with sore feet and an aching lower back. The effects of Ohren's liquor had worn off long ago, leaving her feeling slightly dizzy and exhausted. Compounding her sense of unease was the fact that, although she had danced with different men all night, she hadn't once glimpsed Rainere among them. She used the respite in dancing to study the ballroom and search for the prince in the crowd.

Festooned in a rococo style, the ballroom's ceilings were fantastically high, giving Adele a crick in her neck as she examined the paintings above her head. The walls and columns were ornately gilded, and mirrors had been used cleverly to make the room feel bigger still. Columns lined both sides of the two longest walls and the spaces between them were draped with a sheer, shimmery fabric.

Adele grabbed a drink off a passing tray and drained the glass in one gulp. The fruity punch was fizzy and made her sneeze. Sniffing, she turned her attention to the crowd. Both women and men were dressed in vibrant colors and fabrics, and sparkled with jewels of every size and color. The clothes were very old-fashioned to Adele's eye, full skirts and tight corseted bodices, gloves and hair piled up high. The men mostly wore shoulder capes in their family colors with tight-fitting jackets over slim velvet trousers, cut close to the leg. They generally wore their hair shorter, cut to shoulder length or higher, but weren't averse to a ribbon or jeweled decoration in their hair.

One young woman passed into Adele's line of sight in an incredible ensemble that took her breath away. The lady wore a plunging V-necked dress with a stunning multilayered skirt. From top to bottom, each layer was slightly darker than the last as if she walked within a purple cloud. Her bodice and shoulders were covered with tiny amethysts, which glittered beautifully as she swayed elegantly through the crowd. Adele found herself staring so intently it took her a moment to realize that the young woman was looking right back at her. Embarrassed, Adele waved before she remembered the "no waving" rule. Too late, the young woman thought she was being summoned and made her way over to curtsy in front of Adele, her skirts spreading prettily and settling again with the movement.

"Your Majesty, I humbly bless your reign."

"Thank you," said Adele still feeling awkward though she had heard the phrase all day. "Um, that is a beautiful gown you are wearing. I was told everyone is wearing the colors of their family tonight and as your dress is purple, I guess that means you are St. Lucidis, like me?"

Adele could feel herself prattling as the crowd around her fell silent, listening in on their conversation. It was making her paranoid.

The young woman flushed with pleasure at the double compliment. She dropped her head and her long blonde hair fell forward to frame her face in silky waves. Her clear blue eyes sparkled in the lights and she smiled broadly at Adele.

"Thank you, Your Majesty. My name is Lady Olivia Templeton, of the St. Lucidis Templetons. The is a dress I designed myself. It's a particular pleasure of mine, and I'm glad it pleases you."

"It really is lovely," replied Adele, reassured by the young woman's polite response and happy smile. "Perhaps you could come and help me with my wardrobe one day. I could use some advice. Desperately, actually." She gestured at her own gown, feeling self-conscious.

Adele had never seen a more radiant smile than the one that lit up Lady Olivia's face. She really was a very beautiful girl.

"It would be an honor, Your Majesty!"

A waiter waltzed by with a tray of more fizzy drinks, pink this time.

"Can I offer Your Majesty a punch?" asked Lady Olivia, taking two glasses off the tray and offering one to Adele.

Adele took the cool drink with a smile, but before her lips touched the glass she felt a hand clamp on her elbow. Almost spilling her drink, she turned in irritation to face Ohren.

"Your Majesty might be better served with a drink of water," said Ohren quietly but firmly. Adele internally bristled at the insult but meekly handed the pink drink to the high wizard. The surrounding gawkers melted away at a glance from Ohren. Adele gave Lady Olivia a rueful smile.

"It was lovely to meet you, Lady Olivia, I hope I'll see you again soon."

The lady gave another deep curtsy, and with a beautiful smile at Ohren she took her leave.

Adele was tired and sore. She was upset that she hadn't seen Rainere yet and was wary of the intensity with which Ohren studied her now. She tried not to flinch from the tall wizard as he leaned down to speak to her, but his breath seemed to enter her ear and his words swirled unpleasantly in her head. She shifted uncomfortably and Ohren finally released his grip on her elbow but he still stood too close to her.

"It has been noted you haven't yet danced with Lord Orgustus. It is very important that you do so tonight, Your Majesty. It will show everyone in the court the clear bond between the old guard led by Lord Orgustus and your new reign."

"Shall I go and ask him to dance then?" Adele asked attempting to step away.

"No, Majesty, that would shift the balance of power to Lord Orgustus. No, he must come to you, and request his royal couplet with you in front of everybody."

"How do we do that?"

"I have organized for another gentleman to dance with you now, someone Lord Orgustus dislikes intensely. The affront to his honor of having this prince precede him should spur him to take his dance with you."

Adele was astonished at the pettiness of the plan.

"Seriously? Orgustus won't see through that? Surely he knows you would want him to dance with me and will be ready for you to try and push him."

Ohren gave a wry grin. "He really hates this prince, and I'm positive he will rise to the occasion, if only to have the chance to humiliate his enemy before the court."

Adele was shocked that she had to be part of such a schoolyard prank. As Ohren steered her over to a space behind two columns she thought to ask, "Does this prince know he is being used like this?"

"Not at all," answered Ohren quickly. "Now remember: Look like you are having a wonderful time, and then Lord Orgustus should pounce on you straight away. Good luck!" And with that, Ohren melted into the crowd again.

*Good luck?*

Adele already dreaded the whole situation, but as she prepared herself for yet another gray-haired gentleman with clammy hands and a leery smile, she felt her heart stop beating as she turned to stand in front of the most beautiful man in the room.

Tilburn was already halfway through his presentation speech.

"...you are honored to receive a request from Queen Adelena herself for a moment of your company and a turn about the dance floor. What say you, Your Highness?"

"It would be my greatest pleasure," answered Prince Rainere as his dark eyes fixed on Adelena and caused her stilled heart to hammer painfully in her chest.

In a daze, Adele followed the prince onto the dance floor. They faced each other and bowed, never taking their eyes off the other. The music started and Adele took the step forward into the prince's formal embrace. Her pulse raced as she felt his hand close over hers and the other settle lightly on her waist. She was only tall enough to reach his chin and had to look up at him as he looked down at her.

"Queen Adelena..." His voice was deep, rasping slightly at the edges.

"Prince Rainere," she whispered as tears came unbidden to her eyes. *So, this is what having a dream come true felt like.* Adele was afraid that if she spoke anymore the tears would fall, so she stayed silent gazing up at the strong, beautiful face of her Dream Man come to life.

She felt the strength in his arms as he led them in the dance's stately steps and turns. Of all the astonishing things that had happened in the last week, finding Rainere was the only one that had made her happy. Her heart sang, and the tears dried up as she calmed down enough to enjoy the feel of being in his arms. *If only they could be alone.* Adele almost blushed when she thought of all the times she had so thoughtlessly tried to kiss him in her dreams...but now the real man stood before her. *What must he think of her?*

*He always tried to kiss me back,* she reassured herself. *And he looks as happy to see me as I am to see him.*

Adele shivered as Rainere pulled her slightly closer to him. She could feel his breath on her cheek. A bolt of desire rocketed through her and she couldn't look away from his dark-green eyes. This all just felt so familiar, and so right.

Lost in her own world, Adele did not notice the ever-widening circle of empty space around herself and Rainere as the crowd backed away from the couple and stared, whispering and throwing scandalized looks from behind their fans.

"Adelena, if I may?" the prince's voice was low. "I must see you. We must…I need to talk to you about…" He stopped, obviously desperate to say something discreetly. He lowered his voice even more.

"I think I can help you."

Adele's breath caught in her throat. He could help? Did he mean get them home?

"I think the wiz—"

Prince Rainere straightened up suddenly just as Adele felt a light tap on her shoulder. She turned around and into the full force of Lord Orgustus's glare.

"Your Majesty?" he spat the words out through clenched teeth. "May I have the honor of this next dance?"

His lordship had taken the bait.

Adele looked helplessly from one man to the other as the penny dropped. So. She had found the one man in all the kingdom whom Lord Orgustus hated as completely as he obviously hated her. Now she and Rainere had that in common, too.

Adele felt torn. She knew what Ohren wanted her to do. She also knew her hesitation made everything worse, but to step away from Rainere and into the arms of Lord Orgustus seemed impossible right now. Rainere made the decision for her and moved back, letting his arms drop. She felt a chill where his hands had held her. Adele almost cried out with disappointment.

"Rain…Your Highness," she said quickly. "Please make an appointment with my majordomo. I would be happy to have a chance to chat about this further."

Adele tried to smile as Rainere bowed to her, but Lord Orgustus snatched at her hand and pulled her into his arms, already turning her about the floor.

*This man is such a jerk*, thought Adele furiously as she narrowly missed stepping on her own dress. She looked for Rainere over the lord's shoulder, but the prince had already disappeared into the crowd. He was gone again, just like in her dreams.

"What?" she snapped. Lord Orgustus was talking to her.

Lord Orgustus raised an eyebrow at her tone.

"I merely remarked that it is rare for a Marchant to ever 'chat,' Your Majesty. Plotting, scheming, and disseminating is more their style. They are not to be treated with lightly, you know," he said archly. "You would be wise to stay away from that one altogether. Some say he is a warlock of some middling power, though not as strong as his grandfather was."

Adele tried to keep her footing on the shiny marble floor as Lord Orgustus whirled her expertly around.

"What's a warlock?" asked Adele, somewhat breathlessly.

Lord Orgustus looked down at her, his expression curious. Adele was annoyed with herself for noticing how handsome he was now that he wasn't glaring anymore.

"I keep forgetting Your Majesty is so new to our world. Don't they have *any* magic where you are from?"

"Not that I've ever seen," answered Adele honestly. "Definitely not like magic is here, as a part of the everyday world. In my world wizards and witches are just in children's stories."

She tried not to stare up at the lord as he pulled her in so close to him that his chuckle vibrated through her chest.

"That must be some kind of paradise where human beings do not have to live at the whims and fancies of those with magic," he mused, his blue eyes speculative as he stared down at Adele. "A warlock is worse even than a wizard. He is everything that a wizard isn't supposed to be. They work with the Dark Magic as well as the Light Magic: rarely for the good of society and always to strengthen their own power."

He glanced about to check if they had any eavesdroppers before he leaned down closer to her ear.

"It is said that they capture the souls of little children to fuel their evil spells and charms."

Adele looked up to see if he was making fun of her and found Lord Orgustus's face too close to her own.

"The younger the better," he whispered.

"Oh!" gasped Adele, shocked.

The lord threw back his head in a big booming laugh at her reaction.

"Of course you cannot believe everything you hear about Marchants," he sneered, the expression ruining his good looks again. "Truthfully, this Prince Rainere is just a sad little relic of his ancestors. The sole heir and genetic dead-end to a great long line of the worst warmongers, murderers, and criminals the kingdom has ever seen. Being immortal makes him sterile, you know, and what's a monarch without heirs? I'd feel sorry for him if he wasn't a Marchant." He smiled as he gave Adele a particularly vigorous spin, sending her reeling and falling into him.

Adele felt sick to hear Rainere described like this by such a horrible person as Lord Orgustus.

*Warlock. Immortal. Murderer.*

None of this matched with what she saw in the eyes of her Dream Man.

Adele tried hard to find her feet and slow her racing heart. She needed Rainere to be everything she thought he was. She needed to be able to trust him. He was the only thing she could be sure about. He was the only thing she had from home.

Thankfully, Ohren came and rescued her from another dance with Lord Orgustus before her dizziness turned to nausea. The lord bowed low to her and kissed her hand as she took her leave. His lips were hot, and Adele felt a childish urge to wipe the place where they had been on her skin.

"Please tell me this night is over, Ohren," begged Adele quietly as they walked to the edge of the crowd. The headache from earlier tightened its grip on her head.

Ohren chuckled. "I should say even I would be tired after being spun around the floor by Lord Orgustus like that. I thought you were going to fly away at one point."

Adele made a wry face. "I stepped on my own feet at least twice to try and keep up. Prince Rainere was much more polite with me."

She gave Ohren a sideways glance to gauge his reaction to her mention of the prince.

Ohren only smiled warmly down at her.

"Only a few more people to meet, Your Majesty, and then you can make your gracious exit, I promise."

"Really?" groaned Adele. "You wouldn't happen to have anything left in your little silver bottle, would you?"

Ohren laughed, and the sound of it made Adele smile despite her headache. He sounded like a much younger man when he laughed.

"It's probably safer to stick to water right now, Your Majesty." He grinned and Adele squirmed slightly. Had she embarrassed herself that much?

A flash in the corner of her eye made her head snap around, but it was only the midnight blue of a cape swimming about a young man's shoulders. Adele wondered where Rainere was, or if he was watching her.

"I can help you," he had said.

Well, whatever it was Adele had to do tomorrow, she was definitely going to try to find him. She smiled to herself. It sounded so much like a fairy tale but finally she had found a prince who had offered to rescue her from the insane predicament she found herself in as queen of a fairy-tale kingdom.

She couldn't believe it, yet she was living in it.

Hopefully, Rainere had some shining armor and a white horse hidden away somewhere—or at the very least he would have some answers for her.

Tomorrow couldn't come fast enough.

# CHAPTER TWENTY-TWO

## "He Let Her Name Kiss His Lips"

Rainere watched as the cretinous Lord Orgustus twirled the queen around the dance floor. Even in the isolation of the Grey Palace, he had heard about the campaign of lies the Regent continued to run against his family name of Marchant. Old hatreds died hard here, in the heart of the kingdom.

Rainere couldn't help but notice all the pointing and staring from the other couples in the crowd, as they moved aside for the spinning royals. Lord Orgustus was running his mouth off and laughing obscenely at his own jokes, but Adelena looked like she was holding on for dear life.

Rainere felt a growl building down low in his chest. A dark jealousy gripped him as he watched the lord bend low as if to kiss Adelena but move at the last moment to whisper in her ear. He held her closer than decorum would ever allow…closer than Rainere had. Rainere snarled.

Oh, the things he could do to that arrogant buffoon, and no one would ever know it was him…or at least not until he had returned to the safety of the Grey Palace.

But that would leave Adelena here alone and unprotected. She would be at the mercy of the Wizards Council and the political games of Lord Orgustus.

Adelena.

He let her name kiss his lips and calmed himself. He had felt her in his arms, trembling like a tiny bird and smiling up at him with her eyes so wide.

*If only he could take her away with him, tonight!* But there were dangers for her at the Grey Palace, too. At least here, in the heart of the Wizards' Court, the Spider Empress could not touch her. Rainere felt another surge of emotion as he saw Ohren interrupt the dancing. He had managed to avoid the wizard's company during the last two days, and he hoped his run of luck would continue. The last thing he needed was Ohren interrogating him on what he knew of this ridiculous prophecy. No doubt, Rainere himself would be the only scapegoat for the "forces of darkness" quoted in the first chapter, and if Ohren suspected he knew anything about it then his chances of getting close to Adelena would become very remote. They would have to keep their knowledge of each other a secret from the high wizard and his court.

Despite the caution he needed to use with Adelena, Rainere felt the heavy hand of the Gods guiding him here in the Golden Palace. It was the original and ancient seat of power for his ancestors, after all, and it was in this very palace that the Gods had blessed the reign of every one of the great Marchant kings. Perhaps Grotto had been right all along. Maybe he did belong here—this was his home, too, more so than for any of the imposters who lived here now.

Rainere watched closely as Ohren led the queen away with him, leaving Lord Orgustus to be swallowed up by a crowd of his cohorts and cronies. Rainere resisted the urge to follow Adelena, and instead made his own surreptitious escape from the ball. He would find Adelena tomorrow. Now he just had to get through the rest of the night without her.

# CHAPTER TWENTY-THREE

## "The New Court of Queen Adelena St. Lucidis"

Adelena woke to the sound of her children's laughter as they played with their puppies on the floor. She rolled over to check the clock radio—a habit that wouldn't die. The gray light coming in the window told her it was probably just before dawn. She did a quick calculation. *Ugh, only four hours' sleep. That wasn't nearly enough.* Adele snuggled back under the covers of Natalie's bed. She'd slept in the nursery, as Aaron had woken in the night with a nightmare and Adele hadn't bothered to go back to her own cold bed but instead climbed in with Natalie, the least wriggly of her children.

Now, Adele was regretting that decision.

She felt a wet nose touch her cheek and got a blast of hot puppy breath right in the face.

"Ewww!" she complained to the giggles surrounding her.

"Hero Dog wants you to get up, Mummy, doesn't he?" crowed Aaron. "He's kissing you."

"And so does Princess Tra La La," said Natalie, dumping her puppy on Adele's chest.

"Bunny!" yelled Stella enthusiastically.

"So we've managed to name the puppies, then?" Adele groaned as she rolled out of bed, wincing when her head pounded, but managed to force a smile when Caitlin popped her head in the door.

"Good morning, Your Majesty! Ready to start the day, my bairns?" she sang.

The children shrieked in response, and the girls headed over for cuddles. Adele was too tired to be jealous of their affection for the sweet nanny this morning.

"Your Majesty, the high wizard sent a message to say he will be stopping in soon. Shall I fetch Ladies Cara and Lisbeth to dress you?"

Adele gave her pillow one last longing glance.

"Why not?" She sighed. The day had already started, after all.

*    *    *

Adele and the children were sitting down to breakfast when Ohren burst in through the double doors, startling the stewards and making the children cheer.

"Good morning, royal family!" he boomed at his happy audience.

Stella threw a friendly piece of toast at him, which Ohren managed to catch before the sticky topping could touch his beard. Natalie and Aaron clapped their approval.

"Children!" scolded Siobahn, or "the bossy nanny," as she had been dubbed by the children. "Show some respect for High Wizard Ohren."

Adele was inclined to agree, but she bristled when anyone else admonished her children, so she just smiled at Stella.

"Oh, I think Stella was worried the high wizard needed more breakfast. It *is* incredibly early," Adele remarked, pointedly.

High Wizard Ohren's eyes twinkled as he watched the children regard the power play between their mother and the nanny. Stella wore a smug smile. Mummy always won.

"Oh, I wouldn't mind at all, if only someone would throw me a cup of tea to go with my toast," he answered mildly.

Natalie got the joke first, and her giggles got the other two going again. Soon toast was being thrown under and over the table, and Siobahn only just managed to save the teapot from Natalie's overexcited clutches.

Adele could tell that Ohren enjoyed the antics of her children. Her heart warmed to the old wizard as he chuckled with genuine affection while Stella threw berries to the puppies behind her chair. Adele smiled, too, and so she was caught off guard when Ohren leaned over and murmured to her without taking his eyes off the children.

"Majesty, we have a very important meeting to attend this morning." He shifted slightly to dodge a flying bread roll. "You had better prepare the children for your absence today."

Adele felt the now-familiar dread return to the pit of her stomach. Though she felt the children would be relatively safe with the nannies and Mrs. Ollenby, still, anything could happen. She pushed away her plate, appetite gone.

*       *       *

Adele tried to stop herself from running back into the nursery, where Stella was wailing with grief at having to be separated from her mother so early in the morning. It killed Adele to leave her baby when she was so upset.

Ohren looked at the queen with interest as they walked away from the royal apartments. Adele was obviously struggling with her own tears.

"Have they spent every day of their lives with you, Your Majesty?" he asked curiously.

"Pretty much," Adele answered, wincing when Stella renewed her howling with fresh vigor. "Natalie has school, of course, but the other two are home with me most of the time."

Ohren nodded. "It makes for a very strong bond, I can see. Are they as close to their father?"

Adele hesitated before answering. She probed the sore part of her heart where Justin used to live. It didn't hurt as much as she thought it would.

*Because of Rainere*, a voice whispered in her mind, and a shot of electricity flew up her spine in anticipation of seeing him again.

"They do love their father," she said slowly. "But they are used to him not being a part of their lives. He was, is, always so busy with work, you see."

"I can only imagine he is missing you all so much right now…"

"Two weeks," interrupted Adele, wanting this conversation to be finished. "He'll notice we are gone in two more weeks. He and I are not together, you see…we are divorced."

She stared straight ahead and quickened her pace. She couldn't hear Stella anymore and didn't know if that was better or worse.

Ohren took the hint and dropped the subject of Adele's husband, easily stepping up to keep pace with her.

"Apologies, Your Majesty. Right now I should be preparing you for this first meeting."

Pale-faced, Adele nodded.

"This meeting today is a general meeting with all the princes and heads of houses. You will need to tread lightly with each. Tilburn has speeches prepared for you to make to each of the Families."

They met Tilburn at the intersection of two corridors, and after a quick greeting, he remained silent, joining their party with his own two squires in tow.

Adele fought a wave of anxiety when she realized the sheaf of papers Tilburn carried were actually all speeches. There were at least fifty pages there.

"…after which we will break for a quick recess, and then the individual appointments will begin this afternoon. I will not lie—this will be a grueling day, but it is so important to cement relations with each house and give them your total assurance that you will maintain the status quo in the kingdom. We simply want to quash fears and sooth nerves today, not make any proclamations," continued Ohren.

"How can I quash their fears when I have so many of my own?" snapped Adele, a slightly hysterical note in her voice. "And why do I need to be here for the whole day if I just have to promise to do nothing and let the kingdom run itself?"

They had reached their destination. Adele had not been to this part of the castle before. The carpets were heavily patterned with dark colors, and the walls were lined with huge portraits of serious-looking men and women in heavy gilt frames. These were real kings and queens of Unisia, and Adele quailed beneath their painted stares, already feeling like a fraud.

Absently, she noticed the nervous twitching of the stewards at the doors, as they remained undecided as to whether or not they should open the doors for the hesitating queen and high wizard.

Never had so many people relied upon her word for action, from tiny things like opening doors to enormous things like running a kingdom.

Ohren gently pulled Adele around to face him.

"Your Majesty," he said, his voice low yet firm. "It is crucial that we keep the families calm and happy right now. The day will come when we will need to rely on the goodwill that you have fostered today. You must not fail in your duty."

Adele couldn't breathe. Anxiety crushed the air from her lungs. Unfortunately, Ohren took her silence for assent and nodded to the stewards to open the doors.

The meeting room was sumptuous. Gold and lavender silk lined the walls, and gilded furniture glittered in the sunlight flooding through the three sets of French doors that led out to a tree-lined balcony. A large oval table filled the middle of the room, with seats for twenty. Every chair was already filled except the two largest at the head of the table.

Adele's eyes took a moment to adjust to the light after the relative dimness of the hallway. As she stepped into the room, Ohren behind her right shoulder, all the dignitaries stood in silence. Adele immediately got the impression she should say something. She opened her mouth to speak when—

"Welcome, princes and heads of the St Lucidis, Caparell, Belvoir and Marchant families." Ohren's sonorous voice boomed the greeting, but Adele was sure all the gazes of these important men were focused on her alone. She became horribly aware that she was the only woman in the room.

Ohren's warm hand on her back guided her to the chair at the head of the table. The chair was quickly pulled back so she could adjust her large skirts. As soon as she sat, the rest of the table sat as well. There was probably more twitching of capes, clanking of heavy gold chains of office, and huffing than might have been truly necessary, but the tension in the room was palpable. Only Ohren remained standing during the minute-long hubbub, gently placing the speech notes Tilburn had handed him in front of Adele. He cleared his throat and instantly all eyes were on him.

While the gentlemen hung on every word of Ohren's welcome, Adele had a chance to look at the men before her. She searched the table until she found Rainere. He was sitting unnaturally still and wearing a cold expression, staring at a point above her head. Adele guessed that the reason for his tension was Lord Orgustus seated immediately next to him. She cursed silently as the lord caught her gaze and stared until she looked away.

A round of polite clapping as Ohren's speech ended roused Adele from her focus on Rainere. It was her turn.

*Dammit, I probably should have listened to the wizard*, she thought belatedly as she stumbled to her feet and shuffled her stack of papers.

Feeling dizzy with nerves, Adele began the first page of the fifty given to her. Thankfully the handwriting was large and clearly printed for her to read. Knowing Rainere was watching helped calm her, and she managed to finish the first part with only a few mistakes. She even managed a quick smile as she sat down.

Next to speak was the Ruling House of St. Lucidis. Lord Orgustus climbed to his feet wearing a look of cool amusement on his face. With a wide theatrical gesture, he encompassed the whole room in thanking Adele for her heartfelt speech. Adele shifted uncomfortably in her seat. His sarcasm was unmistakable.

"It is no small wonder that our *precious* Queen Adelena has been returned to us through the miracle that is magic, by our High Wizards Council, under the *esteemed* direction of High Wizard Ohren," began the lord, his voice loud and his tone pompous.

Lord Orgustus turned to Adele, and though his smile was warm, his eyes were cold. She fought the urge to shiver and withstood his glare with a determined one of her own. He couldn't hurt her with Ohren and Rainere in the room.

"And let us thank the Holy Gods that we live under the direction of such an *enlightened* Wizards Council who can make such *complex* decisions for our kingdom of Unisia without ever having to bother us with *any* of the details involved."

He paused, and Adele could feel Ohren pull himself up in his chair. She risked a glance at him, and saw he had locked gazes with Lord Orgustus, his expression furious. Orgustus himself looked equally fierce. Adele felt her stomach drop. This was not going well.

"As the head of the ruling family of St. Lucidis, until very recently, that is, I am *extremely* grateful that my authority by birthright, and all powers of decision making, were taken right out of my hands by Wizard Ohren—" He waved his hands in the air to belabor his point.

The tension in the room became suffocating as every person at the table sat up in horror of what Lord Orgustus was about to say.

"—and put right into the tiny hands of our long-lost queen. A woman who many of us had thought had fallen victim to a Marchant regicide one hundred and forty-five years ago. But no! Here she is, good as new, speaking our own King's Tongue, no less, even though she is said to have grown up on a far-off, distant world. A queen who, though she looks like none of my line, is said to be a full-blooded St. Lucidian."

Lord Orgustus turned his lion-eyed gaze back on Adele. She could see the calculation in his eyes. Although his cheeks were pink and his voice loud, Adele could tell that he was a man completely in control of his passion. He knew exactly what he was doing.

"And I am also grateful to our high wizard for not inviting me to the Ceremony of the Blood. As I understand it, it was held very late at night in the basement of the University, and not on palace grounds, though that would have been more traditional. *But* as always I will trust that our most *revered* High Wizard Ohren would not lie to this court and kingdom about something as important as the origins of our new queen. My faith in his word in unshakable, and I would never for a moment want to suggest that he has simply put a puppet on the throne, in the guise of an heir, in order to wrest absolute power of the kingdom for himself..."

Adele wasn't sure what happened next, but, all of a sudden, guards were standing on either side of the lord as he leaned across the table yelling at Ohren while the other aristocrats fell into chaos shouting among themselves. Adele only caught fragments.

"Treason!"

"Seditious fool!"

"You tell 'em, son!"

Adele sat back in her chair. Her heart was pounding at the atmosphere of violence in the room as Orgustus was dragged out, still shouting, by the guards. Adele noted they weren't in the livery of her Queen's Guard. Ohren remained standing until the lord had left and looked as though he was barely restraining himself from following. Tilburn flapped around the table.

"Please, gentlemen! Please remember yourselves, our queen is present."

Adele looked over at Rainere but he was sitting back comfortably in his chair, his expression neutral and his hands folded in a teepee in front of his chest, as he watched the chaos before him.

Prince Bertrand of Belvoir looked as though he was thoroughly enjoying himself as his fellow aristocrats shouted and huffed at one another. Bertie realized the Marchant prince was watching him and gave Rainere a formal *'how do you do'* nod. Rainere inclined his head back at the elderly prince and leaned across the table to say something too low for Adele to hear, but she saw Bertie throw back his head and laugh uproariously.

*Maybe Rainere has another friend at court?* thought Adele as she watched the curious connection between the two men. *So not everyone hates the Marchants, at least.*

Eventually the princes and lords settled themselves, still muttering and shooting dark looks at one another.

"Please, gentlemen! If anyone has an issue they wish to discuss with High Wizard Ohren, this is *not* the forum today. Make an appointment for a separate interview." Tilburn glowered around the table, daring anyone to take umbrage with his request.

"My door is always open," said Ohren, smiling, but Adele wondered why suddenly everyone had to look at their laps or at something on the wall instead of at the wizard's kind face.

*Are they really all that scared of him?* thought Adele, checking Ohren's expression for a threat, but finding none. *Then why is it just Lord Orgustus who will stand up to him?*

The politics were completely beyond Adele's comprehension.

"Very well, then," huffed Tilburn, satisfied with the silence. He pulled his waistcoat down smartly. "We shall continue. Your Majesty?"

Adele rose and, after checking that Rainere's eyes were on her, made her second speech outlining her earnest hope that the family of Belvoir would remain active and supportive within the new Court, *and blah, blah, blah...*

Adele tuned out what she was reading and just concentrated on pronouncing the difficult legal terms. It looked like Latin, but she couldn't be sure of anything in this world.

Thankfully, when Bertie stood up he had nothing but nice things to say and even got a few chuckles with his speech about Old Blood in the new court. Only the decrepit Prince Claudio of Carparell rolled his eyes, but perhaps, hoped Adele, that might have been a tic, as he was quite ancient.

Ohren called for a recess after Bertie sat down, and servants cascaded into the room, carrying tray after tray of sandwiches and cakes. Large carafes of wine and water circulated as the princes and lords got up to stretch their legs.

Adele leaned over to Ohren as soon as she could.

"How am I doing?" she asked him anxiously.

"Very well, Your Majesty," he answered giving her a distracted smile. "You are a natural. Now, please excuse me..."

Adele felt annoyed with Ohren until she saw that it was his brother who had walked into the room. Adele hadn't seen Ohren's twin since the first coronation. Despite her unpleasant memory of him, she was fascinated by how completely identical the two men were. It was extraordinary to see them standing side by side. If it wasn't for the clothing, Ohren might have been standing before a mirror.

The two brothers were in the middle of an intense discussion when Orestes's gaze flicked to Adele and caught her staring at them. He nodded once and his expression was guarded but respectful. Adele wondered at the change in his attitude toward her, before her gaze was inexorably drawn back to Rainere. The prince was sketching something on a piece of paper, his hand moving in graceful, fluid strokes. Adele felt an urge to see what he was working on, but Ohren got to Rainere before she could stand. Adele noticed that Rainere quickly slipped the paper under another sheaf by his side.

Tilburn placed a plate of food under her elbow and refilled her water cup. As he rearranged her notes, he gave her new instructions now that their party had been joined by High Magistrar Orestes. Thankfully, the changes were only minor and Adele didn't have to do much more than indicate her respect for the constitution of Unisia.

The meeting started again at an apparently invisible signal from Tilburn, and Adele's plate of food was whisked away untouched.

Orestes sat in Lord Orgustus's empty chair. But Prince Rainere looked more uncomfortable now than when the lord had sat there. His eyes were trained on the table in front of him, and his jaw twitched as he ground his teeth. It distracted Adele to see Rainere so obviously unhappy. She was so looking forward to hearing him make his own speech, even though he looked like he might run from the room.

Before Rainere could speak, Adele had to endure Prince Claudio of Carparell's long-winded and tiresome speech. She smiled as she caught Bertie trying to hide a big yawn.

Finally it was her turn, and with as much warmth as she could, Adele read out her welcome to the last prince of Marchant. The words meant nothing to Adele, but they started a muttering and lots of chair shifting among the other gentlemen. Instantly she felt paranoid. Who had she insulted?

But wait.

Why did the speech talk of "negotiations to rejoin" and not the "open invitation" to the other families? Too late, Adele remembered her quick history lessons with Ohren. The Marchants had been expelled from Court all those years ago.

Adele tried to keep it together, but she heard a sharp keening in her ears as her hands shook the papers she held. She rushed through the rest of her speech, too embarrassed to lift her eyes to Rainere's.

When Rainere rose, however, she couldn't help but look at him. He stood tall and proud, his chin high, every inch a prince and, despite it being the contrary, he looked like the youngest man in the room.

"Your Majesty, Queen Adelena, Princes and Gentlemen of the court, Magistrar and High Wizard. As the last remaining prince and sole surviving heir of the Marchant family, I look forward to commencing negotiations for the reentry of the Marchant family into the new court of Queen Adelena St. Lucidis."

Adele looked about the room in consternation, as the mutterings grew louder and the looks grew darker. Unfazed, Rainere continued, his raspy voice carrying over the noise of his peers.

"Unfortunately, however much we might wish to, we can make no financial contribution to the Crown, as the reparations after the last civil uprising reduced our family holdings to the single title of the Duchy of Black Mountain and the Grey Palace contained therein."

An uncomfortable silence fell heavily over the audience. Rainere's gaze swept the entire table before coming to rest on Adele. Her heart thumped loudly in response.

"Yet we would offer all that is ours to the Crown of Unisia and our undying service as a Prince of the Realm in exchange for a fond and genuine relationship with the Crown."

Adele smiled and opened her mouth to speak.

"The Crown accepts Prince Rainere's kind offer," Ohren broke in, his voice hard, "and we will consider new terms in due course. Now if that is all, gentlemen, we will adjourn for the day. All requests for interviews have been reserved with the queen this afternoon. I bid you a good day, and remind you that all the families are welcome to the dinner being held in the ballroom tonight."

After the fuss and pomp of the day, Ohren's farewell was abrupt, but everyone seemed happy enough to stand up and end the meeting. Adele took her cue from Ohren to rise and head out. She took his arm gratefully, as her legs had pins and needles from sitting for so long. As they passed Prince Rainere, Adele wanted to catch his eye, but the prince was deep in conversation with Orestes, though he was leaning as far back in his chair as he could to avoid being close to the high magistrar.

"Like a mongoose chatting to a snake," muttered Ohren, glaring openly at the two men. Adele had no time to ask him what he was talking about before Prince Claudio begged for a minute of her time and kept her talking for so long she never even saw when Prince Rainere left the room.

# CHAPTER TWENTY-FOUR

## "Walking in the Sun"

Rainere felt like howling, or smashing something, or maybe hurting the high wizard so badly that he couldn't ever walk again. Ohren certainly deserved it all, and more, after the way he had treated the prince today at the meeting.

"Master, stop fidgeting—I'm trying to pin these sleeves," snapped Grotto for the umpteenth time.

"You were right, Grotto," growled Rainere. "I have no stomach for these games and courtly politics. That wizard will let no one say his piece in front of the queen."

Rainere rolled his shoulders and fought to control his anger.

"Couldn't I just kill all the other princes and force the Wizards Council to recognize me as the only member of their precious new court of Queen Adelena? Wouldn't that be simpler?"

Grotto sat back on his heels.

"Yes, and look at how far that attitude has taken the Marchant family now," he chided, pulling himself to his feet and adjusting the prince's new jacket. "We are destitute, with only one surviving heir and one property."

Grotto caught Rainere's eye in the mirror.

"Perhaps if your father had learned to play nicely with the Wizards Council instead of tormenting them, we wouldn't be in this mess."

Rainere shrugged off the new jacket and headed for the window to look out over the palace gardens, still bathed in the late-afternoon sun.

"She's so close, Grotto," he sighed. "So close and yet they always have her completely surrounded by people and their magic. How can I win her to me when they have given her everything already? She has a kingdom, and ultimate authority in her crown. What can I offer her?"

"But win her you shall," answered Grotto in a firm voice. "You have an advantage those wizards never thought of. She already knows you - knows you and wants you. When you see her tonight, you will win her heart and secure your invitation to court. Then you are merely steps from marriage and putting the Marchant family back on the throne where you belong. Finally! I have waited so long for this day, master, and if the Spider Empress is to be believed, fate will secure your future as king."

Rainere picked at the gilding on the windowpane with his thumbnail. Grotto was becoming obsessed with this prophecy.

"You make it sound so easy, Grotto. But though I know her, her heart is still a mystery to me. She might not…when she comes to know me, it might not…"

"Pah!" snorted Grotto. "What is a woman's heart but a plaything to be caught and won? Flattery and toys are the way to earn her heart. Jewels, trinkets, charms…a woman's affections can be bought very easily, master. They have given her a kingdom!"

Grotto cackled unkindly.

"It's like putting shoes on a dog. She is out of her depth here, and just a puppet for the High Wizards Council. But she could be your puppet, my prince. Yours to command when you are finally crowned king and can legally wrest the power from her."

Rainere thought of Adelena sitting at the head of the table today, her voice soft and sweet as she read her lines. She had looked so nervous. Her full lips had trembled and she'd often chewed her bottom lip to hide the movement. A slight frown had pulled down the smooth skin on her forehead as her intelligent gaze had taken the measure of all before her. It was as if a fire had flashed through his blood whenever she caught his eye. He was sure she had been watching him as he watched her. The idea that she might feel for him as he did for her made his head spin.

"I could never hurt her, Grotto. If she would consent, I would keep her as my queen, by my side," Rainere said quietly.

"Keep her, don't keep her—it will be your choice as king, master." Grotto sniffed. "Now, I have to take this jacket to the tailor, so I'd advise you to rest and eat a little before your interview with the queen tonight. You need to look your very best. Women are ever swayed by a fair face."

Rainere heard the door slam as Grotto left their suite. No doubt, a guard would follow him about the palace on his errands. Old habits died hard when it came to the Marchant family, and the prince saw signs of mistrust everywhere in the Golden Palace. He and his servants were watched like chickens in a pen.

Rainere itched to be back in his Grey Palace. He had been born there and spent almost every day of his life walking its empty corridors and many rooms. Though smaller than the Golden Palace, it contained twice as many mysteries.

He remembered a time, before his father had died, when the halls had been bustling with servants and the kitchens always smelled good. They'd had visitors then, and parties in the ballroom. But after his father…well, there had just been him and Grotto. No one had come to call, and all the servants had left as the pittance that was his inheritance had run dry. There had only ever been the Grey Palace and Grotto before Adelena. His heart thudded at the thought that there might be more for him now. Something more than political exile, more than magic…something that loved him in return. Adelena and he were connected across time and space by a bond he couldn't explain, even with all his knowledge of science and magic. Maybe the Spider Empress was right when she said the Hidden Child was his destiny. If Adelena really was the Child of Prophecy, of course.

The prince's eyes drifted to the couples and small groups walking about the sunny gardens. *So many people everywhere.* He wondered what it would feel like to walk with Adelena in the sun, laughing with friends.

He shook his head to dispel the notion.

Bizarre. His thoughts were being jumbled by the energy of all the people here. That was all.

"When I have Adelena by my side, we will rule from the Grey Palace," he told himself. "The Spider Empress can take this golden snake pit, and I won't care if she eats them all."

# CHAPTER TWENTY-FIVE

## "Finally—They Were Alone"

Adele sat back in her chair by the fireplace in the palatial interview room. It was a balmy night, but Adele had asked for the fire to be lit because it was cozier. The interviews she was conducting were supposed to be informal affairs, and Adele had enjoyed having a glass of wine or two with Prince Bertrand and his extended Belvoir family. She had met his surprisingly young successor, Lance, a gangly boy of sixteen with bright red hair and freckles, who had nevertheless impressed her with his maturity and poise. Bertie, as Adele now felt completely comfortable calling the old prince, had kept her laughing with his stories of a misspent youth in the Golden Palace and the hijinks of his now-staid fellow princes in the other families.

"Don't let them fool you, my Queen Adelena," Bertie had said as Tilburn tried to usher the group out well past their allotted time. "Those old boys had some real spirit in them sixty years ago."

He'd squeezed her hand in both of his, and Adele had resisted a very real urge to give him a hug.

"Thank you, Bertie," she said with sincere affection. "I'll have to remember that the next time they're all tutting and rolling their eyes at me."

Bertie laughed with a boyish chortle.

"They do that to me too, my queen!" He said, as he gathered the rest of his family and left.

Adele smiled at the fire, remembering some of Bertie's stories. Apparently, Prince Claudio of Carparell had been a real ladies' man in his day. She thought of his hanging jowls and the disapproving glares of his watery blue eyes, and shuddered.

She sipped her wine but accidentally spilled some when a loud knock came at the door. Tilburn poked his coiffed head through.

*How does he get his curls to stay so tight all day?* She wondered, before registering his apologetic expression.

"What?" She asked, already disappointed.

"I'm so terribly sorry, Your Majesty, but there is just one more appointment before you are finished for the night."

Adele didn't bother to hide her dismay, and her majordomo had the good grace to look chagrined.

"I do apologize for not telling you earlier, Your Majesty, but the scroll only came this morning, and I never thought he would actually attend the interview, as it were. Then when he did show up, I thought if I made him wait long enough he might leave…as it were." He cleared his throat noisily. "But he…er…didn't leave, that is."

Adele sat bolt upright, her heart thudding. There could only be two men who made Tilburn react like this. It was either Lord Orgustus or Prince Rainere waiting for her behind that door. She swallowed down on her suddenly dry throat.

"I'm sorry, Your Majesty." Tilburn ducked his head at her stricken expression.

"Send him in, then, Tilburn," Adele croaked and downed the last of her wine. With a cough and a slight shudder, she refilled her glass and poured another for her guest. She tried not to notice how much her hands were shaking.

Tilburn stepped out into the antechamber to welcome the newcomer. Though she was waiting for him, Tilburn's knock still made her jump out of her skin.

"The Marchant Prince Rainere, humbly requests a private consult with Her Majesty Queen Adelena. Shall it be granted, Your Majesty?" And for the first time that night, her majordomo actually sounded like he was asking a real question and not making a statement.

Adele made to stand then thought better of it and sat back down again, then wriggled to the edge of her chair. She took a deep breath and fought to control her excitement.

"It shall," she answered.

"Anything you need, Your Majesty? Anything at all?" asked Tilburn. "More refreshments, perhaps?"

"No, thank you, Tilburn…" but her voice drifted off as the prince stepped into the room from behind the little man. It was a shock, once again, to see her Dream Man come to life before her very eyes.

Rainere stood tall, like a dark angel, looking elegant and intensely somber in his black velvet suit. He carried a square of silver silk in the top pocket of his long jacket and wore a Marchant crest on his arm, its shining silver threads glittering in the lamplight. His shoulders were broad for his slim frame and he held his hands clasped behind his back as he bowed to her. Long hair hung on either side of his face, framing his perfectly pale skin and illuminating the blue shadows under his eyes.

"I could take notes of the meeting for Your Majesty, if you would like?" Tilburn offered.

"Thank you, Tilburn, but we will be fine," said Adele, dragging her gaze from Rainere to Tilburn's frown. She nodded and forced a smile.

With many backward glances, Tilburn reluctantly left the room.

Finally—they were alone.

Adele felt sick and a little dizzy as her anxiety roiled with the wine in her stomach. After all those nights of dreams and this last day knowing he lived here, in this new world, what could she say to him?

Suddenly the fire felt just too hot. It was stifling. Without looking at the prince, Adele got up and walked to the window. Closing her eyes, she let the night breeze cool her hot cheeks.

*You've got to say something!* She snarled at herself. *Just, please, don't blow this.* An image of Justin's face flashed in her mind.

Adele breathed deeply, and opened her eyes. The breeze lifted the wisps of hair at her neck that had escaped her braided hair. A hint of vanilla scented the air. A fierce flash of desire overcame Adele. The very moment she had dreamed about for years was before her now.

She turned and gasped when she saw that Rainere had moved to stand just a few feet away from her. The power of his gaze sent her pulse racing as her stomach dropped away. He was just so perfect and so real. Unconsciously, she moved toward him and committed to memory the new details of his face that she hadn't known before. The way the firelight threw shadows under his cheekbones. The fine dark arch of his eyebrows. The way his eyes seemed to glitter with her own reflected desire. His mouth with its perfect lips parted to speak.

"Adelena, my…queen…" His voice was husky and sent a thrill down her spine.

Adelena didn't realize she was stretching up on her toes, or putting her hands behind his neck, but she could feel his cool breath on her cheek and watched his lips part to speak again. It was like so many of her dreams. In every one of them, another inch closer and their lips would almost touch, then the wind would blow in and she would fly back to her bed, and her 3:00 a.m. reality.

The agony of unrequited passion was exhausting.

As a gentle breeze swirled in the window and around them, a tiny sigh escaped Adele and, as if it were his cue, Rainere bent his head and their lips touched.

*Finally.*

The planets spun and the stars flew in and out of alignment as they kissed. The prince's breath felt cool but combined with her heat it seemed to ignite the air itself, sucking all the oxygen out of her lungs.

Yet still they kissed.

Adele felt Rainere's strong arms encircle her and pick her up as if she weighed nothing at all. She wrapped her own tighter around his shoulders, feeling the flex and ripple of his back beneath her hands.

She had no idea of how much time had passed when she finally pushed herself back and off his delicious, rolling kiss.

"Rainere," she gasped, steadying herself with her hands on his chest. "I—"

Adele realized she was sitting on the prince's lap, her gown puffed up between them. She pushed down the velvet layers and tried to catch her breath. Adele felt a thrill of energy ripple over her skin and looked up in surprise.

Rainere's smile was as pure and light as sunshine.

"You are so beauti—" was all she could manage before she leaned in to taste his smile. His mouth molded to hers and Adele moaned as her body responded on its own.

How she pulled him down to the floor she had no idea, but when she became conscious again she was lying on the plush carpet with Rainere running hot, sweet, little kisses down her neck to her bare shoulder. He held himself up so as not to crush her.

"Rainere," she sighed happily, his name a song.

Rainere looked down, his dark eyes almost hypnotizing her. She raised her hands to hold his cheeks. His skin was smooth on his chin where it had been freshly shaved. Adele breathed in deeply. He smelled of wood smoke, deep spices, and snow on the wind. A hot burn was stoked low down inside of her.

"Adelena," he whispered, reverentially placing a kiss at the corner of her mouth. "How long have I yearned for you…thinking you were only a phantom sent by the Gods to drive me mad."

Adele ran a finger along his sharp cheekbone.

"And I always thought you were an angel I dreamed up to save me from my loveless existence," she whispered back, not even slightly recognizing herself but feeling more real and whole in Rainere's arms than she had since waking up in this foreign world.

Recognition bloomed in Rainere's eyes.

"I, too, have been alone, my dearest, *cara mia*." He stroked a finger across her lips. "But now we have found each other across the stars, finally we can be together."

His smile faltered when he saw her eyes fill with tears.

"They brought me here, Rainere," she said quietly. "The wizards brought me to this world and they are holding us here. Ohren said we could never go home."

Rainere frowned.

"Us?"

"My children and I," answered Adele with a nervous glance at the door. She pushed herself up on her elbows as Rainere shifted to sit beside her. "You said last night that you could help me. Can you get us back home?"

Adele grabbed Rainere's hand as he looked away from her.

"Please, Rainere," Adele begged. "I was told that you were a wizard, too, or a warlock or something. I know everyone is scared of your power and your Marchant magic, but I know nothing about these things. I think you are the only person who can help us escape."

Rainere looked down at Adele's small hand gripping his own. The Ring of Office sat, dark and huge, on her delicate finger.

"We have only just found each other, and you want to go away again?" His voice was low, husky with disappointment.

He looked up at Adele, and the hurt and confusion she saw there drove a knife through her heart. She cursed herself. The one perfect, powerful moment of romance in her whole sorry life, and she ruined it by telling the man of her dreams she wanted to leave him.

But the children. They needed to get home.

"I didn't know you had children," said Rainere softly, tracing the bones on the back of her hand. The touch made her shiver. "How many do you have?"

"I have three," she answered. "Three little ones. My daughter Natalie is six, my son Aaron is four, and the baby Stella is just two. They have adjusted to life here on this world, but they don't belong here, Rainere. None of us do." She gripped his hands with both of hers, desperate to make him look at her and understand why she had to go.

"Rainere, I know that everyone here thinks that I am this long-lost heir, hidden on another world, but I'm not, Rainere—I'm just an ordinary person. I'm not a wizard, I have no magic, nothing. I'm just a mother to three stranded children in a world we don't understand."

The tears slid down Adele's cheeks as she tried to force Rainere to understand.

Rainere finally looked up at her. His gaze was inscrutable.

"You don't believe that you are the Hidden Child of the Prophecy?" he asked.

Adele pushed herself to her feet and threw her hands in the air. She started to panic slightly. What if Rainere was just like Ohren?

"Prophecy! I had never even heard of such a thing until I came here. No one believes in prophecy where I come from, or in wizards or warlocks or magic or any of this craziness."

Adele walked back to the fireplace and threw herself into a chair, glaring at the flames.

She felt more than heard Rainere get up and settle in the chair opposite her, but she couldn't look at him.

"Rainere, when I saw you at the coronation, I felt like there was a chance...that you might be the reason I'm here."

She paused as her voice broke.

"But it's all messed up because my children are here, too, and it's not safe for us. All this royal family business...it just isn't real. It can't be real. I don't know how I can get free of this mess, and I don't know how I can get us home. You have to help us if only because no one else will."

Rainere sat forward just as Adele buried her face in her hands, her silent tears turning to sobs. He moved to kneel in front of her and gently pulled her into his arms.

Adele resisted for just a moment. But the smell of wood smoke and vanilla surrounded her, and Rainere felt so good and so strong. She had to trust somebody. She had to let her guard down with somebody who knew her, even if it was only in her dreams. She needed someone on her side, just for once, and this prince was the closest thing she had to home.

Adele's arms crept around Rainere's chest as she sobbed onto his velvet-covered shoulder, and as she finally got a chance to say what had been screaming around her head since waking up in Unisia.

"Oh Rainere, I'm so frightened! They want so much from me. I'm not a queen, for God's sake. I don't care about their dark days that are coming. I just want my children to be safe home again. I just want us all to be safe."

Adele cried until the tears ran themselves out and were replaced by little hiccups. Rainere was still on his knees, holding her and stroking her back. It felt wonderful.

Adele sniffed and pulled her face from Rainere's neck.

"I'm so sorry." She sat back, suddenly too aware of how red and puffy she must look, and how badly she needed a tissue.

The prince silently handed her a handkerchief, his dark eyes taking in all of her.

Adele sighed and tried to blow her nose quietly. Why could she never be glamorous or appropriate? Here she was with the most beautiful man she had ever seen and she threw herself at him like a tart and then cried all over him.

"I'm such a fool," she whispered.

*Rainere probably thinks I'm as crazy as everyone else does now*, she thought bitterly.

She dared a glance up at him to confirm her suspicions.

Rainere's eyes were soft and his mouth quirked up at the side. He ran a finger along her chin.

"You missed one," he said quietly, the rasp of his voice exciting her pulse again.

Adele saw the teardrop on the tip of his finger and almost gasped when he put it between his lips.

"It's sweet," he said in mild surprise.

Adele giggled.

"You're just saying that…"

His embrace surprised her with its suddenness and strength. His nose was buried into the nape of her neck.

"I don't care what anyone says, either, or who they think you are, Adelena. We will be together, and I will help you be wherever you want to be. This I vow to you," he whispered fiercely. "You can trust me."

She could feel his heart thudding against her chest, keeping time with her own racing one.

She reached her arms around his body and squeezed him hard.

"Thank you. Thank you, Rainere!" She fought back more tears but of relief this time.

Rainere released her and sat back on his heels. His eyes searching her face, as he gently caught the wisps of loose hair out of her eyes.

"They are going to think I've done something dreadful to you," he said, brushing her bottom lip with his thumb.

Adele turned into his hand, nestling her cheek in his palm.

"I'm so glad you are here, Rainere. You are the one thing that has been good about this whole…madness. Finding you just feels right." Adele struggled to make her words come out in whole sentences. She turned and kissed his palm.

"You are even more wonderful than all those nights I dreamed of you."

Adele smiled up at Rainere, reveling in her joy at finding him. She didn't let another dark thought cross her mind when he leaned in slowly to kiss her.

She was here. He was here. They had each other right now.

It was too soon when Rainere pulled away.

"Someone's coming," he whispered, and flew away faster than she would have thought possible to sit on the couch by the window.

Tilburn knocked loudly and entered, calling out, "Your Majesty, I'm terribly sorry to interrupt, but there is a minor family emergency which requires your attention just now."

His eyes searched the room before he found Prince Rainere comfortably leaning back on the couch, legs crossed and looking a picture of easy calm.

Adele quickly closed her open mouth and hoped Tilburn didn't notice her burning cheeks or wet eyes.

"Is it Stella?" she asked, smoothing her hair.

"It's all of them, Your Majesty," replied Tilburn drily. "And it's quite a scene, I've been told."

"Fine, I'm coming now," answered Adele, standing too quickly and grabbing the back of her chair until the blood had a chance to rush back up to her head. She waved away Tilburn's polite concern.

"It's just the late hour," she said before turning to Rainere. His eyes were so dark they smoldered at her, threatening to hypnotize her again. Adele hid a smile.

"Thank you for taking this interview with me, Your Highness," she said, trying to be formal. "I look forward to seeing you again before the week is out. I do apologize for having to cut our time so short, but duty calls."

Adele watched with hungry eyes as Rainere approached her and swept into a deep bow.

"I look forward to building further relations between the Marchant family and your new court, Your Majesty. I'm delighted to have had the chance to enjoy your personal acquaintance tonight and thank you most humbly for your time."

Though his words were submissive, his tone was anything but. Adele felt another wave of desire flood through her as the prince took her hand and kissed the back of it.

It was too late to ask when she would see him again, or make another appointment. Adele cursed herself and the time she had wasted crying all over him as she watched Rainere walk out of the door and away from her.

Adele followed Tilburn back to the royal apartments in a daze. Her mind felt pushed to breaking point.

Rainere wanted her as badly as she had wanted him for so long. *If only they had met in her world, where she belonged and where the children were safe. But...what would she do if the situation were reversed and Rainere had wanted to leave her world and return here? Would she help him to leave her? Could she let him go?* Adele shook her head.

*It doesn't matter,* she told herself. He had promised her he would help. He had *vowed* that he would.

Adele didn't realize they had reached the door to her rooms until she felt Tilburn's light touch on her shoulder.

"Majesty, we are here." He smiled kindly at her distraction. "Don't worry about him, Your Majesty, the Marchant prince has this effect on everyone. He is a decidedly...intimidating man."

Adele could only smile wanly in response as she stepped into the room to the shouts and squeals of three hysterical children.

"Duty calls, indeed," remarked Tilburn, giving her a *better-you-than-me* look, and made a quick exit.

"Mummy!" shouted her children in unison, and instantly enveloped her in their need and noise. She pushed away thoughts of another sort of ending to her night and began to settle her children.

# CHAPTER TWENTY-SIX

## "Gorrik and His Master"

Gorrik sat in his comfortable chair by the fire, sipping at a tiny glass of Firewhiskey. It didn't make his old bones jump anymore, like it did to the young ones, but he enjoyed the feeling of warmth in his blood. The fire in the grate had barely taken the chill off him, even on this warm night.

"Ahhh, that's the ticket," he groaned happily as the golden elixir melted the ice holding his muscles and bones stiffly. He lay back in his chair, eyes closed, and instantly dozed.

Scratching noises at his window woke him a moment later. Gorrik looked over to see a pointy little black face at the window.

"Meow!"

"All right, all right, master, I'm coming," grumbled Gorrik as he levered himself out of his armchair. "Of course you want to come in just as I'm getting comfortable."

Gorrik went to the little window and pulled the latch. A strong breeze blew in and ruffled his wisps of white hair. Gorrik cocked his head to the side.

"What's that?" he asked, his expression as of one intently listening.

The skinny black cat delicately stepped through the window and butted against the hand Gorrik still held to the latch. He purred loudly until he got Gorrik's attention again.

"Meow-ow!" he cried quietly, begging for a scratch around the ears.

"Well, isn't that interesting, master," said Gorrik, coming back to himself. "The North Wind is a right gossip, but it looks like Ohren was correct. That new queen of ours definitely takes after her father."

He chuckled darkly and scratched his cat under the chin as it purred throatily.

"But despite what that boy wizard hopes she'll do for him, blood will out. The flesh wants what the flesh wants, and those St. Lucidis royals ever strayed to the forbidden side."

"Meow," the cat agreed and stared up at Gorrik adoringly, his sea-green eyes almost glowing in the dim light.

Still chuckling, Gorrik closed the window and turned to head back to his chair. The cat followed him and leaped up onto the old man's lap as soon as he had settled himself.

"You might well ask if I will tell Ohren this bit of news, my little master?" said Gorrik, already closing his eyes as the last of the Firewhiskey worked its soothing magic. "But I think we'll keep it to ourselves until we see how this plays out. We don't want to upset things right now, and of course the boy wizard will ask how we know. No, this secret will keep for a bit."

His chuckles faded and soon turned to soft snores. The little cat watched the old man intently for a moment before curling up in a tight ball. Then, he too, was soon asleep.

# CHAPTER TWENTY-SEVEN

## "A Lesson in History"

"Your Majesty, wonderful news!"

High Wizard Ohren came striding over to the royal family in their dining room, where they were all sat down to breakfast. He narrowly avoided stepping on a puppy as it darted into his way, and his subsequent twirl to avoid falling over sent the children into fits of giggles. Adele gave the older man a little clap as he dropped into a chair at the table, dignity intact.

"Nicely done, Ohren."

"Not as nimble as I once was, Your Majesty, but thankfully I can still save myself from a vicious puppy attack." He frowned in mock anger at the big-eyed pup cowering under the table. Stella struggled to get down and join her puppy, which Adele allowed, much to the consternation of Siobahn, who immediately wanted her off the floor.

It had been one of *those* mornings.

"Good news, Ohren?" prompted Adele.

"Yes, Your Majesty, quite." Ohren looked positively ecstatic. "It is time for your magic training to begin! We had been waiting until your blood had settled before it was safe to proceed. But now that we know it has, we can explore how strong you are."

Despite herself Adele was quite pleased…just a moment before her self-doubt crept back in. If Ohren could show her that she had magic powers of some kind, wouldn't that mean he had been right all along, and she did belong here in Evendaar?

Maybe he would try to trick her into believing she had powers that she didn't really have?

Adele smiled brightly at the wizard and hid her thoughts.

"That sounds like fun. Can the children join us at training?" she asked as they started clapping and chanting, "Magic! Magic! Magic!"

Ohren clapped his own hands together with glee.

"Absolutely! All right, children, who would like to come to a smelly old classroom and try to sort out dust from dirt with Mummy?"

Their little faces fell.

"Or," suggested Ohren with a shrug, "who wants to go on boring pony rides at the garden party today, and eat lots of awful-looking sweets?"

"Sweets! Ponies!" shouted Natalie and Aaron, instantly excited again.

"Bunny!" yelled Stella from under the table, getting into the spirit.

"There you go, Your Majesty, the children just don't want to come." Ohren grinned and held his hands up in defeat.

Adele rolled her eyes at the wizard's lame trick and kissed her children as they hustled out to get dressed and down to the garden party with the nannies. Today, Stella seemed happy to leave her mother without the tears of yesterday. Adele tried to ignore the hollow feeling that left in her chest. Mrs. Ollenby bustled in and grabbed quick hugs before the children ran out.

"My word, that's an excited bunch," Mrs. Ollenby puffed as she sat at the table. She allowed Adele to pour her a cup of tea while a maid hovered close by, nervous about the lack of protocol. The queen was always insisting on pouring her own tea, though, and Mrs. Ollenby had given up trying to argue with her about it.

"Might I inquire, Mrs. Ollenby, about your business with the queen this morning?" asked Ohren politely. "I had intended to take her for some initial magic instruction."

"Oh, I am sorry to inconvenience you, High Wizard," replied Mrs. Ollenby, not looking at all sorry. "But we have the royal procession to prepare for, and only a few days to finish it all in."

"But her blood has settled," argued Ohren with a polite frown.

"Then she can take her instruction with you tonight," answered Mrs. Ollenby sweetly.

"Sorry, she has her St. Lucidis and Carparell interviews tonight," called Tilburn as he made his way over, leading a conga line of liveried servants carrying piles of boxes and pulling trolleys behind them. "No time free there."

Ohren was going pink in the cheeks.

"Couldn't we do both planning and instruction this morning, then I can have the afternoon at the garden party with the children?" asked Adele.

Both Ohren and Mrs. Ollenby turned to her in horror and started protesting at exactly the same time. Adele couldn't help it. She laughed. The sound of it filled the room and echoed into the hallway.

Adele clapped her hand over her mouth as the whole room went silent.

"Oh, I'm so sorry," she muttered, embarrassed.

Ohren smiled at Adele warmly. "Never apologize for laughing, Your Majesty."

Mrs. Ollenby chuckled. "You know, that is the first time I have heard you laugh since you arrived here. Such a bright and infectious laugh it is, too!"

Adele smiled in relief and sipped her tea. She had felt different since she had left Rainere last night. Calmer, and somehow lighter.

Before Ohren could get in first, Mrs. Ollenby had the breakfast things cleared as Tilburn simultaneously started dumping charts, diagrams, and dress designs on the table in front of her.

Ohren groaned theatrically and acquiesced to the change in his morning plans with bad grace. He stomped out of the dining room muttering under his breath.

"Now, Your Majesty," began Tilburn, "this royal procession is incredibly important to you and your family. Now that you've been crowned and have created your new court here at the palace, it is time to go out and meet your people."

"My people?" repeated Adele stupidly.

"Yes, Majesty, the people of your kingdom. The townsfolk, the farmers, the landed gentry, the church folk. All these people make up your kingdom, and they are all terribly excited to see their new royal family." Mrs. Ollenby beamed, and Tilburn nodded encouragingly at Adele.

"Oh-kay," she agreed slowly, looking from one to the other. She hadn't once thought about the world of Unisia beyond the Golden Palace. It was a shock to have to do so now.

"Wonderful! Now the people will be expecting a fabulous spectacle that they can tell their future grandchildren about. That means preparing the dress carriages, planning the procession itself, organizing the staff to accompany you, and gowns, gowns and more gowns. Sumptuous, elegant, and gorgeous gowns to stun all those in the town squares and beyond. Jewels as far as the eye can see! Of course, the children will have to be dressed just as beautifully, and will have their own staff and carriages. Oh my word, there is so much to be done, it doesn't bear thinking about it all!" Mrs. Ollenby took a breath and dabbed at her pink cheeks with a delicate handkerchief.

"It's going to be expensive," warned Tilburn.

"It's going to be fabulous!" trilled Mrs. Ollenby, giving Adele the very clear impression that Mrs. Ollenby had waited her entire life for a moment such as this.

The morning passed in a flurry of fabric samples, carriage decoration ideas, color combination choices, and a thousand other issues to do with the politics of royal hierarchies and which houses and estates the procession would visit. All of which Adele ruthlessly delegated to anyone with an opinion. By midday, Mrs. Ollenby was nearly at breaking point.

"Now, Your Majesty, please think very carefully about this next decision. Please! Your choice of horse says a lot about your connection to the other families. Who will you please by choosing their special breed above all others?"

Mrs. Ollenby threw some sketches of beautiful horses down in front of Adele.

"Well, what do you recommend?" asked Adele innocently.

"Majesty," pleaded Mrs. Ollenby. "It's not my decision. It's a very important one and only you can make it."

The poor woman was close to tears of frustration, so Adele looked carefully over the pictures to placate her.

"I don't know anything about horses but these are all very pretty. Maybe one from each family's stables. Then everyone's happy," she suggested.

Mrs. Ollenby looked like she was trying to gather strength from a spiritual source. She shook her head firmly, bouncing all her curls.

Adele relented.

"Okay, no. Well, the St. Lucidis white are too bridal-looking. The Carparells dapple gray are nice but I think they look kind of untidy. The chestnuts are pretty with their black manes. I think they would be nice in all the parades."

Mrs. Ollenby smiled in relief.

"Lovely decision, Your Majesty. I'll contact the Belvoir stables immediately." She added more notes to her overflowing pile of scrolls.

"It's just a shame that there are no black horses," Adele mused. "They've always been my favorite since I read *Black Beauty* as a girl."

Mrs. Ollenby looked at Adele with an odd expression.

"Your Majesty, the only family who breeds black horses is the Marchants, and they cannot be used by anyone but Marchant drivers. They are an especially aggressive breed. It's my belief that His Highness the prince still breeds horses, though, if you would like me to inquire?" Her expression was enough to tell Adele it wasn't a good idea.

"No, no, it's fine," said Adele. "I was just checking, that's all."

Mrs. Ollenby brought out another huge folio of dress designs and another of fabric swatches. Adele groaned.

"It's for the Belvoir Racing Carnival Ball, Your Majesty, held in your honor this year. I need your full attention for this," Mrs. Ollenby begged.

Adele sighed mightily. "Fine, just let me take a minute, first."

She got up, almost stumbling on her cramped legs, and trudged to the bathroom.

As Adele was washing her hands and dreading going back to Mrs. Ollenby, she had an idea. She poked her head outside her bedroom door into the antechamber that led into the main corridor outside the apartment.

It was quiet in the antechamber, and Adele saw just one of her stewards loitering by the main door, chewing his nails and kicking at the edge of the carpet.

"Hollis! Hey, Hollis," she called quietly, fearing Tilburn was nearby. "Could you please tell the high wizard to meet me here in my bedroom? Not in the main room. Just here. And Hollis, don't tell anyone what you are doing, okay?"

Hollis nodded once and dashed off.

Adele felt silly sneaking away from Mrs. Ollenby and all her duties like this, but there was only so much she could take of picking ribbon trims and choosing which aunt of which prince to invite to sit in the royal carriage on each day of the procession.

Quicker than she would have thought possible, Ohren arrived at the antechamber door.

"Aha," he whispered gleefully when Adele gestured him to silence. "Follow me, Your Majesty, I'll take us where no one can find us."

Outside in the corridor, they walked as fast as dignity would allow. Adele could only admire the formidable frown that Ohren wore as they negotiated the crowds in the palace hallways, frightening everyone who looked interested in speaking to them. She didn't even open her own mouth until they were in a deserted part of one of the palace towers.

They climbed several sets of stairs leading up. Each landing lost the luxury of the last as carpets became floorboards and plaster walls became unadorned stone. Only a few bits of threadbare furniture decorated the landings, and even the air smelled dusty with neglect. Eventually, Ohren stopped in front of an ordinary wooden door on an ordinary-looking floor of the tower. With a smile and a welcoming gesture, he opened the door to the room in which Adele would discover her magical powers.

Adele stared around the chamber, noticing its dusty tables and chairs and dirty windows. It was clearly an old classroom that hadn't been used in years.

"You hang out here a lot, Ohren?" she asked, accidentally kicking over a pile of paper rubbish and old apple cores. Well, that accounted for the smell of rotten fruit.

"Hmmm, what? No, not at all. I just thought it would be a useful cubbyhole today," he answered, and started busily setting up an old wooden bench with two stools on either side. He collected a handful of dust from the ledge of a window and then a handful of dirt from his own pocket and, using his finger, mixed the two together on the benchtop.

"Sit," he instructed. Adele took a seat, mystified.

"Now let's begin." Said Ohren, sitting opposite her.

"Wait!" Adele held up her finger. "Tell me first how my blood has settled. What does that even mean?"

Ohren's expression hardened slightly with impatience.

"When we brought you from Earth, the High Wizards Council performed the Ceremony of the Blood. You heard about it, yes?"

Adele nodded slowly.

"It was something to prove that I was a St. Lucidis princess."

"Exactly. We take a sample of your blood, not very much at all, and burn it over the Sacred Fire. The magic in your blood releases certain colors as it's heated. Your blood burned gold, proving your St. Lucidis heritage, and because of the strength of the magic in your blood, your blood has kept burning since we placed it over the fire several days ago. But since last night it settled from a blaze to a smolder. That's how I know how strong you are and that it is time to begin your instruction."

"Wow, that's very cool." Adele was shocked. So there was actually proof that she was who they said she was.

"Can I see it? My burning blood?" she asked.

"Maybe later," Ohren answered, avoiding her eye. "The Sacred Fire is over at the University and it is tightly protected by magic…it would take an effort we don't have time for right now."

"Okay," agreed Adele, forcing a smile. Ohren's reticence reminded her uncomfortably of Lord Orgustus's accusations yesterday at the meeting that the Blood Ceremony had been some kind of hoax. She shook her head to dispel her reservations. Ohren wouldn't do that to her. *He was one of the good guys, right?*

"Now, can we begin?" Ohren beetled his eyebrows at her, daring her to interrupt again.

Adele gulped a little. *What on earth was going to happen?*

"The first step is always the hardest, and magic is no exception to this rule. First one must believe absolutely in the possibility of that which you wish to achieve." He paused. "Understand so far?"

Adele nodded. "Believe in magic. Got it."

"Manipulation of Matter is one of the most important and useful of all the lessons to study. From the simplest action of sorting materials with different points of origin from each other, to separating the clouds from the sky, it is used in almost every form of magic."

Adele was getting excited. This sounded like serious stuff.

"Now this pile here is made up of dirt I brought in from the garden in my pocket, and this is dust that I found in this room. Both are similar in size but with different points of origin. Isolate each particle from the other and put them in two piles. Dust here. Dirt there."

Adele poked the mess with her finger.

Ohren frowned at her.

"I'm not asking you to use your hands, Adelena. Use your magic."

"Adelena? That's my first name, you know, Ohren. Getting a bit familiar, are we?" joked Adele, her eyebrows up in surprise. She could tell that Ohren was going to respond with an apology right away and set him straight.

"Please, just call me Adele," she smiled. "I'm sure it's fine when it's just the two of us."

Ohren smiled and nodded before frowning again.

"Adele, if you please." He gestured at the pile of rubbish between them. "I would like you to have a try first by yourself, and then I will help you if you need it."

"Um…okay." Adele felt ridiculous. "Let's see…"

She pointed at the pile and muttered, "Separate."

Nothing happened.

Ohren smiled encouragingly. "Try something else."

Heartened that she wasn't totally embarrassing herself, Adele closed her eyes and placed her hand above the pile. She breathed deeply.

"Separate."

She opened her eyes. Nothing had changed.

"Instead of trying to separate the materials together, try focusing on just the dirt and call it to you," suggested Ohren, watching her closely.

Adele took another deep breath. Eyes closed, she imagined the dirt glowing. She held her hand out again. "Dirt, come."

She opened her eyes. "Hey, I did it!" she exclaimed, looking at her dirt-covered hand.

"No." Ohren shook his head. "Your hand dipped into the pile. Brush it off and start again."

Suddenly, Adele wasn't sure if this magic instruction was going to be any more fun than choosing lace trimmings for carriage cushions.

After almost an hour of frustrated effort, Adele's patience finally snapped.

"Okay, Mr. High Wizard, you do it! Show me how it's done."

Ohren frowned at her petulance.

"I thought you would never ask, Adelena. You know the human eye takes in more information than the brain can process at any one time. But with magic in your system, you can train yourself to learn by observation alone."

Adele was too annoyed to fully enjoy Ohren's only moment of actual instruction, so she just sat back with her arms folded, waiting to see this dammed pile of dirt be finished off.

Ohren placed his hand over the pile and a pale glow emanated from underneath it. The dirt and light-gray dust quickly and quietly leaped away from each other and sat in two neat piles. He hadn't uttered a word or done anything else she could see. With a sweep, Ohren put the two piles back together and mixed them. Brushing off his hands on his gray robes, he looked up at Adele.

"I did it slowly so you could see the process. Now you try." He nodded expectantly.

Adele dropped her head to rest on her arm on the table.

Ohren's answering chuckle only made her feel slightly better.

"Ohren, this is useless," said Adele, sitting up and glaring at the pile of rubbish. "I have never seen magic or used magic or been close to magic in my life. I have absolutely no idea what you want me to do with this stuff. It's like asking me to breathe with another type of air! I didn't know there was another type of air, and I sure as hell don't know where to find it to breathe it."

Ohren sat back in his chair and looked at Adele curiously, his head cocked to the side.

"So it's a belief in magic that is holding you back, or, should I say, a lack of belief?"

Adele shrugged. Despite her complaints, she was feeling like a failure. Ohren had been so confident of her magical powers he had almost convinced her she had them, too.

"Maybe if you tell me what I'm supposed to feel like when I feel the magic in me. That might help," suggested Adele.

Ohren frowned and turned to face the window but not before Adele caught his look of disappointment.

"Magic is as natural to our bodies as breathing is," he said. "One could say, it's like another way of thinking about the world. We use magic to change and manipulate the area and people directly around us, whether to heal, or correct, or enable…" Ohren drifted off from his textbook instruction. He gazed out the window in his own little world.

Adele let him be for a moment before she gave a quiet cough.

"Adele, there is something very important you must understand," said Ohren as he suddenly came to and turned to face her. Adele almost flinched from the intense look in his eyes.

"Our world of Evendaar was created by the Gods several thousand years ago. That makes us only a newborn in terms of the age of the stars surrounding us in the universe. But to help us, their creations, survive the new world, the Gods gave us the Gift of Magic. Those strongest in magic were instructed to build our communities and increase our population, creating a peaceful society based on the merits of strength, justice, and beauty. As the human race flourished in Evendaar, we all split into the different tribes that each of the Gods created. The most powerful among those tribes were given extra gifts by the Gods who watched over them. Here in Unisia, the Goddess Serena gave us the Celestial Skies star chart and, to a chosen few, the Gift of Prophecy. These tools were given to help us watch out for any danger that might be near in our future. As I told you before, living so close to the World of the Gods has made us a target from those entities who hope to enter their world."

"Entities?" interrupted Adele.

"Entities like Evil and Darkness." Ohren's expression was hard. "While our world was still young and vulnerable, the Gods left doorways so that they could enter and leave as they saw fit. It was here that other beings or entities crept into our world and hid in the dark places, where the Gods wouldn't see them. Hidden as they were, the Dark Entities grew stronger and multiplied. When the Gods left us to travel back to their own world, the Dark Entities came out of their hiding places and tried to take over Evendaar. The human race barely survived the attacks and was forced to defend themselves by forming armies and creating weapons to defeat them.

"One family stood out in the new settlement of Unisia as the strongest and most capable as leaders and fighters. They used their magic in creative and ingenious ways to defeat the Dark Entities, and it was this family who finally led the human race to victory here in Unisia. When the war with the Dark Entities was won and the Goddess Serena returned to us, she saw that the Dark Entities had almost destroyed the human tribe she had created, and so she gave the victors the Gift of Immortality so that they could pass on their knowledge to the generations who would follow. Then there would always be one family with the knowledge of how to defeat the Dark Entities."

"The Marchants," whispered Adele. She realized she was gripping the fabric of her skirt tightly. She released her fingers and wiped uselessly at the sweat marks that now marred the yellow silk. She had a horrible feeling that Ohren was going to tell her something about the real reason that she was here in Unisia…a reason that has nothing to do with carriage parades and ball gowns…the Dark Days.

Ohren looked pained as he described the history of his world.

"The Marchant family ruled over the other three families because they were favored by the Goddess. As they had created weapons and fought in the early stages of their conception, their magic changed from the rest of the other families. It changed from a gold to a green energy that released more power than before. "

Ohren illustrated his point by showing Adele a ball of golden light balanced on his palm before it disappeared in a delicate cascade of gold sparkles.

"The Marchant family was proud of their special magic, and the Gift of Immortality from the Goddess, and jealously guarded the bloodlines that carried these gifts. They chose to breed only with certain lines of the other families, those who they thought would bring them extra qualities like strength and endurance, and, of course, those especially strong in magic, like the St. Lucidis family. They then decided that these bloodlines would be the royal lines in each of the other families. The four family hierarchies were born, and the new Marchant rulers built a fort with their magic to house all of their family and the royal lines of the other families."

Ohren looked around the old classroom.

"It has been a long time since the Golden Palace has been described as a fort, but in those times the population was small and the people were still terrified that the Dark Entities would return. As the years passed, the Marchant family gained in strength and power. Under their rule, the population built up to healthier numbers and began organizing a new society for Unisia. But the Marchant rulers were not content with their own thriving colony and began to covet the settlements of the other humans in neighboring parts of Evendaar. The other tribes of humans and creatures had been blessed with different gifts, by their own Gods, and the Marchant kings were determined to take those gifts either by commerce or force. Some tribes fell to the conquering Marchants, while others fought back and remained separate. War and weapon production became the backbone of the economy in Unisia and helped speed our development as the strongest human settlement in the land. Over thousands of years, the Marchant family ruled Evendaar with an iron fist. No one could hope to defeat them, other than the Marchants themselves. However, the very thing that kept their magic so strong and pure was ultimately their downfall.

"Generations of inbreeding had reduced their numbers and warped their minds. The Blood that carried their Goddess-given power became rare and skipped whole generations within the Family. Still, the Marchants remained favored by the Goddess Serena. The ruling King at the turn of the millennium, King Raingar, begged the Goddess to let him colonize another world, to increase his power and save his family from dying out entirely."

Ohren sighed and rubbed his hands over his face as if to block out the knowledge. When he looked back at Adele, his blue eyes were clouded with worry.

"We do not know if it was by the grace of the Goddess or perhaps the superior magic of the Marchant king, but he managed to create a means for traveling to another world, where humans also existed. That was when the exodus started. At first, it was only a few leaving in small family groups, but when word spread of a rich world free of magical creatures, in which technology and the wealthy flourished, then more and more of the Marchant families left Unisia. The Marchant king crowned his son as the new king of Unisia and left him in charge when the royal family left. King Rainov the Cruel was a powerful warlock and an ambitious ruler. It was he who found a way to block the portals to the other world so his father, Raingar, couldn't ever return to Evendaar and take back the crown of Unisia. He wanted complete and sole dominion over Evendaar for his own family line.

"But the St Lucidis, Belvoir and Carparell families had different ideas. They had rejoiced at the Marchant exodus to the other world and had banded together in secret, led by the St. Lucidis family. They employed the greatest wizards in each family to overthrow the last Marchant king. Though as an immortal he could not be killed, he and his family were forced into political and social exile, and the St. Lucidis family claimed the Golden Palace and the throne as their own. Unfortunately, the royal line of the St. Lucidis who claimed the throne still had many ties with the Marchant Family in exile. Just one Marchant generation later, when King Rainov's son, Prince Rainold, tried to get the exile order reversed, King Octavius, your father, was sympathetic to his request—"

"And that's when I was born, and was sent away," said Adele. She was overwhelmed by the picture of Unisia she had just been given by Ohren. "Did you send me to the same world that the Marchants had gone to? Was that Earth?"

Ohren nodded slowly, gauging her reaction.

"It was. I…we didn't think that you would be there for very long, and as the world was free of magic, we didn't believe you would be at risk from the Marchants already there." Ohren sat back in his chair. "To be perfectly honest with you, Adelena…we were just a group of young wizards, and it seemed like our only option to keep you safe. As the only St. Lucidis heir it was crucial we keep you safe from the other wizards of the Carparell and Belvoir families. I knew where a portal was and how to open it. I had seen how beautiful the world was there. I just had no idea that time would move so differently and that you might not be able to be brought back by the same means. The portal we had used collapsed behind you, leaving your stranded."

He sighed, and Adele reminded herself to breathe as well.

"And the prophecy?"

"The prophecy came about at the time the first St. Lucidis King took the Throne: King Orelieus, who was father to Octavius. The King was a deeply religious man who worshipped the Goddess Serena faithfully, if a little zealously. He started the Church of Serena in the belief that it would call the Goddess back to Evendaar and that he would be blessed by her as the Marchant victors had been blessed in the past. The King did not believe that prophecy was a gift reserved for only the chosen few with magic. Anyone could be blessed with visions or hear the words of the Goddess in the form of prophecy. The leaders in his church encouraged any and all to come forward if they believed they had been visited by the Goddess.

"As you can imagine, it led to many fraudulent claims of prophecy and visions of the future. But there was one…a young girl stumbled into a country monastery claiming that the Goddess spoke to her constantly. The priest on duty faithfully gave her hospitality and wrote everything down that the girl said. On the first night in the church nursery, as the clock struck midnight, the girl awoke, calm and smiling, and rose from the ground. Sitting cross-legged in midair, she spoke to the shocked priest and said she was the Goddess Serena, and she had a message for the King. It was the Prophecy of the End of the World. King Orelieus had all of his best wizards and student wizards study the text as gospel, trying to discover the signs, which would help them prevent the calamity that was predicted. It was only when we sent you away as a baby over a hundred years later that I realized it was I who had set the prophecy in motion. I activated it when I hid you from the world of Evendaar, and made you the Hidden Child."

In the silence that fell, Adele could hear the soft faraway sounds of the garden party where she knew her children were playing. The floorboards creaked as the slanting beams of sunlight warmed their old timbers, and the slightly hitched breath of Ohren filled her ears. Adele stared at the wizard before her. She took in his old face, his expression so solemn and sad, and his radiant blue eyes, now clouded with dark memories of the past and the specters of the future.

"You brought me back here to fix a mistake you made one hundred and fifty years ago. You think that you might be the reason the Dark Entities will be back to try and take over Evendaar again, and the prophecy told you that I would somehow be the one to fix it all," said Adele woodenly. "Is that about right?"

"It's even more complicated than that, Adele," said Ohren leaning forward, his elbows on the table. "Magic is dying out in our world. Every generation born gets weaker and weaker. If we do not find a way to strengthen our family bloodlines, then soon we will just be prey waiting for the Dark Entities when they emerge from hiding, or something even more horrific that we have no knowledge of yet. That is a fact." He stabbed at the table to emphasis his point. "I only had the prophecy to guide me when I decided that you must be brought back. A celestial formation in the sky gave me my one opportunity to create the portal through which we retrieved you. If I hadn't taken that chance, then we wouldn't have you back and we would still be at the mercy of the prophecy. Do you understand? I had no choice. The people of Unisia and Evendaar needed me to make a decision. I couldn't let you go again. We need you, Adelena!"

Well, one thing was perfectly clear to Adele.

Ohren was never going to let her and her family go home.

Ever.

"We need to awaken the magic inside you, Adele. It's a part of who you are and how we function in this world. Your magic will also help you to know how act, and react, as the prophecy unfolds, and it will help you succeed. It is imperative you have all your gifts at your command as you move forward as our queen."

Ohren's expression softened as he took in Adele's troubled frown.

"I'm sorry that we couldn't have brought you back under better circumstances Adele, but…" He leaned forward and took her hand. "Please know that you are not alone. You have so many people around you who want only the best for you, and to help you learn how to be the queen we need you to be. You will never be alone." He squeezed her hand.

Adele's stomach rumbled in response.

Ohren smiled.

"I think that is enough instruction for the day. We should get you back to finish those vital decisions you need to make for the royal procession," he said, rolling his eyes.

He pulled her to her feet and led her out the door.

Adele gave a wry smile. After what Ohren had just told her, she cared even less for the details of pomp and ceremony. What she did care about were the people's lives that Ohren had endangered when he pulled her out of her world and put her in this one. He had put all of his eggs in her proverbial basket because of this prophecy, which *he* caused to activate, and now he had left her no choice but to act as their queen.

She had never felt more trapped. Though she wasn't wearing her crown, Adele felt her neck bend under its weight.

Rainere was mixed up in all this, too. After what she had learned today, it was no wonder nobody wanted him back in the Golden Palace. But just because his family had been so evil, that didn't make him evil, too. He wasn't just the sum of his bloodline.

He was an outsider, just like she was.

Adele thought of Lord Orgustus and how much he hated her for appearing in his world. He obviously knew nothing about why she was really here. Was the prophecy a secret, or did Ohren just make that up for her benefit?

She turned her head slightly to watch the wizard's profile as he walked next to her back to the royal apartments. With his long gray beard and vivid blue eyes surrounded by laugh lines, he certainly didn't look like the evil wizards of her stories at home. He chuckled too often and played so kindly with the children, but did that mean she could trust him with her family's safety? He had proved he would do anything for his kingdom. He had already sacrificed her once for the good of his world, and then had brought her back again to face an uncertain future here. How far would he go to ensure this mad prophecy was fulfilled?

As Adele smiled back at Ohren when he caught her eye, she tried to hide her thoughts from him.

*The first thing I need to do is find a copy of this prophecy and read it for myself,* Adele promised herself. *I need to know what's coming next, now that I know that Ohren will be doing everything to follow it.*

She shivered at the thought she was now living a destiny written for her hundreds of years ago in Unisia. An unfamiliar growl of rebellion stirred in her chest.

*Ohren might think he has me cornered in this golden cage, but I want to know what Rainere thinks about the prophecy. He is the only person in this world who hasn't asked me to be something I'm not, and the only one who has promised to help me. I need to see him today.*

Now that she had resolved to actually do something, Adele felt pleased with herself. For too long she had let herself be swept along in the shocking newness of life on this world and the bustle of the royal family routine. It was time she started making some decisions and finding her own way out of this mess. Her knight in shining armor might actually ride a black horse instead of a white one, but that didn't mean he was any more evil than she was supposed to be good. He had offered to rescue her, and Adele was going to make sure that he could.

As she settled down back at her dining table with a miffed Mrs. Ollenby and a slightly hysterical Tilburn, Adele returned to her chores with new enthusiasm. It had only just occurred to her that her royal procession would take her to the Grey Palace for four whole days. She would be with Rainere, alone, and that would give them plenty of time to work out how to send her and her children home.

When Tilburn presented her with letters of invitation to a private dinner the following night for the Marchant, Belvoir, and Carparell princes and Lord Orgustus, Adele took the chance to quickly write a note to Rainere in the bottom left-hand corner of his letter. She didn't know how he would manage it, but she had to see him privately tonight.

She felt a thrill of excitement at the idea of being alone with him again. Who knew what would happen if they had hours instead of minutes together?

# CHAPTER TWENTY-EIGHT

"Sex and Politics."

After getting back from his interview with Adelena, Prince Rainere had lain awake most of the night staring at the clear night sky and its sparkling stars. He could imagine that Adelena would like the stars like this. They glittered like her eyes did when they were filled with tears.

Waking much later, Rainere grumbled as Grotto pulled back the curtains with sharp tugs. Midmorning sun streamed into the room and hit him in the eyes. Squinting, Rainere found Grotto snatching the tray of coffee and toast from the maid, only to crash it down on the night table next to Rainere's head. The maid wisely fled.

"Something on your mind, Grotto?" asked Rainere as he sat up in bed and stretched languidly.

"Not at all, master," snapped Grotto. "You just came back, hours late from your first interview with the queen, all dazed and confused as if you'd been drugged, and refused to speak to me."

He slopped coffee into a cup and thrust it at the prince.

"I have no concerns at all."

Rainere regarded his manservant with an amused expression.

"Dazed and confused, Grotto? Hardly," he said archly. "I was merely surprised by my conversation with the queen. We had much…in common, and much to discuss."

Grotto did not like the dreamy look on Rainere's face at mention of the queen. He did not like it at all.

"For instance, did you know she had children? Three of them, in fact."

Grotto snarled.

"Of course I knew, master, it's all the palace can talk about! Her children are heirs to the throne now, casting many St. Lucidis in their shadow. I can tell you, these heirs are a complication we do not need right now. Did you not wonder, maybe, who their father is and where he is? If he is a strong wizard, perhaps he might follow them here to this world. Did you talk about that with the queen?"

"No," answered Rainere with a frown. "I didn't think about their father. But it is no matter, Grotto. There is no magic in their world, so he couldn't possibly follow them here."

Grotto moved away grumbling something that sounded like "Don't be so sure," and started arranging Rainere's wardrobe for the day.

"She is like no one I have ever met, Grotto," mused the prince quietly.

"That's because she is…" Grotto paused, struggling to keep a civil tongue in his head. He bit back his caustic comment and tried again with the distracted prince.

"Did you ask the queen how it was she came to be the Hidden Child, master? Did the wizards tell her how they brought her back, or why? Do they know that you and the empress tried to retrieve her, too, at the exact same time? Did you discuss *any* of this with her?"

Rainere pushed himself back on his pillows and wrapped both hands around his cup. It was almost as warm as Adele's skin. A small smile played over his lips.

"Master!" snapped Grotto.

"She doesn't want to be queen, Grotto," answered the prince, slightly exasperated. "What's important is that all she wants is to send her children home." He paused. "And she wants to go home, too."

He looked up at Grotto and his dark eyes flashed.

"I don't think she has any idea what the wizards really want with her. She is frightened and alone, but she will do anything to protect her children. That much is clear."

He almost smiled again, as he remembered the proud tilt of her chin as she spoke of her children, and the softness in her eyes.

Grotto looked unimpressed.

"She would say all that if she wanted you to think she was harmless."

Rainere relived the feeling of Adelena trembling in his arms and sobbing her heart out on his shoulder. No one had ever made him feel so needed or so strong. He had sworn to help her be wherever she wanted to be. Rainere pursed his lips. Now he just had to make her want to be with him instead of going back to Earth.

He sighed deeply.

*She was much more fragile and sweet than she had appeared in his dreams. Yet her kisses…he could taste her fire on the tip of his tongue.*

She was such a conundrum, but puzzles were the prince's primary fascination in life. She would be so wonderful to solve…

"Master, how is it you are going to get the queen to commit to a political relationship with you?" asked Grotto, breaking Rainere's daydreaming. "How open is she to your romantic attentions?"

Rainere almost blushed, looking down at his cup.

"I think she is open to me," he said quietly.

With an enormous strength of will, Grotto refrained from rolling his eyes. His master might be an immortal Marchant prince and a fiercely powerful warlock, but he was a babe when it came to women. Rainere had lived like a monk since his Immortality had been inflicted on him one hundred and fifteen years ago.

Grotto clasped his hands behind his back and pressed his lips into a thin line. How was he to explain the foibles of women to a man who was still such a boy?

"Well, let's start there, shall we?"

Rainere looked up at him.

"Do you think I should try and take advantage of her…romantically, I mean?" Rainere frowned. "Even if I do, how will that tie her to me? I need a greater pull than just…me."

"There is no greater pull than physical desire, Your Highness," answered Grotto. "Besides, the woman has three children. Believe me, she knows how it all works between men and women."

Grotto stood over the prince and refilled his cup.

"What you need to do, master, is convince her you are the only man who can give her what she wants." He held up a finger to stop Rainere from speaking. "And if she wants to go home, then that is what you promise her. It is of no concern to you that it is not magically possible. All that matters is that *she* doesn't know that. You can hold all her hopes in your hand."

Rainere frowned doubtfully.

"Master, she wants what you can give her, not you as such." Grotto's voice was cold. "These are the ways of women, master. They fall always for the highest bidder."

"But Grotto, she just wants what is best for her children. She only asked me if I could send her home. I don't believe she seeks anything else from me."

Grotto arched an eyebrow. "Did she ask you for this mighty favor before or after she gave herself over to you?"

"No," frowned Rainere, then remembered their conversation had come after her fierce and wonderful kisses.

"Well…maybe after she gave…a part of herself," he replied hesitantly.

Grotto smiled grimly. "Do not waste your time feeling the pangs of conscience for a woman, master. She wants what you can give her as much as you want to give it to her…it's only their tricksy nature that makes them pretend otherwise. This one is no different from any other woman. But you must control this game. Give her only what it takes for her to commit herself to you…remember your lessons in warcraft?"

"Allow the enemy to take only that which you wish to give," answered Rainere, his voice hollow and his eyes flat.

Grotto nodded. "So what shall you do now?" he prompted.

"I will take her and convince her to make me her king, in return for sending the children home," the prince replied dully.

"I know it seems simple enough, master," said Grotto as he turned back to arranging Rainere's wardrobe. "But believe me, you may still have to make a real effort to charm this woman. However, if she is as frightened of power as you say, offering to take it out of her hands might just win her gratitude."

Rainere made a noncommittal noise and slumped down further in his bed.

Grotto made perfect sense. Rainere needed only to take control of Adelena while she was vulnerable to him and convince her to put him on the throne as her king, and all would be set to rights. She would be safe from the Spider Empress. She would have him, and he would honestly try to send her children home for her. As a king, he would have the power of the Wizards Council at his disposal, whether they liked it or not. Of course, it would be impossible to send Adelena home, too. She would belong to him.

Then when all of that was over, he could abdicate the throne and take Adelena to live at the Grey Palace with him, leaving the kingdom to the Spider Empress with all her sick and twisted plans.

He dreamed a delicious fantasy where he and Adelena could live quietly together forever, studying magic and conducting experiments day and night.

And her kisses…he felt weak just thinking about them. The way her hands traveled over his body, small but so sure. If only they had had more time last night…

"She needs me," Rainere agreed quietly. "I just have to show her how much I care for her…to make her believe in me."

Grotto was glad he had his back to his master as he winced at the prince's words.

*Of all the stupid…it's as if he has no idea how much he is worth to the Spider Empress, so obsessed is he with this imposter queen,* Grotto thought, completely frustrated.

Grotto had tried to teach the prince the philosophy of war and the art of political combat, but sex and politics were beyond his capabilities. Grotto prayed the prince could keep his head when this queen started begging him for favors after giving him her body. Greater men than the prince had been brought low by a fair face.

Grotto ground his teeth.

Oh, and Marchant princes could always be relied upon to take the body's need over those of the spirit.

Still, Grotto had always had such high hopes for Prince Rainere. Grotto was determined that he would return the prince and the ancient glory of the Marchant family to the throne in his lifetime. Only then would he have fulfilled his ancient promise to his original master, Rainere's father.

It was just unfortunate that Prince Rainere now had to play the only game Grotto couldn't teach him from books. All their lives were at stake now that the prophecy had been set in motion, and events had taken hold. Even Adelena's, and all her blasted children's.

When the queen's note arrived later that night, Rainere was frozen by indecision.

"This is not an official summons," he pointed out to Grotto as they both pored over the little handwritten note in the corner of the scroll. "What would she wish to see me about tonight?"

Grotto raised his eyebrows. "At midnight, in her private chambers?" he asked pointedly.

"No. Really?" Rainere was surprised. "Already?"

"I hope you remember how it works, Your Highness," said Grotto, earning himself a baleful glare from the prince. "Because it's time for you to catch yourself a queen."

Two spots of color rested high on Rainere's cheeks as he carefully dressed himself for the midnight rendezvous. Despite Grotto's base opinion of Adelena, Rainere could not imagine her to be as conniving as the old manservant had suggested. Her eyes were so clear of guile, her smile so open. Rainere wasn't at all sure if she would even offer herself to him tonight. Perhaps she just wanted to talk? Then, at last, he would have the chance to explain how joining herself to him would protect her and the children from the shadows of the Spider Empress and the machinations of the Wizards Council.

Staring at himself in the mirror, Rainere couldn't help but notice how much better he looked after the Gift had restored his strength a week ago. His eyes were brighter, and the ring of silver which circled his pupils, undulated with reserves of the power that floated through his veins. He hadn't noticed a ring around Adelena's pupils, despite the fact she very probably would be filled with the strength of old St. Lucidis blood. Perhaps tonight he would see it shine gold?

Though he had never been vain, Rainere felt a kind of relief that Adelena should see him now, when his cheeks were fuller and his skin held a tinge of color. It pleased him that he would appear attractive to her.

Rainere frowned. At least, he hoped he was.

Grotto watched his Master staring at himself in the mirror, skittish as a bride on her wedding night, and his heart felt a pang for his young charge. Rainere could do with some advice right now, but it wasn't Grotto's place to give it. It was a father's place, and Rainere hadn't had a father since he was a babe of five years. In lieu of anything else to do, Grotto had remained silent, giving the prince time to prepare himself for the night ahead.

As the clock neared midnight, he alerted his master to the time with a quiet cough. Grotto watched as the prince left for the queen's chamber through a secret door in the bookcase.

The entire Golden Palace was riddled with secret passageways and doors like this. For fifteen hundred years, the palace had stood as the home of the Marchant royal family, and it was Rainere's true birthright. No amount of gold gilding and purple curtains were going to change that fact.

Grotto wished the luck of the Goddess went with his master. That young man was the last and only hope for the survival of the Marchant family. Without him, there was nothing left for Grotto.

Nothing at all.

# CHAPTER TWENTY-NINE

## "Adele Finds Her Magic"

Adele paced her room in a fever of indecision. Had she done a terrible thing inviting Rainere to her room tonight? What would he think of her? What was the proper etiquette when you met the man you had been dreaming about for years in his alien world?

Who could even answer that bizarre question?

Adele giggled hysterically to herself and then choked it off just as quickly. She had to calm down.

After flopping into the sofa by the balcony doors, she took a sip from her glass of wine and then another. A minute later, she was up pacing again, her heart in her throat.

As the hour of midnight ticked over and then slowly passed by, Adele felt like crying like a little girl.

He wasn't coming.

Adele threw herself on her bed and buried her face among the dozens tiny pillows that decorated it.

*I am such an idiot! Why would a man as beautiful as him, a prince, want me? Maybe it's because I kissed him first? Maybe because I cried all over him? He must think I am insane!*

Adele shook her head and dried her eyes. The emotions were all too much after such a trying day. She should just go to sleep and pray he never mentioned the note ever again.

*The note! Maybe the note got lost?* Adele's heart flew into her throat again.

A tiny click had come from a bookcase near the doors, which led out to the living rom. Adele turned to check, but in the dim candlelight, she couldn't see anything. If Rainere was coming, surely there would be a knock at the door.

*I'm just imagining things*, she thought, falling back on her pillows and trying to calm her crazy pulse. She shut her eyes tight and willed herself to go to sleep.

Another click sounded in the quiet room, and she sat bolt upright in bed.

There in the shadows, as if out of her dream, stood Prince Rainere.

With slow steps, he came toward her. Adele caught her breath as her anxieties melted away in the fire that now heated her blood.

He was here, with her. Completely alone.

Rainere stood before her, his raptor gaze pinning her where she sat.

She watched silently as he shrugged off his jacket and dropped it to the floor.

*Oh God, this is really going to happen!* The thought fluttered frantically around her head like a butterfly in a jar.

Rainere's long fingers undid the three buttons of his waistcoat, and then slowly undid the buttons of his black silk shirt. As his clothes slid to the floor, the picture-perfect musculature of his body was revealed. Adele had never seen such a stunning body this close before. She watched, hypnotized, at the play of his muscles under the smooth white skin, as he climbed onto the bed and came to rest leaning over her.

Adele cradled Rainere's face in her hands.

"Tell me I'm not dreaming," she whispered.

Rainere leaned down and laid his lips softly on hers.

Both their heads turned sharply at the sound of a voice just beyond the front door in the antechamber.

"My guard," breathed Adele.

With a snap all the locks in the room turned. Adele sat up in shock and saw the pale-green glow all the doors now wore.

"Magic," she whispered with a grin.

Rainere gave her an almost-smile. He looked down at the front of her nightgown and ever so slowly pulled at the ribbon that held it closed.

"Show me more," asked Adele recklessly, stalling for time as her nerves got the better of her after their interruption.

Rainere raised an eyebrow, making her giggle quietly.

"I can only think of one thing I'd like to do right now," he growled, his voice hoarser when he was trying to speak quietly.

Adele looked at him expectantly, her breath hitching.

His hand touched the fabric at her shoulder. There was a sudden flash of heat and Adele's skin vibrated all over as if she had been blown by a dry wind. She opened her eyes to see she was lying in a cloud of white feathers. Adele caught one in her hand. It wasn't a feather at all, but a tiny scrap of lace. She gazed at it in wonder.

That's how long it took her to realize she was now completely naked. Her nightgown had been reduced to a puff of soft ash.

"Now tell me I'm not dreaming," said Rainere, his dark eyes flashing with flecks of silver as the rings around his pupils lit up.

Still vibrating from the touch of the magic, her skin was extra sensitive as Rainere brushed the back of his fingers down her chest to her stomach.

Adele reached up, knotted her fingers in the silky hair at the back of his neck, and pulled his mouth down to hers.

Their kisses were frantic and wild as Rainere covered her mouth with his, making her heart race out of control. He pushed her down into the mattress, crushing her with his weight, and reaching down he immediately searched between her legs with his hand.

His mouth traveled down her throat to her collarbone, his kisses hot and wet.

It was...uncomfortable.

"Stop, please...slower," Adele gasped, as her desperation to have her prince warred with her discomfort that he was taking it too fast. She didn't like it this rough.

*It must be because he thinks I'm a slut, after I threw myself at him yesterday,* was Adele's uneasy thought as she felt the moment get out of control. *He's going to take what he wants, and it's going to hurt.*

She closed her eyes tight as she had so often with men. Closed them tight and waited until it was over. It was just the way it had always been for her when the first rush of lust was extinguished by the primitive act of taking.

This time, however, there was no better place she could go to in her mind. Rainere had been her fantasy, and now she was here, with him, and he was no better than the others.

Disappointment fell like an anvil on her earlier excitement. Her heart started racing with something other than passion, and the ringing in her ears was sudden and loud.

As Rainere's breathing grew heavier and his hands traveled her body unheeded, Adele stilled.

*Oh God, I'm going to faint,* she thought as she fought to breathe with Rainere's weight crushing the air out of her lungs. Panic swamped her...

Suddenly, everything went quiet and dark for Adele.

The ringing in her ears…they weren't bells…but voices…three, four, or five voices, chanting in unison. As she relaxed, the words became clearer. They were singing her instructions, no…commands. They were commands that would help her now. Adele listened hard as the words were repeated in high-pitched tones.

She braced herself and, fixing her hands against Rainere's chest, she whispered the commands with her breathless voice.

Adele felt Rainere freeze and gasp. She felt the vibrations through his rib cage as the command pulled the magic out of her and pushed it into Rainere. Struggling, she shoved him up and off her. With another whisper, she knew that she had pinned him to the bed.

She was safe. She was in control.

Adele sat up and slid her leg over Rainere's torso. She looked down into his face. His eyes widened with shock and anger as he fought her control. His hands clenching and unclenching the sheets by his side. Adele kept her hands on his chest, her fingers pressing into the bones of his rib cage. She knew instinctively that it was important to keep that contact.

Rainere hissed and winced as she shifted on his hips, feeling the press of him, still hard, against her behind.

"I'm sorry, Rainere," Adele whispered, shocked at her own power and dismayed by what she'd done, despite being relieved she was no longer pinned under him and unable to breathe.

She let her gaze travel down his gorgeous body, and sighed. He really was the most beautiful man she had ever seen. But now she had him trapped, furious and dangerous, between her thighs.

"You can't know this," she said, sadly. "But I don't like it rough like that. I need you to be gentle with me. To take your time and kindly…convince me to let you inside."

Rainere writhed under her and gasped in pain as the power she held him down with pinched at his lungs. His eyes were dark and wicked, and he snarled as he fought against her.

Adele watched as the power of her command held the prince captive. She could sense his struggle as she felt surge after surge of energy push up and against her hands. The skin beneath them grew hot.

Adele felt as trapped as the prince was. She didn't know what to do. If she called to her guards, everyone would see her naked and know that she had let the notorious Marchant prince into her bed...but if she let Rainere go, he might hurt her in retaliation, or worse. She was stuck.

The history Ohren had told her today spun around her head, but the history she had with Rainere mixed with those stories, and confused her. One thing she had learned on this world was that not everything was as it seemed.

After years of dreams, Adele had to trust that Rainere wanted her, and would listen to her words as no one else did. He had promised to rescue her. He was hers and she wanted him to kiss her so badly right now. She chose to trust him.

"Rainere, my love," Adele leaned down and whispered in the prince's ear. Rainere moaned softly in response.

"Are you listening to me now?" Adele asked and sat up straight pushing her shoulders back. Carefully releasing one hand from his chest, she reached behind herself to slip her hand into his pants and hold him firmly.

Rainere's expression changed as the realization dawned on him that Adele wasn't finished with him. She was only getting started. He stopped fighting her and froze.

Adele smiled as she sensed Rainere's change in mood. Finally, he was paying attention.

"You have to know, my love, that you are a lot more, man…than I'm used to." She smiled coyly, glancing over her shoulder to illustrate the point.

Rainere's expression grew almost smug, and Adele wanted to crow with relief. He was going to play her game. The fear of reprisal left her, and she felt satisfied in a dark place, deep inside of her.

"You are going to have to take it slowly with me, and I am going to control how you move. Am I clear?" Adele leaned down and gently bit his ear to illustrate her point.

She made to take her other hand off Rainere's chest but felt a surge of his power flow up her arm, sending cold chills all over her body. She laid her hands back down flat, and watched him gasp.

"If you push me too hard, my love, I will take you down again," she whispered throatily, not recognizing herself at all. She felt so strong, so in control.

Adele looked deep into Rainere's eyes and saw the dark joy there that matched her own. This was what she had wanted!

He nodded soundlessly and stared at her mouth, licking his lips in anticipation. Adele released her hold on Rainere and he slowly sat up to kiss her softly, before his tongue traveled down her neck, to her shoulder, and down to her chest.

Adele gasped at the sensation of his hot mouth on her flesh. He warmed her skin where his magic had put cold chills before. As he rose up to meet her, he reached around her to free himself from his pants. Adele wrapped her arms around his shoulders and she knelt to crest the tip of his erection. The sound of Rainere's carnal groan as he felt her pressing against him made her blush hotly. Slowly, slowly she dropped down until she found the rhythm that suited her and he was eventually enveloped, right inside of her.

Adele rocked back and forth as Rainere groaned against her neck. She felt his teeth against her skin and gasped as he gently bit down on her. His hand slid between her legs and his fingers delicately found the place where she needed them most.

As the pleasure built and she arched her back into the motion, Adele saw stars flash before her eyes. The ringing in her ears started again, but now that she knew what to listen for, the words were startlingly clear. This time it was only two words, over and over. As the rush took hold of her, lifting her and freezing thought, Adele whispered the commands and heard Rainere's answering gasp, but whether it was of pain or pleasure she didn't know as she rode a tidal wave of ecstasy longer than she had thought possible.

Finally, she crashed, breathless and shaking, on the shore of reality.

When Adele opened her eyes, she was lying atop Rainere, his heart thudding loud and hard in her ear. Slightly sheepish, she looked up at him and saw the radiant smile she now treasured so deeply spread across his face.

He was happy. She was happy. She had made him happy. A deep breath released itself.

Rainere chuckled and the sound was sweet music to Adele's ears.

"I thought you said you didn't have any magic in you. *Cara mia*, you lied…"

"I didn't know I could do that," answered Adele, feeling smug. She pushed herself off Rainere and onto her back, relishing the cool of the sheets.

She frowned. "Come to think of it, I did have my first magic lesson with Ohren today. Maybe he woke something up in me?"

Rainere pushed himself up on his elbow to lean over her. He raised an eyebrow.

"Ohren taught you that?"

"Ewww! No, he's an old man," giggled Adele and gave Rainere a playful shove. He didn't budge. "He just tried to get me to separate dust from dirt."

"Fascinating," replied Rainere archly. "I imagine I could show you something a bit more interesting, now it is so obvious you are a more advanced student."

He leaned down and kissed her neck, running his hand down her chest to rest just under her breast.

"Where did you learn those incantations, *cara mia*?" he whispered, his voice studiously casual. But he wasn't playing now. She had said she had no magic in her and then she had managed to control him so completely with just a couple of words. "I have never heard them before. Ever."

Rainere looked into her eyes, and Adele could see his natural distrust and confusion. If she had lied about that, what else had she lied about?

"If I could tell you I would, my love," she answered, picking up a lock of his hair and twirling it around her fingers. "All I can tell you is that I heard a voice, or voices, and I felt I wanted to say the words they gave me. I knew somehow what the words were. But it was an instinct, I didn't think about it."

"You are so strong," he whispered, his raspy voice sending shivers across her skin, but when she looked in his eyes again she saw his fear.

"Rainere, I will never willingly hurt you," she said simply, and held his beautiful face in her hands. She couldn't lie to the man who had seen her innermost soul in so many dreams for so many years.

"I love you." She smiled.

Adele didn't think it was possible to actually see someone fall in love, but she knew that was what happened to Rainere in that moment with her honest declaration. All the darkness left his expression and his blinding smile broke through.

"Adelena, I love you, too," he replied, and it was a benediction, and a vow and a command. She felt it all as his power surged and crackled between them.

The second time was gentle and intense, and their eyes never left the other except when the bliss overtook them again.

They rested after and Adele felt like crying at the thought that she might never have had Rainere like this if she hadn't been brave. If she had just acquiesced like she always had with men in the past, letting them have their way, it would have been horrible. But this time she had fought for what she wanted. She had fought Rainere and she had won him. Now he was hers, completely and utterly.

She drifted off into a weird twilight doze, calm but conscious that she had just changed everything she had previously settled in this new world. Rainere was going to be the beginning of a whole new Adele.

# CHAPTER THIRTY

## "The Prophecy Takes Over"

Ohren pushed open the little door to Gorrik's chamber with more force than was necessary, disturbing the two men inside at their lunch.

"Oh, here you are! I've had a devil of a time looking for you all over the palace this morning. Do you know how many people claimed to have seen you 'just this minute' in the kitchens or the library, or at the University?"

Gorrik and Orestes looked at each other, nonplussed.

"What do you make of this, then?" asked Ohren, in an obvious state of disquiet, and threw a letter and small lavender book down on the table.

Gorrik pushed his plate of food away and raised his white eyebrows.

"I'll tell you when I've read it, lad," he answered calmly and took the delicate scroll in his hand.

"Coconut paper?" he asked sniffing the page, and holding it close to his face so he could focus properly.

Ohren threw himself into the only other free chair at the little table.

"Orestes." Ohren finally acknowledged his brother with a curt nod, as he aimed a swift kick at the black cat purring around his legs. The cat scampered off in fright and jumped up on Orestes's lap, settling himself to glare reproachfully at Ohren from a safe distance.

"Ohren." His brother nodded back. "How's your little queen doing today? You started magic instruction with her yet, now that her blood has settled?"

Ohren sighed deeply and slumped lower in his chair.

"I just don't understand it," he answered, a deep frown creasing his forehead. "Her blood literally sparkled with gold when we set it on the Sacred Fire. Her power should be intense, and at least as strong as her father's but she showed no aptitude at all in the most basic of spells."

"What did you do with her?" asked Orestes as he gnawed on a chicken wing. He proffered the plate to Ohren, who took the last one.

"Manipulation of Matter," he answered with his mouth full. "She only had to sort dust from dirt, but we sat there for an hour while she did nothing. She was almost crying by the end of it. So I ended up giving her a history lesson."

He huffed. "I hope she finally understood how important it is that she try harder next time."

"Heavens!" said Gorrik, looking up from the letter. "You mean to tell me you tried something once and she couldn't do it? Throw her off the throne, I say! She's no good if she can't understand something as complicated as magic the first time she encounters it."

Gorrik returned to his reading, neatly avoiding Ohren's glare.

"Why did you make her cry?" Orestes asked, sucking on a bone.

"What? I didn't." Ohren turned his filthy look on his twin, now indignant. "She just looked like she was going to cry. She does it a lot, you know…"

"It's just that you've never really had a way with women, have you," interrupted his brother, his eyes twinkling.

Ohren rolled his eyes.

"For a two-hundred-and-three-year-old man, you can be such a child, Orestes."

Orestes smiled and nodded, accepting the insult as he would a compliment.

"If you boys have quite finished?"

Gorrik set the letter carefully on the table next to the little book, which was open to a page covered in an untidy scrawl:

*THE EMPRESS OF A DARK GOD WILL WANT TO*

*BURN THE BLOOD OF THE LOST CHILD HIDDEN*

*THE CHILD MUST SACRIFICE A FEAR OF THE DARK*

*AND GO WITHOUT A MAGEK TO SAVE THE WORLD*

*FROM AN EVIL PESTILENCE THAT WILL DESTROY*

*ALL LIFE IN ITS PATH*

"Tell me what *you* think this means?" he asked Ohren.

"The letter came this morning with an envoy from the Empress Sanda'hani of Sandar. Our scouts spotted them coming across the border two days ago and escorted them to the palace. At first I thought it was a delegation to introduce themselves to the queen, but this"—Ohren gestured at the letter—"is disastrous. The empress says her Volcano God, Dahk'hani, is unhappy with the new Queen of Unisia and wants to burn her blood in the fires of Mount Dahk'ni. It's a Blood Ceremony, but on a much more primitive level. They are withholding all supplies of the precious Fire Orchid stamens until their God is appeased."

Orestes frowned.

"I can check the trade contract that was drawn up with Sandar at the time of restitution, but as I recall it was pretty vague. They could be well within their rights to insist on this Blood Ceremony."

The twins locked gazes, and a loaded look passed between them.

"But why?" asked Orestes as if he was continuing their silent conversation out loud. "Why would Empress Sanda'hani think we would put any but St. Lucidis blood on the throne?"

"They are looking at the stars, too," sniffed Gorrik, staring at his full plate of food but not eating anything. "They must have seen the Seven Sisters falling into the brief alignment. Perhaps in their culture it is an ill omen, or perhaps they have their own prophecy? Have you spoken with the delegation yet, Ohren?"

"No." Ohren shook his head. "They wouldn't see me but insisted on a meeting with the queen today."

The tall wizard got up and started pacing the tiny room, a deep frown on his face.

"The prophecy is so clear at this point. But that's what's confusing me. A lot of the prophecy about the Hidden Child is so confused and complicated...yet now it could be as simple as can be. One: The Empress of a Dark God is Empress Sanda'hani and her Volcano God. Two: Their Volcano God wants to burn the blood of the Hidden Child in a typical Blood Ceremony. And three: They are withholding the Fire Orchid stamens until we allow the Hidden Child to perform this Blood Ceremony. We need those stamens for the all sorts of different medicines at the hospice, but especially the Summer Influenza tonics. If we don't have them, sickness will indeed spread."

Ohren's cheeks were quite pink now.

Gorrik scratched the side of his nose.

"I can see your point, m'boy, but what do you make of the 'sacrifice a fear of the dark'?"

Ohren threw himself back into his chair. It creaked under his weight.

"Fear of the Dark Magic of the Sandarians, perhaps?" he ventured. "Or fear of the dark inside the volcano? It's too hard to say, because poor Adelena is scared of everything on our world. I can only imagine what she'll make of this. She definitely cannot go without me to protect her, as she has none of her own magic."

He looked up at Gorrik, suddenly inspired.

"Perhaps that's why she isn't able to use her magic yet? It's waiting for this part of the prophecy to pass."

"Perhaps," mused Orestes, he picked up the little book and read the page again, then the page before and the page after it.

"Why is the Hidden Child referred to as *the Lost Child Hidden* in this part?"

"You should remember this from your lessons with me, Orestes. The Old Tongue uses the same word for lost as it does for hidden, *damnum*. No doubt whoever translated this edition of the prophecy didn't want to make a choice," said Gorrik and quickly checked the inside page. "Thankfully this isn't my work. I wrote a few of these translations in my time, you know? It's by a fellow named Berry, and as I recall the man was a bit of an idiot, so the double translation makes sense. But the thing that disturbs *me* the most is the reference to '*a* Magek.' In the long-ago days when the Goddess walked the world, a wizard was called a Magik or a Magek. I think that is what the prophecy is referring to."

"What!" Ohren paled. "I couldn't possibly send her off to the court of Sandar without any help or guidance. It would be like sending a lamb among wolves. There is no way she could resolve a diplomatic situation like this on her own."

"Well, for someone who risked all our lives bringing this Hidden Child back to Unisia, you of all people must realize you cannot pick and choose the parts of the prophecy you wish to follow," said Orestes with a fierce glare at his brother. He still hadn't forgiven Ohren for what he'd done to the three of them. "Everything must be allowed to be as it will be. If our Hidden Child fails us and doesn't secure the next delivery of Fire Orchids, we are all going to be in a lot of trouble. The season of the Summer Influenzas is just a few short weeks away. If we have no tonics for the people…"

All three men sat in somber silence broken only by the deep purring of Gorrik's cat.

Ohren sighed heavily. The decision was clear. He had to let the Hidden Child live out this part of the prophecy without him.

"I will send her to Sandar, then, with no magic and with no one with any magic. And the Goddess help her in the days ahead."

"The Goddess help us all," said Orestes grimly.

# CHAPTER THIRTY-ONE
## "The Sandarian Delegation"

Adele shifted uncomfortably on her chair. She had chosen the gorgeous emerald-green dress she wore for its color, not realizing how low cut it was. Now she sat at a table full of the princes and lords of the realm, too scared to take a deep breath in case her small cleavage should fall out of her bodice. She could see Rainere sitting at the end of the table and hoped he would look up, but he was intently drawing something on a scroll.

She tried to refocus on all the information that Ohren was giving her in a low voice before the start of the meeting.

"...it is vitally important that we secure vouchsafes from the delegation for your safety before we agree to any journeys, Your Majesty. The Sandarians are a quiet and peaceful people, though they are stubborn in their primitive beliefs. Having said that, we must not give them an opportunity to make their ban on the import of the precious Fire Orchid stamens permanent. This will be a very tricky negotiation..."

"So shall we start the meeting, or are Her Majesty and High Wizard Ohren taking care of this state emergency by themselves?" Lord Orgustus called out loudly, silencing all the murmured conversations around the table.

Adele couldn't quite describe Ohren's expression, but she could wait a very long time before he gave her the same look.

"We shall call this meeting to order." Ohren's voice was steely. "We will discuss the letter the court received from the Empress of Sandar just this afternoon. I believe it has been examined by all?"

Accompanied by shuffles and whispers, the letter made its way back up the table to the high wizard.

"The letter requests the presence of our Queen Adelena in Sandar for a Ceremony of the Blood."

Adele's stomach dropped away and she sought Rainere's gaze again. Their eyes met and a flicker of a smile lightened his expression. She almost sighed with relief. He didn't seem the least bit concerned by this political mess, so perhaps it wasn't as bad as Ohren was making it out to be.

"The court of Sandar—"

"Court!" snorted Lord Orgustus. "It's more of a blanket on a beach than a court, isn't it?"

The Prince of Carparell tittered along with the lord.

Ohren continued, ignoring the two gentlemen.

"—wishes to halt the export of the Fire Orchid stamens until we comply with their requests. This is completely insupportable. The kingdom needs those flower stamens for the continued production of the Summer Influenza tonics, now that the season is but weeks away."

"High Wizard, what are our current stocks of the stamens?" asked Bertie with the most serious expression she had ever seen the cheerful man wear.

"Low." Ohren frowned. "Perhaps only enough for one or two thousand people, and most years we will need enough for closer to eight or ten thousand."

A dry and husky whisper came from the man to Lord Orgustus's immediate right.

"Oh Father, it will hardly come to that," scoffed the young lord in reply. Adele thought the ancient man he addressed looked more like a great-grandfather than the father of such a young man. Surely, Lord Orgustus couldn't be more than in his early thirties.

"We'll send the queen off to Sandar and she can repair the situation very quickly."

He turned his sharp blue eyes on Adele.

"I'm sure our queen will know how to handle this most sensitive of political crises."

Adele gulped and looked down into her lap.

*Oh. Crap.*

"Queen Adelena only wishes to fulfill the needs of the court and her people. She will do whatever is necessary, I can assure you," said Ohren, speaking to the entire table of concerned-looking aristocrats. "She will not let us down."

Lord Orgustus leaned across the table to get Adele's attention.

"Your Majesty needn't look so anxious," whispered Lord Orgustus conspiratorially, though his voice carried across the whole table. "I'm sure all your years on 'Er-arth' prepared you for the magnitude of what we are about to do here tonight, repairing relations with Sandar and saving your people."

For one hot minute, Adele fantasized about reaching over to slap Lord Orgustus hard across his smug face. The force of the desire made her hands shake.

"Tell me, please, what exactly was it that you did on your world before coming to Unisia? Were you a law-maker, law-keeper, doctor, politician?"

Lord Orgustus's eyes were like chips of ice as they bored into her. A heavy silence settled over the table as all the gentlemen present listened for her answer. Her eyes roamed the table, but only Bertie gave her an encouraging smile. Rainere was glaring coldly at Lord Orgustus as if he, too, felt the urge to hurt the lord.

"Well, I..."

"Yes," prompted Lord Orgustus unctuously. "You were what?"

"I was a full-time mother to my children," answered Adele, hating the apologetic tone of her voice. "I never had the time for a career or study, as my children are still so little. I didn't have any servants at home so I have always had to run my own house, too...there hasn't been any time for anything else."

"Ah." Lord Orgustus sat back in his chair as though all his worst fears had been confirmed. "A poor housekeeper and nursemaid to her children. Perfect qualifications for running a kingdom, I agree, High Wizard."

He smiled around the table at the rest of the aristocrats, who were muttering among themselves.

"So despite my absolute competence at running the Court of the Golden Palace for the last ten years, and my father before me for forty years, the High Wizard Ohren has replaced me with a nursemaid from another world. Brilliant," he ended sarcastically.

Adele sat blushing furiously as hot tears of anger and shame filled her eyes. *I never asked for any of this!* She wanted to scream at the pompous lord.

"That's enough, Lord Orgustus," interrupted a deep voice from the other end of the table.

Everyone turned to look at the calm visage of Orestes as he sat down to join them.

"If the Gods saw fit to bless us with the knowledge of how to retrieve the lost heir of St. Lucidis and instate her on the throne as our true ruler, then who are we mere mortals to judge our queen for her life before us?" Orestes nodded respectfully at Adele. "I'm sure our good queen will take all our words of wisdom under advisement before she makes any decisions, today and every other day."

He turned to look directly at Lord Orgustus.

"That is, of course, if you have any words of wisdom to offer, my Lord?"

"The Gods!" spluttered the lord, going pink in the cheeks himself. "The Gods didn't put her on the throne, the High Wizard did."

He pointed accusingly at Ohren.

"And this woman—" He turned his glare on Adele.

Thankfully, Tilburn interrupted another long-winded protest from the lord by entering the room and announcing the arrival of the Sandarian delegation.

"Your Majesty Queen Adelena, High Wizard, Magistrar, Princes and Lords of the Realm, may I present the Ambassador of the Sandarian People, the Right Honorable Ripenzo Shale and his entourage…"

Adele didn't hear the rest, as she instantly focused on the Sandarian representatives as they entered the room.

Ripenzo Shale was medium height, well built, with shaggy blond hair and a deep tan. He was good-looking in a rugged sort of way, with deep-set eyes and a strong chin sporting blond stubble. His clothing hung loose on him in a mix of soft blues and greens. He looked as though he were dressed to go surfing or on a tour of India rather than a meeting with royalty. He smiled around the room until he found Adele staring at him and gave her a grin so big and friendly that she found herself smiling back despite her nerves. Ripenzo Shale found his seat without taking his eyes off Adelena.

The other three members of his party were dressed similarly, but all had coffee-colored skin, dark-brown eyes and high cheekbones. The man who sat closest to Ripenzo Shale had a wild mohawk, and a long plait falling over his shoulder that was knotted up with pebbles, bits of bone, and strips of colored cloth. He wore a necklace over his loose shirt that looked like it had been made up of sharks' teeth. He was the only person who wasn't smiling, and he immediately turned his dark eyes on Adele, staring at her boldly without uttering a word.

Ohren was keen to get started once the Sandarian people had found their seats and were made comfortable.

"Gentlemen," he began, with a grand gesture to encompass the table. "We all know why we are gathered here tonight, and it is to discuss with you a matter of trade close to our own hearts."

He paused, smiling expectantly at Ripenzo Shale.

Ripenzo Shale smiled back and remained silent.

Ohren cleared his throat, his smile becoming a polite frown.

"Having received and read the letter you brought from the empress, we were surprised and disheartened by its contents. We would dearly like to see trade relations resume on the transportation of pearls and Fire Orchid stamens immediately. I'm sure it will benefit both nations to see a return to the status quo. What say you, Honorable Shale?"

Ohren was very impressive with his firm *let's have no more of this nonsense* approach, but Adele could see Ripenzo Shale wasn't buying it. Though he continued to smile brightly at the wizard, he didn't seem in the least bit cowed by whom he was speaking to.

*Either he is too stupid to understand who Ohren really is or he is too powerful to care,* thought Adele, mystified by the casually dressed man's attitude. But as always in this world, nothing was quite as it first seemed. Adele decided to accord Ripenzo the respect that another wizard would be due. *Who knew what the man was capable of? He worked for an empress, after all.*

Ohren looked to Adele to back him up. Obviously, the queen needed to say something here. Adele just raised her eyebrows at the wizard— what was he expecting of her?

"Your Majesty," Ohren prompted her more keenly.

Adele felt her heart leap into her throat and had to take a sip of water to help swallow it back down. Knowing her voice would shake as soon as she spoke, Adele threw a glance at Rainere to help ground her again. She caught his dark glance and instantly a warmth spread through her.

For a moment, it was just the two of them in the room. Adele felt her head spin, like she was riding on a carousel. Rainere was the only point she could focus on. She felt his lips on her neck and took a sharp breath in.

The world tilted and adjusted back to normal again. Adele smiled at the Sandarian ambassador.

"Mr. Shale…" she began, not a waver in her voice.

"Please, Mr. Shale is my father," interrupted the beaming dignitary. "Just call me Ripenzo, or Rip, if you like."

Adele nodded.

"Thank you, Ripenzo. I know that the Sandarians have some serious issues with my right to wear the Crown of Unisia, but I can assure you I would be happy to undergo the Ceremony of the Blood right here, right now, if it will confirm for you my happy place as the rightful heir and true queen of Unisia."

Adele pretended not to hear the quiet snort coming from the direction of Lord Orgustus. It was bad enough she already felt like a liar; she didn't need him confirming it.

"Or you can come and see my blood burning now on the Sacred Fire here at the University. It was a proper blaze when it was set alight, I'm told."

Ripenzo Shale sat back comfortably in his chair, his pose relaxed. He certainly didn't look like he was discussing a hugely important trade embargo, or her legitimacy as queen. When he spoke, it was with a loose drawl that reminded Adele of her seaside town at home on Earth.

"Well, thank you, Queen Adelena, for your kind words. It's such a pleasure to meet you, and we from Sandar are very sorry it's not under happier circumstances. But…that's life, you know."

He smiled around the table at the unsmiling Unisians.

"I guess you could say that our empress was a little, er…upset…by your sudden arrival and coronation in Unisia. Not that it isn't a happy occasion, mind you. It's just that the empress is a student of history and panicked a bit at the idea that the Wizards Council might be appointing queens without being absolutely sure about where they came from. So she was hoping that we could bring you before our Volcano God Dahk'hani for a Ceremony of the Blood just so she could welcome you to our world without angering him, or any other Gods."

"Uh-huh, I see," nodded Adele, hoping her face didn't betray how ludicrous she thought the whole situation was.

"So what of the embargo placed on the Fire Orchids?" asked Ohren. "Surely that was an unnecessary measure to take if you only required a sample of royal blood?"

Ripenzo Shale shrugged nonchalantly.

"Far be it from me to explain the decisions of the mighty empress, High Wizard. I was merely sent here to deliver the letter and accompany the Mage here." He jerked his thumb at the silent, Mohawked man beside him.

Everyone turned and stared at the Mage. His dark eyes bored into Adele, making her feel like a bug under a microscope. To avoid his gaze, she concentrated on counting the feathers sticking out of his hair. She got to six before Ripenzo Shale spoke again.

"The Mage is, unfortunately, without the power of speech, having given his voice to the Volcano God Dahk'hani in exchange for his powers as a shaman. The Mage will determine if you are…please excuse the word, worthy, of meeting the empress and if you are exactly who you say you are." He smiled warmly, giving Adele the full benefit of his twinkling blue eyes. Though his words angered all of the men around her, Adele couldn't take offense. It just seemed as weird as anything else in this meeting.

"Now, if you'll all just give our honorable Mage a moment's silence, he can verify the Queen—"

"Now see here," interrupted Ohren, pushing himself to his feet. "No one said anything about using magic in the presence of our queen."

The Mage held up his hand and directed his gaze to Ohren's glare. He shook his head slightly.

"It's not magic as you would know it, High Wizard," answered Ripenzo Shale in a soothing tone, not looking in the least bit perturbed by an angry wizard staring him down. "The Mage is just reading the queen's aura. It won't take a moment and won't hurt. I promise."

His wink surprised Adele enough to make her blink.

Adele felt uncomfortable despite Ripenzo Shale's promise, and she felt a definite prickle of energy run over her skin as the Mage's eyes raked her body where she sat. She kept still as if she were having her photo taken.

The Mage looked away and made a complicated hand gesture to Ripenzo Shale, which looked like some kind of sign language to Adele.

Ripenzo Shale nodded, and his smile was a relief to her.

"Wonderful news, Queen Adelena. Our Mage has confirmed with his own eyes that you are indeed the lost heir and rightful descendant to the throne of Unisia."

*Really!* Thought Adele in surprise. *Maybe I'm going to have to start believing it one of these days if everyone keeps saying it's true.*

"So the Ceremony of the Blood will not be necessary now?" asked Ohren hopefully as he sat back down.

Ripenzo made a masterful attempt to look apologetic.

"I am sorry, High Wizard Ohren. May I call you Ohren?"

"High Wizard is sufficient," replied Ohren, his voice steely again.

Ripenzo Shale nodded and looked almost amused at the wizard's formality.

"High Wizard, the problem we have here is that our Volcano God needs to be appeased, and the Mage here says that Dahk'hani has specially requested blood from the new monarch." He shrugged. "The Mage is the empress's conduit to the Gods. We of the Sandar do not question the Gods."

"What if we gave you a sample of the queen's blood today, then you can go back to Sandar and burn it yourselves?" pushed Ohren.

"I wish it were that simple, I really do." Ripenzo Shale smiled ruefully. "But the queen needs to be present in the Dark Place of the Holy Caves, and the blood must be spilled fresh."

Adele didn't understand why Ohren suddenly clenched his fists on the table, but when she looked up at his face he was staring over at his brother Orestes, their gazes locked for a moment.

"Why would we put our queen through such a trial?" asked Ohren leaning forward on the table, his voice raised in anger. "What guarantees could you give us for her safety? We have just retrieved her from the other side of the Universe, for Goddess's sake, and you think we would just risk her to an underground ceremony with your primitive God? It's madness!"

"High Wizard Ohren," interjected Orestes in a warning tone. "I'm sure you can see why—"

"I understand your concerns, High Wizard, I really do," answered Ripenzo Shale with a bright smile. "But I wish you wouldn't resort to name calling. We Sandarians are quite sensitive about our beliefs, and I'm sure you understand how misunderstandings like this can lead to hurt feelings, and those hurt feelings can lead to irreparable damage being done to trade relations."

Ohren responded with a heavy glare.

"My apologies for any offense I might have caused, but you must understand that we Unisians are sensitive about the safety of our queen and would never put her in harm's way—no matter what the cost."

Ripenzo Shale shrugged, but his expression belied his casual gesture. Adele could see a sharp intelligence in those eyes surrounded by laugh lines.

"Far be it from me to question the ways of mighty wizards, High Wizard, but Sandarians have long memories. Very long memories," he said and turned to Prince Rainere sitting at the opposite end of the table.

Rainere looked up from studiously examining his nails when the sudden silence fell over the table.

Adele held her breath.

"All reparations were paid in full," said Rainere in response to the unasked question. "But if you would like my heartfelt apology to the Sandarian people for their treatment at the hands of my Marchant ancestors for the last thousand years, I would be happy to give it."

Though his expression was neutral, no one failed to pick up on the sneering tone of his offer.

The Mage stood and made a violent gesture in Rainere's direction. Rainere only smiled coldly and nodded politely in response.

Ripenzo Shale put a restraining hand on his Mage, pulling him back down to his chair.

"I'm so sorry, Your Majesty, the past enslavement and cultural genocide of our people isn't generally a laughing matter to Sandarians." Ripenzo Shale gave Prince Rainere a not altogether incurious look. "We didn't expect to see the last Marchant prince at a meeting of the Heads of the Realm, I must say. You'll have to excuse our Mage, he isn't good with surprises."

Prince Rainere waved an elegant hand in Adele's direction.

"Well, I suppose the arrival of a new monarch has us all creeping out of our shells, now doesn't it?" Rainere replied coldly.

Ripenzo Shale's expression hardened as his smile fell away.

"If we could please get back to the matter at hand," interrupted Ohren. "We need to get this issue resolved immediately."

"Well, then, please consider yourselves immediately invited to the Court of Sandar," Ripenzo Shale said, instantly smiling again and banging the table with his hand for emphasis. "And let's get this trade disagreement, agreed upon."

"Is there no other course of action we can take?" asked Ohren in an almost plaintive tone.

"There isn't," said Orestes firmly, giving his twin a loaded look.

"We need the queen on Sandarian soil," insisted Ripenzo with an apologetic shrug.

"So, it's decided, then?" asked Adele just to confirm, and looking around the table was confused why no one except Rainere would look her in the eye. "I will go to Sandar with the delegation for however long it takes for this Ceremony of the Blood, and will return as soon as it is complete. Yes?"

Ohren took a long time to answer. "Agreed, Your Majesty," he said quietly.

"It takes maybe five days to get to Sandar if you travel by carriage, then give it perhaps two days for the ceremony and to recover from your journey, then to travel back home again...so...you will be gone around twelve days all told, Queen Adelena." Ripenzo smiled and pulled out a long scroll from his jacket pocket.

Adele's stomach dropped. Twelve days! There was no way she could leave her children for that long. No way was she leaving them with only nannies and Lord Orgustus in charge at the Golden Palace.

"I will be happy to come as long as my children are welcome, also. They are very little, you understand, and can't be without me for such a long time as that."

"No, Your Majesty, please be sensible!" Ohren barked suddenly. "There is no need for the children to be—"

"They cannot be without me, Ohren," said Adele firmly, and risked a glance at Lord Orgustus. The lord had been suspiciously silent for the entire meeting. He was watching the proceedings with a canny expression that chilled Adele, making her panic enough to blurt out, "So it's settled, then. I will take my family to Sandar and return in twelve days' time."

"And I can assure you the kingdom will run just as well without you as it does with you here," interjected Lord Orgustus, immediately making the most of the situation.

Adele nodded without looking in the lord's direction.

*That jerk really likes to belabor a point.*

"That is wonderful news! Thank you, Your Majesty, for making this decision so quickly. My men and I will travel home at first light tomorrow. The empress will want to be informed immediately of your decision, and preparations can be made for your arrival in a few days time." Ripenzo Shale smiled broadly and raised his glass in a cheer. "To the future of a happy and close relationship between our two nations! Long live the queen!"

The cheering from the Sandarians was heartfelt and much louder than the restrained murmurs from the Unisians at the table. All except Lord Orgustus, who was now grinning with unabashed pleasure at the idea of having the throne back again.

"Cheer up, Ohren," said Adele in a low voice to the wizard beside her. "We both knew I had to go away, and anyway nothing bad will happen with you by my side. We'll be perfectly safe, I'm sure."

Ohren turned to her and she wondered at his pale cheeks and the stricken expression he was trying to hide behind his tight smile.

"But of course, Your Majesty."

# CHAPTER THIRTY-TWO

## "In the Cavern of the Empress"

Rainere swallowed down on his nausea and suppressed a shudder at the taste of bile. He hated traveling such a distance by portal but it had been necessary. The Empress Ka-kik had called and he must come.

Rainere pulled the collar of his cloak up to his chin and glanced about himself in the twilight murkiness of the Dark Forest. A light rain was falling, pattering upon the leaves above his head. He was still dressed in the fine clothes of the Sandarian meeting and could already feel the damp soaking into the delicate fabrics. He steeled himself to enter the dark tunnel in the rocks. An enormous tree grew over the entrance, its roots hanging down in an immovable curtain. Rainere stepped to the side and found the concealed gap, just wide enough to let a grown man slip through. Grotto followed a moment later.

In the tunnel, there was only the sound of their breathing accompanied by the constant dripping of water on stone. Rainere carried a small white light in his hand and it illuminated the thousands of tiny eyes who watched their progress.

The tunnel traveled on and down endlessly, Rainere had to rely on his own memory more than sight to know the correct twists and turns to take in the darkness. A person could get lost in this underground world and never find their way to the light again. Grotto followed close on his master's heels. Rainere knew the old man hated it down in the damp darkness, even more than he did.

It took them the best part of an hour to find the way to the monstrous cavern at the center of the nest.

Rainere extinguished his light as they stepped out of the last tunnel and into the main cavern. Two of the empress's guards materialized in front of him in their human forms and bowed low, clanking their weapons in a sign of respect. Rainere returned the gesture with a nod and followed behind as he was led to the dais in the middle of the room.

Empress Ka-kik was truly enormous for her kind: as tall as the prince himself, but ten times as wide. Her eight legs were thick and muscular, stretching out to the edges of the stone dais. Her abdomen was supported on silk cushions, and her thorax was stretched high as she reared up to greet Prince Rainere. Rainere dropped to his knees before the empress, his arms raised and his head bowed.

"Rise, Prince Rainere," the empress spoke in a voice that both clicked and rasped. "Welcome to our Nest again. It is good to look upon you, Son of The Blood. Rise, so that I may see you better."

Rainere took the chance to surreptitiously suck in a breath from the perfumed scarf he wore at his throat. The smell in the cavern was appalling. Swampy and fetid, the air seemed to carry the very spores of the earth, and already his tongue felt grainy.

The prince rose to stand perfectly straight before the thousand glittering black eyes of the empress. She had painted her fangs a lurid shade of green and the hairs stood out, shiny with glistening poison. Rainere found the sight very distracting and worked hard to continue to stare only at her eyes.

"Thank you, Empress Ka-kik, for the honor of allowing us to take an audience with you…"

"Enough!" interrupted the empress, waving a foreleg in irritation. "Enough of your Marchant formalities, Prince Rainere. We have so much to speak of and so little time tonight. My children shall be hatching soon and we will not abide guests in the Nest during their first feeding."

"Of course, Empress Ka-kik, as you wish." Rainere nodded and tried hard to avoid thinking about what the new children would be feeding on.

"The Lost Child of Prophecy has become queen of all Unisia, has she not? You have met her and verified her authenticity for us, yes?"

Rainere nodded. "Queen Adelena is the Lost Child of the Prophecy, Empress, of that I am now certain."

"Is she strong in the Old Magic?"

"As to her magic, Empress, I cannot be sure that it is anything more than the modern St. Lucidis strain. She hasn't used any magic in front of me. I believe the Wizard Ohren fears that her magic's strength has been irreparably stunted by her time in the other world," Rainere lied smoothly.

"Ah…well, that is inconsequential," the empress rasped. "She is the Lost Child and will find her way to the power, I'm sure. Was the Child open to a relationship with the family of Marchant?"

Rainere nodded once, only a slight twitch of the eyes betraying the emotions that he held so tightly controlled.

"I believe the queen is very sympathetic to our cause."

The empress waved a foreleg at Rainere. A drop of poison flew past his face, but he didn't flinch.

"And what does she want, the Child? What does she want in return for putting a Marchant back on the throne and betraying the court of the Golden Palace?"

Rainere had prepared himself for this question, but still his answer gave him doubts. He pushed his shoulders back and held his chin with a haughty tilt.

"The queen has no desire to wield the true power of the throne, and has no head for politics. To be frank, Empress, the queen is no more than an uneducated girl frightened by this new world she finds herself in. Right now, she is a puppet of the High Wizard and his Court. I believe it will be a simple matter to get the woman to agree to take me as her king and be my escort."

The empress omitted a hissing wheeze, something akin to a laugh for her people.

"You would have her abdicate the throne directly? Ha! I have always loved the audacity of you Marchant princes."

The empress cocked her head to the side, her eyes glittering in the light of the covered flames surrounding the cavern.

"Of course, when she has the whole Kingdom at her feet and the Wizards Council at her back, why wouldn't she step aside for a Marchant husband?" The empress's tone was suspicious, and her sarcasm was clear to all.

"With all due respect, Empress, the ways of the human female mind are far less evolved than your own race. The only thing that the queen desires is to be cared for and protected from the weight of ruling the nation. That, and to go home to the only world she has ever known: Earth."

Empress Ka-kik stiffened. "The Lost Child must never be allowed to return, Prince Rainere."

"Of course not, Empress. The idea is unthinkable," replied Prince Rainere quickly. "But I may have to promise many things of no consequence to secure the lady's hand in marriage."

"It has been said to me that the Lost Child has young of her own that were brought to Unisia with her. Is this true?" clicked the empress.

Rainere felt sweat tickling its way down his spine under his heavy black cloak, his silk shirt stuck to him uncomfortably in the heat of the cavern. He swallowed but his mouth was dry. How did the empress know that about Adelena? Did she have her own spies in the Golden Palace?

"I believe she has three infants with her," he said. "I have yet to meet any of them, but I'm sure it is only a matter of time."

If the empress's expression could have been interpreted in human terms, one would have said she looked at the prince in admiration.

"I am so glad of the day we saved your life, little prince. You have been so helpful to me and my family for so many years." She paused. "Not all Marchants have been so respectful of the ancient bond between the Marchant clan and the Spider People. But you, you remember the vow you made to honor me so many years ago."

She raised her forelegs and clicked her fangs.

"Tell me again what it was you promised in return for our care…"

Rainere tasted the dirt and mold in the air. It made him want to gag, but not more so than the empress's ritual humiliation of him.

"I vow on my immortal life and the blood that flows in my veins to be of service to the Empress Ka-kik and her people when she has need of me. I make this vow in return for the succor of the Gift of Life in my hour of greatest need."

The empress wheezed, delighted.

"You would have died the Endless Death that day if we hadn't found you at our door," the empress gloated, her voice carrying a malevolent tone. "I could have eaten you and spat out your bones, grinding them up for my Magix. You soul would have been mine but instead…"

Rainere knew his line.

"Instead you gave me the Gift and let me return to the land of the living."

"Yes," replied the empress, satisfied with the prince's memory. "You arrogant Marchants with all your God-given immortality, you never thought about your souls, did you? Though your minds give up eventually, the spell seals your soul into your bones so you can never be free of this world you love so much."

Prince Rainere worked hard to keep his expression cold and still while the wheezing laughter of the empress echoed around the chamber.

"And you all need the Gift to stay alive, just like us, just like all the Children of Darkness." Empress Ka-kik worked her face into a ghoulish grimace. "And it is with your help that we will rise again and rule the world above us, my little Marchant prince. You will marry the Lost Child and kill the wizards who would stop us bringing our Shadows into the Light. Our Dark God will reign over the land once again, and the prophecy will be fulfilled."

With her last cry, a loud clicking and rustling began among the crowd surrounding the dais. Her guardsmen were clacking their weapons together in excitement.

The empress was distracted from her celebrating as a large black spider with orange markings approached her, its belly low to the ground in respect. He whispered to the empress in their breathy, clicky language. Empress Ka-kik stood, raising her immense abdomen off its bed of rotting silk pillows.

Though he felt Grotto flinch behind him, Prince Rainere remained perfectly still in front of the monster.

"Prince Rainere Marchant, I must ask you to leave, now that the Hatching begins. You will take yourselves out of our nest immediately to avoid any unfortunate accidents."

"We thank you for your time and patience, Empress," said Prince Rainere.

"You are welcome, Prince Rainere," said the empress, lumbering off her dais. "But know I am running out of both. You will have your bride off the Unisian throne by the next full moon in three weeks' time, or I will be creating a new prophecy. Just. For. You."

Prince Rainere bowed deeply to hide his pale cheeks.

"I understand, Empress."

"One of my Lesser Children will show you out," the empress said over her shoulder as she gestured to the tunnel they had come in through.

As quick as dignity would allow, Prince Rainere and Grotto turned and headed back into the dim wetness of the tunnels. Even with Rainere's white globe of light shining brightly, both men stumbled several times on the path. The brown spider they were to follow was barely the size of Rainere's hand, and it steered clear of the light's range. Fortunately, Rainere knew the way out as well as in, and after a little less than an hour he had led them into the cold of the fresh night air.

"We need to get back to the Golden Palace, master, and get you cleaned up for another rendezvous with Queen Adelena," grunted Grotto, shaking off the cobwebs that covered his head and shoulders. He gave his master a heavy look.

"And this time you need to secure more than her virtue."

"Yes, of course," answered Rainere quietly as he conjured the portal that would take them back to the palace.

The only bright light in this whole sordid business of power and politics, Rainere thought, was getting to spend more time with Adelena. Despite what he had said to the empress, he would keep Adelena as his escort and love her until the end of his days. As he stepped toward the swirling green of the portal, he could almost taste her kisses, and smell the sweet scent of her skin. She would be safe in this nasty game of prophecy, or he would give his life trying to protect her.

Rainere snarled at the memory of the empress's humiliation.

*There are other vows I can make, too, Empress,* he thought bitterly. *You might have my life in your hands, but the Lost Child has my heart now.*

Roughly, Rainere grabbed Grotto's arm and the two men disappeared in a swirling flash of sparks.

*　　　*　　　*

The small brown spider scuttled up the leg of the empress and whispered in her ear.

"Good, they have gone," she answered in their native language. She waved a foreleg at a yellow-striped guard, calling him over.

"Oki, my favored son of the First Hatched. Show me your human form."

Oki shuddered and his black-and-yellow fur rippled as he morphed quickly into an upright figure. His eyes were too large to be naturally human and his head was an odd oblong shape, but his body was tall and heavily muscled, covered only in a little black-and-yellow fuzz to betray his spider heritage.

"That Marchant prince has given me much to think on," hissed Empress Ka-kik. "If this new St. Lucidis queen is as weak and powerless as he seems to think she is, then perhaps it is we who should make the first move on her? Perhaps we can win her to our cause without the meddling of the Marchant prince?"

Oki bowed before his mother.

"Go now to the Golden Palace and find this new queen, our own Lost Child of the Prophecy."

The empress touched Oki's face with her enormous foreleg.

"You are certainly the most beautiful of all my sons and the favored one of all my First Hatched. Certainly, you can charm this frightened girl with your strength and handsome face. Promise her our protection and bring her to me, where I may deal with her without Marchant interference. Go, my son, do this thing as quickly as you can."

A shrill scream rent the fetid air of the cavern.

"Ah, my hatchlings have started their feeding. I mustn't miss it." The empress gave Oki another affectionate pat before turning and lumbering off down a tunnel behind the dais.

Oki turned and raced from the cavern into the same tunnel that Rainere and Grotto had walked down.

The honor his mother had given him was immense. No Spider People had entered the forbidden doors of the Golden Palace for hundreds, if not thousands, of years. He would be the first to treat with the infamous, human Lost Child of the Prophecy.

Perhaps if he were successful in his quest, his mother would give him permission to eat Queen Adelena after she was no longer useful to them?

Saliva pooled in his mouth. He had never eaten a queen before. The status that would give him in the nest would be immense.

*"Oki the Queen Eater…or Oki, Devourer of Queens…"*

Fantasizing wildly about his future, Oki morphed back to his spider form and scuttled up and out of the tunnels much faster than the humans had earlier.

Outside, in the dark of the night, Oki skipped over the scorched earth where the prince's magic had been and slipped into the ancient portal that lay between the two realities, just to the left of it. He made his way towards the Golden Palace, fame, and fortune.

# CHAPTER THIRTY-THREE

## "A Political Proposal"

Adele paced her bedroom, too wired to sleep. It was well after midnight and the dark whispers of anxiety swirled in her head.

She was still going over the events of the dinner in her mind. Ohren hadn't wanted to discuss the plans for the voyage to Sandar, and had only left her at the door to her chambers with a brusque "we'll discuss this tomorrow."

His tone had made a shot of adrenaline rocket through her system. She had never seen the gentle wizard so angry before, and she came away with the feeling that he blamed her for how the meeting had ended.

*But I can't leave my children behind, no matter what Ohren might think,* thought Adele as she paced around her glass bed, absentmindedly following a golden line on the carpet's pattern. *And I cannot be sure they would be any safer here without me, than they would with me on the road.*

She shook her head to clear her frantic thoughts.

*Besides, I'll have Ohren and the Queen's Guard with me; they should be able to protect us from everything dangerous. Surely?*

She was so distracted she didn't even hear the soft click as a door behind her closed.

"Adelena." The whisper came from the corner of the room, and Adele shrieked in fear as a dark figure materialized out of the shadows.

"Oh, Rainere, it's you!" she gasped. She put her hand on her chest to keep her pounding heart in place and staggered back against the bed.

In a few long strides, Rainere was by her side and swept her up in his arms, holding her trembling body against his own.

"Sshhh, *cara mia*, it's only me. I'm sorry I frightened you, my beloved," he murmured and stroked her hair against her back.

"No, *I'm* sorry, Rainere," Adele whispered. "It wasn't you, I just feel...I'm just so worried about this trip to Sandar. We leave the day after tomorrow, you know. I just—just—"

She sniffed and pushed herself away from him with an embarrassed smile.

"I just hate this time of the night, that's all...I'm sorry to cry all over you again."

Adele wiped at where her tears had touched Rainere's shirt. She noticed that most of his buttons were undone already and he wore his waistcoat open. She could see the smooth expanse of his chest through the gap and breathed in the warm, clean scent of him. A warmth surged inside her.

*Get a grip, Adele,* she admonished herself, as she turned her eyes from the vision of his naked skin. *First you cry on him, then you want to jump him. You have got to stop acting like a crazy person with this man!*

Despite her best intentions, Adele jumped a mile when there was a knock at the door.

"Are you all right, Your Majesty?" one of her guards called softly.

Adele froze and looked up at Rainere, her eyes wide and frantic. He nodded slowly.

"I'm fine," she croaked. "I just, er...kicked my toe. I'm off to bed now. Goodnight."

"Goodnight, Your Majesty."

Rainere stroked a finger down the side of Adele's face and graced her with one of his almost-smiles she so loved.

"You are a terrible liar," he whispered, leaning down close to her ear.

"Well, I was distracted," Adele whispered back. "Normally I'm much better than that."

She turned her head to bring his lips closer to her own but then a crash outside the antechamber door made her flinch again.

"There are too many people here tonight. They are all packing for the trip to Sandar. We're going to be caught," Adele whispered, disappointment curdling the desire in her.

"We could go somewhere else," murmured Rainere. "There is a secret way. You would have to hold my hand the entire time, though. It would be dangerous if you let go."

Rainere frowned down at Adele, and she almost couldn't stand it. How could he be so handsome and yet still human? Was an immortal still human?

She thought of her children asleep in the nursery. Stella or Aaron would probably be waking up soon for a cuddle.

*But that's what the nannies are for, isn't it?* Thought Adele, quashing her sharp spasm of guilt. *I need this, right now, with Rainere. It'll just be for an hour...*

Adele nodded.

Rainere led her over to the wall by a large mirrored bookshelf. He reached out and pointed a finger at a tiny depression in the wall just behind the cupboard. A narrow door swung open.

Adele gasped when she saw the rough stone hallway revealed beyond the secret doorway. She made to step through but Rainere pulled her back.

"Careful," he whispered. "The pathways are protected by magic. Only those of The Blood can pass. Marchant Blood," he added when saw Adele open her mouth to protest.

"You must hold my hand, and do not let go until we get to my chambers."

Adele nodded, eager to be going anywhere private with Rainere.

*God, I feel like a teenager,* she thought as she stifled a hysterical giggle. Though she couldn't remember a time when she'd ever had this much fun when she was going through that awkward stage.

She took Rainere's hand and was pulled under his arm as he protected her from the shimmery green magic that hissed and spat as they passed through the door. The door closed behind them with a soft click.

Rainere led them through a confusing and dark network of corridors hidden in the walls of the Golden Palace. Adele was amazed at how extensive they were. They passed hundreds of doors shimmering with green magic, which opened only God knew where. Adele thought of her children but was comforted that the doors only opened for Marchants, and she knew the only one around.

After fifteen or twenty minutes of brisk walking, Rainere came to a stop in front of a small door. The door opened at his touch, and he pulled Adele through after checking that there was no one on the other side.

Rainere's room was like every other guest suite in the palace, but it had been very recently furnished in black velvet and silver brocade in an effort to make him feel more at home, surrounded by his Family's colors.

"This is beautiful," said Adele admiringly as she spun around in the center of the room, taking in the Gothic ambience of the decorations. It was so romantic. She moved to the large open window to check the view. She saw only the dark shadows of the garden below but was satisfied it would be nice in the daytime.

"It's not the traditional Marchant quarters, but it will suffice," was all Rainere said as he came up behind her and gently pulled the hair off her neck. She moaned softly with pleasure when he slipped his arms around her waist and pressed against her. She could feel his barely restrained desire.

"Rainere…" She turned to face him. Their mouths joined and Adele's heart skipped as Rainere picked her up and carried her to the bed. He placed her down gently, cradling her head on his hand. She ran her hands down his shoulders and pushed off his shirt, reveling in the smooth strength of the tightly packed muscles of his stomach.

"Adelena…" Rainere tried to pull away but Adele followed his mouth with hers. "Adelena, please…I need to talk to you."

"After…" moaned Adele, reaching down his front and trying to free herself from her nightdress at the same time.

"No, *cara mia*, now." Rainere was firm but gentle as he disentangled himself from her arms. He moved to sit on the side of the bed next to her. He rubbed his hands over his face and didn't look at her.

Adele pushed herself up on her elbows, curiosity overcoming her disappointment at Rainere's change of mood. The prince ran his hands through his hair and looked across the room to the billowing curtains as they moved in the night breeze. He seemed very unsure of himself, and he opened and closed his mouth several times before he could bring himself to speak.

"I have to ask what this…" He gestured to the bed they were on. "What all this means to you?"

Adele frowned and tilted her head. *Wasn't it obvious?*

"It means…I want to be with you…um, here."

Rainere looked back down at his hands where they rested on his knees.

"Because when I first met you, during the royal interview, you told me you wanted to go home, back to your world with your children. You asked for my help, remember?"

"Yes." Adele chewed her bottom lip.

"Is that still what you want from me?"

He turned slightly but didn't quite face her.

"You want to leave me and go back to Earth…and your children's father?"

Adele frowned in confusion for a moment. *Father?*

*Oh. Right. Justin.*

She had yet to tell Rainere about Justin, but it was perfectly natural that he would ask about him.

"Rainere," she said gently, and leaned forward to kiss Rainere's shoulder. "My husband, the children's father, left me."

She paused, waiting for the pain of that statement to stab her in the heart, but…surprisingly…she felt okay.

"I'm not married to Justin anymore. He isn't a part of my life, like that, at all now."

She tried to calculate the amount of time they'd been away, and the time differences between their worlds that Ohren had told her about. Perhaps barely a day would have passed.

"He wouldn't have even noticed we'd left yet."

"You don't love him then, this…Justin?" asked Rainere. His lip had curled over the name of her ex in a way that suggested His Highness might be jealous. Adele was surprised at how pleased that made her.

She shook her head. "Not like I love you."

The truth of her words lifted her heart and made her smile.

"Rainere, I love you…and I always kind of have, ever since I started dreaming of you years ago."

Rainere still wouldn't look at her, though a smile ticked at the corner of his mouth. Too soon, his expression became sad.

"Yet you would leave me today to go home," he replied. "I think you know how I feel about you, Adelena. I love you deeply, despite our differences and despite my bloodline. But if you would have me do it, I will try to send you home before we go much further…"

He gripped the fabric of his trousers tight in his hands and his knuckles were white. Adele could see the pain she was causing Rainere and had to make it stop.

*But how can I promise him something I'm not sure I want? The children need to go home, even more than me,* she thought, pulled apart by indecision. She decided to stall.

"Rainere, look at me," she begged gently. He turned his magnetic green eyes on her.

*Okay, that isn't helping,* she thought as the blood started to rush down and away from her head.

"I will need to go home for my children—but not right now." She paused, trying to remember how to breathe as he stared deep into her eyes.

"I need to get to Sandar first to fix this problem with Empress Sanda'hani and get her to send the Fire Orchids here again for the people when the Summer Influenza comes. I feel awful that my arrival could mean that thousands of people might die of an illness that the Orchid tonic prevents. And it would all be my fault."

"But afterward?"

"Come with me!" blurted Adele. "Come with me to Earth. We can be together there where no one cares about queens or the Marchant name. We can be normal. We could be a…family."

Rainere's expression dropped.

"But there is no magic on your world of Earth," he rasped sadly. "Adelena, I am a creature of magic. This Immortality Curse I wear binds me to this world. Without magic I would surely die. It's who I am."

"Oh." Adele wanted to cry, as her last hope for a compromise died. Why was this all so impossible?

"But even if I stayed here with you, Rainere. I am St. Lucidis, and you are a Marchant. We would never be allowed to be together. We would always have to keep our relationship a secret. There's no future for us like that," Adele argued, though she hated herself for it.

She was dying to throw herself into his arms and stop this horrible conversation. But she couldn't. The world was what was keeping them sneaking about like naughty teenagers, and she was far too old to be playing around like this with the man she loved.

Rainere turned away.

"There could be another way," he said but his voice was low, and unsure.

"What?" asked Adele, as her heart leaped.

Rainere turned to face her again, his expression solemn.

"Marry me," he said bluntly, as his eyes watched her carefully.

Adele gasped.

"Marry me and put me on the throne as your king." He moved closer to take her hands and cradled them in his own.

"We have already lain as man and wife, Adelena, *cara mia*; this next step is but a formality. If you put me on the throne, I will have the power to change the law forbidding Marchants from marrying outside The Blood. We can be together in the open. No more secrets."

"You want to marry me?" asked Adele dumbfounded by his bombshell. Did sleeping together mean so much in Unisian society? Adele shivered as though with a chill.

*Marry again? But it was so miserable the first time!*

Adele felt trapped and panicky like she had the first night she had slept with Rainere and he had pushed her too hard and too fast. This man just didn't know when to stop.

"Rainere, I—" Adele paused. Rainere was trying to help her here; she didn't want to hurt his feelings. "You haven't even met my children yet. If we are going to be a family, then that will take time. I can't marry you until I know that they will be happy with you and me together. And what about Ohren? There is no way he will let us marry that easily, he and the others would try and stop us—"

"If you want to leave and go back to Earth, then that's what you should do," interrupted Rainere brusquely, but Adele could see the pain in his expression. As always, it mirrored her own.

"I want you and I want us to go home," she said miserably. "I know it's impossible, but that's what I want."

Rainere's look was heartbreaking.

"I just want you." He reached out and wiped a tear that had escaped down her cheek. He placed it to his lips.

"But I want your happiness more than my own. If you want to leave, I will help you get home as I vowed. But if you would stay with me, Adelena, I can promise you again that I will spend the rest of my endless life making you the happiest bride in the world."

He leaned forward and kissed her lightly on the lips.

"I love you, Adelena, you are my life now."

Adele kissed her prince back. She had nothing she could say that would give him as much joy as that simple touch. She let him pull her nightgown over her head and throw it aside.

How could she tell him of her terror of getting married again so soon after getting divorced? The hurt of Justin's rejection was just too fresh for her to believe that it wouldn't happen again.

*But Rainere is a dreamy prince from a land far, far away, and he loves me…maybe it would be different this time? Maybe it would be right?*

*But he was also a Marchant.*

Adele knew enough history now to know that a Marchant king on the throne would send the entire kingdom into a huge panic. Just look what had happened when the Sandarians had heard that a new St. Lucidis queen had been crowned. Everyone was terrified of the name Marchant. Maybe something terrible would happen to Rainere if she agreed to this. He might be hurt—or worse—as Ohren and the court fought her decision.

As their kiss deepened and Adele felt Rainere's tongue dart into her mouth, she shivered. She had only known Rainere for a little while, but already he held her heart in his hands. To imagine a life on this mad world without him was unthinkable. She needed to protect him from his own passion and sense of commitment to her. They couldn't marry, so she would have to promise something else to make him feel safe with her. But what?

"Adelena, your answer?" Rainere pulled away, breathing heavily. His eyes were too serious.

Delicately, she laid her hand on Rainere's naked chest and whispered the Command.

The effect was instant.

"Oh *cara mia*…oh, don't…stop…oh, don't stop that…" he groaned and fell back on the bed, overcome by the exquisite pain as her power coursed through him and he became helpless to fight it.

Adele exhilarated in her power over the gorgeous man stretched out on the white silk sheets in front of her. She could better feel now the push and pull of the magic in her hands and studied the way the pressure built and released slowly, and the way each release made Rainere writhe and moan. It was so exciting to be reminded that she had really changed, that she had something inside her now that was special. It helped her believe that she might, in fact, just be the lost St. Lucidis princess, as ridiculous as it sounded. But if she really were a princess, then maybe she would be worthy of a prince like Rainere, and maybe he really could be hers…and they could be together.

She climbed atop him and leaned down to kiss the fluttering pulse at his throat.

"I love you, Rainere, never forget that."

She kissed him on his perfect mouth and gently let go of the power that bound the two of them.

As soon as it was released, Rainere flipped Adele onto her back and settled between her legs. She almost shrieked at the speed of the movement but giggled as Rainere looked down on her with a wicked expression on his face.

"That is a delicious trick of yours, *cara mia*," he growled throatily, pinning her to the bed. "But I think it's time I showed you some of my own."

A thrill of nerves and anticipation shivered through Adele as Rainere pulled her arms over her head with just one of his hands, leaving the other one free to roam her body. She writhed under his control as his soft pinches sent shots of electricity shooting through her.

"*Cara mia*," he murmured trailing kisses from her jawline down her neck. She wrapped her legs around his waist and felt the length of him push up into her, almost but not quite there. This time she had been ready for him. His deep groan at being inside her made her ache and arch up into his body. She felt herself getting lost in the delicious scent of him. The cold, smoky fragrance that was Rainere's own enveloped her, making her eyes close with heady pleasure.

"Oh, Rainere," Adele gasped. "I could just stay like this forever."

She smiled as Rainere looked down at her. In the flickering candlelight, she could see the silver rings of magic circling his black irises. He truly was the most beautiful man she had ever seen.

And now he wanted to marry her.

Despite her reticence to make such an incredible decision after only a couple of days with him, one part of Adele longed to acquiesce. If she married Rainere, then she could surely share the burden of ruling Unisia, which she was so ill equipped to do by herself. Maybe if she said yes now, he might even come to Sandar with her, saving her from dealing with this angry empress all alone.

But he could never leave this world with her. She and the children would be stuck here in Unisia.

*But was that so bad?*

She thought of their tiny, crumbling bungalow in the suburbs, the mountains of bills, and the ex-husband who didn't want his family anymore.

*What would she really be taking them back to?*

The man who was now covering her breasts in kisses had always been so precious to her. Every night he had been there for her, waiting. Now that she knew it had all been real…well, that meant they were fated. *Surely? Star-crossed lovers who had finally found each other across the entire universe. Now they could be together. Forever.*

Rainere moved down lower on her body, his hands sliding down her ribs and stomach, following the curves of her form until they reached her inner thighs. Trailing kisses across her stomach until he reached the heat between her legs…Adele gasped as his tongue brushed her most sensitive point.

"Oh God," she groaned.

"Adelena, I love you. Please, tell me yes." Rainere's voice was muffled from between her thighs.

He flicked his tongue rapidly against her swollen flesh, making her gasp and moan. She glanced down and saw he watched her writhing with the pleasure he gave her. His dark eyes flashed and burned into her. A jolt of wild energy coursed through her, setting off the chime-voices and their sweet song in her ears. But this time she didn't need their command. Rainere was breaking her apart all on his own.

Already she was so close to the edge...

"Will you marry me?" growled Rainere persistently. He slipped a finger inside her, then another, pushing them in hard and making her back arch. His long fingers found the invisible point of ecstasy deep within her.

"*Cara mia*, please..."

His tongue caressed her without a break as his hand massaged, gently then harder, in turn.

The rush was coming...and like waves crashing on the shore Adele was lifted up and carried away...

"Yes. Yes. God. *Yes!*"

He reared up and pushed himself inside of her just when she thought she would pass out from the exquisite sensation of it all. He was already at the pitch of his own pleasure. Adele heard his answering cry as if from a great distance. She clenched him deep inside her and held him until he collapsed...the instinct to breathe deserted her while she lay surrounded by his huge and gorgeous warmth.

Adele felt her body reverberate with the aftershocks of pleasure for minutes after they had finished. Her flesh ached where Rainere had bruised her but even the pain felt delicious in the glow of sated desire.

Though she knew she needed to get back to her own room, she just couldn't seem to make herself move right now. Adele only opened her eyes again when she felt Rainere shift beside her.

He sat on the edge of the bed in just his unbuttoned trousers. Lifting his long hair off his back he swung it over his shoulder and stretched his arms up over his head releasing a satisfied groan. The enormous tattoo which covered his back seemed to roil and roll with the movement of his muscles. Never having looked at it closely before, Adele watched fascinated as the black ink swirled in an intricate pattern up to the prince's neck, licking around the sides of his ribs and hipbones, before reaching down to the top of his sculpted buttocks.

Adele reached out to touch a swirl above his hip, but Rainere flinched away from her hand.

"It's beautiful," said Adele quietly, and smiled up at him. "You're beautiful."

Rainere gave her a quick look she couldn't read. He seemed pained by the compliment.

"No one has ever accused me of that before." His voice was hoarse with emotion. He looked up at her again. "I don't suppose anyone ever thought that before you did."

Adele grinned and flopped back onto the pillows. "I find that impossible to believe…there must be hundreds of women throwing themselves at you every day." She shoved him with her foot. He didn't move.

Rainere gave her an incredulous look.

"You do know who I am, don't you? Any woman of good sense would be terrified to find themselves alone in a room with me, let alone allow themselves to be ravaged in my bed. I am the evil Marchant prince, devourer of babies, and defiler of grandmothers," he growled playfully and climbed back on the bed to rest over Adele, holding himself up so as not to crush her. His arms were like steel pillars made flesh.

"Women of good sense, eh? Well, what does that make me?" Adele smiled, pulling a lock of his hair and twirling it around her finger.

"Wild, courageous, and completely insane—why do you think I want to marry you?"

Adele really didn't want to ruin the moment, but her emotions betrayed her expression. This was going to be so complicated.

Rainere sensed the change in her mood immediately and dropped next to her, resting on his side. He held his face close to hers.

"I will love you forever," he whispered, kissing her on the lips. "You never have to fear me, Adelena."

Adele pulled out of the kiss but kept her face close.

"But I won't live forever, Rainere, not like you will with this." She ran her hand over the tattoo that peeked over his shoulder. "I am not immortal."

"I didn't want to be immortal, either," said Rainere softly, running a gentle finger along her cheekbone. "They came for me at night..."

Rainere paused and closed his eyes against the memory that swam into his mind.

"They came in through the window of the Great Library. Grotto couldn't help me...no one could." He paused and looked down at the webs of scars on the back of his hand where it rested on her chest. "I had no idea they were still alive. I had thought...I had been told that I was the only one left. The last Marchant. But they are still out there, somewhere up in the Black Mountains. I don't know where, exactly, but it was cold so it must have been high up." He paused again.

"Who are they, my love?" Adele gently pressed, desperate to know more about the mysterious man she loved so much.

Rainere turned to Adele, and she almost flinched from the pain she saw in his eyes.

"The Eldars," he whispered. "The Eldars are the oldest Marchants left alive. They must be thousands of years old by now. Only they can draw the immortality spell…only they could do this to me."

Adele couldn't hide her shock.

"But if these Eldars did this to you, then everybody must know you aren't really the last Marchant…"

Rainere wiped his hand across his face and glared down at Adele.

"As far as these fools in the Golden Palace are concerned, I did this to myself. It's been too long since anyone spoke of Marchant magic for this generation to understand what we are and are not capable of. No one else knows…and Adelena, you mustn't speak of this to anyone. It's been my terrible secret alone to keep, but since you are to join my family then I have to tell you that the Eldars still exist. For centuries, they have controlled the Marchant family and worked to keep The Blood pure. Only as a reigning King of Unisia will I be able to change their laws and unite with you as husband and wife. Otherwise…"

"Otherwise what?" asked Adele, alarmed to discover a new danger for her family in Unisia.

"To be honest, I'm not sure." Rainere frowned. "Our union could never be fruitful, as the immortality spell renders me sterile. We could never have a child of mixed blood together, and it is really only a child who would be at risk."

Rainere squeezed her hand and brought it to his lips for a kiss.

"I would hope that we will be safe, but changing the law ensures they would not come for us."

Adele had a thousand questions to ask Rainere about his past and his Family, but only one mattered.

"Are my children in danger if I'm with you, married or not?"

"Adele, I will not lie to you. Your children are in danger every day, not because of me but because of you. They have displaced the entire court of the Golden Palace just as you have usurped the St. Lucidis Regents who ruled before you. The high wizard has brought you from Earth to play a very dangerous game of politics and prophecy."

"Do you think I shouldn't trust Ohren? He is the one who did this to me, after all. I know he is using me to help save the kingdom from these Dark Days that are coming…but is that all he is using me for? What do you know about the prophecy, Rainere?"

"I know that it is beyond both our powers to control it, *cara mia*," Rainere soothed her, pulling her in to lie on his chest. "But you are the queen, and that is your biggest burden and blessing right now. I also know the high wizard thinks he understands the prophecy, but things are not always what they seem with such ancient puzzles. In Sandar you will be safe, free of the court and free of the spi…free of the shadows that reign in Unisia."

Adele felt Rainere's heart thud suddenly beneath her cheek. She looked up at him.

"I feel safe with you, my love."

"Adelena, *cara mia*…" The prince's voice was a soft rasp. "I can protect you from them all when you take me as your husband. The Eldars, the court of the Golden Palace, Lord Orgustus, the other wizards. Everyone who would seek to take advantage of you and use you for their own ends."

He turned her chin with his finger to look deep into her eyes.

"But more than that, I will love you with every ounce of my strength, every single day of my endless life. You will have nothing to fear ever again with me by your side. But until we are married, I am just the Marchant prince in exile, helpless to protect you if I can't be near you."

His hand stroked her back, anchoring her as new nightmares flooded her mind. His words had soothed her but Adele still cringed at the idea of marriage. What would her children think of him?

At the thought of her children, Adele remembered that she should be getting back to her quarters in case someone discovered her gone, if they hadn't already.

Reluctantly, she pulled herself off Rainere's chest and climbed off the bed to hunt for her nightgown. She felt uncomfortable, but also pleased that Rainere never took his eyes off her as she strolled around the room. She caught sight of herself in a full-length mirror by the dresser and paused for a moment to appraise what she saw. In the dim candlelight, her round hips looked soft, her butt was full and high. Her boyish figure had been softened by her three pregnancies; and despite the stretch marks and extra curves on her thighs, Adele was happy to see a body that could make a prince desire her. She pushed her dark hair off her face and enjoyed the look of her kiss-swollen lips and hot pink cheeks. She gave herself a lopsided smile. *Well done, girl!*

Once she'd found it, Adele pulled the white, silky nightdress down over herself much more slowly than was necessary, reveling in Rainere's admiring gaze. No man had ever looked at her like that. It made her feel beautiful and desirable.

Adele turned to the door and screamed as she came face to face with a gaunt-faced specter. Her hand flew to her mouth as she recognized, too late, his black servant's livery.

"Grottonski, leave! You have upset Her Majesty!" ordered Rainere calmly as he pulled his trousers up and slid off the bed.

The thin man, his face twisted in a snarl, immediately turned to leave.

"No, please, I'm sorry," blurted out Adele. "You just surprised me, that's all."

Adele was utterly mortified and completely aware that it was obvious why she was in the prince's private chamber. She hoped the horrible man hadn't seen her doing her reverse striptease.

She blushed furiously, now in embarrassment.

"Queen Adelena, this is Grottonski, my manservant," said Rainere, coming up behind Adele to make the introductions. "He doesn't warrant an apology, but should offer one instead."

Adele watched as the man before her dropped into a deep bow. She could see his scalp between the greasy strands of black hair that were plastered to his scalp. It revolted her.

"My sincerest apologies, Your Majesty, if I startled you." Grotto's voice was deep and cold.

His face was all odd angles and hard lines, but his eyes were his strangest feature. Their color was an almost iridescent green, and they had a beautiful, nearly feminine, almond shape. Unfortunately, their pleasant effect was ruined by the emotion that clouded them. Adele tried to smile, but it died on her lips as she recognized the hate in his expression.

"I am taking Her Majesty back to her rooms, Grotto," said Rainere as he propelled Adele toward the little narrow door beside the fireplace.

"I shall await your return, master." Grotto bowed again but sent Adele another deathly glare as she slipped out of the door under Rainere's arm.

Adele shivered as her bare feet hit the cold stone of the secret corridor.

"I don't think your manservant likes me much," she remarked as they hurried back down the dusty corridors.

"Who? Grotto?" Rainere glanced down at Adele's frown. "He doesn't like the chances I take to be with you, but he has no right to decide whether to like you or not. You are a queen, and he is just a humble servant."

Adele silently reflected on Rainere's answer. He saw the world so differently from her. He had grown up in a palace with servants to wait on him, and where no one questioned his will or word. He had been born and raised as a prince. Though he lived on the outskirts of society, it was still a world he understood. Throw in being an immortal wizard, and there wasn't really a long list of things that they had in common to balance all the differences.

With an effort, Adele pushed that uncomfortable train of thought away and tried to lose herself in their parting kiss.

This, they definitely had in common.

After Rainere had left, Adele pushed the secret door closed with its soft click. She went and sat on the side of her enormous glass bed, her feet dangling off the side like a child's.

*Did I really just promise to marry Rainere?* She thought in a daze. *Does he really want to marry me after only meeting me a few days ago?*

Though the question itself seemed ridiculous, Adele knew there was so much more to their relationship than just the last few days they'd spent together. Something stronger and more powerful than lust had brought them into each other's arms.

*We were both outsiders in our worlds, and now we can make a life together, and finally be part of something wonderful. Maybe our marriage would heal the rift between the Golden Palace and the Marchant family? Perhaps our love will fix these Dark Days coming in the prophecy?*

Despite her misgivings, Adele smiled at the thought. Nothing on this world had felt right until she had met Rainere. Now she felt strong enough to actually try and be the queen Ohren wanted her to be…and maybe she could do it all with Rainere by her side.

A knock at the door startled her from her reverie.

"Your Majesty?" A blonde, coiffed head poked around the door.

"Yes, Mrs. Ollenby?"

"Oh, good you are finally awake," said the older lady with a smile. "We have got so much to do today, and there are a thousand decisions only you can make for this journey to Sandar."

Adele stifled her groan and jumped down off the bed. She couldn't let herself wonder at how she was going to cope with the day after another sleepless night.

"Just let me freshen up and I'll be there in two minutes."

# CHAPTER THIRTY-FOUR

## "Ohren's Sacrifice"

Ohren snatched the letter from the footman, Spencer, and quickly dismissed the man. He shut his door with a firm push and threw it down on the table with the others. He had a tidy collection.

"Another note from the queen?" asked Orestes, picking poppy seeds out of his teeth with a splinter of wood. The cake he was eating lay in crumbs on a plate before him.

Ohren only frowned in response and strode over to his window where he had a partial view of Queen Adelena's balcony. The shouts of the royal children carried faintly on the breeze. Ohren huffed heavily and tried to squash the rope of guilt that curled up from his gut and threatened to strangle him.

*Why had that stupid woman insisted on taking the children with her? Surely, she should know that the children would be safer in the Golden Palace than on the road or in the desert lands of Sandar?*

Ohren gritted his teeth. It must be a joke of the Gods that just when he was prepared to sacrifice the queen for the good of his nation, he must risk losing all the heirs to the throne at the same time.

*But it was more than that...*

Ohren had become very fond of the children. Their silly antics and unadulterated joy whenever he walked into the room always made him smile. He made an excuse every day to see them, and take the time to play with them and their growing puppies. Even after just a few weeks, Aaron had lost all of his shyness and greeted the wizard like an old friend, saving up all his oddest questions for Ohren to answer, such as, what did magic smell like? And, had he ever heard the stars sing? Or, most recently, was there a fairy who collected lost baby teeth living in Unisia?

Natalie often used him as furniture in her overly complicated games, sitting him on one of the children's tiny chairs to be "the giant" or the "grandfather" of her little dolls. He was happy to do it, as it meant that the baby Stella would climb onto his lap to cuddle and pull gently on his beard.

Ohren felt the memory like a sharp stab in his heart.

*Stella*. Her golden curls and rose-pink cheeks reminded him poignantly of another baby he had adored so long ago. His only sister had been born many years after him and Orestes, and as a boy Ohren had taken such pride in looking after her. She had been the prettiest baby in the palace, and clever…she could count her fingers and toes before she was even two years old. Her magic had been so strong that Ohren had had to keep a close eye on her all day in case she hurt herself or someone else. He had loved that little girl more dearly than anyone else, ever. Stella was the image of his little sister.

Ohren sighed heavily again.

"Feeling guilty, Ohren?" Orestes's voice was only slightly mocking.

Ohren knew his twin felt as powerless as he did in this situation. Powerless but, unlike Ohren, also blameless. It was always Ohren who had to make the hard decisions, and it was he who bore the hardest consequences.

"It would be perfectly natural, of course," continued Orestes. "I mean, you risk our lives to bring the Hidden Child home and then sacrifice her to the first Dark God who asks for her presence in his demonic rituals. You must feel like a complete fool right about now."

"It's hardly a demonic ritual, brother. The Blood Ceremony is quite ordinary in every culture, the same as ours. Besides, you know I have no control here. We must follow the prophecy…"

Both men fell silent staring off into their own worlds.

"I feel awful," sighed Ohren, finally. "But Adelena must face this trial on her own without a wizard's help. I can't know exactly when she should be away from me to allow the prophecy to run freely, so I just have to stay away altogether. But brother, the risks are insane! What if the Sandarians find out that she isn't really…? What if they can discover the one thing we need to hide from her? We have no idea what that bloody Mage is capable of!"

Orestes looked grim. He knew exactly what his brother spoke of. The situation was impossible, but now completely out of their hands. The prophecy had to run its course.

"Perhaps it will be for the better that she is far from the Golden Palace if the Sandarians discover the truth about her? Then the blame for her death will fall far from your door," Orestes suggested hopefully, but his expression was morose. "If only the children weren't with her. If anything should go wrong, Ohren, then we will lose any chance to…"

"I know." Ohren interrupted his twin and shook his head sadly. He looked at the pile of letters Adelena had already sent him asking for his help today. "But little Queen Adelena is more scared of leaving her children in the Golden Palace with Lord Orgustus here than she is taking them to a distant land and into a tribe of barbarians."

"You should keep that pompous fool on a tighter leash, Ohren." Orestes frowned. "I've told you he is more dangerous than his ignorant blustering would suggest. He is a serpent in wolf's clothing, brother."

"He is irritating, I agree," replied Ohren. "But if everything goes well with Adele after this trial in Sandar, well, we shouldn't have much more use for the Honorable Regent any longer. I shall deal with him then."

"Hmph, better late than never, I suppose," grunted Orestes as he lifted himself from his chair and headed for the door. "Well, I shall leave you to your maudlin guilt and go take care of my responsibilities. Should Adelena fail in her duty, then I'm sure even in these dark times a good lawyer will always be needed."

He gave Ohren a quick grin to belie the black humor of his comment before stepping out and shutting the door behind him.

Ohren's stomach tied itself into another painful knot. If Adele failed in her dealings with the Empress of Sandar, there might not be a society left which required any order at all.

# CHAPTER THIRTY-FIVE

## "Oki, the Devourer"

Adele lay in bed, staring at the ceiling. The light of near-dawn illuminated only the shadows of the things around her. It would be her last night in a bed for at least five days while on the road to Sandar, and she didn't want it to end just yet.

Adele ran over her list of major anxieties for the day:

> One - Ohren hadn't replied to any of her messages yesterday, and she still had no idea why he had decided not to accompany them to Sandar.

> Two - She was leaving for Sandar today with only her three children, their three puppies, her six-man Queen's Guard, two nannies (the children's favorites, Caitlin and Seraphina), and Tilburn in tow, as well as drivers for the three carriages they were to take.

> Three - She had no idea how to negotiate trade agreements with foreign empresses, and if she failed to secure the Fire Orchid stamens for Unisia, then thousands of people would die when the Summer Influenza arrived in a few weeks and it would all be her fault.

> Four - She hadn't seen Rainere all day yesterday or last night, as she had constantly been surrounded by people who had needed her say-so on everything from the color of their sheet sets to the number of toys the children could bring.

> Five - She had only climbed into bed an hour ago, exhausted but too manic to sleep…and still no sign of him. Maybe he was rethinking the marriage proposal? Would that be a good or a bad thing?

It was too overwhelming. Adele pulled a pillow over her face and miserably prayed to go to sleep, just to stop the hysterical thoughts swirling around her head.

A snap sounded, then a soft clicking noise. Adele threw back the pillow.

*Rainere, finally!*

She scanned the room for her dark prince, paying special attention to the deepest shadows, but it was mysteriously quiet. Adele's heart rate slowed again and she fell back on her pillows. She tried not to feel completely crushed that he hadn't come.

She heard a sharp click and a low hiss.

"Oh, this is just ridiculous!" she said out loud and pulled herself out of bed. Either Rainere was playing tricks or she was completely mad, both of which required her to be standing.

But before she had taken a step, Adele froze. Her heart stopped beating as she gazed in horror at the unholy creature before her. A spider the size of a dog sat in the middle of the red-and-gold carpet on her bedroom floor. As her brain fought feebly to come up with a plan of action, her eyes took in every horrifying feature of the creature. It was deeply black with bright yellow stripes across its abdomen and thorax. It had yellow tips on its pincers, which moved when it opened its mouth and emitted a loud hiss. Despite the lack of light, its eyes glittered at her as it raised one muscular leg.

Adele was surprised and relieved by the volume of her scream as she leaped back up onto the bed. She had had this nightmare before but never been able to wake up before the spider had crawled up her leg.

The spider stopped hissing and began moving its legs one at a time in some sort of weird dance, turning this way and that.

Adele screamed again just as Captain Lucky and Queen's Guardsman Owens came bolting into the room with their swords drawn. Lucky was the first to see the spider. The creature lifted both its forelegs, rearing as if to strike.

It was too much for Adele.

"Kill it!" she shrieked hysterically. "Lucky, kill the thing!"

Captain Lucky looked at Adele in shock. "Majesty?"

Adele composed herself only enough to enunciate her words.

"Kill. It. Dead. Now!"

The spider dropped to all its eight legs and took a step backward, almost as if it understood the command.

With a grim expression, Captain Lucky pulled a dagger from his belt and with a sure aim threw it hard. It struck the creature square in its back. The spider opened its mouth but no sound came out. Captain Lucky walked cautiously toward it and, with a quick motion, cleaved the spider in two with his sword.

Adele watched the whole process with an escalating sense of hysteria. Only when she was sure that the spider had stopped twitching did she leap off the bed and grab the empty water jug on the nightstand. She heaved into it once, then twice. She sat back shaking like a leaf in the wind, careful not to look at the mutilated body of the creature.

"I'm so sorry gentlemen," said Adele as she carefully put the jug back on the nightstand, and wound her shaking hands in her lap. "But I've had a dreadful case of arachnophobia since I was very young, you see. Spiders make me kind of hysterical, and that one"—she gagged slightly—"was just too damn big."

Captain Lucky was still rather pale himself and exchanged a glance with his shocked lieutenant.

"I would say that is a very healthy fear indeed, Your Majesty." He smiled but it didn't reach his eyes. "We will take the creature's corpse to the High Wizard Ohren. He'll know what to do with it."

Adele had a terrifying thought.

"You don't think there are more of them in the palace do you?" she asked in a strangled voice. "They aren't common here, are they?"

Captain Lucky shook his head.

"Your Majesty, it's my belief that a Spider hasn't been seen in the Golden Palace since the time of King Rainov the Cruel."

"Oh well, that's good, then." Adele was going for casual but her voice broke on the *good* and she sounded like she was going to throw up again. "But could you quietly do a sweep of the apartments for me? I'd hate for the children to find a monster like that in their room, as well. But don't tell anyone about this, will you?" She gestured at the jug on her nightstand. "I know everyone thinks I'm pretty fragile at the best of times."

"Yes, Your Majesty, of course not. It will be as you wish." Captain Lucky and Owens both snapped smart bows.

Still shaking, Adele escaped to the bathroom to calm down in private.

*This would never have happened if Rainere had been with me*, she thought, irrationally furious now that the first shock of fear had passed. She crawled into the empty bath, holding herself tight, and cursed Unisia and all its mad creatures a thousand times.

*            *            *

Captain Lucky waved Owens over to the body as he grabbed a soft rug off a nearby chair. The tall QG loped over to his younger senior officer.

"See that the corpse gets to the high wizard now, will you. And Owens, keep this very quiet—only QG to know. We don't want to start a palace-wide panic."

Owens nodded and prodded the body with his toe.

"Have you ever seen anything like it, Captain?" he asked. "When you were at the Accadaemia, maybe?'

"No, never…well, only in the history books. But I thought they were just a myth." Lucky hesitated and looked up at Owens, the realization of the gravity of what he'd just done dawning in his eyes. "I've just killed a mythical creature."

"Well, it was on the queen's orders, no blame there, man," grunted Owens as he hefted the blanket-wrapped bundle into his arms. "And a damned heavy creature it is, too. This one weighs as much as a grown man."

Lucky watched Owens leave and turned back to discreetly search the rest of the apartments. He pretended he couldn't hear the queen quietly sobbing in her bathroom.

*This new queen is a magnet for trouble,* thought Lucky, still a bit shaken himself. *A Marchant prince in the Golden Palace and now a spider right out of my ancient history books! What next?*

Lucky crossed himself with the Sign of the Goddess and concentrated on the job at hand, starting with the royal nursery.

# CHAPTER THIRTY-SIX

## "Pick a Side"

Grotto shook the prince awake. Rainere had been in a semi-slumber ever since Adele had left him the night before. He had wanted to check on her several times, but Grotto had warned him that she was surrounded by too many people all day and then at night, too. He had tossed and turned with dreams of her, her kisses, her hands, and her tears before finally falling into a heavy sleep in the early hours of the morning.

It was entirely too frustrating being away from her for a whole day and night. How would he survive with her being gone so long in Sandar?

Grotto shook the prince's arm again, and finally Rainere raised his head off the pillow and growled at his manservant. But before he could lie back down, Grotto shook him again, more fiercely.

"Master, she has killed him," he hissed.

"Who?" asked Rainere blearily.

"That whore queen, Master—that whore has killed Empress Ka-kik's son Oki!"

Suddenly very much awake, Prince Rainere sat up in bed.

"But why? How could she? Why was the empress's son here in the Golden Palace already? I told Ka-kik to wait for my word!"

Grotto's eyes flashed with barely contained fury. All their plans stood on the brink of ruin.

"All of that means nothing now," he snapped bitterly. "This will mean war, master, so you had better pick a side."

# CHAPTER THIRTY-SEVEN

## "On the Road"

Adele sat against the seat in the carriage. Another bump in the potholed road sent her ink pot flying. It covered the new folio she was reading with vivid purple.

Adele swore quietly, causing Tilburn to look up in horror.

"Oh, come on, Tilburn," snapped Adele. "Surely you've heard a woman swear before."

"Yes, but I've not heard a queen use that gutter language," sniffed the little man, his tightly coiffed curls shaking in disapproval.

The conversation lapsed into an irritable silence.

They had been on the road for three days now, and the land had been getting steadily more arid since they had left the lush green forests and swaying grain fields of the kingdom of Unisia. The temperature had been getting much hotter and the air in the carriages was horribly stale and stuffy with no breeze to blow through.

Adele sighed, and pulled the curtain on the window aside. She could hear the children whining and arguing in the carriage behind her own. She had been horror-struck at the thought of leaving her children without her for the two weeks she had to be in Sandar, but their behavior now had her contemplating leaving them by the side of this dusty, old road.

"Why is this road so bad, Tilburn?" Adele asked. "I would have thought the only road that led to a neighboring nation would be better taken care of."

Tilburn shrugged, still miffed with her.

"There is no money in it, Your Majesty. The Sandarians come onto kingdom territory to deliver the Fire Orchid stamens, and that is only a tiny cargo. There is no need for the kingdom to pay for any extensive work to be done here."

Adele could see his point, but her numb backside still protested all the bumps and bruises it had suffered.

"I think I might get out and walk for a bit," she said, ignoring the new folio that Tilburn tried to hand her. "It might help my mood—and my language."

Adele gave Tilburn a grin and was relieved to see him smile back.

She jumped down from the slowly moving carriage, pleased that she had argued to wear the masculine pants and shirt ensemble while they were on the road. Mrs. Ollenby had been scandalized at the idea of Adele dressing like a man, but Adele had argued that it would be more practical for traveling, and easier to dress herself with none of her ladies-in-waiting accompanying her on this trip.

Feeling free and comfortable, Adele sauntered up to Captain Lucky, who was in a quiet conversation with one of the other guards. Adele remembered his name was Pepper because of his dark-red hair.

The men's conversation broke off when Adele approached.

"Good afternoon, Your Majesty," said Captain Lucky and dismounted to join Adele on foot.

"Good afternoon, Lucky, Pepper," Adele answered and choked slightly on the dust that the horses were kicking up.

"Thought to go for a little stroll, Your Majesty?" asked Lucky politely.

"I think Mr. Tilburn and I just need a little time apart," answered Adele with a rueful smile. "It can get a bit close in those carriages."

Adele ran a hand down the neck of Lucky's beautiful chestnut.

"I wish I could ride a horse, it'd be so much nicer than sitting in the stuffy carriage all day."

"D'you not know how to ride, Your Majesty?" asked an incredulous Pepper. "I thought all ladies knew how to…"

He went silent at a sharp look from his captain.

"On Earth we drive everywhere," admitted Adele, awkward as always when describing her home world. "Cars are like mechanized…um, wagons or carriages, no horses needed."

"Like those clanking engines they use at the flour mill?" asked Pepper curiously.

"I'm not sure, I've not seen a flour mill before," said Adele, making a mental note to try to find one soon. "But they are very fast and make traveling so much easier than lumbering along like we are doing."

All three turned at the piercing shriek of Stella and watched as a tiny shoe flew out the window of the children's carriage.

*Whatever it iss that Seraphina and Caitlin are being paid, it isn't nearly enough,* decided Adele. She cringed at the wailing that ensued and waited for the inevitable cry of "Mummy!" that would follow it.

"Would you like to learn how to ride a horse, Your Majesty? Because, if so, I would be happy to give you your first lesson." Lucky smiled broadly, and Adele felt a little surge of excitement at the idea.

Why not? She had always wanted to learn, but growing up in cities it had been impossible for her to see a horse, let alone ride one.

"Let's do it!"

Captain Lucky led Adele and his horse out of their small party and to a stump at the side of the road.

"This will be a handy mounting block," said Lucky, pulling his horse in by the stump. "Now, if you hold the reins like so…"

Adele listened attentively as Lucky showed her how to mount and sit in the saddle. He went to great lengths to avoid touching her, which made showing her some things a bit difficult, but because his horse, Redfire, was so well trained, Adele didn't feel frightened at all. She spent a happy half hour riding and getting a feel for walking with Redfire until the children finally noticed her and demanded her attention again.

Reluctantly, Adele climbed into the carriage with the children and right into their overtired and cranky barrage. Adele envied the puppies, who got to travel underneath the carriage, walking in the shade and only coming inside for naptime.

"The poor mites are so bored, Your Majesty," said a harried Caitlin. "I'm afraid I've run out of ideas to entertain them."

Adele thought longingly of the electronic devices she normally planted in her children's hands on long car trips. Aaron was the worst. Full of little-boy energy, he bounced on seats and fell on his tired sisters, asking a million questions and making up songs about spit and poo that had Natalie screaming for her mother to silence him.

"I have something to discuss with the queen," shouted General Ohrig as he drew up alongside Adele's window.

"What is it, General?" asked Adele, glad of any distraction.

"Hmmm, what? Oh, nothing." General Ohrig gave her a blank look. "Just had to get away from the incessant babbling of QG Pepper. That man could talk underwater, I'm sure of it."

Adele craned her neck out to see her Guardsman looking a tad forlorn as he was avoided by all the other QG's. She had noticed that only Captain Lucky seemed to be friendly with Pepper. He was a bit of a talker.

Just then Aaron started up with a particularly loud rendition of "The Poo goes Down the Toilet," complete with sound effects.

"Maybe I have a solution to both our problems," said Adele.

Ten minutes later, with the girls quietly playing in the children's carriage, Adele returned to her own to find Tilburn dozing on a pile of scrolls. She smiled and settled back against her bench, picking up the last document Tilburn had handed her. A blessedly cool breeze blew through the window carrying with it the pleasant chatting of Aaron with his new best friend, Pepper.

"But why is that your mummy's name? Did she pick it when she was born?" Aaron was asking as he sat in front of Pepper, riding on a dappled gray. The *why?* was automatic in response to any new information Aaron was given.

"Well, it's interesting you should ask that," replied Pepper, honestly pleased. "Her name is very unusual in our family…"

Adele returned her attention to the scroll in her hand, the "Brief History of Marchant Law and the Sandarian Resistance Fighters." Adele skimmed it until she reached something interesting.

*"…for the hundreds of years that the Sandarian people were held as indentured slaves, there had always been a strong and persistent underground resistance. The core of the resistance movement was always to be found among the Fire Orchid farmers, for they were the most harshly treated by the Marchant overlords.*

*"Life as a farmer was a precarious existence, as one could die in any number of unfortunate ways. If the farmer managed to avoid the gas and steam geysers on the volcano fields, then he or she would have to contend with the overlord, and the constantly changing quotas of stamens which would need to be collected to receive rations and a bed for the night.*

*"The Marchant Overlords were often the criminal and mentally unstable members of the different Marchant Clans who were punished for their indiscretions by being exiled to the isolated and hot Sandar volcano fields. There was no hope of return to the Royal Court for these Marchant exiles, so they ruled Sandar as their own personal fiefdoms, with dangerous and inventive cruelty.*

*"The main aim of the Sandarian Resistance was to smuggle as many women and children out of the Fire Orchid farms as possible to the surrounding jungle and*

*into the care of their Spirit Guardians. Not much is known of these Guardians, as the knowledge is forbidden to those of foreign blood, but historians believe…"*

Adele looked out the window as the breeze dropped again.

Slavers, overlords, inventive cruelty…would she ever find anything redeeming about Rainere's family? It was no wonder the Sandarian delegation had been so rude at the meeting.

If she put Rainere on the throne as the king, she could only imagine how upsetting it would be to the Sandarians. Apparently, two hundred years of freedom wasn't enough for them to forget the evil done to their nation by the Marchant family.

Maybe it was time for those bonds to be healed?

Maybe it wasn't?

Adele chewed her bottom lip and tried to regain the light-hearted feeling she'd had the moment before she had read the scroll, but it was no good. Rainere loved her with a passion that took her breath away, and the responsibility of that was heavy. But the people of Unisia needed her to make the right choice for them. It could mean the difference between life and death for them if the Sandarians decided to never give another Fire Orchid to Unisia after their marriage.

"Ah, Majesty, there you are…er-herm." Tilburn woke with a start and immediately pretended he had never been asleep. It would have been funny, if she hadn't felt so anxious.

"Do you have any other scrolls on the history of Sandarian and St. Lucidis relations after the War of Liberation?" asked Adele. "I want to know how the other families treated the Sandarians after the fall of the last Marchant king."

Tilburn shuffled through his papers and found a handful to give Adele. He smiled, pleased she hadn't noticed him falling asleep for a moment, and happy she was taking her research seriously.

Adele got straight to work.

# Chapter Thirty-Eight

## "Home in the Grey Palace"

Prince Rainere stared far off into the distance, Grotto knew not where.

The prince still wore his traveling cloak and gloves, as they had just walked into the Grey Palace, finally home after more than a week away. But there was to be no rest, it would seem, as Schiss had met them, in his human form, at the door with an important message from the Spider Empress.

Grotto felt sick to the bottom of his stomach.

*Why, when these plans had been so carefully laid, was everything falling apart? Did the prophecy mean nothing anymore?*

The empress had sent word that she was in mourning and would not take any outsiders into the nest while she grieved the death of her favored son, Oki.

Schiss had delivered the official message from the empress and also let Rainere know that the nest itself was in an uproar. With the high-ranking Oki dead, the rest of the Favored from the same Birth Cycle were all killing one another, warring for the position at their mother's right side. Empress Ka-kik was beside herself with grief and had sequestered herself in the Birthing Chamber eating all the Offerings of the Gift her children had brought her seeking favor, and eating those others who came too close.

"I have never seen the nest like this before," sniffed the skinny little Schiss. "I almost kissed the foot of the empress when she told me to go to the Grey Palace and let you know not to enter the tunnels while she grieved the loss of that beast, Oki."

Schiss trained his round eyes on Grotto.

"I, for one, am glad that Oki is dead, Grottonski." Schiss smiled and managed to look slightly scary. "He ate almost my entire Birth Cycle, did I ever tell you that? Hundreds of brothers and sisters. All gone, every one of them! I was lucky to make it out alive that night. Yet the empress never punished him. Not him…not the beautiful Oki. Handsome Oki! Oki the Blessed! I tell you, I tell you, and I tell you again, I will kiss that Queen Adelena's foot for killing Oki. Yes, I will…"

"And she will step on you with it, you fool," Grotto snapped. "She killed Oki and she will kill you, too."

"We don't know that, Grotto," interrupted Rainere, coming out of his reverie to send a hard look to his manservant. "We have no idea why Adelena killed Oki…perhaps he frightened her, or threatened her. No, we have no idea why she would kill such an important member of the empress's court. But I'm sure she had a very good reason."

"He *was* a murderous cretin," offered Schiss helpfully. "Perhaps in her infinite wisdom as a queen she could sense that?"

"Wisdom!" sneered Grotto. "The only thing that Queen—"

"Enough, Grotto!" shouted Rainere. His voice thundering through the entrance hall made the servants freeze in their tracks as they carried the luggage in from the carriage. Schiss threw his hands over his delicate ears.

Grotto dropped to his knees and bowed his head low.

"Master, forgive me," he whispered. "I had no right to speak as I did. Forgive me, master, I had no right. Forgive me, master, please."

"You will not speak of her at all," hissed Rainere, his face a mask of fury and pain, as he struggled to control his rage. "She is my…she is *mine*. I will have no servant defile her name in my presence. Am I understood, old man?"

"Master, forgive me," Grotto intoned and kept his eyes trained on Rainere's shoes. If they came toward him, he had to be prepared to drop and roll, with only his arms to protect his head.

But Rainere did not advance on his cowed manservant. Instead, he turned to the frozen man-spider who stared in fear at the angry wizard before him.

"Schiss, I understand that it will be dangerous for you to continue living at the nest while your many siblings are warring. I will offer you a roof to live under until the empress should have recovered herself enough to regain control." Rainere kept his voice smooth, though his suppressed fury caused him to shudder once, slightly, as he clenched and unclenched his fists.

"Thank you, m'liege, that is so extremely very kind of you. I would be happy to live under your roof." Schiss bowed but kept his eyes cautiously on Rainere. Angry wizards were not to be trifled with.

"I didn't say it would be my roof, Schiss," said Rainere, a mirthless smile tugging up the corner of his mouth. "Tell your mother, the empress, that you will be spying on the Queen Adelena for me on her journey to Sandar, while she is in Sandar, and then when she comes back to me...I mean...when she returns to the Golden Palace. I need to know she is safe while on this quest to the Empress Sanda'hani for the Fire Orchids."

He held up his hand for silence as Schiss opened his mouth to protest.

"You will tell a lesser minion to pass the message along to the Empress Ka-kik, so that by the time she has received it, you will be far gone on your duties for me. Once a day, you will report to me to let me know that the queen and her children are safe and well. You will, naturally, use the ancient portals to travel, and let me know where you are. If the queen is ever in any danger, you are to tell me immediately. The Wizard Ohren believes he is following the prophecy by sending my...Queen Adelena to Sandar, but the fool has the wrong empress. I have no doubts that Adelena will fare well, but I will not risk having her out of my sight for so long."

Rainere gazed out the open front door, and searched the view beyond as if he might be able to divine where Adelena was from the steps of his own palace. He had left the Golden Palace three days ago, the very day she had left for Sandar. He'd not even had the chance to kiss her hand before they were parted.

"It will be hard enough not being close to see her myself..."

"Errr-hehgm." Schiss cleared his throat phlegm loudly. "I should be happy to leave on the morrow, m'liege, and will very, very much be happy to follow your command. I just think it might be difficult to remain hidden in Sandar; you see, there is a Mage there who..."

Prince Rainere turned his unseeing eyes on Schiss, completely uninterested in his presence any further.

"You will leave now. I will not have Queen Adelena out of my sight for any longer than she needs to be. Tell the nest, and then go to her. But remain hidden until we can be certain that she will not kill you out of hand."

Schiss gulped and his round eyes bulged.

The prince turned and strode up the sweeping staircase of the enormous entrance hall of the Grey Palace. His cape swept over both his shoulders as his black hair rippled down his back.

"Get up, Grotto," he called back over his shoulder. "We have much to do, and just a few weeks before the next full moon. It's time I started taking this cursed prophecy more seriously."

# CHAPTER THIRTY-NINE

## "Pretending to be a Queen"

The following days on the road were more pleasant as the children discovered that riding lessons with Captain Lucky and QG Pepper were as much fun as Adele found them.

It was nice getting to know the rest of her Queen's Guard as well, now that they had nothing but time on their hands while traveling the long road to Sandar.

Captain Lucky had proved himself to be unfailingly polite and pleasant company. He was a gentle teacher, and under his tutelage Adele found herself growing into a confident rider. There was no getting around the fact that he was an extremely attractive young man and looked every bit the Captain of the Queen's Guard, but Adele felt an affection for him that was only maternal. He was a young man any mother would be proud of. After just a few days in his company, Adele understood why he had been promoted to the position over the more senior members of the Guard. Not only was he incredibly professional, but also he was the most educated of all the men, apart from the general, and had attended the Accadaemia for several years before entering the army of Unisia. What he lacked in military experience he more than made up for with his quick mind and considered responses. She also appreciated that he never once mentioned the episode with the spider that had happened before they had left.

General Ohrig mostly kept to his own company but was always happy to converse with Adele about the kingdom lands that they were driving through. He seemed to know everything from the plant species along the road to the habits of the birds that flew above them, and the invisible borders between the title lands that they passed on the King's Highway.

Though he was naturally very serious, the general often showed a dry and sardonic wit that reassured Adele the man was just as human as she was.

QG Leith was a lanky young man in his early twenties with a quiet, easy way about him. He quickly became a favorite of Natalie's, as he could show her how to plait the grasses that grew by the side of the road into crowns, bracelets, and belts. The youngest boy in a family of all girls, Leith was very tolerant of Natalie's chatter and gentle with her feelings when she declared her undying love for him at the end of the third day.

More than once, Adele caught Seraphina smiling the guard's way with a blush on her cheeks. Though he didn't share the elegant features or charm of Captain Lucky, Leith carried himself well and had the proud bearing of a soldier.

QG Pepper joined QG Leith as one of the youngest guards in the retinue, but unlike Leith, his inexperience showed in his constant questions and endless anecdotes about his family and their farm in the high country outside the capital, Concordis. Adele thought he was very sweet with his wide-eyed innocence and young man's enthusiasm, but it didn't stop her from occasionally hiding in her carriage and pretending to nap when he got started on one of his long tales about his uncle or aunt or cousin who had invented the something-or-other and changed the course of farming history in Unisia.

The other two QG's, Owens and Bear, stayed away from any casual interactions with the royal family. Owens was older than the other guards, maybe in his early forties. He was tall and slim, with a narrow face and a distant expression. Sitting astride his horse with his hands folded over each other and his body moving in a loose sway, he reminded Adele of the cowboys she had seen in the movies at home.

QG Bear, on the other hand, Adele was happy to avoid speaking to. Bear had a definite roughness about his character. Whether it was his sour expression or his tone of ill-disguised hostility, Adele couldn't be sure what she liked least. But she never allowed the children to go near him, and made certain she was never alone with him. It gave her the shivers whenever she caught his blue eyes staring at her. That was when she decided that though his frown was intimidating, his smile was downright scary.

Late in the afternoon on the fifth day, the royal party finally reached the end of the road, and met the broad sweeping sand dunes of the nation of Sandar. Adele gazed upon the golden sand as it glimmered in the sun. She could just make out the enticing shimmer of an aqua-blue ocean in the distance beyond it.

"How shall we proceed, General?" asked Captain Lucky when all the men had assembled.

"We all go together, don't we?" Adele was surprised there would be another way.

"No, Your Majesty, I think you should proceed with myself, Captain Lucky, QG Bear, and Mr. Tilburn. We will leave QG's Owens, Pepper, and Leith to guard the children and nannies. That way we can get a feel for the sentiments of Empress Sanda'hani before we bring the children in."

Adele felt her stomach drop.

After the holiday atmosphere of the last few days, her return to playing at being a queen was almost painful.

Adele adjusted the heavy skirts of her gold brocade gown. She had only had Caitlin to help her dress in the cramped confines of the carriage, and she was pretty sure she looked as wrinkled and disheveled as she felt. Adele wiped her already-damp handkerchief over her forehead and neck. Makeup was impossible to keep on in this heat, but she had done her best as, unfortunately, she would never get another chance at a first impression with Empress Sanda'hani of Sandar. Adele prayed she would be okay. The whole of Unisia was depending on her.

General Ohrig touched her arm to get her attention. The skin on his hand felt rough and callused.

"Horses will be no good on this sand, Majesty," the general noted.

Adele almost opened her mouth to protest. She was pretty sure she had seen horses walking on sand before. *Didn't horses love the beach?* But Ohrig and Lucky were talking strategy now, and she felt too intimidated to say anything.

"It should be a mile or so to the empress's court," said Tilburn, who was standing at her shoulder with the map that Ripenzo Shale had given them. "It'll be a hot walk with this sun overhead."

"Shale said for us to come straight over as soon as we arrived," said Ohrig. "And so we shall. Lucky, get the water bags to bring with us."

Adele sighed deeply then noticed General Ohrig giving her a sidelong look, a smile hitching up the side of his mouth.

"What?" she asked, instantly self-conscious.

"Feeling unprepared, Your Majesty?" His question was bold, but over the last five days, Adele had come to appreciate the general's honesty. He spoke his mind without a lot of unnecessary protocol. He was honest, real, and she felt that she could be more natural with him.

She smiled grimly.

"Only slightly," she replied sarcastically. "I've never had the fate of a nation resting on my shoulders before. I have to tell you, General, I don't know what the hell I'm supposed to do if this all goes wrong."

She paused.

"Ohren should be here doing this. Do you have any idea why he didn't come with us to Sandar?"

General Ohrig shrugged one shoulder.

"Because Sandarians hate Unisian wizards," he stated matter-of-factly.

"Really, is that true?"

The general shrugged again.

"It's common knowledge, but that doesn't necessarily make it true, I guess."

"Why didn't he just tell me that himself, then?" Adele mused to herself, completely mystified.

"Wizards!" said Ohrig "Who knows why they do what they do?"

General Ohrig and Adele looked out over the sand dunes as faint strains of music wafted to them on the breeze.

"Majesty, may I give you some advice that works just as well on the battlefield as it does in the court?"

"Please, General, fire away," Adele said.

"When an enemy has you outnumbered on foreign terrain, there is only one thing you can do: outclass them. Use every weapon in your arsenal. As it stands your weapons are dignity, diplomacy, and your ability to search a person's soul with your eyes."

Adele raised her eyebrows in surprise at the list but stayed silent.

"Remember, when in the enemy camp, any information is good information. Gather as much intelligence as you can for the potential of a second offensive."

The general gave Adele a tight smile.

"And then pray to all the Gods who may have followed you from your world."

Adele tried, but her mouth wouldn't smile back.

When General Ohrig gave the signal, Adele, accompanied by Tilburn, Captain Lucky, and Bear, all set off across the hot sand toward the empress's camp on the shoreline.

The sun beat down on their unprotected heads. Only Adele was shaded by the tiny parasol Tilburn had insisted on bringing. Her skin sweated and itched beneath her heavy dress, making her more than aware that she hadn't had a bath in two days. Her last wash had been in a cold stream by the side of the road, which the children had thoroughly enjoyed but Adele had found less than satisfying.

Adele tripped and stumbled across the soft sand, which squeaked, powder soft, beneath her court slippers. Her eyelashes felt like they had woven together to protect her eyes from the glare of the sun. Already her mouth was pasty from the dry heat radiating off the sand, and the adrenaline making a constant circuit of her veins.

She shot a look at General Ohrig and almost went over on another ankle. His fearsome squint matched her own, though he did manage to keep his feet better.

*This is it, Adele. Time to be Queen Adelena,* Adele told herself. *Just approaching a hostile nation on behalf of my kingdom on a Thursday morning. Sure, it's not quite the same as fretting over the price of organic vegetables at the supermarket but it's similar, I'm sure.*

Adele stifled a hysterical giggle.

Despite her anxiety she was feeling strangely exhilarated. Maybe it was the armed men by her side, or maybe because she was at the beach, but Adele felt almost hopeful as their little group plowed across the dunes, then down and along the shoreline of the beach to the empress's court.

The heat of the day was cooled marginally by the light breeze that came off the water, closer to the shoreline. The sea lay almost still, sparkling in the afternoon sun like a mythical creature that had been put to sleep.

The empress's court was a collection of candy-colored tents erected at the midpoint between the water's edge and the thick green forest above it. A golden corridor of tents linked the two, so that one could walk completely shaded. Adele was distracted by the laughter and chatter of children playing in the shallow waters under a large pavilion. Its four poles stood in the water, and a palm-frond roof shaded the little children and their caretakers. It took all of Adele's self-control not to head in that direction first.

The sumptuous tents glistened in the sun, and the gentle tinkling of wind chimes reached the sweating Unisians.

"I hope they give us a drink before they send us packing back to our carriages," muttered QG Bear to Captain Lucky. He was silenced with a look from General Ohrig.

Adele tried to put the QG's lack of humor down to his wearing full ceremonial armor and leather pants in the sun, instead of a lack of faith in her diplomatic skills. Her stomach roiled, anyway.

Adele felt General Ohrig's light touch at her elbow. An armed guard of eight men had surreptitiously formed a barricade in front of the largest tent, closest to them. It had to be the royal tent, and home of the Empress. They stopped. Adele felt her pulse race.

*This is it!*

She wiped the sweat from her eyes to appraise the large, silent men in front of them. They were not weighed down with the heavy gold armor of her guards but instead wore light leather braces which crossed their chests. A gold cloth sarong, tied with a leather belt, reached to the knee. At the waist they carried two daggers, each with three prongs and a bone handle, like a small trident. Each guard wore a sword on his back.

The Sandarian guards were so large that Adele couldn't see behind them into the dim light of the tent, but she thought she caught a glimpse of someone familiar.

General Ohrig stepped in front of Adele and gestured Tilburn forward, but Adele barely heard the flowery and overly long speech as she concentrated on controlling her breathing. The chime-voices started to sing softly in her ears.

As soon as Tilburn had finished, the guard line in front of them broke neatly in two and stepped back smartly, four to each side. Ripenzo Shale stood between the lines, his arms extended in welcome, and a broad smile on his face.

"Welcome, everyone! Come in out of the sun, my friends," he said, beckoning them into the tent. "Why didn't you take the forest path? It's a lot cooler than coming across the beach all that way. You must be parched!"

"We had no idea there was another path, Mr. Shale," replied Tilburn acidly. "I'm afraid we had a little difficulty reading the map you gave us."

"Well, never mind all that now," said Ripenzo, waving away their troubles with his hands. "You are here now and need a drink. Please help yourselves."

It took a moment for Adele's eyes to adjust to the dim light of the shade, but soon she could see clearly just how luxuriously decorated the tent was. Hundreds of silk cushions were scattered on the soft carpets, while small low tables held scented candles and bowls of flowers. A servant stepped forward with a tray of sliced fruit and cups filled with icy-cold water. Adele gratefully took a cup and finished it quickly. She knew from experience that no one else in her party would drink until she had finished hers.

It felt so good to be in the shade again.

Ripenzo Shale edged around the group until he was at her shoulder. He smiled and leaned in close. He looked so cool and calm, his blond hair tousled and his clothes fresh and unwrinkled. He smelled like lemons. Adele felt like a sweaty heap of rubbish next to him.

"You gave me a bit of a shock at how fast your entourage traveled, Queen Adelena," he said with a grin. "Normally Unisians take days to prepare to leave their grand palace. We thought that, as queen, you would take weeks to get here."

"I travel light and fast when I have to, Ripenzo," replied Adele, and reached for another cup of water. "This matter is hugely important to me, and Unisia."

Ripenzo cocked his head to the side, his expression canny.

"Do you mean proving you are St. Lucidis, or getting more Fire Orchid stamens?"

"Both—they mean the same thing to me," Adele answered shortly, not liking his line of questioning or his knowing gaze.

"Didn't bring High Wizard Ohren, I see," said Ripenzo, but his casualness was too studied to be natural. "That *is* unusual."

Adele copied General Ohrig's earlier nonchalance and shrugged.

"I have decided the high wizard doesn't need to be involved in this matter. He has other things I need him to do back at the palace."

Ripenzo smiled and Adele got the distinct impression he didn't believe a word of it. Though why not, she had no idea.

"Empress Sanda'hani will see you now," he said, and proffered her his arm as if they were going to dance.

Adele waved back a concerned General Ohrig as he made to follow her and tried to swallow her heart back down into her chest. Ripenzo led them along the tent corridor closer to the shore. A low dais had been erected for the empress, facing the water.

Adele took several deep breaths and tried to prepare herself to meet a fellow queen. Ripenzo gave her arm a squeeze and then let go to bow deeply to the figure on the dais.

"Your Majesty, may I present the new queen of the kingdom of Unisia, Queen Adelena St. Lucidis."

He gave Adele a wink as she stepped forward, making her blush.

Why did he have to be so casual and friendly? This was a really important meeting.

A beautiful woman turned to stare at Adele.

Adele bit her lip to keep from squeaking in fright.

Before her sat a true queen. Empress Sanda'hani sat with a graceful and elegant dignity. She was tall and broad across the shoulders, which lent a steadfast quality to her regal bearing. She wore her black hair long and down, over the flowing robes that left her arms bare and accentuated her voluptuous curves. Her coffee-colored complexion made her sea-green eyes all the more striking as they stared at Adele out of a beautiful face. She didn't look happy.

"Rip, please go and entertain the children while I am occupied with Queen Adelena. They missed you while you were gone."

Adele followed the empress's sight line and saw that she had a clear view down to the children cavorting in the gentle wavelets. Adele quickly turned back to the empress.

"Your Majesty, it is wonderful to meet you." Adele gave a shallow curtsy and stepped on her dress.

"Please." Empress Sanda'hani waved away any formalities. "You have had a long journey from the kingdom; you must be tired, yes?"

The empress gestured at a bank of cushions on another dais similar to her own. Adele noted it was lower than the empress's and was surprised at herself for caring about that.

"Your Majesty," began Adele, praying her voice would stop shaking soon. "Thank you so much for inviting me here like this. It is very kind of you. I hope we can resolve the issues between our two nations today."

"Today!" replied the empress, raising a sharp eyebrow. "You would give us just one day to solve this matter?"

Adele went pale.

*Crap.* This wasn't going well, already.

She cleared her dry throat and suddenly really needed to pee.

"Of course, we can take as long as we need to," Adele croaked, forcing a smile.

Empress Sanda'hani was no longer looking at her but stared past Adele down to the water.

Adele heard the chime-voices start singing as she fought to retain her fragile self-control. Miserable, she felt like she had lost before she had even begun to play this ridiculous game of politics. She knew nothing about Unisia and even less about how things worked here in Sandar.

*I should never have come,* Adele thought morosely. *And Ohren should never have let me come here on my own. I'm going to ruin everything for everyone.*

Despite her despondency, Adele figured she could at least make her children more comfortable while she attempted to scrape her dignity off the sand.

"As a very new inhabitant of this world, may I say, Your Majesty, that this is the most beautiful beach I have ever seen. It is such a wonderful sight for my homesick eyes to see the ocean again. I thought we had left beaches behind when we were brought to Unisia."

The empress looked at Adele with new interest. "Yours was a coastal tribe?" she asked.

"In a way…" Adele agreed, smiling. "My children and I are never happier than when we are on a beach somewhere."

Adele looked back down to the water when a servant appeared as if from nowhere and whispered to the empress.

"Queen Adelena, you have brought your children here with you?" This time both the empress's eyebrows went up.

"Yes, all of them, and their pets," said Adele ruefully. "I'm sorry Your Majesty, but I hate to leave them for any length of time. They are still so young, and this world is still so new to all of us."

Empress Sanda'hani graced Adele with a radiant smile.

"Please," she said. "Let us bring your children from the caravans you arrived in. They must be tired from their long journey and, perhaps, would enjoy a swim, yes?"

"Your Majesty is very kind." Adele smiled, relieved she wouldn't have to ask to get her children now. She gave General Ohrig a wave and let him know it was fine to retrieve the children. Ohrig delegated the mission to Bear, who jogged away up the canopied path to the forest with several of the empress's servants.

"My man will show your people the way through the forest so they do not have to come over the sand as you did," said the empress.

"Yes, Ripenzo said there was another way, though his map wasn't quite as detailed as we would have liked."

The empress stopped smiling, and her eyes took on a distant gaze. "Indeed. He can be a bit of a trickster, that man."

Adele was served more chilled water and sweet fruit as they waited for her children to be brought over. The puppies were pulled along on leashes by Bear, who did not look at all happy with his dog-walking duties.

Adele could hear Aaron and Natalie well before she could see them, but little Stella had fallen asleep against Caitlin's shoulder by the time they reached their mother.

"Oh, such a sweet little baby," Empress Sanda'hani cooed quietly at the sleeping Stella, and gently wiped the damp curls off her hot little brow. Adele instinctively warmed to the empress.

Adele insisted that Natalie and Aaron greet Empress Sanda'hani respectfully before she allowed them to strip off their clothes and dash down to the water in their underpants. Caitlin and Seraphina trailed nervously behind them, reminding the children of all the sea monsters that might eat them.

Empress Sanda'hani smiled indulgently at the children's high spirits.

"You were right when you said your children have a great love of the ocean, Queen Adelena. Most kingdom-dwellers are afraid of its salty depths, but your children leap and play as my own do."

Adele smiled in acknowledgment of the intended compliment, watching proudly as her children fell in playing with the five Sandarian children, who looked to be around the same age as her own. Ripenzo Shale was leading a game with lots of splashing and Aaron and Natalie shrieked with joy.

It was not to be a day for business after all, as Empress Sanda'hani seemed as reluctant as Adele felt to sit down formally and discuss why the Unisian royal family was at their beachside court.

Adele was mystified, but relieved that she and Sanda'hani spoke of nothing consequential to their kingdoms for the entire afternoon. Instead, they discussed their children's births and infancies, and how Adele's were adjusting to their new life in Evendaar. As their mothers got to know each other, the children held sand castle competitions in the shade and swam in the clear green water. The younger members of her Queen's Guard were quick to strip off their armor and joined the children on the shore, while General Ohrig, Bear, and Owens remained within a cautious distance of Adele, prepared to act should they be needed.

Finally, at an invisible sign from the empress, the rest of her court emerged from the nearby jungle to join in the late-afternoon gathering. Then Adele and the children had a chance to meet the empress's four sisters and various other relatives as they wandered in under the tent. The empress had no husband that Adele had met, and she didn't know if it was too rude to ask the empress about her marital status, despite the fact that she had children.

Soon the afternoon merged into early evening, and a grand party was organized for the royal family and their entourage. Adele had felt awkward and uncomfortable in her big dress, and the empress had offered Adele one of the gauzy flowing gowns that the ladies of their court wore. When she returned from the wardrobe tent in a beautiful, diaphanous gown of ten different shades of pink, she almost skipped with joy. The freshwater bath had been no mean gift, either, after the stress and travel of the day.

As the sun dipped low on the horizon, dinner was arranged on long, low tables set up on carpets on the beach. Adele was thrilled to see grilled lobsters, prawns, and raw oysters served alongside fresh salads and fruit. The smell of barbecued seafood mixed with the scent of salt and hot sand made Adele feel as if she were home again.

The only black spot on the whole lovely afternoon was the righteous indignation of Tilburn, who wore his most scandalized expression for hours on end. The informality of the Sandarian court was appalling to him, and he gasped in horror when a barefoot Adele decided to go paddling with a naked Stella. Adele could only keep him busy unpacking the carriages and overseeing the care of the horses.

Adele's tired and happy children were put to bed with the Sandarian children in a large breezy tent close to the main column of tents. They slept on huge soft cushions with silk sheets as gentle breezes blew in the warmth that still radiated off the sand.

After a second cool bath and thorough hair washing, Adele dressed in another light gown, this time a blue one, to rejoin Sanda'hani for after-dinner drinks and, maybe, she thought, a more formal discussion.

But again Sanda'hani was in no mood for business, filling and refilling Adele's cup with more coconut rum than she could handle. Before she knew it, she'd had too much and was giggling like a fool as Ripenzo Shale's jokes became funnier and the candlelight glittered brighter than before. The evening then flashed by with lots of laughter and Adele accidentally knocking her drink into the general's lap, and then trying to help him clean it up, much to everyone's amusement.

The early hours of the morning found Adele sitting alone on a blanket on the beach, staring at the half-moon and the thousands upon thousands of stars spread across the night sky.

*Is Rainere is looking at the moon right now?* she thought blearily. *Does he love the beach as much as I do?*

Adele thought of Rainere and all at once a strange mixture of melancholy and adrenaline swept through her, making her hands shake.

She had promised to marry him!

He had asked and she had agreed, albeit slightly under duress.

"What have I done?" whispered Adele and hugged her knees close to her chest.

*Finally I truly fall in love, and he turns out to be a prince on an alien planet, and a social outcast! What are the odds of that? Ever?*

Despite knowing she loved him with all her heart, Adele just couldn't see putting a Marchant prince back on the throne as something anyone in Sandar or Unisia would want.

Anyone but Rainere.

Adele felt hot tears prick her eyes, and because she was slightly drunk and already morose, she started to think of her ex, Justin. She could never remember feeling the way she did about Rainere for Justin. Even in the early days of their romance, she had been very conscious of making a "choice" with Justin, and working to keep him interested in her. Always changing herself to meet his needs and his desires, despite her own.

*Justin was just too different from me,* she thought, sniffling. *Happier and so much more confident. He was always the wild man at the party. I was just happy to bask in his golden glow. God, I was so pathetic! I was just so desperate to mold myself to him and have the family I've always wanted the poor guy couldn't live up to my expectations. But now the children and I are stuck in this strange world in all kinds of danger and I cannot afford to make any more mistakes with our lives.*

*Rainere truly loves me and I need to do whatever I can to find my way back to him but on my own terms. I just think our marriage will be impossible.*

The idea, so clear now under the dark velvet sky, helped her tears to spill over.

*I love Rainere but without him here right now I'm the only person I can really trust. I have to be brave and clever and utterly unlike myself. The children need me. Rainere needs me…*

She thought of the beautiful lines of his face and the gentle pulse at his neck that was so delicious to kiss. She felt warm inside and wiped at the tears that fell from her eyes.

Adele felt the hard claws of an addiction forming, and she sighed, wincing in pain at the deep craving for his touch again. One thing was certain. If Rainere wanted out of their secret relationship, then he would have to leave her first.

*Stop it!* she admonished herself as she felt her cheeks blush in the dark. *I should be focusing on tomorrow and the Ceremony of the Blood. Who knows what's going to happen then.*

Though she still felt a complete fraud, she was anxious to pass this test…failure was just too awful to contemplate.

Resolved, Adele staggered only slightly as she made her way back up the beach to the tent where her children gently snored, and put herself to bed. She slept soundly for the first time in days.

Unseen in the shadows, General Ohrig waited until the queen was safely tucked away before swapping shifts with Captain Lucky.

"What a day, eh, General?" whispered Lucky. "I cannot believe the way our queen has won over the Sandarians. It looks like she really will pull all this off."

Ohrig frowned. "She certainly is unconventional, but the queen has done much to make us proud today. Despite the fact she can't hold her liquor for pennies. But if she doesn't pass this test tomorrow for whatever reason…"

"We'll have to fight our way out, I guess," whispered Lucky even more quietly.

"Women and children out first," agreed Ohrig grimly. He clapped Lucky on the shoulder.

"Night, Captain."

"Night, General."

# CHAPTER FORTY

## "The Truth About the Past"

As Ohren strode down the corridor to his chambers, his thoughts weighed heavily on his mind.

The queen and her family would have arrived in Sandar by now if the journey had gone well.

For the five days since the royal family had left the Golden Palace, Ohren had not slept a wink. The guilt of letting Adele go off into Sandar, with only her Queen's Guard to protect her, was eating away at him. *If the worst should happen and the Sandarians became hostile, or if she should fail to fulfill the prophecy...*had he been wrong to stay away entirely?

The questions spun around his head but no answers were found.

*I did what I had to with the knowledge I was given,* he told himself for the umpteenth time, trying to assuage his screaming conscience. *The prophecy will protect her if she can succeed.*

But the faces of Natalie, Aaron, and the tiny Stella lingered in his mind. He had no idea what methods of execution the Sandarians favored...had he brought them all home to Unisia only to send them to their deaths barely a month later?

Ohren was distracted by a sharp odor outside his laboratory door. The door was slightly ajar and the smell was coming from inside.

He cursed himself. He hadn't been inside his lab all week. He must have left out food or one of his potion experiments which, by the stench, had definitely gone bad.

As Ohren touched his hand to the door handle, a little black form streaked past his leg, making him curse out loud.

*Damn that cat of Gorrik's!* thought Ohren crossly. *It gets into the strangest places.*

As the cat sprinted off down the hallway, Ohren saw that it carried something dark in its mouth.

Disgusting animal! It was probably attracted by the rotten smell.

Ohren went to push the door open but a shout made him turn. A young man was running toward him down the corridor. Ohren watched curiously as the boy almost tripped on the little cat, while he waved and shouted to get Ohren's attention.

"High Wizard! High Wizard Ohren!"

"What now?" muttered Ohren as the boy came to a stop in front of him. He was no more than sixteen, and his hair flopped into his eyes as he bent over to regain his breath.

"High...Wizard...Ohren," gasped the boy. "I was...sent to...fetch you...Master Gorrik...sir...needs..."

"Spit it out, boy," snapped Ohren unkindly as he took in the boy's red cheeks and the Accadaemia robe that hung off his shoulders. Had he run all the way from the University? That was at least five miles away, outside of town.

The boy straightened up and valiantly tried to control his panting.

"Master Gorrik sent me to tell the High Wizard Ohren that his presence is immediately required at the Accadaemia...sir."

Ohren noted the badge on the front of the boy's robe. He was a first-year apprentice wizard. Ohren's eyes narrowed. If this was Gorrik trying to trick him into coming in to teach the apprentices, he was much too busy for this.

"What's your name, boy?"

"Orlando, sir—er...High Wizard," stammered the boy, quailing under Ohren's stare.

"Orlando, did Master Gorrik say what he needed from me specifically?" asked Ohren, in a tone that suggested it better be something important.

His eyes were starting to water from the smell from his laboratory. No doubt, this was going to take days to clean out.

The boy nodded. "He said to tell you that 'the prophecy has turned, and for the love of all that's holy you must come now'."

Ohren felt the blood drain out of his face.

It was just about the worst news he could have heard.

Without another word, Ohren turned and fled down the corridor in the same direction the cat had gone. He had another way to get to the University, which would only take a few minutes. Turning a corner into a dead-end corridor, Ohren took a moment to check that he was alone before he leaped into an almost-invisible doorway. The light sparkled greenly as he passed through.

Ohren pushed ahead blindly in the darkness, shuddering as the portal deposited him into Gorrik's office at the University. The old man sat at his desk, staring into the distance and twisting an old amulet he wore around his neck. When he saw Ohren panting and pale before him, he slipped it back into his robes and stood up.

"What is it?" asked Ohren, but the guilt in his eyes betrayed him.

Gorrik's normally mild expression was stony. His frown brought his wrinkled brow so low it almost covered his eyes entirely.

"Come with me."

The two men made their way down to the basement rooms beneath the enormous Accadaemia building in silence. Ohren followed a step or two behind the older man despite Gorrik's slow and shuffling pace. As they descended deeper into the bowels of the Accadaemia, it became cooler and a smell of damp pervaded the air. They had left the more populated corridors far behind and saw no one else as Gorrik led Ohren down yet another steep staircase of old and mold-covered stone. Ohren's gut constricted painfully. He had prayed so hard that this day would never come. He stared at the back of his old teacher's head as Gorrik slowly and carefully led them down to the Chamber of the Sacred Fire.

A guard rested before the door of the Chamber, but stood to attention when he saw Gorrik. Ohren noticed the guard's glassy-eyed stare. He'd been hypnotized. Ohren was disturbed, but not surprised, by Gorrik's decision. Hypnotized guards could tell no one of what they saw or heard on duty.

"Don't let anyone else but myself and High Wizard Ohren into this room," said Gorrik in a loud, clear voice.

"Yes, master." The man nodded, his voice wooden, and stepped aside to let the two men enter.

"So, Ohren…" began Gorrik as Ohren reluctantly entered the chamber. Both men stared at the large crucible in the center of the room where Adelena's blood burned over the glowing flames of the Sacred Fire. The high wizard groaned.

"Do you have something to tell me?" Gorrik asked, his tone a mixture of steel, fear, and disappointment.

Ohren swallowed. "Gorrik, I can explain…it was very complicated at the time…"

Both men stared at the dancing smoke of the queen's blood, which up until very recently, had burned a bright gold. Now…now an acid-green cloud twirled and curled above the crucible.

"You have put a Marchant on the throne," whispered Gorrik, horrified. "And worse still, she is a Half-Blood."

Ohren made a sound somewhere between a cough and a whimper.

"You stupid boy." Gorrik turned to face Ohren, and in his eyes, Ohren saw every one of his old friend's five hundred and eighty-odd years of life.

Ohren couldn't stand to look at his old teacher and dearest friend, and his eyes were inexorably drawn back to the dancing green smoke of Adele's blood.

"We only had enough power to send one child across. The baby we sent was still the King's daughter, just…just to another woman…"

"A Marchant of The Blood?" interrupted Gorrik. "Goddess help us all, who was she?"

Ohren flinched at the horror in Gorrik's tone.

"No one in the Golden Palace Court but me knew King Octavius was having an affair with Princess Rainella …"

"Rainella? Prince Rainere's mother?" groaned Gorrik. "Do you mean…?"

Ohren nodded miserably. "Adelena is half-sister to the reigning Marchant prince."

Gorrik paled in the dim light of the chamber as he suddenly remembered the gossip the North Wind has whispered in his ear so recently.

"But Ohren, do you know what you have done, letting the prince into the palace with her here? They have met, they have…been together."

Ohren looked confused. "But that's impossible!"

"Nothing is impossible when it comes to Marchants, Ohren. Didn't you learn enough about that when you were a boy?" Gorrik snapped. Ohren had no business knowing how Gorrik knew about the liaison between Adelena and Prince Rainere. Listening to the Wind speak was a talent known only to his people, and few others. Ohren wasn't the only person with secrets to keep.

"I was young and loyal to my king," whispered Ohren, sounding like a much younger man, ashamed and unsteady as the mistakes of his past were laid before him in the green glow of Adele's blood.

"You were in love with a Marchant, too, as I recall," said Gorrik with a hard look at the wizard.

Ohren flinched away from Gorrik and pulled himself over to a wooden bench at the side of the chamber, where he sat down and held his head in hands, his elbows on his knees. Eventually he dropped his hands, but his head stayed low.

Gorrik moved to sit beside Ohren, resting his old, gnarled hand on the wizard's back.

"Tell me," he said softly.

"When I was still working for you as a student teacher at the Accadaemia, King Octavius called on me for a secret mission to help curb the civil unrest we all knew was brewing in the kingdom. He told me he had intelligence that the Marchant clans were organizing a rebellion. He knew...about me...and wanted me to infiltrate their ranks, trading on my reputation and the St. Lucidis name. He said that the peace of the kingdom relied on the information I could get him, so he could quash the rebellion before it began. I knew he had been close to the royal Marchant clan, and that they had entertained him several times. It was common knowledge that he experimented with Dark Magic himself, but I had no idea that he was having an affair with Princess Rainella until after she was with child. Octavius pleaded with me to send the baby away when the time came...he knew it was too dangerous to leave the baby in Unisia as a Half-Blood. The queen, Olivia was pregnant at the same time, and despite my begging her not to, she said she wanted to keep this child. Octavius promised me that he would leave Rainella to stand by Olivia and stay as father to her child if I did this thing for him. I believed he really loved Rainella, much more than he ever did Olivia...he was desperate to save Rainella from the wrath of the Eldars...if they found out that a Half-Blood had been born, they would have killed everyone, both Rainella and Octavius, and the baby as well. Then Olivia would have had to rule alone, and then she would have been at the mercy of those vicious sons of hers..."

Ohren took a deep breath and slowly let it out. He slumped back against the damp stone of the wall.

"I only did what I did to protect my king, and to keep the kingdom in the hands of the royal line of St. Lucidis. I didn't know that Olivia was going to die after her baby was born. I thought I was protecting her as well...Prince Rainold told me how to open the portal, and gave me The Blood I needed for it..."

"Good Goddess, Prince Rainold knew about his wife and the King!" Gorrik shook his head at the shambles Ohren had been embroiled in. "But what of your sister's child, Ohren? What happened to Queen Olivia's baby?"

"It could not have been more perfect timing," said Ohren, his voice heavy with regret. "The babies were born within minutes of each other. With the coup going on in the palace, I could slip away and take the baby girl Prince Rainold brought me through the portal in the King's own apartment and then straight to the ceremony we were performing downstairs..."

"What did you do with Olivia's daughter?" insisted Gorrik, his voice growing louder as Ohren's grew quieter.

"I gave the baby...Olivia had had a son...I gave him to Prince Rainold to give to the Eldars...he said they somehow knew that a Half-Blood had been born, and the prince told me that if they were given the child immediately then he could convince them not to kill the baby as he could prove that The Blood had skipped a generation, like it sometimes could. Then the child would be no threat to them. He promised me because the baby was pure St. Lucidis it would work and Olivia's son would be safe..." His voice trailed off.

"And you believed him? You fool, Ohren. That baby boy was the only true heir to the St. Lucidis throne, and you committed him to death the minute you handed him to Prince Rainold!" Gorrik was furious. "So was it the Eldars who killed Princess Rainella and King Octavius in the end, anyway?"

Ohren closed his eyes against the pain of the memories. The coup had been horrific. *So much blood shed, the walls spattered with gore, and dead bodies in every room.* But the St. Lucidis family had fought with more savagery and ruthlessness than any other family. Olivia's sons had held the line, and St. Lucidis had retained the throne, albeit with no one of the royal line left to sit on it.

"I didn't even know when the Eldars entered the Golden Palace. I was down in the lowest chamber sending the baby away, along with you and all the other wizards. No one was protecting Octavius…none of us who could have helped him were there when they came."

A fire burned in Ohren's eyes as he stared into the past.

"I was the one who found him. He had choked to death on his own blood. He was lying next to my sister…Olivia." Ohren's voice broke as he unburdened his heavy conscience.

He blinked and seemed to recover himself somewhat.

"Rainella had died in childbirth, I was told, and Rai—Prince Rainold was forced into an Early Death."

"Because he was already immortal by then, of course." Gorrik paused, piecing together his own memories of the time and what Ohren had just told him now. "So little Prince Rainere was left an orphan and the sole surviving member of The Blood."

"His father the prince made me swear, on his death bed, to protect his son with my life and give him whatever aid I could against the Eldars." Ohren wore an odd expression and his tone was almost jealous. "He was so worried that they would seek revenge on him for allowing Princess Rainella to betray their family with a St. Lucidis man. He was so sure that they would come after his true son, Rainere."

Gorrik gave Ohren a sharp look.

"But I would not help the boy regain political power," added Ohren hurriedly. "The prince abstains from taking the Gift of Life since he became immortal, and insists I provide him with the Blue Tonic every few years. It's the only thing I have ever really done for him. Of course it will kill him eventually." He shrugged. "But it's his choice, not mine. I'm just fulfilling my oath to his father."

"He didn't look close to death when I saw him in the hallway the other day," muttered Gorrik, pinching his bottom lip between two fingers. "Maybe he has changed his tastes."

The two men sat in silence, one steeped in his memories of the past and other furiously trying to fathom the future.

"I'm so glad that your sister died in childbirth so that she never had a chance to learn of your betrayal, Ohren," said Gorrik quietly, and the bitterness in his tone was unmistakable.

"I held her at the end, you know," whispered Ohren. "I held her in my arms as she lay bleeding out on that glass bed. She was so fierce, so fierce right until the end. I promised her the baby would be safe…but when she died I just didn't care anymore. The baby was the one who had killed her. It was just another of her wretched sons who had stolen my beautiful girl's life away. I didn't ever want to see it again."

Ohren slumped against the wall. The grief of his sister's death was still raw after a hundred years. Gorrik looked down on his friend and his expression softened. The boy was still suffering more than anyone for his actions.

Gorrik gave Ohren's shoulder a little shake.

"Come on, we need to leave. There is much to be done, and there is nothing more we can learn from Adelena's blood now."

Ohren followed Gorrik out of the chamber, leaving the hypnotized guard in front of the door.

As they walked slowly up the stairs, Ohren waited until Gorrik brought up the dark matter now at hand.

"Poor Adelena…those poor children." Gorrik shook his head sadly. "You have sentenced the whole royal family to death now. If only you had told me the truth before you made the decision to follow the prophecy like a child."

"But no, that's not true. Or at least, it doesn't have to be the truth," insisted Ohren much more positively than perhaps the situation warranted. "Her blood burns gold first, and it took almost two weeks before it turned green. Adele and the children will be long gone from Sandar before it has a chance to change. That means the St. Lucidis part of her nature is stronger than the Marchant part. Besides, the Sandarian Mage couldn't see any hint of Marchant about the queen when he did his voodoo nonsense at the meeting."

Ohren attempted a smile.

"The queen also has the Prophecy of the End of the World to protect her. As long as she succeeds in her task and conquers her 'fear of the dark,' the prophecy about her goes on…and Unisia is saved from the days of darkness."

"I know the prophecy," snapped Gorrik. "But I also thought I knew you, Ohren, and you've just reminded me how blind we can be even when something, or someone, hides in plain sight. You lied to me, Ohren, even when you must have known the queen's true heritage would be found out."

"I had only hoped it had skipped a generation…King Octavius's magic had been so strong, I had thought perhaps it would be dominant and would protect her…" Ohren protested weakly but he couldn't even convince himself.

The two men fell silent again as they reached the more populated part of the University. When they entered Gorrik's office, Ohren headed straight for the invisible portal beside the bookcase at the back of the room, but he hesitated before stepping through. He didn't quite turn, but spoke over his shoulder, not willing to catch Gorrik's eye again.

"Gorrik, what I did…it was only ever for the love of my King and love for my family. In the coup, the Carparells would have killed us all…they would never have allowed Olivia's child to live, anyway."

"What you did activated an ancient prophecy and cursed us all," sighed Gorrik, too tired or disappointed to be angry anymore. "When I thought it was for Olivia's child, I could forgive you for that, Ohren. That beautiful woman deserved to have her child survive us all. But in your blind ignorance, you made the Hidden Child a Half-Blood Marchant, and now she is sitting on our throne. For that I will never forgive you."

Ohren nodded, accepting the weight of his responsibility. He did not expect anything other than Gorrik's fury for what he had condemned the kingdom to through his actions, well intentioned though they had been.

The high wizard stepped through the portal and out into the dark corridor of the Golden Palace again, just around the corner from his chambers.

Standing in the dark, he took a moment to let his anguish show. Silently, he moaned and rubbed his face. His beard tangled in his heavy gold rings and his breath caught hard as he swallowed down on a sob. He couldn't remember the last time he had actually cried, but it must have been decades ago. Obviously, he was out of practice. He put his hands against his chest where the sobs boiled and burned him, too thick to be released.

He had to find his brother. Orestes needed to be told that Gorrik now knew what they had done one hundred and forty-five years ago. Orestes would be furious and fearful that their awful secret had been discovered, but as always, he was blameless. Orestes had only ever been following his brother's lead, trying to protect Ohren from his own bravery and stupidity.

A memory of holding the baby princess swam before his eyes. She had been so red and so quiet. Her body had still been covered in the waxy white and blood of Rainella's womb. Olivia's baby had screamed lustily as Ohren had wrapped him, so much bigger and stronger than the King's daughter. He hadn't looked at the boy-child again when he had handed it to the prince. But before he had put her in the portal, Ohren had named the baby: "Olivia Adelena Serena St.

Lucidis," blessing her with the name of his beloved sister and fastening the name charm to her head with a kiss.

Now all his betrayals and lies had been for naught, as he had probably sentenced her and her children to death at the hands of the Sandarian Court. No matter what he told Gorrik, he couldn't have faith that the prophecy would guide her even though it continued far past this chapter. If only he could be with her now…

Ohren wandered up to his laboratory, but the rotten smell still leaking out sickened him. He pulled the door shut and kept on walking. He had to find his brother before anything else went wrong.

# CHAPTER FORTY-ONE

## "The Mage and the Cave"

The stench really was incredible.

Brimstone.

Adele tried to breathe through her mouth, but the urge to gag was getting stronger.

She looked over the charcoal gray of the bizarre landscape in front of her. Adele jumped in fright as another rumble beneath the surface shook the fragile crust of volcanic soil she was standing on. She wiped away the sweat on her forehead with the back of her hand. The smell was making her dizzy, and she could barely hear Ripenzo Shale's chatter over the chime-voices ringing softly but constantly in her ears. It was putting her on edge thinking she might need to use her magic soon.

*My magic,* Adele silently reminded herself, which had only ever been used to subdue and play with Rainere in bed. *Well, as long as the person attacking me is naked and lying down, everything should be just peachy!*

Nevertheless, she clutched at the hope that she could cause enough pain to be able to escape. Her eyes sought out the Mage. He was the only person who really scared her here in Sandar.

The Mage was already far away, hopping across the lava field, avoiding the columns of steam and hot ash that came bursting out of the tiny geysers intermittently, his mohawk bobbing and flashing in the late-afternoon sun.

She really should keep up with him. Adele almost groaned aloud thinking how much she wanted this day to be over. After waking late to the bright midmorning sun, and a horrible hangover, Adele had had nothing but coconut water to drink all day. Apparently, it was to purify herself for the ceremony, but she was queasy enough not to mind at all. Ripenzo Shale had had a hard time convincing General Ohrig that only he and the Mage would accompany Adele to the caves. General Ohrig had tried to insist on coming himself, but the Mage was adamant no one else should come; and as the argument persisted long into the day, Adele made the executive decision to just get the whole business over with and acquiesce to the Sandarians' wishes. Apparently, the Mage's dislike of Unisian wizards crossed over to a dislike of Unisian military personnel as well.

Adele cursed her bad luck as, now, she had to travel over these dangerous lava fields with the sun sinking in the sky, and the idea of a night spent camping with the Mage and Ripenzo Shale after the ceremony. They would have to wait for morning to travel back to the Sandarian court. Hence her hope that subduing a naked attacker might not be so fanciful.

Adele swore as she tripped and stumbled badly. A warm arm caught her around the shoulders.

"Easy there, Your Majesty," cautioned Ripenzo Shale, pulling her against his chest until she was back on proper footing. "This is tricky ground if you don't watch your feet."

"That's the understatement of the year!" muttered Adele as she shrugged off his arm, embarrassed.

Ripenzo laughed his easy laugh. The sound was so incongruous, given Adele's mood.

She tripped again and bit down on her lip, hard. The pain almost made her burst into tears, but she refused to cry in front of Ripenzo and that awful Mage, if he ever looked back. No sooner had Adele made her resolution than she fell again, this time bashing her knee on a sharp rock and tearing the delicate fabric of her gauzy dress.

*Dammit!*

Adele sucked her bottom lip and tasted blood.

Suddenly, it was all too much.

Giving up, Adele sat down on a ledge to examine her knee properly. When she saw the amount of blood oozing down her leg, her eyes automatically filled with hot tears. She had a terrible, adolescent urge to throw her hands in the air and trudge back to the court of Sandar and her children, leaving that stupid Mage high and dry. This was just all too horrible. She had no idea what was going to happen to her in some dark Holy Cave with that Mage, and now she had blood everywhere.

Ripenzo Shale knelt in front of her, resting his hand on her shoulder. Adele dropped her head to hide her wet eyes.

"Oh, that looks nasty," he said with a sympathetic grimace. "I'll wrap it for you now, but we should get the Mage to fix it up for you properly at the caves."

Ripenzo yanked his shirt out of his pants and, with a sharp pull, ripped a strip off the bottom. With gentle hands, he wiped the cut and then wrapped it firmly with the cloth. Adele couldn't look at him until she had control of herself again, which didn't seem to be coming easily. She winced with embarrassment as a tear slipped off her cheek and dropped onto his hand.

Ripenzo looked up in surprise. He pulled Adele's chin up with a bloodstained finger.

"Hey! Hey, it's all right, Queen Adelena. Look at me; it's going to be all right."

His tone was odd, too intimate somehow. Adele wanted to but she couldn't look away from him.

"It's not going to be as bad as you think, I promise." Ripenzo smiled and his blue-eyed gaze held hers. He was too close. Adele could see his lips moving toward hers.

She blinked and pulled back.

"Don't!" she said sharply.

Ripenzo sat back on his heels, not all perturbed. His smile was so understanding and kind that Adele instantly felt like a jerk. Maybe he hadn't been about to kiss her?

Right now, Ripenzo Shale was as close as she had to a friend out on this lava field. She should be nicer to him. He was only trying to help her.

"I'm sorry to snap," said Adele, wiping away the rest of her tears with the back of her hand. "I'm not myself today…and this knee really hurts." She forced a smile. "I'll be okay, though, thank you for wrapping it."

"You are welcome," said Ripenzo as he got up and pulled Adele to her feet. "I don't want to be too forward, but I honestly think it might be a good idea if you would hold my hand right now, if that's all right with you? We will be heading downhill soon and the way gets a bit treacherous if you don't know where you're going. The sun is sinking too, so we'll lose our light."

Adele grasped Ripenzo's hand firmly in her own. She tried to ignore the shiver that wanted to wriggle down her spine. The chime-voices shrieked once and then went blessedly silent.

Adele sighed in relief. *Finally*. They had been giving her a headache.

"Let's go." She smiled at Ripenzo and was determined not to notice how beautiful his indigo-blue eyes were.

As they walked, Adele became uncomfortable with the silence between them. It just felt awkward, not speaking to someone while you were holding their hand, more romantic somehow.

"How long have you been with the Sandarians?" Adele asked just to make conversation.

"What makes you think I'm not a Sandarian myself?" Ripenzo replied with a quick glance over his shoulder as Adele paused to struggle over a pile of loose stones.

"Just—ow—because you look and sound nothing like them," she said bluntly and winced as she managed to kick the big toe of her good leg.

"Don't I?" answered Ripenzo, but his tone was guarded.

Adele worried that she'd offended him. "I'm sorry if you are Sandarian, too; I just wondered, that's all…"

"I've been with the Sandarians ever since Empress Sanda'hani rescued me from slave traders off the Wild Coast, north of here." He glanced back again but too quickly for Adele to read his expression. "That was five years ago."

"Oh, really! I didn't know there were slave traders in the kingdom," she said, shocked.

"The Wild Coast is *not* the kingdom," said Ripenzo. "And the slave trade runs out of other nations."

"How did the empress rescue you?"

Ripenzo shrugged. "She bought me."

That shut Adele up.

Everything she had thought about Empress Sanda'hani was suddenly thrown into doubt. The empress had slaves? The very idea made Adele sick…and the smell of brimstone almost pushed her over the edge.

"You are her slave?" Adele couldn't keep the disapproval out of her voice.

Ripenzo Shale threw back his head and laughed, his golden hair glinting in the last rays of the setting sun.

"I've been in worse prisons," he said, chuckling. "Though technically you could say that I am a slave to love now."

He waggled his eyebrows suggestively and Adele couldn't help but smile at the silliness of the gesture.

"So you and the empress are together…like a couple," Adele asked, just to be clear.

Ripenzo agreed with an open grin. "A couple…of lovers."

Adele's smile spilled over into a giggle. Ripenzo gave her a cheeky wink and joined in with a chuckle of his own.

*How did he do that?* He made her feel so comfortable after she had been so frightened just a minute ago. She gave his hand a squeeze before she could stop herself.

"I could never be her official escort, but we have a wonderful arrangement, if you know what I mean?"

Adele rolled her eyes at his comic leer.

"I know what you mean, really…I understand," she said with a smile.

They descended the last bit of the hillside in silence, as it was tricky to negotiate the slipping shale in the growing darkness. Adele managed to make it to the entrance to the caves without further mishap, though her knee throbbed horribly.

By the time they got there, the cave mouth had been lit by at least a dozen tiki torches which sparked and smoked with a pungent aroma. Adele coughed and peered into the cave, but it was too deep to see the back of it.

"Is he in there?" she asked, her eyes searching for the Mage. Suddenly, her heart started beating erratically again.

"He'll be in there, probably in the third chamber, where all the important ceremonies are held," answered Ripenzo.

Though it still felt weird to hold hands with a man she barely knew, Adele didn't want to let go.

"Have you been in that chamber?" she asked, looking at Ripenzo for reassurance.

Shale nodded and his eyes reflected the firelight of the torches in an odd way. They flashed at her like a cat's. His expression was somber.

"Yes, but it won't help you to speak of it now," he said quietly.

He suddenly smiled and became normal again.

"Go, go, Queen Adelena," he urged her with a friendly shove. "Get it over with and you can be out here, eating dinner, in a few minutes. I make a mean pineapple stew, you know." He rattled the backpack he carried in a cheerful way. "It really won't be as bad as you think it will. I promise."

Reluctantly Adele let go of his large hand and clutched her two smaller ones together in front of her chest.

*What I really need here is Rainere, or Ohren*, she thought as she slowly entered the smoky dimness of the cave. *I do not belong here!*

Adele glanced over her shoulder to check if Ripenzo really was going to wait for her, and he gave her an encouraging smile. The second time she glanced back, he laughed.

"Go on, Queen Adelena, I promised to wait and I'll wait."

"Promise you'll come running in if you hear me scream, too?" asked Adele making a lame play for humor.

Ripenzo Shale cocked his head to the side, his expression frozen for just a moment.

"I promise I will come running in if I hear you scream," he said formally.

Feeling slightly more secure despite the weirdness of her situation, Adele walked forward through the cave to the tunnel she could now see at the back.

The cave itself appeared to be formed by an ancient lava flow. The walls were all black and glittered with tiny silica crystals. The floor was natural earth, dry and sandy. Adele left the first cave and entered a pitch-black tunnel with a bright light at the end of it. Adele had the most disconcerting feeling of walking into a television screen as the square of light at the end of the tunnel got closer and closer before it turned into a rough-hewn doorway. Adele was reluctant to step through despite the creepiness of the tunnel, only because she couldn't find the source of the light in the cavern. The air just seemed to glow of its own accord. The chime-voices started tinkling in her ears, and Adele's breathing ratcheted up to just-below-panic pace.

There was strong magic here and it felt...dangerous. Adele hugged the wall as she traced her way across the cave to the entrance to the third chamber. Thankfully, there was no tunnel, and the light was provided by a blazing fire set up just off-center in a shallow pit in the floor.

Despite being so close to the lava fields, the cave was cold, and Adele instinctively moved toward the fire. She stopped when she saw the Mage rise up from behind the flames like a skinny ghoul.

He had taken his shirt off, and she tried not to stare at his knobbly frame, covered with all its ugly scars and primitive jewelry.

The Mage gestured for Adele to sit next to him and went back to preparing the bowls of ingredients he had in front of him for the ceremony.

Adele slowly sank down in the sand next to the Mage but not too close. Her sore knee protested the movement, and she sat with an awkward thump.

The Mage erected a metal stand over the fire and didn't seem to notice as the flames licked at his hands. The stand had three long metal legs spiking out from a triangle. At each point of the triangle was a circle of wire to hold a small bowl, one for each of the bowls the Mage was preparing. He poured what looked like salt from a little bag at his waist into the last bowl. The other two had a handful of little twigs and leaves in them. One was left empty.

This didn't look too bad so far. The scariest thing in the room was the expression on the Mage's face. He had a look of such fierce concentration that despite her desperate curiosity about her part in this ceremony, Adele was afraid to interrupt him with any questions. He placed all the bowls into their little resting places above the fire, and almost immediately Adele was reminded of Sunday roasts as the smell of toasting rosemary and sage filled the air.

The Mage took a fourth bowl and wiped the rim of it with his saliva. Adele wrinkled her nose at the sight of his gray tongue. It looked sickly and diseased. The Mage then carefully placed the last bowl in the center of the triangle, in its own little circle. Adele heard a hiss as the saliva steamed a little.

The chime-voices in her ears whispered a clear word of command.

The Mage leaned across and grabbed Adele's wrist, yanking her arm over the fire and holding her wrist over the middle bowl. Adele gasped as she saw the black stone knife in his other hand.

He was going to do it now.

Adele steeled herself for the pain but the slice was swift and cold. It was only when she saw her blood dripping into the bowl that a whimper escaped her. The Mage held her fast, his fingers tight around her wrist. Soon the bottom of the bowl was covered as her blood oozed and dripped out of her. Adele began to feel lightheaded and nauseous.

*Surely, the Mage had enough blood now?*

Her sleeve began to smoke, and her body, held too close to the fire, was beginning to burn.

Adele whimpered again and tried to pull her wrist back but the Mage held it in a viselike grip.

The chime-voices shouted the same word of command.

Adele looked up at the Mage from her bleeding wrist, and he grinned and bared his blackened teeth with their chipped and broken stumps.

Adele looked away and was horrified to see the Mage now had an erection poking out of his low-slung pants.

Revolted, Adele tried to pull away more strongly. The Mage was grunting excitedly now and pointed at the fire with his knife. Adele looked at the smoke of her blood that floated up to curl about her slowly dripping wrist.

*Wait. Wasn't it supposed to be gold smoke? Isn't that what Ohren had said?*

But as Adele watched the green smoke twirl and dance above the bowl, she felt ill. The Mage had done something to her! He had tainted her blood with his disgusting saliva, and had changed the color. That had to be it!

Adele watched as the acid-green smoke separated into three tendrils and floated out over the burning herbs and salt.

This wasn't just a Ceremony of the Blood, this was a spell. Adele could see the smoke transforming into the sparkling shimmers that Rainere's magic always caused.

A movement to her left made her look back at the Mage. She fell back in shock, finally pulling her hand free, as he stood over her with his leering grin and the black stone knife held high over his head...she gasped as he plunged it down toward her heart.

The word of command roared out of Adele, burning her throat like liquid fire. She instinctively put her hands up to push the Mage away, but her hands stuck fast to his skinny chest and he gasped his hot foul breath into her face as he fell on her.

With a shriek, Adele shoved the Mage onto his back and scrambled astride him as he shook and shuddered beneath her.

The command escaped her lips over and over, like a prayer, as she pushed her magic down into the man who had just tried to kill her. Adele was too panicked to observe the life slowly leaching out of his body...as his skin became gray and papery...as his eyes widened and bulged, looking up at her in agony…as he opened his mouth to gasp out his last breath.

Suddenly, he was still.

Adele could feel her magic blasting away into a body that no longer held a soul. It was like dropping rocks down a dry well.

Trembling all over, Adele pushed herself off the dead Mage and crawled away from him as far as her shaking limbs would take her. When she hit a wall, she pushed her back against it and pulled her knees up to her chest. She rocked and shuddered trying to calm herself. Occasionally she whispered the word of command that had taken the life of the Mage, but it only made her jump as the energy shot through her.

*What have I done?* thought Adele, disturbed beyond panic. *I've killed a man. A Mage. I'm a murderer! How could I do that? How could I kill somebody? Why aren't I dead?*

A noise at the doorway distracted her and she froze when she saw Ripenzo Shale step slowly into the cavern. Adele took in his look of fear and shock. She surveyed the cave with his eyes. The fire still burned brightly and her blood smoked, sending writhing tendrils of green up into the air above the bowls of blackened herbs and glowing salt.

The Mage was laid out like a shriveled skeleton, the black stone knife still clutched in his left hand, the blade glinting with her blood. He looked like one of the mummies of ancient Egypt with only its skin and bones preserved.

*Oh, sweet Christ.* What was Ripenzo going to do? Maybe he would try to kill her, too?

Adele pushed herself to her feet and leaned back against the wall for support. She could still feel the energy of the command zapping and surging through her limbs, giving her a weird feeling of strength, despite her shaking legs. She watched Ripenzo Shale warily as he slowly approached the fire and then stepped around it to the corpse of the Mage. Leaning over the body, he looked up at her.

"I heard you screaming so I came running," he said calmly. "Like I promised I would."

He eyed her hands, which she held out before her, defensively, in case he ran at her.

Ripenzo settled on his haunches by the fire.

"Do you want to tell me what happened here?"

Adele cleared her throat. It still burned horribly from the word of command.

"This wasn't a Blood Ceremony," she croaked. "He was casting a spell. I don't know what it was for…but all I know is he did something to my blood so it didn't turn gold, but see"—she pointed—"the smoke is green now."

Ripenzo smiled and the sight of it eased a bit of the fear in Adele's chest.

"Then you told him to lie down and go to sleep while you screamed for me?"

Adele took a step away from her defensive position against the wall, and toward Ripenzo.

"Your wrist, it's bleeding," he said, his expression concerned. "I can take care of that for you."

Ripenzo's kindness took her fear of him away, and Adele made her way to the fire and slumped to the side of it, as far from the Mage as she could get. Ripenzo's hands were cool on her hot skin.

*I hope I don't have an infection from that disgusting knife*, she thought as she realized she was sweating. She shuddered as she caught sight of it, still being held aloft by the dead Mage.

Ripenzo handled her calmly and carefully, keeping his movements slow and gentle so as not to startle her. Adele was embarrassed. She knew how she must look to him.

"What did you do to the Mage?" Ripenzo asked her quietly as he tied the end of a hastily made shirt-bandage.

Adele shook her head. The too-fresh memories flashed like visions in front of her eyes.

"He had that knife…he was smiling at me…his, thing, was up…I thought he was going to kill me, or rape me, or both."

"But you stopped him," pressed Ripenzo gently. "How?"

"I don't know," whispered Adele and shook her head to dislodge the memory. "I have a certain magic inside me…and when he came at me…I just felt what I had to do…the chime-voices told me…I just felt what I had to do. I couldn't stop until he was dead…I just couldn't stop."

Ripenzo Shale nodded and smiled as if she'd given him a perfectly coherent and reasonable explanation. He squeezed her shoulder in a friendly way and moved to crouch next to the Mage. He started running his hands over the body and going through the few pockets the Mage had on his belt and pants.

"What are you doing?" asked Adele.

"Looking for clues," replied Ripenzo, continuing to search. "If he wasn't performing a Blood Ceremony, then it might be good if we could find out what he was really doing."

The logic of his answer floored Adele for a moment. She really needed to do the same as Ripenzo and sort herself out. The situation was bad. She was stuck in a foreign nation on an alien world with her three children, and only six guards to protect them all. She had just killed the Sandarians' only, and no doubt treasured, Mage.

Now what?

Adele thought of General Ohrig's advice from yesterday about gathering knowledge.

"What will Empress Sanda'hani do to me if she knew I'd killed her Mage?" she asked.

"I'm not sure," said Ripenzo, frowning and trying to roll the Mage over to check his back pockets. "Sanda'hani is not a bloodthirsty woman, but I can promise you it wouldn't be good. The Sandarians believe in blood-for-blood retribution."

He managed to wrench the black stone knife out of the Mage's clawed hand. After examining it, he shoved it in the belt of his own pants. Then he pulled a small, flat box out of a pocket in the Mage's belt. He frowned more deeply.

"Hmmm, this looks valuable," he said, fingering the lid. "It's not a metal I recognize, yet it's very old. What's inside, I wonder?" He gave the box a shake and sniffed at it, recoiling at the smell.

"Maybe you can open it?" He offered Adele the box, which she took gingerly from his hand. Immediately the seam around the box glowed green, and when she pulled the lid came right off.

Ripenzo and Adele peered inside. A flat black spider curled up inside the box, a gray stripe down its back. Black eyes glittered up at Adele, and she shrieked as the pincers moved, slamming the lid back on tight.

"Rare, indeed," remarked Ripenzo, looking up at Adele in surprise.

"I hate spiders," said Adele by way of explanation. "They've frightened the crap out of me since I was a little girl."

Ripenzo cocked his head to the side. "But you could open and close the box. What does that mean do you think?"

"The magic…I guess I'm good with green magic. Not only Marchants use green magic, I'm sure. The Wizard Ohren said my magic should be very strong," said Adele hurriedly, getting up and dusting herself off.

It was time to stop trembling and make some decisions right now. The most important one she had to make was if she could trust Ripenzo Shale.

*Blood for blood,* she thought. *I cannot let them hurt my children for what I've done.*

"Ripenzo, I realize that you're conflicted here, and don't need to believe me, but I promise you I didn't kill the Mage on purpose. I'm not a murderer." She was going for firm and calm but her voice was too loud. "I was going to let him have my blood but not more...I couldn't just let him kill me."

Ripenzo nodded, but she noticed he edged slowly away from her around the fire.

"What I need to know is, what are you going to do about this? What will you tell Empress Sanda'hani?"

"I've been wondering the same thing," answered Ripenzo, his honesty shocking her. "You've killed the empress's only Mage. This is not something she will easily understand or forgive. Even if we explain that he tried to kill you first, you are a foreigner with a lot to lose if the Mage had proved you weren't a true-blood St. Lucidis queen."

His eyes traveled to the curling green smoke above the fire, which seemed to be betraying her pure St. Lucidis heritage as they spoke.

"It would be hard to convince Sanda'hani you were able to overcome her all-powerful Mage without the use of Dark Magic. Which would only mean one thing: that you killed the Mage with Marchant magic."

They both looked down at the body of the Mage. His face was frozen in an expression of agony, his eyes wide and his mouth open. The gravity of the situation hit home, and Adele gasped as if she'd been punched in the stomach.

How the hell did she know how to use Rainere's magic? Was it because they'd had sex? But that was crazy!

"But if you told Sanda'hani you saw—"

"But I didn't see anything," replied Ripenzo reasonably. "I only came in after I heard you screaming."

Adele was crushed.

"Anyway, I'm just a slave in her court. My word won't count for much if Sanda'hani thinks Dark Magic was used here. You could have bewitched me into believing your story after you killed the Mage."

"Then we can't tell anyone," whispered Adele, reality warring with her sense of ethics. "We have to hide the body and pretend he left us, or me and—" She stopped, her mind spinning hopelessly.

She looked up at Ripenzo, and he shrugged. "It's the only way we both get out of this alive, I guess. Unless you are going to kill me as well, to stop me telling Sanda'hani what you have done?"

Ripenzo smiled at Adele's stricken expression.

"No? Then I suggest we get rid of this body and work out what we are going to tell the empress."

Ripenzo nodded at the Mage's feet, directing Adele to pick them up, as he moved around to pick up the shoulders. Though she was loath to touch his filthy ankles, Adele was surprised at how light the Mage was. She easily held his legs straight and followed Ripenzo as he walked backward through the only other doorway in the cavern. It led down a fairly steep path to yet another cave and then another beyond that. There were little moving lights on the ceiling and walls, which glowed just brightly enough to light their way.

"Do you need to stop, rest?" panted Ripenzo as he wiped the sweat from his brow with his shoulder, in an awkward gesture. They had been walking for not even ten minutes.

"I'm fine," answered Adele, surprised Ripenzo was struggling so much. She had covertly admired his well-muscled shoulders and back when he had gone swimming with the children yesterday. The Mage really wasn't heavy at all, though he was a tall man. The only annoying thing was that her bandage had come loose and her cut wrist was touching the filthy skin of his foot.

"Great, it's just around this corner," Ripenzo said, the strain obvious in his voice.

"Do you want me to take the head?" asked Adele, trying to be helpful.

"No, no, I'm fine," replied Ripenzo quickly. "Let's just find the last cave."

They continued on down through another tunnel. Adele heard an eerie rushing, whistling noise, like the wind through a chimney on a stormy night. She felt odd little warm and cool breezes swirl about her.

"Almost there," gasped Ripenzo.

As they came out of the tunnel into the last cavern, Adele's mouth dropped open in shock. It was enormous, truly enormous.

The ceiling was covered in thousands of the glowing dots that cast a strange, pale fluorescent light on the cave. It was by this light that Adele could see that half the floor of the cavern fell away into a sheer drop, and it was this enormous void that the warm and cool breezes blew up from. Adele had to almost shout to be heard over the noise of the wind.

"Shall we drop him down there?" she asked, pointing at the edge.

Ripenzo nodded and indicated with another nod where they should put the Mage down on the ground.

"Stand back," cautioned Ripenzo. "These winds can blow strong enough to take you over the edge."

Adele backed right up and watched as Ripenzo crouched to cautiously roll the Mage to the cliff's edge, and then push the body off. He looked down into the darkness, but it was impossible to tell if the Mage had landed at the bottom yet.

Ripenzo turned back to Adele. "It's done," he said. "Though we should probably get out of here before the Spirit Guardians realize what we've done."

"Where are the Spirit Guardians?" asked Adele, looking over her shoulder and walking backward toward the entrance they had come in.

"All around us," replied Ripenzo, casting his own worried gaze about the cavern. "They are the breezes you can feel."

Adele freaked. She turned and ran headlong up the dark tunnel, her feet slipping on the floor of solid lava rock. She ran blindly up and through each of the tunnels and caves, stopping only to kick over the Mage's stand in the third cave. Her blood bubbled gently in the bowl, and the herbs and salt were near ashes but she wanted it all destroyed. She tried to kick out the fire but for the first time noticed it burned without fuel. Sure, logs and stones sat in the flames but they didn't burn or smoke or even glow.

The Sacred Fire. Adele remembered Ohren's words when he had first told her about the Ceremony of the Blood. Adele waited for the chime-voices to give her a word of command to destroy it, but they remained silent.

*Then I guess it's not a threat*, thought Adele, but she jumped when she heard a loud whistle coming from down deep within the tunnel she had just run out of.

Where the hell was Ripenzo? Surely he wasn't too far behind?

Adele's screaming nerves wouldn't let her wait and she bolted out of the caves. She felt only sweet relief as she reached the sulfurous air of the outside. The stars glimmered naturally above her head, and Adele could hear the calming swell of the ocean floating in on the breeze.

Looking around, she spotted the little camp that Ripenzo had set up for himself while he had waited for her. She dropped down by the fire to warm her shaking body. Her mind was scattered and frantic, as the memories of her awful night churned her insides.

*I'm a murderer*, Adele thought despondently, incredulous that it had really happened. *I've killed someone!*

She jumped a mile when Ripenzo Shale walked out of the mouth of the cave a few minutes later.

"So, you are fast as well as strong," noted Ripenzo with a wry smile, and dabbed at the sweat on his forehead with the bottom of his torn shirt. "I thought you were leaving me when you bolted like that."

Ripenzo threw himself down beside Adele, lying on his side, his body almost curled around the little fire. His posture looked completely relaxed, and it had a calming effect on Adele. Surely he couldn't lie down like that if there was more danger coming?

The two of them rested, staring into the flames, silent with their own thoughts.

Adele wondered if she looked any different. When she got back to the Sandarian court, would anyone be able to tell by looking at her that she had killed a man? Would her children be able to tell she had taken a life?

Ripenzo shifted next to her and she cast him a sidelong glance.

What about Ripenzo Shale? He was a slave and the lover of Empress Sanda'hani. What if he accidentally confessed to the empress one night when they were in bed? Heaven knew she had promised to marry Rainere during an orgasm. Anything could happen with Ripenzo and his conscience when she went home.

A deep sigh interrupted her dark thoughts.

Adele looked back at Ripenzo and saw his expression was heavy with sadness.

She thought immediately of the first time she had seen Ripenzo and the Mage together, and their silent hand communications.

"Was he your friend?" asked Adele softly.

"No, he wasn't my friend, but he was special to me, in a way," answered Ripenzo. "He was teaching me the ways of the Sandarians and helping me become a part of them, their culture, their tribe. He is the one who showed me what Sanda'hani would want from me, he…"

Ripenzo trailed off and wiped his hand over his face.

"It's going to be difficult without him, that's all."

"I'm sorry, Ripenzo." Adele felt sick at what she had done. "I've really screwed this up for both of us, haven't I?"

Surprisingly, Ripenzo chuckled and pulled himself up to sit next to her. He put his arm around her shoulders.

"Don't worry, my queen. There is always a bright side to every dull coin. When Sanda'hani tires of my talents, it could be very useful for me that the Queen of Unisia herself owes me a rather large favor." Though his tone was light, his words were not. "I'm sure you'll be able to come to my aid one day if I ever have need of it."

Adele sighed and hugged her knees. Ripenzo was warm, and his arm resting around her shoulders felt good. The chime-voices had started whispering again, but the voices were low and Adele found it hard to panic after the trauma she had been through this evening.

"I've been thinking about what we can tell Sanda'hani tomorrow, when we get back to the court," said Ripenzo, and Adele felt his rib cage press in against her arm. "I'll say that the Mage was pleased with the test and that the God Dahk'hani told him to go on a spirit quest to commune with the ancestor spirits. That way you have at least a week before he will be expected back at court."

Ripenzo turned to look at Adele, his eyes glimmering in the firelight. That was a blue a girl could drown in. Adele felt his breath on her mouth.

Their faces were far too close.

Adele blinked and Ripenzo was looking back at the fire. Calmly. As if he hadn't just been about to kiss her.

*How did he do that?*

Adele turned to watch the fire as well. Out of the corner of her eye, she saw Ripenzo smile. She could feel his body pressed into the side of hers, his arm holding her shoulders, and his hand gently stroking her arm. Adele felt in no danger of being forced to kiss him, and when she wasn't looking directly in his eyes, she felt no desire to, either.

Yet why didn't she want to move out of his arms?

*He reminds me of Justin,* she thought, the realization turning her stomach slightly. *He has Justin's hair, his wicked smile...*

But there was something else about Ripenzo that Justin had never had. Something "other" or almost alien about him that Adele couldn't quite put her finger on.

*Maybe because he is being nice to me,* she thought bitterly. *I am a sucker for a pretty face. Throw in a rescue mission, and I'm yours.*

She felt Ripenzo breath in deeply next to her and almost shivered at the intimacy of the movement. This wasn't right, and not just because she wasn't ready to betray Rainere. She didn't want to touch any man the way she touched Rainere, and the way he touched her.

*Rainere.*

The thought of him gave Adele the push she needed to wriggle out of Ripenzo's arm in the pretense of lying down to go to sleep. She was cold now and the ground was sandy but she tried her best to get comfortable.

"Good idea," agreed Ripenzo and she could tell by his voice he was smiling again. He was only silent for a moment before he said, "You know, for someone so afraid of spiders you do incredibly well when confronted with scorpions. I was going to wet my pants when I saw them all over the caves, but you just kept on going." He chuckled. "It was one of the bravest things I've ever seen."

Adele sat up. "What scorpions?"

"The ones with the little glowing eyes," replied Ripenzo and gave a theatrical shudder. "They lit up the caves. I have never seen so many in all my life. I was just waiting for one to drop into my hair." He shuddered again and grinned. "Maybe they were afraid of the woman who had just killed their Mage."

Adele felt the blood run out of her cheeks. Those lights were scorpion eyes!

"That. Is. So. Disgusting," she whispered, horrified, and looked into the mouth of the cave where thousands of scorpions had covered the walls and ceilings of the deeper caves. What would stop them from coming out now?

"They won't go near the fire, don't worry," smiled Ripenzo with a reassuring wink. He settled himself by the fireside, using his little bag as a pillow. He made a loud noise of satisfaction when he got comfortable.

"Sleep well, Queen Adelena."

And with that appeared to go immediately to sleep.

Adele hugged her knees again, jumping at every small noise from the darkness around them, and every faint breeze that ruffled her hair.

She didn't sleep a wink all night, but stayed up and kept their tiny fire burning bright.

# CHAPTER FORTY-TWO

## "Lies and Broken Hearts"

They set out at first light back across the lava fields.

Adele had had to wake the soundly sleeping Ripenzo Shale, where he gently snored next to her. She tried to ignore the petty satisfaction she got from poking him awake with a stick, in his foot.

But even after such a rude start, Ripenzo soon regained his good humor and began describing the long and involved dream he had just been woken from.

There wasn't much to breakfast on, so they had packed up camp quickly. Adele was anxious to be back at the court with her children as soon as she possibly could. Spending the night awake and alone had left her with nothing but a stiff back and a deepening sense of impending doom.

The gray dawn brightened into a beautiful morning, and Ripenzo Shale actually whistled while he strode over the rocky ground. He gave her a bright grin every time he caught her looking over at him as she struggled to keep up.

"I have a free hand to hold yours if you like, Your Majesty," he offered yet again.

"No, I'm fine, thank you, Ripenzo. I'm managing better today," said Adele firmly, narrowly avoiding going over on her ankle for the second time in a few minutes.

She was lying, of course. Her wrist burned and her knee was a purple mess of bruises. Her bottom lip had puffed up overnight and hampered her speech a little now. It had cracked again and bled a bit down her chin. But the worst of her injuries rested where no one could see. Adele felt heartsick with guilt and fear about what she had done last night. In the cold light of day, she had a horrible feeling that she had made a dreadful mistake killing the Mage. Had she just overreacted in fear of a scary situation? Perhaps the Mage had really meant her no harm?

The poison of self-doubt had been slowly gnawing at her all night as her memory played tricks on her and redrew the images of the fight in her mind.

Adele looked up and realized that Ripenzo had gotten a little ahead of her. She stared at his back as he hopped and leaped over the lava flow, sure-footed as a child. She saw a dark glint at his back as the sun reflected off the Mage's knife.

*He helped me last night, but how can I trust him?* she thought, accidentally biting her sore lower lip and starting it bleeding again. She licked and tasted her coppery blood. *Is he really the man who would turn on the woman who saved him from slavers? And if he is, then how can I possibly trust him with my secret? How do I know he isn't skipping back to the empress now ready to tell everything and use that knife as proof of my guilt?*

Adele tripped again, and her hands started shaking as adrenaline and fear rocketed through her tired body.

*How can I trust anyone on this world?* she thought morosely. *Ohren seemed like a good guy, but he sent me here alone, probably knowing what I was in for with that disgusting Mage.*

A horrible thought brought her up cold.

*Did Ohren know that the Mage would try to kill her? Did he arrange it? He was an all-powerful wizard, after all—surely he knew everything that might happen to her in Sandar?*

Hot tears sprang to her eyes, and Adele clapped a hand over her mouth. Was there no one she could trust?

*Rainere.* Her heart fed her the answer immediately. *Rainere is the only person I can trust. He loves me. He wants to marry me. He is the only one on my side here.*

The thought strengthened her enough so that she could stumble forward and across the last of the lava field. Ripenzo Shale was waiting for her at the edge to help her down onto the sand. She cautiously made her way over to him and took his proffered hand as they climbed down the high edge of the rocks to the beach.

Ripenzo gave her a curious look as she wiped off her tears with the back of her hand.

"Did you hurt yourself again?" he asked.

Adele shook her head. "I am just feeling terrible about last night."

Ripenzo cocked his head to the side in his usual gesture.

"But you shouldn't feel guilty. You killed a man who was trying to kill you. At least, that's what you told me," he said, his intelligent eyes closely examining her expression.

"I know," snapped Adele. Why did his appraisal make her feel so anxious? "But excuse me, I've never killed anyone before and now I feel awful. Have you ever killed anyone?"

"Not that made me feel as bad as you obviously do," answered Ripenzo.

"Well, then you can't know how I—wait. What?"

"We had better get you cleaned up a bit," Ripenzo said with a smile, deftly changing the subject. "Everyone is going to think we've been in a fight if they see you covered in blood and dirt like this. The ocean is cold, but it'll do the job and it will wash out that nasty gash there."

Ripenzo reached out and gently took her cut wrist. He examined it closely. Adele watched him as he delicately brushed some sand off and prodded the skin near the gash. She blinked and almost missed the quick kiss he laid on the hot skin.

Adele yanked her hand back but Ripenzo only smiled his open smile at her.

"It's not infected yet, but get it clean and we'll wrap it again back at the court," he said cheerfully.

Adele nodded and turned immediately to head down to the water. She glanced back over her shoulder at Ripenzo but he just gave her a grin and a wave.

Had she imagined the kiss? It had been so quick. Maybe her overtired mind was playing tricks again.

Ripenzo was right. The water was almost icy, but as she waded out she felt the warmer currents of the water that had been heated by the volcano under the seabed. She ducked under the soft waves, clothes and all, and doused herself thoroughly, scrubbing at the blood and dirt that felt encrusted on her. Taking a deep breath, Adele dived under the waves again and with a few powerful strokes, swam away from the shore deeper into the dark-blue ocean.

She checked over her shoulder once and saw Ripenzo, so small on the shore, give her a halfhearted wave. She didn't wave to him but flipped to her back and floated on the top of the water, relishing the peaceful feeling of being cool and alone. The sun shone down on her and the chime-voices whispered sweetly in her ears, their chanting so constant since last night that she didn't even notice it anymore. It was just like having a radio on in the background. She rested for a few minutes.

Adele heard a shout from the beach. Ripenzo was there but now he had five guards with him. She could see the sun glinting on their weapons.

Adele's stomach dropped. *Surely, they couldn't know about the Mage already?*

But, no. There was General Ohrig waving at her. He was the one shouting.

Adele swam leisurely to shore, enjoying a brief moment before gravity and her conscience pulled her back down to reality.

As she climbed out of the water, Ripenzo Shale gave her a happy grin. In fact, all the Sandarian guards were smiling at her broadly. Only General Ohrig quickly averted his eyes.

What was going on now?

Adele looked down to see what was amiss and only then realized the gauzy layers of her dress were clinging wetly to her body, outlining every curve.

She flushed, embarrassed, and pulled at the fabric to separate it from her wet skin but only seemed to make it worse.

"If Your Majesty is ready, we shall…return to, uh…the court." General Ohrig's voice was brusque and he couldn't look her in the eye.

"Yes, of course, General," agreed Adele quickly. "Ripenzo—"

"Mr. Shale can walk ahead of us with the other guards," said General Ohrig firmly. "Your Majesty, if you will kindly wait a moment back here for me."

Ripenzo grinned. "Oh I don't think there is any need to walk in formation, General Ohrig. It's too early for protocol out here."

"Walk. Eyes front," ordered General Ohrig, and this time his voice was steely.

Ripenzo acquiesced with good grace and jogged to join the other guards who had turned smartly and were now walking back the way they had come. When they were a sizable distance away, General Ohrig gestured for Adele to walk next to him, though he kept his eyes averted.

"How did everything go, Your Majesty?" asked Ohrig quietly.

"It went as well as could be expected. Provided you expect to be sitting in a dirty cave with a crazy person and have your blood dripping into a bowl," answered Adele, testing herself by answering with a mix of truth and lie. Her voice stayed steady and light, which

343

surprised her. "The Mage was happy with it all, I think...but after the Ceremony of the Blood, he drank something weird and went into a trance for a few hours."

"Weird?"

"Something strange—herbs, I think. It made his eyes roll back and he stared at the fire for a while before he passed out cold."

"I see," said General Ohrig, and Adele heard the protective disapproval in his voice. It had almost killed the general to let her walk away with two men he didn't know well to a place he didn't know at all, and with no protection from her Queen's Guard.

"He wasn't there when I woke up this morning," said Adele and that was the truth. She decided enough had been said.

"Well, we are glad to have you back with us, Your Majesty. Empress Sanda'hani has prepared a feast today in anticipation of your success, but I think we should head back to Unisia tomorrow, if you agree?"

"And bring the Fire Orchid stamens home," nodded Adele.

Maybe this would all be worth it if she managed to save thousands of lives in Unisia when the Summer Influenza swept the kingdom again. One life of a disgusting Mage for thousands of innocent people. Surely that would balance out her guilt?

*Wasn't that how the world worked?*

The heat of the morning sun dried her hair and clothes quickly, and Adele was decent again by the time they reached the Court of Sandar. The crowd of tents had swelled enormously, and men, women, and children thronged the area beneath them.

"They all came out of the jungle this morning," murmured General Ohrig as they entered the camp. "Apparently they were all in hiding until the announcement of your true heritage could be made."

"Oh." Adele was shocked at just how many people had joined the royal party. There must be at least a thousand or more on the beach.

Instinctively she searched the groups of laughing children on the shore for her own. It took a minute but she found them under a pavilion in the waves, with the figures of Caitlin, Seraphina, and QG Pepper grouped around them. She breathed a profound sigh of maternal relief.

General Ohrig led Adele over to the empress's tent, which had been raised to accommodate at least a hundred extra guests. The walls had been rolled up and the large crowd spilled out the sides. Adele tried to wear a look of innocent exhaustion, which would be expected after her long night, but her face suddenly didn't feel like her own.

As she ducked under the awning into the enlarged tent, Adele saw Empress Sanda'hani standing on a large wooden dais like a small stage. Ripenzo Shale stood at her right hand and a large crowd pressed in all around her.

The expression on the empress's face was fierce. Adele's nerves almost failed her.

"Queen Adelena Olivia Serena St. Lucidis, queen of the kingdom of Unisia and overlord of the Green Lands. My trusted advisor, Ripenzo Shale, has told me everything that has transpired last night in the Holy Place of our Spirit Guardians."

Adele swore internally and looked wildly at Ripenzo. This time he didn't smile.

*He couldn't have!*

"And I welcome you to our land as the true queen and heir to the royal throne of Unisia. Long may your reign prosper and the friendship between our two nations flourish and strengthen as the years pass."

Empress Sanda'hani continued addressing the rest of the murmuring crowd, while Adele tried to swallow her heart back down into her chest.

"Our beloved Mage was summoned by our Spirit Guardians to bring the queen's blood to the Holy Summit of Dahk'ni so our God Dahk'hani can taste the blood for himself and rejoice with us that once again a true St. Lucidis heir sits on the throne of Unisia. The Mage gave this precious token of his faith to our Ripenzo Shale as a sign that we should accept his truth and wait for his return."

Empress Sanda'hani held up the tiny box with the spider hidden inside.

Adele was too surprised to even gasp. That had been a clever move. Ripenzo Shale seemed to be very good at covering every base. Adele glanced over at him again, but Ripenzo was smiling adoringly up at the empress.

Adele was relieved when the empress's speech ended with loud cheering and applause from all the Sandarians in the tent. Adele smiled and nodded at everyone, moving up on the dais to embrace Empress Sanda'hani and thank her for her trust and faith. She smiled and waved to the crowd of happy, cheering people, her own guards among them.

It wasn't as hard as Adele thought it might be, pretending not to be a Mage killer.

A huge celebration had been organized, which started with an extravagant feast of seafood and other more exotic foods from the rain forest. Adele enjoyed her first full meal since the day she'd arrived in Sandar. Despite not sleeping a wink last night, she felt skittish with restless energy, and swam and played with her children all day until they retired for their afternoon nap with the rest of the children of the Sandar court. The magical combination of the salt air, sunshine, and a big meal meant Seraphina and Caitlin had an easy time of dragging the children away from their mother.

While she was bidding farewell to her children, Adele didn't notice when the court cleared out of the big tent, and Sanda'hani's stage was taken over by a large band of musicians and a troupe of dancers. Crowds of ordinary Sandarians packed into the shaded space and beautiful music spilled out across the beach. The gentle rhythms and soft melodies of the wooden drums and pipes were matched perfectly by the dancers, whose bodies undulated and rocked in a way that was almost hypnotic to watch.

As Adele found herself getting lost in the beauty of the performance, she heard her name being called over her shoulder.

When Tilburn approached her, Adele couldn't help but notice his slight sway and sporadic hiccups. His hair was slightly askew, and the curls definitely sat farther over one ear than they normally did.

*I knew it! It's a wig*, thought Adele, finally solving the mystery of Tilburn's impeccable curls.

Adele tried to hide her smile as Tilburn straightened up before her in a valiant effort not to seem as drunk as he clearly was. Adele looked over his shoulder and saw her QGs Bear, Owens and Pepper sniggering away together and casting glances in her direction. When they saw her gaze on them, they instantly disbanded and wandered away in different directions.

"Yours Maj-eshty, the Empresh Shanda'ah-ha would like the company of your pleashure for a meeting…for a moment," Tilburn proclaimed with all his normal dignity, if not comprehension.

"Very well, Tilburn," said Adele, fighting her smile even harder. It was so rare to see Tilburn be anything other than completely in control of himself. "I thought I saw the empress go over there. Is she in that golden tent?"

"No, she is in her golden tent," corrected Tilburn firmly. "I will accompany you, Your Maj-eshty."

The little man bowed and then turned and walked in the opposite direction.

Adele pointed to QG Owens who had been oh-so-casually walking past again, and gestured to him to retrieve Tilburn from entering the main tent, where the little man could be seen dancing and swaying through the crowd.

Adele made her way over to the Empress Sanda'hani's tent. She had seen Ripenzo Shale disappear into it with the empress earlier in the afternoon. But the tent had opaque sides to give the empress some privacy, and Adele had no idea what had passed between them.

*Stay calm, stay very calm,* she told herself, but as she neared the tent, her heartbeat ratcheted up to panic pace. Adele adjusted her gown and pulled her salt-ruffled hair back into a loose braid. She quickly practiced a look of innocent shock, but without a mirror it was hard to be sure she didn't come off as horribly guilty. There was nothing for it. Adele squared her shoulders and licked her dry lips as she approached the golden tent of Empress Sanda'hani.

A servant dressed in a blue sarong announced her arrival and pulled a silken curtain aside for her. Adele ducked in through the doorway. The air in the tent was scented by sweet candles and reminded her of the incense burned at her coronation ceremony.

Sanda'hani was reclining on a bank of golden pillows and smiled warmly when Adele entered. She gestured for Adele to sit on another generous pile of pillows close to her own, and made sure her guest had a drink in her hand right away.

"Queen Adelena, I feel like I haven't seen you all day! I hope you have been enjoying the festivities to honor you?"

"It's been wonderful, thank you so much. I am very touched by your generous hospitality, and the care you have taken with my children and myself, since we arrived, Your Majesty." Adele forced a smile over her dry lips. "I had no idea what to expect when we arrived in your land, but I don't mind telling you I think my children and I are in love with your beautiful beach and the court here."

Empress Sanda'hani threw back her head and laughed. The sound was so light and free that Adele felt herself relax just slightly.

"I can only imagine what those wizards and princes in Unisia told you about our primitive ways and barbaric customs. The Picnic Court, I hear we've been called." The empress smiled and rolled her eyes to soften the joke.

Still smiling, Empress Sanda'hani reached under a cushion behind herself and pulled out a small wooden box. It was made out of coconut shell and was decorated with intricate carvings of flowers and sea creatures. Reverentially, Sanda'hani opened the lid. Inside were at least a hundred tiny black filaments.

The Fire Orchid stamens.

Adele looked up at the empress, her eyes wide.

"That is enough to save every one of your people for this year, and the next, when they are made into the precious tonics."

Adele took the box in her hands and stared down at the tiny black stamens. They were so small to be so important to her nation.

"Will you have enough for your own stocks and your own people?" asked Adele, looking back up at the empress. "I hear this Summer Influenza is incredibly dangerous."

The Empress Sanda'hani dropped her chin and smiled up at Adele, but her expression was curious.

"That's very kind of you to think of my people as well as your own, Queen Adelena, but the Summer illnesses of the Unisians do not affect us here in Sandar. We have been genetically inoculated against these things by our previous masters." She shrugged. "One slim benefit of being ruled by the insane Marchant autocrats. They didn't want their workforce dying by anything other than their own hands."

Despite Sanda'hani's friendly tone, Adele was reminded that they were both monarchs discussing the safety of their people, and not housewives gossiping over a fence about the health of their families. So much depended on both of them being able to play their parts properly...so many of her own people's lives depended on Adele.

"Empress Sanda'hani, I cannot tell you how pleased and proud I am to be recognized as the true queen of Unisia and to be able to put your mind at peace. It is wonderful that our two nations can once again return to the mutually beneficial relationship of before."

Adele saw Empress Sanda'hani open her mouth to speak, and her pleasant expression turn wry. Adele knew what the empress was about to say before she said it.

The Unisian–Sandarian relationship was entirely one-sided and had been for hundreds of years. The Sandarians provided the kingdom with Fire Orchid stamens, pearls, and silk for little, or no, profit. Adele had been shocked at the rough state of the road that linked the two nations. In return for their precious trade, the Unisian court did…what? It only left the Sandarians in peace to govern themselves without Unisian interference. Adele thought it was very poor recompense for the effort she knew the Sandarians took to harvest the rare and delicate Fire Orchids that grew on the dangerous lava fields close to the rim of the larger, and active, geysers. And it was even more wondrous to her that they would do this for the kingdom now that she knew they didn't even need the orchids like Unisia did.

"And that is why I would like to negotiate a new trade agreement for the Fire Orchid stamens," Adele began. "In return for a steady supply of the flowers, throughout the year, I will commit to building a new and better road between our two nations to allow more movement of people between our borders. I will also commit to paying a price of one gold piece per ten stamens, as well as freight costs. Lastly, I will be halving the tax on importing pearls and silk into our kingdom of Unisia so that those merchants who wish to trade with your Sandarian suppliers can do so without the normal crippling penalties."

Adele sat back slightly breathless but very pleased she had remembered everything she had planned to say after reading through all the documents on Unisian–Sandarian trade relations. All these items she had just promised had been asked for and refused by the Unisian regents for years. Adele hadn't had a chance to consult with anyone on what it all meant for the royal treasury, but she would deal with that later.

It was too important right now to bond Empress Sanda'hani to her with good will and strong financial ties. Adele needed the empress to depend on her.

"For as long as my reign may last, I will ensure the Sandarian people get what they deserve from the Kingdom of Unisia," said Adele firmly, emphasizing the *'my reign'*. "I would also welcome a Sandarian ambassador at my court to make sure that any Sandarian issues will be recognized and respected by the Unisian court, if that would please you?"

Empress Sanda'hani smiled and a pretty dimple deepened on her cheek.

"I thank you for your kind words and will look forward to approving the technicalities of these agreements as soon as Your Majesty has them drawn up." Though her words were formal, Empress Sanda'hani looked like she wanted to clap her hands with glee.

Adele sat back, hoping it was all going to be enough to ensure the empress's loyalty one day…or, say, in a week's time when her Mage didn't return from his Spirit Quest. Empress Sanda'hani poured them both a tiny cup of coconut rum.

"To the good health of Queen Adelena St. Lucidis, long may she reign!"

Adele smiled at the toast and sipped at her rum, but she choked when she saw Ripenzo Shale enter the tent.

"May I join, Your Majesties?" he asked, his ever-present grin broad.

"Come here, my love, sit next to me." The empress reached out to take Ripenzo's hand. Ripenzo let himself be pulled down beside Sanda'hani, wrapping his arm around her and placing a hand suggestively on her knee.

"Can you believe I found this gorgeous man languishing in the pit of a slave market on the west coast?" Sanda'hani asked, squeezing Ripenzo's chin in her hand and kissing him lightly on the lips. She turned back to Adele smiling proudly.

Adele made a noncommittal noise and forced a smile as Ripenzo leaned in to kiss the empress on her shoulder, all the while keeping his indigo-blue eyes on Adele. His gaze made her skin crawl.

"I have made it my mission to search all the slave markets of Evendaar for any Sandarian or descendant of my people, who might still be trapped in the bonds of slavery outside of Sandar. When I found Ripenzo here, I had been searching for months, thinking perhaps that I had found everyone who could be found. But no, he was still out there, waiting for me." Sanda'hani squeezed Ripenzo's hand, and they shared a smile.

Adele felt sick to her stomach.

"We have been together ever since..."

Adele tried to say something cheerful, but the words caught in her throat. Something was not adding up here. Confused, she compared the blond, blue-eyed Ripenzo with the cocoa-coloring and big-boned beauty of the empress.

*They were the same race?*

"Would you like to spend the night with him?" asked the Empress Sanda'hani with a smile.

"What?" spluttered Adele. She had not expected that.

"He's really very good at pleasing a woman." Sanda'hani chucked Ripenzo under the chin as one would a cat, and though her gesture was gentle Ripenzo flinched from it and cast his blue eyes over Adele. "He must have learned all his wonderful tricks in the brothels of Outer Tar, where I found him. Please, take him. What's mine is yours."

"You know, that's very, um, kind of you to...offer him like this...but I will say no right now, if you don't mind. Not that he isn't...it's just that I'm here on business, so..."

Adele stumbled to her feet. All sense of her previous self-possession disappeared under Ripenzo Shale's mocking gaze.

Adele escaped the tent and the empress's company as fast as she could, spluttering apologies. With burning cheeks and the laughter of Ripenzo Shale ringing in her ears, she hurried away to check on her children, still at rest in their tent.

*God, what was that all about?* Adele thought. She was sure the empress had been sincere in offering Ripenzo as a gift to her.

But that wasn't the reason for her disquiet.

The expression on Ripenzo Shale's face when the empress had sung his virtues in the bedroom had shaken Adele to her core. She was suddenly certain that Ripenzo Shale was a very dangerous man.

Adele found her family and sat quietly with the children until they awoke from their naps an hour later. The peace of their sleeping expressions gave her a measure of tranquility after the stress of the day.

It was the last moment that Adele had to herself that afternoon. The festivities raged on, and as the sun went down, the music became wilder and the coconut rum flowed more freely. The party didn't stop until well after midnight.

Despite no sleep the night before, Adele still felt too wired to rest. Every time she closed her eyes, she saw the leering grin of the Mage or Ripenzo Shale winking at her. It was a horrible combination.

As silently as she could, Adele crept out of the tent, leaving her children sleeping with their nannies. She gave Captain Lucky a nod and took the lantern he offered her with a whispered thanks.

The moon was only half full, but it lit the shoreline enough for Adele to see little crabs scurrying about on their mysterious crab-business. She heaved a deep sigh and sat down on the dry sand just above the high-water mark.

*Rainere, if you can hear me,* she prayed silently, *I miss you, my darling, and I love you. I cannot wait to be with you again.*

Footsteps behind her interrupted her thoughts, and Empress Sanda'hani dropped a cushion on the sand next to Adele and settled on it before Adele could say a word.

"Forgive me for intruding on your private time, Queen Adelena," said Empress Sanda'hani quietly. "I will leave you to your contemplations as soon as you answer the question which has been keeping me from my own sleep."

Adele turned to look at the empress's profile. She was frowning at the tiny waves licking at the shore.

"What passed between you and Ripenzo in the time that you were away with him? I thought perhaps you had lain with him, but now I am not so sure...your eyes are always seeking him out yet you do not speak to him easily and your expression is sometimes...excuse my honesty, but it is as if you are frightened of him."

Adele took a deep breath in and let it out shakily. A thousand frantic thoughts twirled chaotically around her head.

Never had so much relied upon her ability to lie as well as she needed to right now.

Adele tried desperately to arrange her thoughts.

*"Everyone is going to think we've been in a fight if they see you like this...*

*...it could be very useful for me that the Queen of Unisia owes me a rather large favor...*

*...you will have a week before the Mage will be expected back..."*

What would Ripenzo say when the empress asked him this same question?

What had he already said?

She remembered his constant closeness, the intimacy of his touches, and the way he had looked at her when he was kissing the empress on the shoulder earlier.

He was dangerous, yes, but he was also a slave, bought by the highest bidder. She couldn't afford to let him get his story in first to the empress.

"How did you hurt your lip?" asked Empress Sanda'hani softly. She gently touched Adele's bottom lip with her finger; it came away with blood on it.

Adele looked up at the empress through her lashes and didn't have to fake the fear behind her tears.

"Ripenzo, he…" She choked, closing her eyes to find the strength to say what she had to. "He thought I would…that I had wanted to lie with him. When I said no, he—he fought me. When he pushed me down onto the ground, my knee hit a rock and my face…"

Adele raised her dress to show the dark mass of bruising on her leg.

"When I cried out…it seemed to excite him."

Adele looked out at the ocean shimmering in the moonlight.

"He said he knew Unisian women liked it rough, and that he was going to give it to me. The Mage pulled him off when I screamed, but Ripenzo was in such a fury…they fought but the Mage managed to get him under control."

Adele glanced at the empress. Her expression was hard and cold as carved stone.

"He apologized after the ceremony. He said that after all he had suffered in his life, he sometimes gets inexplicable urges toward Unisian women…apparently he was treated badly by one mistress. I said I understood but…the episode has made me very wary of him."

"Queen Adelena," said Empress Sanda'hani, touching Adele's shoulder and making her turn to face her. "I will have him beheaded in the morning."

Adele's stomach lurched.

"No!" she gasped in horror. "No please—he is a broken man, he isn't responsible for his behavior. Also the men with me, General Ohrig and my guards, will demand a public hearing. I would be humiliated…it would cause an international incident! Please, let's just keep this between us women."

"But we are not just women, Queen Adelena," said Empress Sanda'hani fiercely. "We are those chosen by our Gods to rule our nations. No man has the right to defile us, or touch us without our permission."

Adele licked her lips and tasted blood on them.

"If I could take him home with me," mused Adele, "I could tell my men you had given him to us to take back as the Sandarian ambassador to Unisia. Then I could deal with him…discreetly, when I get back to the Golden Palace."

"Better yet, I will give him to you as a gift in return for favorable trade negotiations. He will need to be symbolically chained and handed over with the other goods. More than anything he will hate to be treated as a slave again."

Adele quailed slightly when she heard the deep running bitterness and fury in the empress's voice.

*Dear God, she actually loves Ripenzo*, thought Adele as another black mark engraved itself on her conscience.

"All right," agreed Adele, her voice shaking. "He comes with me tomorrow morning in chains. I have an extra horse for him to ride."

"Let him walk," spat the empress. "He is only a slave, after all."

"I'm so sorry to tell you all of this, Empress Sanda'hani," said Adele softly. "I had no intention of confessing what happened in the Holy Cave, but you caught me at a vulnerable time…"

"He is always with my children, they love him," whispered the empress, and Adele was not sure she was meant to hear that.

*Oh Christ, I've destroyed her trust in men. I'm making her question her faith in her own judgment,* Adele thought, starting to feel hot as shame burned her from the inside out.

Empress Sanda'hani got up from the sand, but before she left she placed her hand on Adele's shoulder.

"Always keep a man as a slave, Queen Adelena. Never let them think they can take your power, because then they will. Even the sweet ones…don't make my mistake." The catch in Empress Sanda'hani's voice stabbed Adele through the heart.

Numb at what she had just managed to do, Adele waited for a few minutes after the empress had left before she walked back to the tent where her children slept. In the soft glow of the lantern light, she checked they were all well. Maternal love welled up from deep within her and quieted the clamoring of her stricken conscience.

*They are worth every second of this guilt and horror,* thought Adele fiercely as she looked down on their sweet and innocent faces. *I will kill a thousand mages and break the hearts of a thousand empresses to keep them safe. They are all that matter to me in this world, and they are all that ever will.*

Adele settled down next to her babies, making sure she could touch each of them.

Yet, still, sleep eluded her.

# CHAPTER FORTY-THREE

## "She Must Not Return"

"So it's decided, then?" asked Ohren, looking around the small wooden table at Orestes and Gorrik. An empty bottle of Firewhiskey and three metal cups the only decorations.

The two men exchanged glances. One was incredulous; the other just exhausted.

"What? Were we taking a vote?" asked Orestes, glaring back at Ohren. "Because as far as I'm concerned, we are just cleaning up another one of your godbedamned messes again."

Ohren bravely stared down his furious twin.

"The queen cannot be allowed to return to the Golden Palace until the problem of her heritage can be solved."

"Ah, now that's a bit of magic I would love to see," interrupted Gorrik with a halfhearted chuckle. "How to turn Marchant green to St. Lucidis gold...how to turn a black dragon into a white lion."

"It's impossible, you fool!" spat Orestes, but his anger was directed at Ohren. "You cannot undo what you have done. This is why I said not to crown her when she was returned to us. You should have waited!"

"I know that, Orestes, don't you think I know that?" Ohren's voice was low but betrayed him with a slight twitch of hysteria on the last word. "I cannot change who she is but I can *hide* it. I can try and disguise her true identity from everyone who doesn't need to know."

Gorrik shook his head and, absently, stroked his hand down the back of the cat on his lap.

"A Marchant half-blood on the throne—Goddess help us all. You really have screwed us good and proper this time, Ohren. You've screwed us well into the ground now, my boy. If Prince Rainere ever finds out who she really is, he will jump on the throne quicker than you can say *'the throne of my sister is my throne first'*!"

Gorrik shook his head again and his milky eyes looked sadly at the twins before him. He had known these wizards since they were babes in arms. It was impossible for him to be angry with either of them, despite their stupidity.

"Look, the queen should be finished in Sandar today," said Ohren, stubbornly sticking to the point of their late-night meeting. "I will send a rider in the morning to meet her on the road and tell her to head over to the Belvoir Estate. Bertie will be hosting the racing carnival in five days' time, and she and the children will be safe there."

"Because of the curse," said Orestes, the inspiration of Ohren's suggestion suddenly dawning on him. "No one can use magic within the boundaries of the Belvoir Estate!"

"Meaning no one will ever be able to tell what sort of magic the queen possesses as even the Rings of Power around her eyes will be dulled. Gold or silver, it won't matter, as everyone's will look the same regardless," said Ohren, smiling cautiously around at his old brother and older teacher. "As the carnival lasts just over a week, we should have enough time to search the libraries to find a way to disguise Adelena's Marchant background for as long as we can."

"That's quite a good idea, m'boy," said Gorrik slowly, and pinched his bottom lip between his fingers. "But what will you do if the Marchant prince decides to attend the racing carnival himself?"

"What? That will never happen," said Ohren firmly, shaking his head. "No Marchant has attended the racing carnival for at least three hundred years, well before my time."

"It would be extremely unlikely," agreed Orestes. "I cannot imagine that the prince would extend himself like that where he has no power. Not even a Marchant can use magic within the borders of the Belvoir Estate, and that's beside the fact that the curse would nullify the effect of his immortality spell. He would age just like everyone else when he was there, and perhaps there would be an even worse reaction. He would have to be stupid or suicidal to risk such exposure."

Orestes looked back at his brother for confirmation. Ohren nodded.

"Ah, of course," said Gorrik sarcastically, addressing the black cat on his lap. "And we've never know a Marchant prince to be stupid or suicidal, have we, my little master?"

The cat only meowed sweetly in response and shoved his head passionately into Gorrik's old hand.

"So we are agreed?" Ohren asked the table again. "Tomorrow I will send a rider to intercept the queen and her entourage and tell them to change direction for Belvoir Estate. I will also send another rider to Bertie to let him know to prepare for the queen's early arrival. All going well, she should arrive at the Belvoir Estate sometime next week."

"Providing she is still alive after her Ceremony of the Blood with the Sandarian Volcano God," sniffed Gorrik, catching Ohren's eye. He was satisfied to see the high wizard pale somewhat and lose his confident expression.

"Yes, of course," agreed Ohren quietly. "If she and the children are still alive."

# CHAPTER FORTY-FOUR

## "The Hidden Child Loses a Fear of the Dark"

"But I don't want to go!" howled Natalie as Caitlin tried to stuff her into the carriage yet again.

Stella sobbed in Adele's arms and Aaron kept trying to bolt from the carriage and dash back down the beach, only to be scooped up by Captain Lucky and put back again. It was terribly amusing to the crowd of Sandarians who had gathered to see off the Unisian royal party, and their laughter and chatter wasn't helping the children keep their feelings under control.

Adele gave Empress Sanda'hani another warm embrace and squashed Stella between the two of them, making the baby giggle, despite her tears.

"Come back soon, my sweet baby," cooed the empress.

"I lub joo," smiled Stella and reached out to plant a wet kiss on Empress Sanda'hani's cheek.

The empress melted at the simple words and looked at Adele with a deeper affection.

"You look after these beautiful children and you look after yourself, Queen Adelena," the empress said quietly. "You be strong for everyone. Remember my words from last night, yes?"

"I will," whispered Adele and fought the tears that sprung, unwanted to her eyes. She purposely avoided looking at the man chained and bound by manacles to the back of her carriage train.

Adele handed a more cheerful Stella to Seraphina and climbed into her own carriage.

The drivers prepared themselves quickly but set off at a slow pace down the loose dirt road out of the Sandarian jungle.

Most of the court had come out to see them off, and the older children ran by the carriages yelling and throwing fragrant flowers into their windows and at the horses, making her children laugh.

Adele saw that her six QG's rode in stately formation on either side of the three carriages. She leaned out to General Ohrig, who was just outside her window.

"Are we going to talk about that?" the general asked, nodding in the direction of Ripenzo Shale as he sauntered along the dusty road, his wrists held before him in irons. Ripenzo caught Adele's gaze and smiled broadly at her, cocking his head to the side.

"I'll tell you later," muttered Adele as one of the Sandarian children ran up to her and handed her a bunch of pink flowers. General Ohrig raised his eyebrows but remained silent.

*This had to be the slowest good-bye parade ever.*

"Have you seen Tilburn anywhere this morning?" asked Adele, changing the subject. "I thought he'd be in this carriage waiting for me, but he's nowhere to be seen."

Just then, they heard a shout behind them.

"Speak of the devil," said Adele, and General Ohrig returned her grin.

Tilburn was running as fast as his legs would carry him, his shirttails waving behind him and his hair held firmly in his hand.

"Wait! Wait!" he shouted.

All the QG's gathered around their general to watch the little majordomo catch up with them.

"What's that chasing him?" asked Pepper.

"That's not a what, it's a who," said General Ohrig, squinting in the bright morning light at the figure chasing Tilburn down the road.

"Ha ha! Pay up," said Owens to Bear, and held out his hand.

"Hang on," said Bear crossly. "We don't know if he got lucky yet."

Just as Tilburn was closing in on the slow-moving carriages, the large figure chasing Tilburn finally caught him. The woman was one of the tallest Adele had ever seen, certainly taller than most Sandarian men, and they were not a short people.

"Are you sure that's a woman?" she asked, squinting at the pair as Tilburn was crushed in a bear hug and covered in passionate kisses.

"Her Majesty has a point," agreed Bear quickly. "I think that that is a man, too."

"No one said he had to get lucky with a woman," corrected Owens. "Just that he *got* some."

He cast a quick glance at Adele.

"Apologies, Your Majesty,"

"No need," replied Adele automatically.

Everyone stared in fascination as Tilburn slowly untangled himself from his lover's embrace.

"Good-bye, Tilly," the woman called out, and Tilburn jogged away from her without a backward glance. "I will pray to Dahk'hani that I now carry your child."

"Oh, he got some all right," smirked Owens. "Pay up, Bear."

A reluctant Bear handed over three coins, wincing as he did.

"And you, Leith," insisted Owens, catching the younger man's eye just as he was about to pull his horse around and leave. "I remember our little wager as to the predilection of our majordomo here. If you would be so kind?"

He held out his gloved hand and Leith dropped two coins in it, blushing furiously.

"To be fair, I would have been in on that bet, too, Leith," said Adele, smiling sympathetically at her young guardsmen.

"I shall promise to include you in the next wager, then, Your Majesty," offered Owens magnanimously, while clinking his full purse of coins.

"I'll get you at cards later, anyway," growled Bear and pulled his horse away to join Leith at the front of the carriage train. The rest of the men returned to their positions as Tilburn awkwardly climbed into the moving carriage.

"Good morning, Tilburn," said Adele, looking at him over the scroll she had snatched up not a second before.

"Your Majesty," replied Tilburn stiffly. "My sincere apologies for my tardiness, I can only hope you can forgive me, and accept my promise that it will never happen again."

"Never mind, Tilburn." Adele smiled. "It can happen to the best of us."

Tilburn accepted her forgiveness with a curt nod and flaming cheeks. He proceeded to take the next hour to tidy himself, fiddling endlessly with his wig until the curls were perfect again.

*     *     *

It wasn't until they stopped to make camp in the evening that the question of Ripenzo Shale came up again.

Adele asked the general to call the guards together to explain the situation to them in as much detail as she could safely give them. Adele decided to stick with the simplest lie.

"I know you are all wondering why Mr. Shale is accompanying us home," began Adele, knowing full well that Ripenzo could hear her speaking. "Well, Mr. Shale is in the very unfortunate position of being a slave in Sandar. Inasmuch as the Empress Sanda'hani values my friendship with her, well, she decided to gift Mr. Shale to me…as a present."

"But what are the chains for, Your Majesty? Is Mr. Shale dangerous?' asked Pepper, his eyes round with surprise. He earned himself a sharp jab in the ribs from Leith.

"Obviously," Adele continued despite the interruption. "I have every intention of setting Mr. Shale free once we are well inside the kingdom boundary line. I do not believe any man should be a slave, nor do I wish to keep one. Any questions?"

Leith nudged Pepper in the ribs again as he opened his mouth to ask the same questions. Adele gave him a hard look and he wisely closed it again.

"Good," said Adele, nodding and looking around at everyone without catching any eye. "Please go ahead and finish setting up the camp. I'll help in a minute."

General Ohrig walked away with his men but gave her a heavy look over his shoulder. Adele knew Ohrig would require a better explanation later. But right now, she was at a loss to explain why the empress would gift the Queen of Unisia her favorite concubine and ambassador. The attempted rape story would just mean Ripenzo's immediate death, and despite the danger he posed her, Adele did not want any more blood on her hands today, or ever again.

She wandered over to where Ripenzo was sitting on a tree stump, picking grasses at his feet and weaving them between his fingers.

"May I sit down?" Adele asked Ripenzo quietly.

"You are free to sit wherever you wish, mistress," Ripenzo said, smiling, though the humor never reached his eyes.

"I'm sorry, Ripenzo, but I really had no choice." Adele sat down on a fallen log next to his. Their knees were close enough to touch.

Ripenzo turned his eyes on Adele and though she saw no malice in them, there was a coldness that chilled her to the bone.

"Oh no, mistress, you have many choices in your life. You see, you are a queen. And me, I am just a lowly slave. But you are my cleverest mistress yet, because you didn't even buy me with money. You bought me for the price of a few lies." He grinned mirthlessly again. "And now you've bound me up so tight in all your lies I have no choice but to go along with them, too."

Adele felt his words fall like blows on her head. She knew everything he said was true.

"I can never go back to Sanda'hani again, she hates me now," he whispered sadly, and dropped his head. "I can never see her beautiful children again, or the beach…my home is gone."

"I'm so sorry, Ripenzo," whispered Adele, gutted by the pain she had caused Ripenzo when he had only ever tried to help her. "I will set you free, though, I promise. You never have to be a slave, ever again. You will be free."

"Free to do what?" Ripenzo gave her a sharp look. "Free to live as a poor itinerant? I have no trade, no property, no money. In Sandar, I lived as a prince, as a royal plaything. I was learning the game of politics by the side of an empress. I was learning so much more with the Mage—" He cut himself off.

"Then come with me. Come to the court of the Golden Palace," said Adele, guilt making her desperate. "You can stay in my household, help me…if only you promise to never…if you promise to…"

Ripenzo laughed, and it was his big, easy laugh.

"Loyalty from the slave you bought with lies. Tsk-tsk, Your Majesty. Don't you think that's a bit much to ask?" Ripenzo grinned but then it died slowly on his face. "Besides, I already made those promises to you, and it wasn't enough for you to trust me—you had to ruin my life, too."

"There is only one other choice I can make here, Ripenzo, and I don't want to make it," whispered Adele, her voice low and hoarse with guilt.

"Go with you or die, is that it, my queen?" asked Ripenzo softly.

Adele didn't lift her eyes from the ground.

"Well, you drive a hard bargain, Your Majesty, so if I have to choose, I choose…to go with you!"

Adele's head snapped up. "Really!"

Ripenzo nodded, grinning, back to his old self again.

"At least if I'm alive I can see what it's like to live as a free man for once—when I'm not jumping to your beck and call, that is."

Adele smiled wryly at the sarcasm, then frowned.

"I'll make sure you are treated well, Ripenzo. You will have a home at my court until you decide you would like something else. It won't be nearly as bad as you think it will, I promise," she said, echoing his famous last words before she had gone into the cave with the Mage.

Astoundingly, Adele and Ripenzo burst out laughing at the same time. After the incredible tension of the day, it just felt so damn good to laugh.

When their hysterics had died down to chuckles, Ripenzo gave Adele a wink.

"When are the shackles going to come off, do you think, Your Majesty?"

"Tomorrow," promised Adele with a sympathetic smile. "As soon as we are far from Sandar eyes."

Ripenzo nodded and went back to pulling the grasses at his feet. Adele smiled and gave him a quick pat on the shoulder. As she walked away, she never turned back to see the curious expression that passed across his face before it was quickly hidden again.

The next day's travel passed happily. The children were not yet bored of the road and the day was warm without being too hot, as it was in Sandar. By nightfall, they had reached the stream that had been their previous bathing place, and everybody enjoyed a wash and a long drink.

Despite Adele wanting to do it casually, Tilburn insisted on making a fuss of Ripenzo Shale as his iron manacles were removed from his wrists. The children cheered and gave him bunches of flowers, which he took gently from their hands and patted them on their heads.

Then Ripenzo stood on the back of a carriage and gave a little speech about how happy he was to be free to work as many hours as he could for a pittance, how he was now free to pay taxes, and spend any penny left over on women he had no chance of winning.

He had all the men laughing, even Ohrig. Uncomfortable because she was literally everyone's boss and in charge of salaries, Adele only chuckled along nervously, coughing slightly as she went.

After a delicious meal flavored with Sandarian spices, everyone settled down early for the night. As the children slept beside her in the tent, Adele quietly sat up, unable to sleep yet again.

That was four nights in a row now that she had not slept at all. It was bizarre and almost frightening how alert she was. Adele lay back down and tossed and turned, thinking of everything that had gone wrong in Sandar and everything she had done.

*Before he tried to kill me, the Mage turned my blood green. How could he do that? And if he could do that, could others? Could Rainere?*

She couldn't forget the memory of the blood smoking and changing into green sparkles before her eyes. Like Rainere's magic, Marchant magic…Dark Magic.

Adele tried to push away the memory, but the Mage's leering face appeared in her mind's eye to take its place.

*My hands were stuck to him. I couldn't have pulled them off if I had wanted to.*

Unconsciously, she raised her hand to her throat. The command had burned coming out. It had actually hurt her. *That didn't make it Dark Magic, though, did it?*

Adele had no one she could ask her thousands of questions of, so she tossed and turned some more, uselessly praying for the morning to come early.

After a long night and a cold breakfast, Adele was helping pack the children and dogs into their carriages when she realized General Ohrig was sending his men out into the surrounding forest. Her stomach dropped.

Adele quickly checked the protected space under her carriage where Ripenzo had slept. The grass was crushed, but he was gone.

Adele opened the carriage door while the forest around her rang with the sounds of men calling his name.

"Mis-ter Shay-yale!"

"Ripenzo Shay-yale!"

"We are leav-ving!"

She saw the little metal box sitting atop a neatly folded piece of paper. With shaking hands, she pushed the box aside and unfolded the note:

*Dearest Queen Adelena,*

*You gave me a wonderful choice but I decided to make my own. After all, you are the one who taught me I could do that.*

*Thank you.*

*Ripenzo Shale*

*PS: There is a storm coming. It's going to be bad.*

Adele registered General Ohrig's presence at her shoulder.

"You can tell them to stop searching for him," she said, not looking up from the letter. "He is gone. Ripenzo has left us."

"May I, Your Majesty?" asked Ohrig politely.

Adele handed the letter to him; it didn't reveal anything her general couldn't know.

Adele pocketed the little metal box and tried not to shudder, knowing what it held.

She walked to a large tree by the side of the clearing and crouched down, turning her back to the camp to cover what she did. Slowly, she pulled the lid off the box, feeling uneasy at the sight of the green that glowed around the lid.

Despite a lifetime of arachnophobia, Adele gently shook the dusty black spider out of the tin and onto the ground. She didn't even flinch when it unfolded its legs and cautiously took a step or two away from her.

"It's all right little guy," she said quietly. "I don't want to kill you or anything else. Ever again."

Adele stood and walked back to the camp quickly. With all the noise in the camp, she couldn't have heard the little crack as the spider disappeared into the tiny portal.

Adele approached her carriage, where General Ohrig stood in front of the door, with Captain Lucky reading the letter over his shoulder.

"It says there is a storm coming, but the sky is completely blue," said Lucky, mystified, gazing up into the cloudless sky.

"It's not that kind of storm," said Adele quietly. "General Ohrig, we need to get home now."

The general took in Adele's grim expression and nodded.

"Saddle up men," he called. "We've got a hard ride ahead."

## *To be continued...*

Continue reading for a sample chapter of The Queen Revealed, Book Two in The World of Evendaar series

# BOOK TWO – AN EXCERPT

## "There's No Place Like Home"

Adele stepped through the gates of the Grey Palace with General Ohrig on one side of her and Captain Lucky on the other.

"Your Majesty! Look!" said Ohrig, pointing ahead of them. "The storm stops at the gates."

"That's impossible," whispered Adele as she gazed around her at the thick snow covering the grounds. Not a breath of wind disturbed the tiny glittering icicles that hung like jewelry from the trees lining the wide driveway. Even the sky above them was clear and black, littered with sparkling stars and a half-full moon, heavy and white above the turrets of the palace.

"General, this is just too strange," muttered Captain Lucky. "It must be the dark magic protecting this place. I don't like it."

"Neither do I, but we have no choice, Captain. The storm is just too strong out there in the forest. We have to think of the children."

Adele heard the men beside her shift and organize the carriages to join them, but she paid them no attention as she walked away up the road alone. Her eyes drank in the sight of the Grey Palace that was familiar and strange all at the same time. The stonework reminded her so much of the baroque architecture of Earth, but with a distinctly alien aspect that was beautiful. She knew this place so well because she had travelled here a hundred times in her dreams when she had still lived on Earth. It had been her happy place during all the lonely nights and bad days of her life as a woman stuck in a loveless marriage with three small children to care for. This palace had been her paradise in all its strange and melancholy glory and this time Rainere would be inside waiting for her.

Adele fought the urge to clap her hands and giggle like a girl. She quickened the pace and almost raced along the wide path. The carriages rattled up to join her at the foot of the front steps of the palace, their wheels sending out sprays of snow that lined the drive. Tilburn cautiously stepped out of his carriage and down onto the gravel. His wig and clothing immaculate despite the bumpy ride.

"I understand that we are here on your orders, Your Majesty," Tilburn said, nervously looking up at the great black doors of the Grey Palace. "But I must beg you to reconsider your decision. No St. Lucidis monarch has stepped foot into the Grey Palace since, well… ever."

Tilburn moved to stand in front of Adele and bring the full force of his disapproval to bear on her, his expression knotting his thin eyebrows and pursing his lips. "Forgive my candor, Your Majesty, but you have no idea what it means politically should you ask for shelter from the Marchant prince. And quite frankly I think we will be safer out in that unnatural storm than we will be by his fireside. And by *we* I mean *you* of course, Your Majesty. You, and the children."

"We had to stop somewhere, Tilburn," said Adele reasonably and stepped aside to guide the children up the steps. "I had the good luck to meet the prince at my coronation a few weeks ago and he seemed very polite. I'm sure he will give us somewhere to wait out the storm if we ask him nicely enough. Now, if we could all just keep our opinions of Marchants to ourselves while we are here?"

Adele turned back to point at her majordomo. "That means you, Tilburn." Tilburn looked momentarily affronted before dropping the act and nodding in grudging agreement.

Adele looked over at General Ohrig to check his mood, but his expression was stony and he only gave her a brusque nod. She almost sighed in exasperation. *Honestly, they didn't even know Rainere, how could they all fear him so much?*

"Look Mummy, stone dragons!" said Natalie slipping her cold hand into Adele's and grinning with pleasure. "They're so beautiful!"

Adele gave her daughter's hand a squeeze. At least Natalie wasn't frightened of the Grey Palace. Nor was Aaron, who was trying to stare up at the roof, cricking his neck backwards and squinting.

"There is a snow man up there, isn't there?" he giggled. "A man with lots of snow!" He pointed. Following his gaze, Adele accidentally stepped back onto the step below her and into Captain Lucky's arms. There was an awkward moment as the captain tried to hold her steady and Adele tried to pull away from him, resulting in the two of them falling into a rough hug and a bark of embarrassed laughter from Adele. She didn't try to look up again.

When the royal party had all assembled behind her, Adele put her hand on the huge dragon-headed doorknocker and tapped three times. The sound could be heard booming through the house. Adele fidgeted in anticipation of seeing Rainere again.

They waited for one long minute, and then another. The guards started shuffling and muttering in their line behind the women and children. Aaron and Natalie blew puffs of steam at each other as their breath came out in white clouds. Adele stamped her cold feet and stifled a grin. *He should be here any minute now.*

They waited some more.

"Maybe no one's home?" suggested QG Pepper in a hopeful voice. "Maybe His Highness is out and just left the lights on for...security purposes?"

"Shut it, QG," growled General Ohrig cuffing Pepper lightly on the head. "The Grey Palace doesn't need security lights. It's protected by the darkest spells magic ever created."

The general caught Adele's eye when she turned. "We should be alert," he said.

"But not alarmed," countered Adele, and raised her hand to knock a second time just as the doors began to swing ever so slowly inwards. Adele's breath caught in her throat, fighting for space with her heart.

The doors had completely opened before Adele could finally make out a single tall figure walking towards them from the dim interior of the entrance hall. He stopped just inside the doorway.

It was Grotto.

Adele's heart sank back down into her chest and she felt the smile on her face turn wooden. Rainere's manservant, Grottonski, was the only other person who knew about her relationship with the prince, and he hated her.

"Good evening," Adele began, before Tilburn almost pushed her out of the way, stepping to the front and pulling himself up as tall as his diminutive height would allow.

"Sir, Her Majesty the Queen of Unisia requests the hospitality of the royal Prince Rainere of Marchant. We have been caught up in a dangerous storm and need to shelter for the time it takes to blow over. We have with us the queen and her royal children in our party and insist that succor be given in their time of need. Of course, it is a great honor to the prince, and Her Majesty expects the best of care, despite the late hour."

During the entire speech, Grotto remained stock still, his face frozen as if carved from the same grey stone that framed the doors. Adele smiled warmly to try and take the chill out of Tilburn's pompous attitude, but Rainere's manservant never spared her a glance. Finally, Tilburn fell silent and looked expectantly at the servant before him.

"This way if it please you," was all Grotto said in his deep, hoarse voice as he abruptly turned on his heel and stalked off into the cavernous entry hall. Tilburn huffed and pulled his vest down with a sharp tug. Giving Adele a quick *I told you so* glance, the majordomo led them all inside, following Grotto.

"Wow!" said Aaron, her son echoing Adele's thoughts exactly as they made their way through the entry hall. "This house was made for giants, wasn't it, Mummy?"

"I really think it might have been, sweetheart," Adele answered as her eyes travelled up to the incredibly high ceilings. Leering gargoyles and fierce griffin-like creatures perched on top of every column and corner, looking as if they might pounce down on them at any minute.

The entry hall led to an even bigger foyer. The floor of the foyer was made up entirely of black and grey marble tiles in a checkerboard pattern. Suits of armor complete with helmets and swords lined the walls. Some polished to a high sheen while others were rusty and beaten up.

Grotto was standing at the foot of one of the two enormous staircases before them. The royal party assembled before him silently, in awe of the somber grandeur of the Grey Palace. The children, sensing the mood of the occasion, clung to Adele's legs.

"This staircase leads to the upper levels of the west wing, and the chambers where you may stay for the time being. The other staircase leads to the upper levels of the east wing. No one is permitted to go there." Grotto glared heavily at their little gathering, daring them to say anything in response to this edict. Then he turned and climbed the stairs too rapidly for such an old man as he appeared to be.

Adele tripped several times on the steps as she couldn't help staring about herself at the intricately carved stone of the balustrade, and the tapestries that lined the staircase. She had never come inside the palace in her dreams before, so everything was as fascinating as it was unfamiliar.

As Grotto led them down a great hallway, Adele couldn't help but notice the air of neglect that hung over the place. The carpet beneath her feet was faded and worn through in patches. The gloomy lighting of the lamps lining the walls only served to highlight the dusty paintings and peeling wallpaper.

"Mummy, this place is so spooky!" whispered Natalie to Adele as they passed yet another full size portrait of a glaring Marchant monarch. "Do ghosts live here?"

Adele hushed her daughter and squeezed her hand. An instinct told her Grotto probably had ears like a bat. Besides, Adele needed all her concentration to remain calm as they moved further into the Grey Palace. Her nerves were growing more fragile as she expected to see Prince Rainere at every turn.

Grotto eventually stopped in front of a set of wide doors. To Adele's surprise they were covered in delicate engravings and glowed a very soft green. Marchant magic protected these doors.

"The royal suite, for Her Majesty and the infant royals," announced Grotto as he pushed the doors open. "Maids sleep in the chamber adjoining the suite. There are closets down the hall for your men-at-arms."

Grotto barely glanced at Adele as he snapped a bow in her general direction and then turned and marched off into the gloom of the long hallway.

Adele tried not to feel completely crushed that Rainere hadn't shown himself. *Maybe he is asleep in bed? It is very late in the evening, after all.* Adele turned to Tilburn to ask him the time, but wisely decided against it when she saw his face.

Tilburn's cheeks had puffed out dramatically and a vein throbbed at his temple. Her majordomo was apoplectic with rage at the casual treatment of the royal family at the hands of a Marchant servant and he was about to express his feelings loudly. Adele quickly pushed Tilburn into the apartment and closed the doors before his anger could explode down the hall.

General Ohrig and the Queen's Guard soon returned from giving the apartments a quick once over. "All clear, General?" asked Adele.

"All clear from a safety perspective, Your Majesty, but I can't say your majordomo is going to be any happier when he sees the state of these rooms."

Adele gave the general a quick grimace as Tilburn surveyed the sitting room, spitting with fury and only managing to speak in garbled half sentences.

"Why, of all the…! How dare they? Abominable treatment of the royal…never have I ever!"

Seraphina had found a tray of refreshments on the dining table and quickly poured Tilburn a goblet of wine. He downed the cup in one draught and carefully put it down on a side table before pulling his waistcoat straight with a sharp tug. His expression showed he had regained some of his self-control.

"Your Majesty, I can only offer apologies for your awful, *awful* treatment at the hands of the Marchant family. It is unforgivable that our royal family should be treated like common houseguests, and not with the honor that your visit should entail. Of course, you will now see why I was so reluctant to put ourselves in this position of asking for hospitality," said Tilburn.

"Tilburn, honestly, it's all right," said Adele, not without a little exasperation. "We have caught the prince by surprise that's all."

They all looked at the trays of food and wine laid out on the dining table. Their preparation didn't entirely support her argument, but Adele decided to look past the point.

"We didn't really have any choice, Tilburn, with that storm out there. And look, the children are happy, at least," Adele said, as she gestured to her three little ones as they careened from one room to the next, screeching happily. The dusty floorboards were perfect for sliding about on their knees. "Let's just get settled and everyone can get to bed. It's been such a long day."

Given instructions, Tilburn finally had an outlet for his anger. He set himself to unpacking the few trunks that the drivers had brought up behind them, ruthlessly employing everyone not of royal blood to dusting mantles and tables, and lighting fires in the enormous grates.

Adele followed behind her children and explored the ancient suite they'd been given. The sitting room was the first room they had entered, but on either side of it were two large reception rooms, one of which was filled with furniture as if it had been set up for a concert. Rows of spindly wooden chairs sat facing a narrow podium where tapestries hung from the ceiling, suspended from horizontal rods, creating a stage area. The pictures on the tapestries depicted scenes of worship and what looked like ritual baptism, but instead of water the white robed figures were walking through a great fire, embroidered in red and gold thread. The acolytes on the other side of the fire held their hands aloft, their clothes burnt away and a green halo about their bodies. Their little thread faces showed expressions of terrible rapture.

From the little naked people dancing about in such wicked glee to the strange writing that ringed the image with letters sharp and unreadable, something about the images felt unwholesome. Adele didn't feel comfortable studying the tapestry with her children by her side so she quickly shooed them away to the next room, which was a large bedroom. A huge canopied bed rested in the center of the room, and several couches of various sizes had been pushed haphazardly against the walls. A large wardrobe sat in the corner. An image of an ugly goblin face had been engraved in the doors and it scared the little girls, so Adele decided that her Queen's Guard could have this room.

The second reception room was all the way on the other side of the sitting room and was almost completely bare of furniture. Tattered grey silk curtains hung at the floor-to-ceiling windows, and a huge stone dragon glared menacingly from above the fireplace, perched as if it had just climbed down from the ceiling. A single leather armchair sat in the center of the room, facing the windows. A stain lay spread at the foot of the chair, marring the floorboards darkly, and Adele didn't want to look too closely to see what had caused it.

Through this empty room, Adele found the bedroom where she was to sleep with the children and their nannies. As she ran her fingers over the heavy black furniture, it felt cold to the touch. Everything was made of iron, and the sharp metallic smell of it filled the room. Adele looked up as Seraphina's lantern threw shadows into the dark corners and studied the walls searching for any hint of secret doors or passageways. Rainere had shown her that the Golden Palace had been full of such secret tunnels when he had stayed there and she guessed that his own home would be the same.

Caitlin bustled into the room with the children running ahead of her and their night things in her arms. Adele helped to bathe the children in the cavernous bathroom attached to the bedroom. The soporific effect of a hot bath was working well to calm their frazzled nerves after a stressful day of travelling, and as they had already filled up on the snacks that had been laid out, the children were ready to sleep quickly.

Adele kissed each of her little ones good night as they snuggled down under the surprisingly fresh sheets of the great bed. The three puppies had piled into their basket under the bed, already snoring. Adele leant down and gave Hero Boy a little pat. The dog stirred and whined in his sleep.

It had been so odd today when Aaron had claimed that Hero Boy had told him about the snow. It wasn't like Aaron to make up stories like that. *Is it possible that I'm not the only one to have magic wake up inside of me, now that we live in this new world?* Anxious, Adele chewed her bottom lip as she headed for the door.

"Are you going to see the prince, Mummy?" asked a little voice behind her.

"I don't know, Aaron. Maybe," whispered Adele, turning back to the bed to see her son sitting up between his sleeping sisters. "You should rest now, sweetheart. I'll be back later though, and I'm going to sleep right next to you, I promise."

"Tell him I like his snow, don't I, Mummy?" said Aaron and thankfully fell back on his pillows ready to sleep.

"I think it's beautiful, too, Aaron," whispered Adele, as she breathed a sigh of relief at the innocence of the comment. She couldn't take any more puzzles tonight. *Perhaps he had heard the QGs talking about*

*Ripenzo's storm earlier,* she thought. *Maybe one of them suggested that it meant snow was coming.*

Adele made her way back into the central sitting room.

"Everything alright, Your Majesty?" asked Seraphina, as the young nanny put down her fork to stand for Adele.

"When you've finished your dinner, could you please stay close to the children?" asked Adele. "The girls are already asleep, but Aaron is still a bit unsettled."

Seraphina bobbed and sat again, ready to bolt down her food and do as she was asked.

"Can't say I blame the little tyke," said General Ohrig as he made his way across the sitting room from the opposite doorway. No doubt he had been looking at the strange set up next door. "I will station guards at your bedroom door and at the front here throughout the night, Your Majesty."

"Do you really think that's necessary, General?" protested Adele. "I'm sure the men are all exhausted from the hard ride today, and everyone could do with a good night's sleep."

She also couldn't think of how she was to sneak away to find Rainere if there were guards all over the apartment. "I'm sure there is no reason to be overly alarmed," she said, making a play for humor.

General Ohrig gave her a skeptical look. "Your Majesty, there is something you should know while we are here in the Grey Palace," he began, but was interrupted by a loud knock at the door.

Tilburn scurried to answer it and stepped back in surprise as Grotto strode past him into the room, searching the group until his eyes alighted on Adele. She almost flinched from the venom in his glance.

"His Highness, Prince Rainere, extends a cordial invitation to Her Majesty the queen to dine with him in the High State dining room this evening," he said stiffly, almost choking on the word *cordial.*

Tilburn was incensed and jumped in front of the prince's manservant. "Surely the prince would not expect Her Majesty to join him for dinner at this late hour, with such little notice?" he asked in a scandalized tone. "It would be most forward and outside all manner of protocols to even suggest such a thing!"

Grotto's expression told the majordomo what he could do with his protocols. "The Marchant *prince* has invited the *queen* to dine with him *this* evening," insisted Grotto enunciating each word and leaning over Tilburn menacingly.

"I accept the invitation!" interjected Adele before Tilburn could explode into righteous fury once again. "Thank you, Mr. Grotto, please tell the prince I can be ready to join him within the hour."

Grotto snapped a shallow bow and turned smartly, exiting the room and banging the doors loudly behind himself.

Adele looked about and saw everyone in the room was staring at her with varying degrees of horror on their faces. She laughed nervously. "What? He's our host! I have to be polite." She smiled as the butterflies began batting against the sides of her stomach. "Besides, I've already told you, I've met the prince before, and he isn't as scary as everyone seems to think."

Adele turned away to avoid General Ohrig's gaze, pretending not to see the hand he raised to stop her as she moved off towards the bedroom.

"Girls, I'll need some help getting ready," she called back to Seraphina and Caitlin. "Please find my nice dress for me, the red I think? And get the make-up and things out. I need to wash the smell of horse and dust off me before dinner."

The moment she had been waiting nearly two weeks for was about to happen. No grumpy general was going to stop her from seeing Prince Rainere tonight. Nothing was going to keep them apart now.

# ACKNOWLEDGEMENTS

I have many people to thank for their help with the creation of this book. Firstly, I need to send much love out to two special women, Monica Hall and Lisa Clausen, who made the original edits for this book and endured the awful spelling and horrific grammar of that first draft to find lots of positive things to say and suggested improvements. Not only did they buoy my fragile ego but they also both inspired me to always do better. I would also love to thank all my wonderful friends and family: Alison Clausen, Cindy Koch, Isabelle Pelletier, Prudence Montague and Nicole Wright. You read and re-read the book, and it was your enthusiasm and criticism of the characters and plot that made me a better writer and this, a better story. Thank you to my family, you all inspire me every day.

Thank you all from the very bottom of my heart.

To find out more about the author A.R. Winterstaar or the World of Evendaar please visit:

www.evendaar.com

A. R. Winterstaar on Facebook